The Salem Chronicles:

A New World

Part One

Chapter 1

As the sun dawned, the signs of autumn were visible on the suburban streets of Salem. The rays of the morning's sunrise touched the orange and red leaves of the trees. Dew clung to the tips of the grass and a faint mist rose, creeping up to the front doors of the homes on the many avenues. The children of Salem were being pushed by their parents to get up and ready; for it was a new start to the school year and for a select number of children they were moving up to the next step in their school life. One such child, a girl named Brianna Eastey, was having a little bit of trouble in sorting out her school bag.

"Mom, have you seen my sports kit?"

"Why'd you need your sports kit on the first day Brianna?" replied Brianna's mom, Gretchen.

"Well, suppose they have cheerleading trials on the first day? I want to be ready," she replied frantically.

Brianna, now fourteen years of age, was about to attend her first day of high school. She had heard many of the rumours that surrounded cheerleading and what it meant to students in high school. It was a highly popular sport and therefore a sport that was extremely hard to be a part of. She had always dreamed of being a school cheerleader and today she felt although it was a necessity to learn about her new school, it was equally as important to show a keen interest regarding the selection process for new recruits in the cheerleading squad. She had done both dance and gymnastics from a young age and as such, greatly desired to combine both of those elements by becoming part of the cheer squad.

Brianna, from a young age, had developed into a girl that was naturally designed to a part of a sport such as cheerleading. She had the frame of a lithe gymnast, with the looks of a dancer, showcasing a pearly white smile, wavy long brown hair and blue eyes.

She raced upstairs and after ten minutes of searching the contents of her room, Brianna knelt down and popped her head under the bed.

"Got it," she called out loud enough for the whole house to hear, swinging the gym bag over her shoulder and running down the stairs. As she passed her kitchen counter she picked up her school bag and lunch for the day.

"Enjoy your first day, darlin'," Gretchen called to Brianna, but she barely heard one uttered syllable as she rushed out the door and raced down the road to the bus stop. She managed to pause by the bright yellow stop sign just in time and signalled to the approaching bus.

She hopped on, showing the elderly driver her bus pass, which he acknowledged with a sleepy 'harrumph', before moving down the bus to find a free window seat halfway down the aisle. As soon as she had settled into a seat and stopped the mad rush her stomach started to flip as thoughts focused on the dawn of a new schooling year. Brianna was not only stepping up from middle school to high school; she was also furthering her schooling career in a completely different state.

She had recently moved from Jacksonville to Salem in the summer. It had left her with a mere three weeks to try and settle in to a new area and gather her bearings in the much smaller town of Salem where the homes and people were fewer and life seemed to be switched on at a much slower pace. She had spent many an afternoon while her parents went off to work, skirting the town and looking at the homes that surrounded her own. In a way she had hoped to find some young people that she could maybe become more involved with but she had not managed to find so much as one neighbour to talk to or any young people that she could become better acquainted with. The move north had happened so suddenly, Brianna had had barely any time to register her feelings towards Salem. She was currently indifferent to the alien town, unsure of its old and rather gothic presence, where everything seemed to creak or whistle as she walked by it through a decaying age that rested over the town. Her main focus since the move was locating a good school that could fit another student into their cohort. Fortunately her grades made her more of an asset and she had had the free choice of the four schools in the local area; one stood out for her and it was to this particular school that she was journeying to on the fine autumn morning.

One day, about four weeks ago, her pop had got a phone call informing him that his job was no longer available in Jacksonville and that the only place that he could keep his job was in an office situated in Salem, Massachusetts. Brianna didn't think it weird that they had to move because of the transfer, but the fact that the business was only locally based guidance centre for those of need in Jacksonville confused her no end. How could there be offices in another state, in a business, which had never stretched further than 20 miles out of Jacksonville?

As Brianna sat in the puttering school bus she sat and observed the many girls and boys hop onto the bus at every stop. Some like her, joined the growing crowd by themselves, but others were busily nattering in groups of two or three. No one paid attention to anyone else; if they were alone like Brianna, they mostly stared out of the bus windows and gazed at the passing suburban scenery. Brianna looked at their faces and soon recognised that quite a few of them had the same frown between the brows that she currently carried. They were all as nervous about their first day as she was.

The bus turned left at the next set of traffic lights and faced a set of wrought iron gates, which automatically opened inwards as the bus slowly approached them. A golden sign just behind the gates read 'Witchcraft Heights' in pearly white lettering, with a witch's hat underneath, erupting sparks out of its apex. As Brianna read the sign her nerves intensified, making her heart flutter sending waves of nerves to the base of her throat.

The name of the school demonstrated once more how town of Salem was linked to a history steeped in magical legend. Brianna had noticed from the first day since her move that a lot of the places in Salem had some link to their magical heritage. Her road was named 'Spellbound Lane', the one restaurant that her parents had taken her too was named the 'Witching Hour' and the clothes store where she had bought some dazzling items was named 'Sparks of Salem'.

The bus continued its slow journey, carrying the students up the elegant winding drive. On either side elm trees lined the road, with their branches arching across the path and joining in a high peak. The autumn sunrise shot beams of light green rays through the leaves and speckled the path beneath them. This almost enchanted feel stopped Brianna from realising that she was on a journey to the school as the path shielded all preying eyes from the school that lay beyond.

As they made their way out of the winding row of elm trees, the road branched out onto a circling driveway, where a tall and proud fountain resided in the middle. The fountains centrepiece was that of a statue. It depicted a small group of respectable schoolgirls and schoolboys. Each character held a wand up high in the air, where water spouted lightly from the tips' of their wands'. The bus drove around the fountain and finally made a crawling stop outside the entrance of a large, light stoned building that stood impressively before them. The bus sunk down as it stopped and let out a noise of exhaustion as its doors opened. Most of the students proceeded to hurry off the bus and rushed up the set of stairs that led to the front doors of the school; Brianna being in no rush, waited until everyone else had left and with a small nod to the driver, she hopped off last.

Brianna followed nervously behind the busload of students, her eyes looking directly at the floor as she made her tentative steps towards the start of something new. She walked up a set of large stone steps and stopped as she reached a pair of tall, thick wooden doors at the top, which were both embossed with witches' hats. As she panned her eyes to the top of the magnificent doors she notices a single word engraved in an arching fashion across the top of the doors, 'Merlin'. As her eyes lowered back down from the solitary word she noticed a sign, positioned just outside of the doorway, which was supported by a small gold stand.

'All Junior's are to report to the entrance hall. You will wait for a house prefect to escort you to the registration chamber.'

Brianna stepped through the impressive doorway and made her way into the entrance hall. It was truly a wondrous school, she thought to herself as she looked around to take in the sheer elegance and beauty of the entrance hall. Her previous school had been modern and lacking in any sense of grandeur or elements of history etched into its walls.   From its high ceiling, drapes of purple and blue were hung in a great sweeping fashion from the centre of the hall to the smooth stoned walls at either side. A reception desk of white stone blocks and a marble top was tucked into the far left corner, which looked minuscule in comparison to the large, polished stone staircase next to it, leading off to places of which Brianna could only imagine.

It seemed that a number of juniors' were starting to congregate at one side of the hall on a round, deep aubergine coloured carpet. Brianna thought it best to walk over and stand among the huddle.

As she waited timidly for the prefect to arrive, a girl with blond hair came and stood next to her. She flicked her slightly wavy locks over her shoulder as she looked in Brianna's direction. At first Brianna noticed a number of freckles on the girls face, but as she refocused her vision on the girl's whole face; she noticed that the girl was smiling at her, so Brianna politely returned the favour.

"Phew," said the girl, "I didn't think anyone knew how to smile in this school! I've being trying to talk to someone for the past fifteen minutes, but everyone is just too jittery. I've moved schools about twenty times I think, so a new start is never anything exciting or new anymore. I just hope this one sticks, it does get a bit boring after a while, my names Kimberley by the way, what's yours?"

Stunned at how quickly the girl named Kimberley had spoken to her it took a good minute before Brianna replied. Brianna couldn't help but notice the tone of command in her voice, but fortunately it wasn't a threatening tone and she felt quite comfortable around her.

"My name's Brianna and this is the first major change that I've had. I've moved across from Whitchurch in England where the weather is colder and the pace of life is slow. Life up here and this school is a completely different challenge; it's almost like stepping into a new world."

"Well I'm the right girl to talk to," said Kimberley, "I'll help you to settle in alright'; don't you go worrying about a thing."

Brianna was about to thank Kimberley and ask her where she had moved from, but stopped as a girl who looked a lot older than the rest of them waved in their direction to get their attention.

"Welcome to Witchcraft Height's juniors'," said the girl. Brianna noticed that this girl had a P

embroidered onto the pocket of the blazer that she was wearing. "I am one of the prefects of Merlin, which is

the name for one of the four houses in this school. I will be escorting you to the registration chamber where

you will meet the heads of houses and consequently be placed into one of the four. In your house you will

share the same classes as your house peers and have a common room that you share with your fellow house

mates."

A small murmuring drifted around as all the juniors' addressed the news with interest and uncertainty.

Brianna caught a few of the passing words and found that they were quickly wondering which house they

might be placed in and what the names of the other three houses could be.

The prefect made her way to the front of the group and led them off from the entrance hall to a

corridor on the left. She did not need to lead the group for too long as she stopped outside a door on the

immediate right, causing a few of the juniors at the front to bump and trample on one another as she had

abruptly halted.

"Alright then," said the prefect, unaware of the collision that had just occurred, "if you could please

enter in a single file fashion and proceed to one of the benches in the room. Fill up from the front and make

sure that there are no gaps, it's always a tight squeeze to fit into that room."

Everyone began shuffling in through the door and Brianna eyed her surroundings. She looked up to the

lowered ceiling and saw intricate carvings of woodland creatures on the coving, which linked the ceiling to the

panelled mahogany walls. On one of the walls there hung four woven banners which were all slightly careworn

and fraying around the edges. Each banner was embroidered with a name that Brianna was not quite familiar

with, Merlin, Morgana, Medusa and Medea. She took a seat next to Kimberley and looked around at the other

students who had taken seats in the rows in front of her. She scanned the backs of girls and boys, but she soon

stopped as one of the boys turned around. As their eyes met he gave a nod in her direction and the small hint

of a smile spread from the corner of his mouth. Brianna returned the smile, feeling a warming glow rise in her cheeks. She tried to refocus her attention on the front of the classroom as four teachers came to stand on the raised platform at the front of the juniors.

"Welcome, new students" said one of the ladies at the front, "we four teachers are the heads of houses at Witchcraft Heights. I am Miss Knoxbury, head of Merlin house. To my left you have Mr Shrewsborough who is the head of Morgana; to my immediate right is Mrs Doubtworth, head of Medusa and also Mr Witcherson, head of Medea.

"The houses are named to celebrate four infamous people who are believed to have dabbled in matters of witchcraft and sorcery. For those of you who were not born and raised within the sacred hollow of Salem, this town has a profound history with that of witchcraft and sorcery and as such we honour part of that history by naming the four houses after four members of the celebrated history. For those of you that are not familiar with the history of Salem and its link with witchcraft, here is a small history lesson on one well-acknowledged moment in our towns past.

"The town of Salem has always had a link to witchcraft. In the 17th century there were a great number of witch trials in Salem that led to great persecution. People in the council believed a few members in the community were performing dark magic on other members in the village. It was believed that those associated with magic were slaves to the devils work and as a conclusion magic was condemned as a punishable sin. In times such as these, magic was seen as an antithesis to the works of God. The gift of magic was believed to give mortals powers far too seductive and dangerous to manage, tempting mortals to complete sinful acts and controlling the world in which the people of Salem presided in.

"In more recent times, the idea of magic is something more of myth and not necessarily something that we as a community believe in. However, we are proud of our town's history and as such we adhere to the history of this town. At Witchcraft Heights, we use the town's magical roots to shape different traditions within the school. The four houses epitomise these traditions and we use four well-noted figures in magical history to place students into houses that they can thrive in and reach their full potential. As well as the use of the four houses to showcase Salem's history, the school dances and charity events of the year often correlate with the history of Salem itself."

Miss Knoxbury stood back at this point and walked to the door on the right of the small room. As she made her way down she made a sweeping gaze that passed over every student. Brianna looked into the eyes of the woman as they looked into her own and she saw the kind lines around the face, slightly deepened through years of experience at the school.

"Okay then ladies and gentleman," said Mr Shrewsborough in a heartily fashion. His nature seemed more youthful than that of Miss Knoxbury, even if his rotund belly and white hair that crowned his head demonstrated otherwise. "If I call your name out in the first block you will form a line behind Miss Knoxbury, thus creating the youngest of years within the house of Merlin. You will be with her until the bell signals for break time so that she may present and provide a rough guide to the school.

"Kimberley Aldridge, Jesse Garon, Xavier Prince, Maria Parker, Casey Jones, Rose Bishop, Michael Proctor, Damien Quests, Caleb Williams, Madison Count, Olivia Dunford, Elijah Stubbings, Danielle Clover, Arthur Pentucket and Brianna Eastey."

Brianna smiled brightly as she shuffled along the bench and followed behind Kimberley to Miss Knoxbury. She was pleased to be with Kimberley, a girl that she had already warmed to, and to also see that the smiling boy Damien was walking along his bench to meet the other Merlin students by the door.

Miss Knoxbury led the students out of the room and into a long and impressive corridor lined with cabinets. Each cabinet was filled with golden plaques and photos of students holding up trophies or wearing medals around their necks. As well as the photos, a series of artefacts cluttered the cabinets, some looking fairly new as they shone and glistened against the lights from the candelabras, others looked old and rusty in comparison.

"This is always a good start to the tour," began Miss Knoxbury, "to the left and right of you we have the photos and relics from the many achievements of past and current students. This school excels in both academic and sporting elements and as such we wish to celebrate the achievements of all our students. All

those who receive a medal or trophy earn their place in one of the cabinets in the Hall of Excellence."

After reaching the end of the Hall of Excellence, Miss Knoxbury continued the class' tour around the

school. Brianna started to formulate a mind map of the school, which was split across four two storey high

buildings. The sheer elegance of the school overwhelmed her as she passed the distinctly different styled

buildings. Miss Knoxbury pointed out the other three buildings as they were led outside. She explained that all

buildings were lined with a different sort of stone walled corridors; some casting warmth to the building whilst

others held a more foreboding atmosphere. They continued the tour, going past key parts of the school such

as the art rooms, outdoor sports facilities, the school library, and an assortment of other different classrooms.

Although Miss Knoxbury was keen and quite happy to explain the different sectors within the school, for

Brianna it was too much information to remember and panicked at the prospect of wending her way around

the school.

"And now, students," said Miss Knoxbury, "we have reached the Merlin common room." She turned to

face a wooden door and pushed with some force on its heavy panels, which held an engraved design of an old

robed man with long hair and a beard. Atop his head was a pointed hat, which was laden with stars, and

crescent moons.

As Miss Knoxbury pushed the door inwards the students all filed in behind her and started to form an

arching procession that faced out onto the impressive room. The common room was large and rectangular,

with a large portrait of the Merlin building. The picture drew Brianna's attention immediately as she looked

directly to the far end of the common room. The simplistic design within the room stated nothing more or

nothing less than comfort. It was a warming room with a deep crimson carpet and dark wooden panelled

walls. The room was bathed in a tinted light of red, blue and purple, which shone from the chapel like stained

glass windows. The room was littered with plush armchairs that were all dotted in little circles around the

room. Along the dark wooden walls were a few bookshelves, which housed a small collection of books.

Brianna could not yet make out the names of the books but she was itching to get her hands on at least one of them.

As the murmurs of approval died down Miss Knoxbury saw fit to carry on.

"This is the Merlin common room and it is somewhere where you are free to relax and rest during your lunch times or for study purposes if you have a free period. You cannot eat in the common room and make sure to treat the common room with respect. Every student is responsible for themselves in here and anyone found abusing this luxury will lose the right to use it." Miss Knoxbury looked around at the new students with a sterner stare than she had previously showcased and Brianna understood the sincerity meant by every word that Miss Knoxbury had said.

"Here are your class timetables," informed Miss Knoxbury, handing out a white sheet of paper filled with a list of lessons for the week. "As Merlin students, you will share all classes with the same house for the first year so it should be easy for you to all remember a timetable together. It is just coming up to break time, after which a Merlin prefect will take you to your third lesson of the day. If you have questions about your timetable or where to go for your classes please feel free to ask either myself or a Merlin prefect."

With that, Miss Knoxbury turned sharply and made her way back out of the engraved door, leaving the new students with some time to get used to their new surroundings. Brianna looked down at her timetable, but was unable to concentrate on what was noted down in front of her. She fidgeted a little on the spot where she was standing, wanting to try out one of the comfy looking red chairs, but not yet confident enough to do so.

The thoughts soon escaped her mind as a student with a P embroidered onto their jumper walked into the common room. This prefect, however, was a boy. He was tall and lean, with dark hair that had a slight quiff at the front. He had a welcoming smile and large hazelnut pools that complemented his olive complexion. Brianna felt herself swooning slightly as she registered the attractiveness of the prefect, but could not help but detect the sense of approachability in his forthcoming demeanour.

"Hi, how you doing? My name's Carter and I'm one of the prefects in Merlin," the prefect announced. "If you'd like to follow me I can take you to your new lockers and then we'll head off to your third period of the day."

All the students followed the beckoning hand of Carter and walked back out of the common room. They filed into a corridor that was positioned straight opposite the Merlin front door, but another avenue that Brianna had not had the ability to previously take in. This corridor was rather narrow and on its walls were situated a long line of wooden lined cabinets. A golden border framed each cabinet with golden numbers hammered across the top of each door. Brianna looked down at her timetable again and noticed a large number 12 at the top of the page.

"If you look at the top of your timetable," Carter nodded towards Brianna, noticing her looking down, "you'll find your locker number is at the top of the page. There's a key in every lockers, so make sure you keep a good hold of it. The caretaker has a short temper at the best of times, and I'll warn you that opening student's lockers' is something that he don't like."

The students shuffled around one another in search for their locker and retrieved their locker keys before stashing away any items that they didn't think they would need for next lesson. After the few minutes of minor commotion the students turned their attention back towards Carter.

"Could somebody please tell me what your first lesson is?" he questioned the group.

"History, with MAS," replied the girl. Brianna was sure that she had stood up when Mr Shrewsborough had called out Madison to follow Miss Knoxbury.

"Okay, that's in the Medusa building, in the lower east corner of the building," stated Carter. He led the students to the other end of the locker corridor and along a slightly challenging memory test as they wended their way through the Merlin building. Eventually a door led out one of the sides of the Merlin building and across a courtyard where a large open grass expanse presided in its centre. They followed the sandstone path around the edge of the grassed courtyard from the Merlin building.

"For those that struggled to keep up with the tour from earlier, this is the quickest way to enter Medusa and as an added hint it is probably the best door to use if you are going to any humanities lessons," informed Carter as he led the group around to a door on the eastern side of the Medusa building.

They had only been shown the outside of the Medusa building on their initial tour and Brianna recalled how Miss Knoxbury had stated that the four buildings had an individual character. As Brianna stepped through the door she fully understood what Miss Knoxbury had meant; the contrast between the two buildings was immediately noticeable as they entered a dimly lit stone walled corridor. The Merlin building seemed to burst full of warmth and light, but the Medusa building exhumed a deeply eerie and cold presence.

The class, shown by Carter, entered the history classroom. There were no windows in the classroom and the room held a musty air as if the ages of history were kept within the four walls itself. The only light in the room was cast from lamps held in brackets around the walls. To give a greater atmosphere the lamps were dimly set and flickered, casting changing shadows on the walls. There were a series of thick oak desks placed in rows facing a grand desk at the front, which was littered with textbooks and odd pieces of paper.

Brianna grabbed a seat at the back of the classroom next to Kimberley. She turned her head and the girl believed to called Madison took a seat in the chair on her other side. Brianna watched the rest of the Merlin class file in. Her eyes caught sight of Damien and they followed behind him as he went to sit at the front of the classroom with a couple of the other boys. As Damien seated his self in the chair her eyes shifted back to the front door as a middle-aged lady followed in behind the rest of the group. She walked rather slowly and in an almost floating fashion to the front of the class before she turned to face the class. She was a petite lady, with short blond hair wound in tight curls around her face. Her clothes were a catastrophic blend of vibrant colours that depicted an array of flowers and birds, casting an overall aura of imagination and creativity.

The teacher gave a small cough and all murmuring stopped immediately.

"Welcome new students'. My name is Miss Ashdown and I am your history teacher for this year," she informed them. "History is a highly demanding subject. It will require all of your attention in order to grasp an understanding of the many stories and mysteries that the ages have to offer us."

She looked around slowly at each individual as if inspecting each student for a certain something before turning to the blackboard to write three large words in white chalk.

"The 'Salem Witch Trials'," she stated, using a long poker to point to the words on the blackboard. "I believe this is a fitting topic for our first topic of the term, yes indeed. I believe one of the best forms of history is a topic that holds some personal link and something holds a relation to the life in which you are a part of.

"To explain what I mean, I would like to ask if anyone here knows of any ancestors that lived in Salem during the time of the Salem Witch trials."

Brianna looked around the class and was surprised to see that six of the students, including Kimberley and Damien, raised their hands.

"Well that is an awful lot for one class," said a surprised Miss Ashdown, "we usually have about fifteen new students a year in this school that have known ancestry of this cruel time. Of course some of you may have had ancestors on both sides of the tale." She sidled over to a book filled cabinet on the right hand side and began to hand out a number of text books.

Brianna noticed that the front cover was slightly careworn and there was a slight curl at the corners. These were books that had been well used.

"The history of witchcraft and its integration with the mortal world," Miss Ashdown began without warning, "is a subject that goes far, far back. It has its place even in the bible, but we as historians will be concentrating on the core facts stemming from the 13th century.

"Witchcraft is something that is believed to be either a gift or curse given to a select number of people. They are given powers beyond the like of which most could only imagine. Some of those that practised magic were believed to use it for the better, such as that of the noted figure of Merlin. Others however were believed to use it for darker purposes so as to influence and control other human beings. In its most evil

form, witchcraft was believed to be a gift of the devil and as such witchcraft has been linked to signing to

servitude with the devil; living a life that is forsaken by sin, where one must suffer in the fiery pits of the

afterlife when the days of their life are utterly spent.

"With regard to its more historically based foundations, the discovery of witches originated in parts of

Europe, where tens of thousands of women and men were persecuted for their association with the dark arts.

For many centuries witches where believed to reside in Europe and Europe alone. However with evolution of

the world and the advancements in methods of transport to the new founded lands, witchcraft soon spread

across the globe. However, it wasn't until the 17th century, when the Europeans sailed the oceans and came to

settle in the Americas, that the superstitions regarding witchcraft and the belief that magic travelled with

them came to light.

"But how did the European superstitions affect the little town of Salem?" Miss Ashdown finished on a

question.

She looked around at the class enquiringly and stopped as one person had slowly raised their hand.

"Wasn't it something to do with a European war that took place in particular areas of America?" said

the boy that Brianna thought was named Caleb.

"That is correct, well done" replied Miss Ashdown, "it is true that the French and English were at war

with one another. They bought their conflict over to the new world and fought one another primarily in the

North Eastern corner of America in a war known as Williams War. One of the towns that the refugees of

Williams War settled in was that of our Salem. They plundered the towns resources and created turmoil for

the towns' people. But now you question how this part in history has a link to witchcraft?

"Well it is believed that when the resources of Salem were drained, conflict arose between the wealthy

and those of poorer origin. Much quarrelling ensued and the villagers of Salem were fuelled with rumours

regarding the powers of witchcraft from the French and English soldiers. The villagers linked the European stories to their new found suffering and they soon believed that witches had plagued dear Salem, draining the village of its resources by order of the devil."

Brianna looked around to see the rest of the class drinking in the information and Miss Ashdown nodded appreciatively at their interest of the town's history. She didn't continue with anymore accounts, but instead set them the task to write up a timeline of the critical historical moments in the witchcraft craze.

Brianna got out pen and paper and started the timeline. As she wrote down the dates of when the Europeans crossed the waters she felt a little shudder as if the sea wind was across her back carrying her across to the Americas. She looked around but nobody had noticed and she carried on with her work.

The bell sounded and the class filed out of the classroom quickly. Brianna turned and spoke to Kimberley.

"I've never fully appreciated history before, but the history of the Salem witch trials is something else. It's much more exciting than normal history."

"I agree," said Kimberley, "my mom was born in Salem, which is why we returned here in the end. She has shown me part of the family tree, but I almost felt drawn to what Miss Ashdown was saying. It was just weird."

They found Carter at the end of the corridor and he led them on to their next lesson. Brianna kept going over the details from the history lesson in her mind, with the inescapable feeling that Salem had a lot more in common with her than she could explain.

Carter asked one of the juniors to inform him of their next lesson and Madison was the one to tell him rather timidly that they had math. He led them back out of the eastern door and walked back to the grassed courtyard that they had journeyed across that morning, but they didn't walk around to the direction of the Merlin building. Instead they ventured through a small tunnel that led them to face a stonewall and Brianna thought that Carter had taken them down a wrong turn. The wall was covered in a plethora of flowers and as they stepped closer Brianna managed to spot a small wooden door hidden in among the flowers and vines, like a hidden secret in the school. Carter pushed on the squeaky door and the students followed in behind.

They could see the other half of the Medusa building as they stepped through the door. They spotted another building tucked away behind a number of short trees that was also obscuring the circular courtyard that Miss Knoxbury had shown them earlier this morning, if her bearings were correct.

"We have the Morgana building at the back of the school," he stated, "the back of the school does have a lot to offer as I'm sure Miss Knoxbury would have told you. The hidden door holds the quickest route to the northern part of the school. This section of the school is usually the busiest and contains all of the paths that lead out to our extracurricular activities."

He walked them down the cobbled path that linked up to the secret door and followed it up to a high arched entrance. The Morgana building was a welcoming contrast to the darkness of Medusa. The high ceiling and wide based corridors made the building feel more like a cathedral than a school building. It was a much larger building than Medusa and it took them a longer period of time to reach the Math classroom where Mr Downswood welcomed them. The first thought that Brianna had of Mr Downswood was that he was a rather boring old man. Harmless as he was, an hour being taught the basics of algebra was not anywhere near as enthralling as the lesson with Miss Ashdown.

The last lesson of the day was held in the Medea building, which again added another ambience to the school. The walls were speckled with light sandstone and large stone tiles that caused an echoing sound across the floor as the juniors made their resounding footfalls to the Music classroom. A very tuneful teacher greeted them by the name of Miss Arietta. She seemed to sing every word that was said and pointed with her arms as if conducting an orchestra rather than communicating with a class of students. As they sat in the classroom Brianna felt her mind wandering even though it was her first lesson. She looked out onto the wondrous view of the school's sports facilities and couldn't wait to spend her first sports lesson in the glorious autumnal sunshine that fell over Salem.

When they finally finished for the day Brianna and Kimberley, who had soon become fast friends, headed back to the locker room together and put away the collection of books that they had been provided with from the lessons of the day. They busily talked to one another as they headed out to the front of the school and said a quick goodbye to Madison, another person who they had become acquainted with, as she rushed out to get her bus. Kimberley bid farewell to Brianna and walked down the path that was stationed alongside the winding front entrance to the school.

As Brianna waited in the queue she espied one of the girls that was also in the Merlin class, "Hello Rose," she called out.

"Oh hello, err..." replied Rose with a rather stuck up sort of attitude that Brianna decided to put down to nerves.

"Brianna," she responded, filling in the gap that Rose was missing.

"Oh yes," she answered shortly.

"That was a fun day," Brianna tried to keep some sort of conversation going, "the lessons were really exciting, particularly Miss Ashdown's lesson. She really is an imaginative sort of teacher."

"I suppose so, if you call talking about stories and old wives tales a lesson," Rose replied rather rudely, "I don't understand to what purpose we will benefit learning about a witch hunt."

"It is the town's history," Brianna replied becoming more and more confused by the behaviour of her fellow classmate, "it's good for us to know what we are a part of."

"Well I think it's a great waste of time, and not remotely interesting," Rose responded sharply, and as the bus pulled up she didn't take a backward glance at Brianna or wish to carry on with any conversation with her.

Brianna was slightly shocked by the less than courteous manner of Rose as she sat in the same seat that she had sat at on the morning journey, milling over all the people that she had thus far met and overly glad that it had been Kimberley not Rose with whom she had an everlasting first impression in regard to the people of Salem. The bus trundled away and Brianna turned to face the school, watching it and looking

back with much wanted desire to not leave at all.

Chapter 2

Brianna woke up the next day for school, bright and energetic. The first day had been a true delight and she had studied her timetable during the evening so much that she knew every lesson, teacher and classroom that was written upon it. She was tremendously eager to return to Witchcraft Heights; she even went as far as to set her morning alarm to wake her fifteen minutes earlier than yesterday so that she didn't have to rush to get to the bus.

"Morning sweetie," called out Gretchen, "gosh, you like as bright as a daisy! What on earth has got in to you?"

"I'm just excited about school, that's all," replied Brianna. "I can't be late or I could lose our team house points."

"Merlin?" said Gretchen, "what are you going on about?"

"My school house, mom," Brianna said exasperatedly, "there are four house teams and I'm in Merlin. It's the nicest house to be in, I'm sure of it. The common room is lovely and I've already made two friends."

"Well that's good to hear. Your dad and I knew you would settle in alright," said Gretchen reassuringly.

"Yeah, that's right," Brianna replied, not really paying any attention to her mom whilst she sorted out some jam on toast, swung her bag over her shoulder and walked down to the bus stop.

She waited at the bus stop for barely a minute, when she saw it turning into her road. The bus slowed as it approached her, its yellow doors opened directly in front of her and she stepped on. She looked around, saw Madison sitting with a spare seat next to her and went to join her

"Hi Madison," said Brianna announcing her arrival, "I didn't know you would be on this bus."

"Hi," she replied, "I'm quite lucky really. Most of the school buses pass by my house so I can jump onto anyone really."

After their encounter during the history lesson, Madison had struck an immediate friendship with Kimberley and Brianna. Madison had a calming nature, which was a welcoming contrast to Kimberley's exuberant personality.

The conversation, which largely consisted over the antics from the previous day, lasted for the rest of the bus journey and stopped just as the bus halted outside the front doors of Merlin, the main building of Witchcraft Heights, where the two girls saw Kimberley and formed the united friendship trinity. The school's students filed in and soon sifted off into their house groups, heading off in the direction of their own common rooms and lockers. Brianna noticed a few older students ahead of her and noticed that one of them was the girl prefect from yesterday. They followed them as they walked in the direction of the Merlin common room, glad that they had someone to follow or Brianna was sure they would have easily have got themselves lost in the maze like environment of the school. As she saw the group chatting animatedly to one another she suddenly wondered how many students there were in her schoolhouse and in the other houses that made up Witchcraft Heights.

When they finally reached the Merlin locker area, Brianna went a short way down the aisle to number 12, inserting the key into the locker's keyhole. It swung open and she looked at the timetable she had attached to the door, to double confirm her already memorized knowledge of her day's lessons.

"English first," said Madison from behind Brianna's locker. "It says it's in Medea classroom 14B, we better head over there quickly."

Brianna got the rest of her things together, placed them in her light blue satchel and slung the bag over her shoulder. They walked across the main entrance hall of Merlin, this time taking one of the western doors that led out onto a winding path. It snaked its way back and forth between a large stone walled courtyard. It was a beautiful place, full of colour due the vast number of flowers that covered both the walls and the gaps between the main winding path on the floor. The sun bore down on Brianna's back, but its weaker rays provided welcoming warmth rather than any discomfort.

The girls went through the main entrance of Medea. Like the contrast between Merlin and Medusa, the Medea building offered another contrasting element to the school. Brianna further inspected the décor of the Medea building and noticed that the hangings on the ceiling were of pale yellows and creams. Like Merlin, the Medea building had its entrance hall with a staircase leading to the upper floor. However, it was not a grand staircase, but a simple curving one that split left and right to the second floor. The girls, believing the English room to be upstairs, turned right as they went up the staircase and followed the winding corridor. They were right in their instincts and managed to locate the classroom towards the far end of the corridor.

They were not the first ones in and as such, meandered in and amongst their classmates to a free table on the furthest side from the door. Once seated, they sat quietly chatting to one another until a jolly looking woman entered the room. She wore a long deep aubergine coloured shawl over a lightly draping fuchsia dress. Her jewellery dripped off of her, bangles, rings and a large pendant necklace. Her outfit gave a sense of jubilance and a rather rich quality.

"Welcome ninth graders, my name is Miss Lotty and I will be your English teacher for your first year at Witchcraft Heights," she boomed to the entire class.

The remainder of the lesson was spent with Miss Lotty handing out a number of battered old books and then getting different students to read sections of the first chapter. They were reading a book titled 'The Wonderful Wizard of Oz', their topic of study for the rest of the first term.

At the end of the hour, the bell sounded and the class filed out. Brianna placed the book carefully at the bottom of her satchel and the three of them headed off to the science rooms over in the Medusa building for their next lesson.

By lunchtime, Brianna had improved her knowledge regarding the school by the slightest fraction as she transferred herself between Medea and Medusa for her lessons. As the sun was still warming the town of Salem, Brianna and Kimberley decided to sit the grassed courtyard in the centre point of the school. Kimberley was very observant of all of the flowers in the vicinity and spent the time telling the other two, rather

impressively, all the different varieties. She depicted their subtle differences and convincingly managed to link

them to a variety of different aspects; including thoughts, feelings and even the elements themselves.

Their fourth lesson of the day was Math, after which all three girls came out with a glazed over look

across their faces. They had presumed that their first encounter with Mr Downswood had been a one off; that

his teaching might have had an off day as can happen from time to time. However, their second encounter

bought together the resounding understanding that he had a true gift. He could send a class into a stupor

within five minutes and as such was labelled as one of the most boring people that they had come across.

They went back to the Merlin common at the end of the day, wishing to rest their tired selves in one of

the plush armchairs by one of the chapel like windows. They supposed that some of the older students must

be distributed among the many areas of the school or had gone home early, as the common room was fairly

sparse, with mainly ninth graders filling up the room.

This was the first opportunity that Brianna had had the chance to relax during this busy day. As the girls

sat among the plush furniture they swapped stories about their own lives.

Kimberley explained that her mom was a rather care free spirit, who always wanted to move around

and often did so on the slightest whim. For Kimberley this was a frustrating affair as she so wished to find

roots and a place that she could settle in. Brianna listened and heard the quiet longing to belong lingering

somewhere ling in Kimberley's tone of voice and realised in comparison how her one move didn't match up to

a lifetime of uncertainty.

Madison was born and raised in Salem; she claimed that all of her family, as far back as could be

traced, had lived within the community of Salem. Her pop and mother had both attended Harvard, where her

mom met her dad. Her dad had originally come from West Virginia, but soon settled and came back to live

with her mom in the little town. Madison explained that the parents, being exceptionally bright, had the same

plans for her. Brianna wondered quietly whether this level of determination and drive had quashed some of

Madison's free sensibility and reduced her to the conformed and slightly timid girl that she seemed to exhume.

Kimberley took charge of the conversation and started to question Madison some more, but Brianna had a more wandering mind and found herself occupying her time by taking a good look at her current surroundings. Her eyes paused as they landed on a notice board that stood next to the front door of the common room. A picture of a purple and silver set of pompoms attracted her attention so she rose from her seat and went to see what was written underneath.

"Cheerleading trials," she read out loud, more to herself than the benefit of anyone else, "Wednesday after school, at the back of the Morgana building."

Brianna's eyes lit up as she finished reading the notice and read it over in her mind to certify what she had just seen. She waved for the other girls to come over and Kimberley and Madison peered over the Brianna's shoulders to read the sign for themselves.

"I'll give it a go," said Kimberley with an agreeable nod, "It would be nice to meet some of the girls from different houses."

Madison shifted, twisting one foot further into the carpet and remained silent. She kept her head low and instead of saying a word she turned around and headed back to their seats.

"Madison, what's up?" Brianna enquired, with a puzzled look towards Kimberley who looked equally as puzzled, "Are you going to come along tomorrow?"

"I don't think so," she replied, starting to blush, "I've got two left feet and absolutely no rhythm."

"That's nothing to be embarrassed about," said Kimberley reassuringly, "you can still come along and support us. You never know, you might want to give it a go."

Madison gave a somewhat weak smile, but after her friends' kind words she seemed a little more relaxed. Brianna carried onto talking to Kimberley and Madison, all the while her heart raced and excitement coursed through her veins at the idea of making the cheer team.

When Brianna got home she rushed up to her room and spent the rest of the evening planning, practising and perfecting her routine. Over and over, she created a cheer chant for the verbal part of the audition, being extra stringent to ensure that the claps and stomps worked in perfect unison with her words. When it got to ten o'clock, Gretchen popped her head around the door to see Brianna still busily working away.

"Come on sweetie, its bedtime. You need to have enough sleep to be ready for tomorrow."

"Yes, mom," she replied with a yawn and pirouetted to turn off her music which made her mom chuckle. She went to kiss her mom on the cheek and lightly stepped over to her bed, snuggling into her duvet. She fell into a deep sleep where dreams of girls leaping across fields with the aid of broomsticks and witches hats taking the place of pompoms invaded her sleep.

*

The following day both Brianna and Kimberley held a slightly greenish tinge to their faces for most of the day. Madison gave them both reassuring smiles and a comforting pat on the shoulder to try and calm her friends' nerves.

As the bell sounded to signal the end of the day, the girls headed over to the Morgana building. On their way, Brianna looked for girls that might be likely candidates for the cheerleading trials, looking at girls huddled in groups and deciphering which ones possessed that overly enthusiastic and dazzling quality. On passing one lot of girls her eyes met one of them, a girl with long black hair that fell like water down her back. The girl noticed Brianna, but returned a slight sneer to her innocent glance. The rest of the group turned around to see who the girl was glaring at and spotting Brianna gave similarly scoffing looks. She decided to ignore the girls, feeling angry that they were so judgemental for no apparent reason and carried on walking past them.

Brianna and Kimberley walked into the Morgana sports hall, with Madison falling behind the two of them to find a seat in the rows of benches that lined the sports hall. The girls walked the length of the dimly lit hall to a table, which was stood out in the enormous sports hall, by a single spotlight. Four girls, all of whom wore a jumper with the letters S and W emblazoned across the front, occupied the table. Brianna and Kimberley walked past each of the four girls who gave warming nods as they passed them, stopping at a girl with her red hair tied back into a high ponytail. She looked up and took notice of Brianna and Kimberley, giving them both a small encouraging smile. Brianna noticed that the girl also had a silver badge attached to her yellow jumper with the word Merlin etched on it in a diagonal slant.

"Names and house please," she questioned the two.

"Brianna Eastey 'n' Kimberley Aldridge of Merlin," Brianna replied, at which the girl gave a greater smile and wrote their names on a sticker. She handed them a sticker each and they planted their names on their tops.

"Thanks girls," she said raising her arm and pointing to a small group sitting on the floor against one of the walls of the hall, "if y'all just go over to join the rest of the try-out hopefuls; we will be shortly with you."

Brianna walked over with Kimberley to join the rest of group. For Brianna, the walk felt more like a trek as her mind began to race back to her practised routine from the night before. She sat on the edge of the crowd, hearing whispered murmurs from the other hopefuls. Some looked older than others and Brianna pondered as to whether everyone had to try-out every year. As her eyes looked out for Madison in the darkened seating she heard a large bang, as the door was swung wildly open. The obnoxious black haired girl and her group of cronies strutted across the sports hall directly to the red haired girl, pointing at herself and the other girls as they received a number of hand written name stickers.

She came to sit directly in front of Brianna and Brianna couldn't help but feel she was trying to block her view from the judge's table, hiding her away from the competition.

"Afternoon newcomers and old timers," said the Merlin cheerleader warmly. "I'm Dakota and I am the head cheerleader of the Merlin house. I, along with the head cheerleaders of Medusa, Medea and Morgana will be selecting the cheer team for this year. For your audition you will need to show us a dance sequence and cheer chant that you have practised. Just give us your best and own the spotlight, for those few minutes it's your time to shine. Good luck."

The short introduction was over and it seemed in no time at all before Kimberley's name was called up to audition. She walked with purpose to the centre spot in the hall; Brianna could see the concentration line that furrowed her brow.

She was astounding; her fluidity of movement and ease at which she carried out her routine seemed a sure winner. Her cheer chant was just as good, with a clear loud voice carrying around the sports hall. A number of other hopefuls followed after Kimberley, some flawless like Kimberley, but others stumbling over their own feet or forgetting their words.

"Zoe Harper," called the Merlin head cheerleader and the girl with the black hair sauntered to the middle of the sports hall, flicking her hair behind shoulders before nodding to start her audition tape. She was good, that Brianna could not deny, but her attitude showed an element of arrogance. Brianna looked over to the judges table and noticed that two of the head cheerleaders did not seem overly impressed by Zoe's egotistical performance and scribbled a couple of notes that looked to be negative, judging by the sour looks on their faces.

After Zoe, Brianna was very surprised to see the pompous Rose walk up in front of the judges. She stuck her nose in the air and barely acknowledged anyone else in the group as she walked past the other candidates. She was not a particularly rude girl, not by Zoe's standards anyway, but she definitely was a rather pompous sort of person. As she carried out the routine, Brianna couldn't help but think she was also a slightly deluded sort of person. Her routine, at a polite push, was average. Her claps were out of time and a lot of her moves lacked that aesthetic quality. What was most surprising was the self-assured look that she carried on her face as she walked back to the group; she wasn't told the truth on a lot of occasions thought Brianna to herself.

A further four candidates showcased their talents in front of judges, including a incredibly athletic boy named Logan who performed a number of highly impressive stunts including the very difficult double twisting double layout. Once Logan returned to an appreciative applause Brianna was called to the centre spot. Her heart was pounding in her throat and her legs felt as wobbly as jelly. It felt to Brianna as if all eyes were already making their judgement on her before she had taken a single step. The walk to the centre spotlight was slow and arduous, but she finally took her place under the hot light and turned to the face the table, which held the four head cheerleaders. She gave one small nod to signal she was ready for the music and then the she began her routine.

Her fears melted away as the music started; she was back in the comfort of her bedroom, dancing in front of her mirror and the company of a few teddy bears. Her jumps and twirls gained smiles from the head cheerleaders and her flying arabesque was received by tumultuous applause. Following on from her routine Brianna began her chant, which was equally as clear as Kimberley's and had much more enthusiasm pumped into it then Zoe had demonstrated. She held her finishing pose with a large grin stuck to her face, breathing out all doubt and worry as she knew that she had given her best effort for the audition.

She walked back over to Kimberley who hugged her to show her belief in Brianna's routine and they sat down with the colour back in their cheeks whilst the remaining ten girls and two boys auditioned for a spot on the team.

"Thank you so much for today everyone, you were all awesome," said Dakota once the last potential had taken their place under the spotlight. "We will let you all know the squad list next week. I want you all to know that even if you don't manage to make the team, your all stars in our eyes" and with that the four head cheerleaders got up from the table and quietly left the sports hall. As soon as the door shut behind them Brianna and Kimberley rushed over to Madison.

"You girls were incredible, you'll have no trouble making the team," said Madison earnestly.

"I hope so," said Brianna and the girls walked off to the main entrance to get the bus back home,

with the previous fears of the audition cleared completely from her mind.

Chapter 3

For the next few days Brianna could think of nothing else but cheerleading. She woke every day since the trials with a panicked feeling, which was often followed by a sick feeling in the pit of her stomach. Every day she nervously went to school and waited for some news on who had made it into the squad. When it had been over a week since the trials Brianna had still heard no news on who had made the team. She had even gone in with the mind to interrogate one of the four head cheerleaders the following Thursday when she could take the suspense no longer, but as she was still new to the school layout she didn't have much luck in finding any of them.

On the morning of the following Friday, Brianna greeted Madison and Kimberley on the school bus. She took the vacant seat by the window and gazed at the passing scenery whilst Madison and Kimberley continued their conversation.

As they met the main bulk of the morning traffic she reverted her gaze back to the occupants on the bus. She came out of her stupor and her tongue struggled to hold back the question that she had persistently been asking for the past week. Once again it was targeted to her two best friends.

"When do you think we will hear about who has made the squad?" she blurted out suddenly.

"I don't know," said Kimberley in a sympathetic tone, "as I have said every day for the past week I'm sure they will let us know soon. You've got to stop worrying about it, I don't think you will have any trouble on making the team and Madison thinks so too. Just try and concentrate on something else."

Brianna nodded in agreement. She knew that what Kimberley was saying made complete sense and was aware that it was pointless for her to keep bringing up the subject. The repetition of her constant questioning day in and day out was becoming tedious for not only her friends, but for herself as well. She resolved to try and put cheerleading to the back of her mind and instead tried to think about the lessons that they were to have that day as the bus drove the past the gated entrance of Witchcraft Heights.

All three girls went right of the grand staircase in the Merlin building and left the building through one of the north doors. This led out onto the circular path that connected Merlin to Morgana; as they followed the path they passed a few students seated on the stone based benches that faced a small fountain in the middle. The students were busy talking amongst one another in their groups whilst they ate their breakfasts in the last few days of warm autumnal air. They entered Morgana and walked right through the building to its northern part so that they could access the changing facilities that linked the school to its outdoor sports facilities.

They had only had one games lesson so far and that lesson had only consisted of an introduction to what sports the school had to offer. Witchcraft Heights was renowned for its American football and athletics squad and both were extremely difficult and competitive extra-curricular activities to become a part of. After the brief introduction to the world of sport the class had started to complete a variety of fitness tests to identify their own athletic ability. The girls knew they would probably have another fitness test today and as such were in less of a rush to get changed. Brianna retrieved her sports kit out of her duffle bag and heard a group of girls noisily entering the changing rooms, causing the door to slam against the wall as it opened. Brianna looked up to see who had made such an entrance and saw that it was the black haired girl Zoe and her friends swinging their bags off of their shoulders and onto a bench in the far corner. Their games lesson was the only lesson in the timetable that mixed different houses in the same class; Merlin and Medusa shared their games lessons together and Medea and Morgana shared theirs on another day.

Brianna's encounters with Zoe had not got off to the best of starts. She had not forgotten their first meeting on the day of the trials, but Brianna chose to believe that the sneering look she had received was as a result of the nerves prior to the cheerleading trials. Since that day however, Zoe had shown that her rude attitude was not due to a nervous disposition but something much more in line with a simple dislike towards herself, Kimberley and Madison. In their first games lesson Madison had tripped during their sprinting fitness test and Zoe and her friends had laughed cruelly while Madison sobbed over a cut knee. As far as Brianna was aware she had done nothing to spark this rivalry. She never had a single enemy back in Jacksonville, only friends and had done nothing but showcased her kind nature and warm personality since her first day at Witchcraft Heights.

Today was no different and Zoe glared at Brianna from across the changing room.

"Well, I'm sure that I will find out soon enough about being successful in the cheer try outs," Zoe said loudly and pointedly in Brianna's direction, "I've spoken to the head cheerleader and she has been very positive about my routine. It is just sad to know that there are those that didn't hit the mark simply because they weren't good enough. In a way it's embarrassing to think that some of them actually thought they stood a chance in the first place."

She finished talking and gave an evil grin that was undoubtedly reserved for Brianna. Brianna felt a little tugging notion on her arm and snapped back to see Madison trying in vain to pull her away from Zoe.

"It's not worth it, it's not worth it," Madison kept repeating over and over and Brianna couldn't initially fathom the reason for the pleading look across Madison's face. It wasn't until she looked further than the grip of Madison that she noticed that she had balled her hand into a tight clench. She took a deep breath and felt the anger subside.

"Good," Madison said soothingly, "she wants to get you in trouble and sink her poisonous words into your mind. Don't give her the response that she wants. Don't let her win."

Those last four words stuck with Brianna as she realised the complete truth in the words. Zoe was vindictive and clearly wanted a reaction from Brianna. Well, she wasn't going to give her that satisfaction. Instead she ignored the unkindly words, stuffed her clothes away in one of the changing room lockers before heading out the back of the sports hall and onto the school grounds.

The journey to the sports field led the students out onto the green fields that took occupancy at the back of the school. The girls joined the path and followed its western direction to the sports facilities. The fields out the back were not maintained like the three courtyards and as such were abundant with violets,

Black-eyed Susans and daisies, which grew freely over the sloping green fields. She walked with Kimberley

and Madison on the snaking yellow sandstone path that was bordered by dark pebbled stones. They chose not

talk much and instead looked around to fully appreciate the natural beauty stretched out before them.

The girls reached the athletics running track and espied most of the junior boys from Merlin and

Medusa hanging around by the finishing line. They walked on the track, avoiding the football field that was

placed in the tracks centre.

As the girls walked down the straight to where the boys were all gathered, Brianna could see most of

the girls following behind them. The boys were all crowded around a tall muscular man with short dark brown

hair that was currently hidden under a red baseball cap; Coach Williamson. From the moment that Brianna

had first met Coach Williamson she could see that he was a typical sports coach. He spent his entire time

outdoors and never spent any of his time in areas that didn't have pitch markings or a running track. He had

been a sports star at one point in his life, but the cruelty of age and time had taken away some of his athletic

youth and build.

"Hurry up girls or you'll be completing suicides in the sports hall as a lunch time treat," he boomed

across the athletics track, his voice echoing to the trailing line of girls that were still walking. Brianna had seen

that Coach Williamson was passionate about his sport from the first moment they had met him and as such he

had a low tolerance level for those students who showed a lack of enthusiasm in his lessons.

When the last straggling few finally caught up with the rest of the group, Coach Williamson gave them

their task of the day; a test of endurance.

"Very simple," he said in short, unctuous tones, "you will see how many laps you can complete of the

athletics track. Run, jog or walk. You have thirty minutes. Go!"

With that, the juniors of Medusa and Merlin carried out their monotonous task. Brianna, Kimberley

and Madison were the most determined of the girls and ran for a good fifteen minutes, before slowing down

to a jog. They managed to catch up with Damien and a couple of his friends who were jogging alongside him.

Brianna held back, careful not to overtake Damien and instead found herself listening in on the conversation that the boys were having.

"So you didn't get on the football team?" questioned a round faced, blond haired boy. Out of the three boys he was clearly not the most athletic. As the other two jogged along at a rather comfortable pace, the blond haired boy huffed and puffed a great deal as he tried to keep up with them.

"No Michael, I told you I saw the captains this morning. They told me that I hadn't been selected for the team," replied Damien, a tone of disappointment ringing in his voice. "He said that a lot of the juniors weren't quite ready to represent the school."

"But you were one of the strongest contenders by a mile. You demonstrated an outstanding drop shot and you were easily the fastest boy in the group" piped in the other boy, with darker features who Brianna remembered was named Caleb. He had to speak down to the other two as he was particularly tall with pointed features from a pointed prominent chin to his sharp steel grey eyes. He looked more suited to the athletic tasks out of the three; Damien had the clear look of an American footballer with wide shoulders and narrow hips.

"Well, I clearly wasn't one of the best. I tried my hardest. Maybe I just didn't fit the bill," Damien replied dejectedly. Brianna had to fight the sudden urge to run up and comfort Damien of whom she had never seen look anything less but cheerful.

"No way," said Michael defensively, his breathing becoming heavier and heavier as he continued to struggle talking and running at the same time. "It was just a biased trial. I mean who's to say that they didn't go and pick all their friends."

"Yeah mate, if they were going to judge it on talent, they couldn't ignore what you had to offer," said Caleb.

The boys finished their conversations and sped up for the last two minutes to race against each other, even though it was more of a race between Caleb and Damien as Michael looked ready to pass out. The girls slowed down to a walk and Brianna and Kimberley looked nervously at each other. Brianna's mind started

to think back to her own performance. If Michael and Caleb had thought Damien had a clear shot at getting in

the football team, was she to suffer the same fate? Were there elements to her performance that would lead

to her demise?

Coach Williamson blew his whistle to signal the end of the endurance run and the students of Merlin

and Medusa traipsed back towards the changing rooms. Brianna was intent on getting back and getting

changed, when Zoe strutted past Brianna. She made a loud comment on her athletic superiority, declaring it a

league above any other girl in the school whilst looking pointedly at Brianna once again. Thinking back to

earlier, Brianna made a conscious decision to ignore the poisonous words and instead set her focus onto a

bigger issue. She decided that she would not rest until she found one of the head cheerleaders to enquire as

to whether she had made the school cheer team.

After a quick change, she raced around the school looking into other classrooms before entering the

cafeteria. She scanned around, eyeing every individual that was sitting at every round table scattered across

the canteen floor. She looked at the pedestrianized queue at the food court and even looked towards the girls'

toilets so as to monitor those entering and leaving its facilities. Brianna started to panic again as she saw no

sign of them and feeling slightly down hearted, headed towards her next lesson. It was a small consolation

that she was to head to her favourite lesson; history.

The walk to the Medusa building for their history lesson was a short one as they used the west side

entrance and followed the corridor all the way down to the history classroom. They were the first group of

students to reach the classroom, with a good five minutes to spare before the lesson started.

"Are you alright?" asked Madison in a slightly worried tone, "you haven't said a single word since we

caught up with Damien."

"Yes I'm fine. It's nothing to worry about," she replied distantly before coming to her senses and seeing

that she was causing an unnecessary worry to her friends. "I'm sorry; I'm getting stupidly worried about these trials again since we overheard that Damien didn't make the football team. I know that I've just got to stop thinking about them so much."

"It's understandable, but we don't actually know how well Damien performed. I feel just as nervous as you about the whole thing, but I truly believe that we have a strong chance of making the squad. All you can do for the time being is to put cheerleading to the back of your mind. We've got too many other things to worry about other than a decision that is out of our control," Kimberley said with wise conviction.

They walked along to the classroom; Brianna tried to make an effort to forget about the fear that was riding in her stomach. The fear of the unknown and failure to develop any knowledge regarding her future at Witchcraft built up inside of her. It settled uncomfortably in her stomach and grew and grew until the fear was all she could think about. At the moment when it seemed the most prominent the lights in the corridor spluttered and died. The darkness engulfed all around her and she felt inexplicably alone. The blackness fed on her fear and she felt lost and helpless as she felt around for some way to progress through the black abyss.

A scream echoed ahead and it was Madison who screamed out among the darkness.

"Madison, Madison, it's alright," Kimberley said in a soothing manner, "follow the sound of my voice, you are only in a corridor, there is nothing to fear."

The panic seemed to subdue almost immediately; her screams vanished and only spluttering of the lights coming back to life could be heard. Brianna looked upon her friends and saw the consoling hand of Kimberley on Madison's shoulder. The fear was no longer in Madison and Brianna believed that it was Kimberley that had a gift to help out those around her; a true and caring gift.

They carried on the remainder of the walk in light and entered the history classroom. As they waited for Miss Ashdown to arrive Brianna thought in the silence how Kimberley had shown in such a short space of time that she wasn't just a bubbly albeit commanding girl. She was also very caring and sensible; she was someone that Brianna could trust to tell anything.

"Good afternoon students of Merlin," Miss Ashdown called out from the depths of the shadows, making a few people in the front row jump.

Maybe it was something to do with the lack of light in the classroom, but Miss Ashdown had a habit of entering the classroom so subtlety that she made no noise or motions to announce her arrival. The Merlin students were no nearer to this accustomed entrance two weeks into their term. In one of their lessons during the second week Olivia had actually squealed and fallen off from her chair at her teacher's sudden arrival.

Miss Ashdown wiped her board from the last lesson and opened her register, ticking off names as they were called out. She closed the folder and then took her usual standing spot by the side of the board.

"Right class, we should all have finished our witchcraft timelines from the thirteenth century to 1692?" she questioned the class.

"Yes ma'am," the class replied collectively, as many of them flipped through their work books to show that they had completed the work.

"Good, good, we will be using them again for a variety of different tasks so make sure that you keep them nice and safe.

"So, as I just said, our timeline ended in the year 1692, when Salem was deep in the belief that witchcraft was taking over the town. In our first lesson we went right back to the roots of magic and discovered how witchcraft evolved from an idea of mere superstition to a great epidemic that spread fear and panic across Europe. We then followed the voyage of superstition across to the new world, where witchcraft rumours began to settle in the north eastern corner of America.

"We shall now delve into the reasons as to why Salem is so heavily associated to witchcraft, looking specifically at the curious events that occurred during the year of 1692."

Miss Ashdown turned away from the class to turn on an ancient looking projector. She slipped a sheet of paper onto the lighted glass and an image was projected onto the board. It was a picture depicting a group of young children standing in court, writhing in pain. Brianna felt disgusted by the sight of the picture, where the artist had illustrated the children with drooling mouths and eyes popping from their heads. As shocking as it was to see the children suffering, it was a small lady in the back right of the picture that seemed to hold her attention a great deal more. The lady was draped in a folded black cloak, embossed with intricate symbols, which swirled and flowed on the fabric. She concentrated on the face and was startled; for where there should be two eyes there was nothing. Nothing but blackness. It glared in the direction of the young children and it scared Brianna far more than the image of the children.

"In Salem, the first account of dark magic was documented when three young girls displayed extremely odd behaviour. This included screaming out blasphemous words and suffering from extreme seizures. The girls were named Ann Putnam, Elizabeth Parris and Abigail Williams. Panic swept through Salem as they witnessed pain that could not be explained through physical sickness. It soon became apparent that the acts of the children were controlled from the influence of Satan himself. Witches had come to Salem.

"The girls later confessed to those that had controlled them. Two of them denied their involvement and pleaded innocence, but Tituba who was a Caribbean slave, professed to be a witch. She claimed that the devil had given her the gift of magic and she obliged to fulfil his duties. Tituba further declared that she was not alone and that there were more witches than could be imagined in the town of Salem."

She took a pause, and pointed down on her register stopping at a few names.

"So, over the next few months many members of the Salem community were questioned as to their involvement with the black arts. A total of nineteen people, mainly women, were sent to the gallows to hang. Others died in jail. It has been recorded that during 1692 over two hundred people were accused of practising the dark arts, yes indeed.

"Now, after looking down the register I have found that your class is one of the most intriguing of classes I have had in a while. If I call your name out I would like you to stand.

"Brianna Eastey, Maria Parker, Rose Bishop and Michael Proctor."

Brianna stood up along with the three other named students with questioning looks at one another.

She felt unsure as to what they had done or what they were going to be asked. Brianna looked down towards Kimberley who merely shrugged her shoulders to show she had no revelation as to what she had done either.

Miss Ashdown gave the four students a smile to show that they had done nothing wrong. "I have asked you four to stand as your surnames are in fact of great importance to this topic. I asked last lesson if people in this group had ancestors that they knew were in Salem during the witches' trials and some of you raised your hands. You four are particularly well linked to the trials. You see your surnames are shared with some of the women and men who were sent to the gallows during the witch trials; Mary Eastey, Bridget Bishop, John Proctor and the two Parkers, Mary and Alice.

"There were others who were hung such as Martha Corey, a seemingly upstanding member of the congregation, but it's incredible to have so many akin to those hung in one class," finished Miss Ashdown with much enthusiasm.

The four students sat down slowly, but none so much as Brianna, who couldn't quite believe that she shared the name with that of an accused witch. She had never thought of her ancestry before, but then there was no need to. She had thought that she was connected with Salem from her first history lesson and now she knew that she was linked to an accused witch of Salem she could finally understand why she felt such a strong connection. She sat while thoughts whirled in her head. The move to Salem was turning into an intriguing mystery, one where destiny had led Brianna and her family to this town. She could think of no explanation as to how her family line was so closely entwined to a place she had only just moved to. It was too vast to comprehend so she settled to dismiss the revelation and instead got to work with the task that Miss Ashdown had set; a research topic into the accused witches of Salem.

By the end of the lesson Brianna had just managed to complete an in depth research on Tituba, the Caribbean slave. She was particularly interested in how Tituba used creatures to frighten others or do her bidding. Animals such as black dogs, yellow birds and black and red cats were common features; all creatures, which she assumed, made their way into future fairy tales. It was quite something to comprehend that this time in history built up a whole genre for future generations to enjoy and imagine.

The three girls finished the day with an energetic drama lesson before wishing each other a good weekend. As she left the Merlin building to wait for the bus to arrive she noticed that Rose Bishop was also waiting down at the bus stop.

"Hi, Rose," she called out automatically.

"Hello," Rose replied. Brianna was slightly curious as Rose seemed fairly guarded at her approach.

"So what did you think about Miss Ashdown's lesson then? It's pretty weird that we might be related to witches wouldn't you agree?"

"I suppose so, if you believe in that sort of thing that is," she said once more demonstrating her less than welcoming demeanour.

"Don't you then?" Brianna was still not too sure about Rose's attitude.

"You're asking me whether I believe in magic. Well no would be the answer there," she answered in her mocking tone, "and as for Mrs Ashdown she is as crazy as they come. As I told you before, I think what we are learning is all rubbish and the fact that you lap it all up demonstrates a rather immature manner."

The bus turned up before Brianna was able to reply and Rose stepped onto the bus without a backward glance. Brianna was shocked for a few seconds, remaining rooted to the spot, before finding a seat on the bus as far away as possible from Rose. Her dislike for Rose couldn't help but surface after being addressed so disdainfully by her for a second time. She didn't think there would be anyone as rude as Zoe in witchcraft heights, let alone in Merlin, but she had definitely found a strong contender.

Some of what Rose said did strike a nerve in Brianna. She had fallen so deeply into Miss Ashdown's stories that maybe she had taken what she had been taught too seriously. She could not explain as to why, but the idea that Miss Ashdown was only telling a fairy tale saddened Brianna. So it was with a slightly disheartened attitude that Brianna set her mind to the weekend, wondering what she was planning to do

with her ancestral discovery from her history lesson.

Chapter 4

Witchcraft heights had certainly made an impact on Brianna Eastey. In the three weeks since she had started she had made both friends and enemies, had trialled for the cheerleading squad and found her favourite subject to be history. Jacksonville to Brianna was already a distant memory and Salem was the town that had always held her heart and soul.

Her connection to Salem had strengthened the moment after her history teacher proclaimed that she was a descendant of one of the persecuted witches of Salem. The fact that she was related to someone in Salem, the town that she had just moved into, began to plant a seed of intrigue on her mind. The inescapable feeling that her ancestral lineage was part of an unfolding plot in her life followed her home that weekend.

She sat up in her room and flicked through the TV channels, but Miss Ashdown's words kept creeping up on her and she found herself thinking of nothing else but Mary Eastey. She sat quietly through dinner, while her Mom and Dad busily talked about their busy week at work. It wasn't until late in the evening that she decided she was going to have to talk to her parents. It was answers that she needed and she needed to find out if they could shed any light on her ancestral lineage. Sadly for Brianna, they were both as surprised as she was. Neither her Mom nor Dad knew anyone in the family to have lived in Salem.

They sat in the living room, discussing the possibility that they had ancestors from the town they had just relocated to. However as the conversation developed, a sense of doubt clouded Brianna's mind. Her parents informed Brianna that they knew where their parents and their grandparent's had presided but could give no input prior to that. As far her Mum and Dad were aware, their family had always lived in England, they believed they had a family history steeped in British qualities and lineage. The only person that they had questionable doubt over his existence was an old Uncle Bertie who wandered across to America with nothing but a small rucksack filled with handkerchiefs and a collection of stamps. It seemed he had been in Salem at one point, but where he was born was not so easily traceable.

"He was an odd one, that old Uncle Bertie," stated her Dad. "I remember some of the strange stories my dad used to say about his brother. Back in England he was always found walking back from the local woodland area and returning with an assortment of strange items. He would also disappear for periods at a time, about your sort of age really. When he returned he would say all these odd sort of chants; none of which made any sense and almost seemed in a foreign language. Soon after his eighteenth birthday he was rarely ever seen, in a note he stated he was venturing across to America. We think he headed to Salem as he kept a journal that we found filled with the word Salem. Well it was there to our belief, but one thing we do know was that he was most peculiar."

So it was decided by the Sunday evening that Miss Ashdown had made a simple mistake. It was mere coincidence; she was not necessarily linked to the witches of Salem just because she shared a surname with a suspected witch. Brianna had been so wrapped up in the world of magic and history of Salem that she had actually allowed herself to believe some of the illusions and fantasy. She took a step out of the unbelievable and saw that Miss Ashdown was merely engaging her pupils in her subject.

She retreated to her bedroom afterwards and looked out into the starry night sky through her window. After a long while she finally fell asleep, as she made herself consider the truth in the matter; that the move to Salem was not some gravitational pull by some greater power but an easily explained job transfer.

*

Monday morning dawned bright and early on Brianna, but it was not a welcomed morning. She had taken long enough to switch off thoughts regarding her family history, but she had then found herself in and out of restless dreams for the rest of the night as her brain kept reminding her of her cheerleading audition.

She dragged herself out of bed, not speaking to her parents as she passed them on her way to the shower. Her mind whirled with the continual feelings of worry about whether today she would find out the squad list, preventing her to stomach any food as it busily bubbled away. She managed to remember her bag and reached the bus stop with just enough time to hail for the bus. She drowsily looked around the bus and spotted Madison and Kimberley sitting on the back row. As she perched down next to Kimberley the exhaustion finally hit her and she managed switch off; catching up on a few winks while the bus meandered through the streets of Salem to Witchcraft Heights. Kimberley nudged Brianna on the arm to wake her as they drove through the main gates.

"Everything alright Brianna?" asked Kimberley, looking toward Madison with concern.

"Yeah I just didn't get an awful lot of sleep last night," replied Brianna, "I asked mom and dad about my surname; we tried to figure out if my family did live in Salem at some point."

"And did you find out whether you were?" enquired Madison.

"Well Mom and Dad don't think so, they said that our family have only ever lived in England," replied Brianna.

"Maybe your parents are right. Miss Ashdown is probably always looking for some connection to Salem's past; to make some connection to shock us all. I mean, just because your surname is Eastey doesn't mean you are definitely a descendent of one of the Salem witches," agreed Madison.

As the three girls headed into the Merlin building they were surprised to see a cluster of girls and a few boys standing by the corridor that they went down on their first day. For some reason Brianna recognised a couple of the girls, but she was not completely sure as to why. As they walked closer to the group she realised where she had seen them before; the girls had attended the cheerleading trials. As she looked around the group, she started to recognise the more of the students and knew that they too had been a part of the trials. She forcefully tugged Kimberley on the arm and pulled her over to the crowd, her brain piecing together what the group of students were waiting for.

Her inclinations were correct as on closer inspection the crowd were looking towards the four head cheerleaders from the trials. The girl that Brianna recognised as the Merlin cheerleader had a piece of paper in her hand.

"Thank you so much for your time and patience," said Dakota, the Merlin head cheerleader. "It has been very tough for us to decide as to who should make the squad this year. If it were possible, you would all have a place on our squad because to us you are all shining stars. The journey that some of you have made to achieve your dreams is by no means at an end and if you are unsuccessful at this point please do not deter from trying again. As it is often pointed out, ever cloud has a silver lining.

"The list I have here are of the students who have made the squad for this year. If your name is called out please go to the registration chamber for further instructions."

Brianna waited with baited breath as Dakota began to read out the list of students who had made the cut. The further down the list Dakota went, the more Brianna started to get worried.

"... and finally," declared Dakota, "our last place goes to Mary-Ann Shelley."

Brianna's heart sank, she hadn't made the team. What Dakota said next was blacked out by a distant buzzing noise; she could not concentrate or think to move as the bell sounded for her first lesson of the day. Brianna looked to Kimberley who looked equally as downhearted; she scanned the group and also noticed Zoe, whose face was screwed up in anger. So many disappointed faces shone through the crowd and Brianna felt heartbroken that she was a part of that group. As the revelation sunk in further she found that her disappointment faded by a fraction and now her attention averted instead to see the joyous faces of those who had made the team.

Brianna was never one to be a sore loser; she had never liked to show resentment and she knew what needed to be done. She put on a brave face, smiled as much as it was possible for her to smile and began filtering through the crowd to congratulate those that had made the squad. After congratulating a set of twins she was cut across by Zoe who stormed past her in a whirl of anger, heading back towards the entrance hall. It didn't surprise her that Zoe had taken this dramatic approach and it did make her feel better that at least someone that horrid had also not managed to be a part of the squad.

Brianna carried on walking through the crowd, which was now beginning to thin as the successful candidates made their way into the registration chamber, before she realised that she was walking in the direction of the head cheerleaders. Dakota immediately spotted Brianna as she had made the quick glance towards her and gave an encouraging smile in return. Brianna was slightly shocked as she then saw Dakota making her way through the crowd with her eyes fixed on Brianna and Kimberley. Brianna tugged Kimberley's arm to make sure that she didn't walk off as she was certain only she noticed Dakota's intentions.

"Hi girls, I'm sorry you didn't make the team this year," Dakota said as she stopped in front of them, "Personally, I wanted to add you two to the team, but one of the other teachers said that you might be needed for another after school club. I'm sure you'll find out about it. I would say more but I've got to go and do my speech," and with that she turned and headed into the meeting room to talk to the newly selected members of the witchcraft heights cheerleading squad; the Salem Witches.

After that short conversation, Brianna was slightly less down hearted as curiosity crept up upon her.

What an odd remark, she thought to herself. The head cheerleader had informed her that she had not been selected for the squad team as, apparently, a teacher had asked for her to be a part of another club. Brianna wondered as to who would request such a notion; considering which teacher would have a great interest in the selection process of students that would attain a solitary club.

She thought Coach Williamson would have a likely candidate, as she had trialled for one of the school's sports teams and he would have a fairly strong link with Dakota. On the contrary, Coach Williamson had not yet spoken to Brianna or Kimberley in any of their lessons and indeed made no attempt to talk to the girls outside of the lesson. Then her mind reverted back to the first lesson and the tiny belief that Coach Wlliamson was linked to the squad choice was promptly quashed. She remembered how they had sat in front of him as he boomed out the list of available sports in the school. He had left cheerleading to the bottom of the pile and chortled against the athleticism of cheerleading. He believed that girls should complete more taxing sports such as athletics or baseball. Brianna realised he would be the last sort of person that would want to give attention to cheerleading.

It wasn't until the third lesson of the day that the girls managed to talk among one another about the squad announcement. They sat in their history with Miss Ashdown and she had soon set them off on the task to complete the research project about the Witches of Salem. The girls all huddled around a table, with their books open so that they looked like they were engaged in their work.

"I wonder which one of the teachers' told Dakota to skip us from the selecting process," said Brianna.

"I reckon that Merlin cheerleader was fibbing Brianna. Why would a teacher interfere with team selections? Surely they would want everyone to have a good chance to get into a school team?" Kimberley responded.

"Maybe," replied Brianna slowly, "I just wish it were true. At least it would be a consoling reason as to why we didn't make the team. Why would she bother saying that to us if she didn't mean it?"

"Maybe we weren't the first girls she spoke to though," reasoned Kimberley in a depressing tone, "she could have said it in passing to any number of other unsuccessful students."

"I'm not so sure about that Kimberley," interjected Madison, "the head cheerleaders were mainly staged at the front the whole time; I didn't see them going around to everyone. I noticed they didn't speak to Zoe. Not that I'm sorry she didn't get a look in."

"You girls didn't get in either?"

Brianna and Kimberley both jumped at the stranger's voice and looked around to see who was intruding on their conversation. As Brianna turned her head she was surprised to see Damien staring right back at her. She tried to respond but somehow her voice was misplaced deep within her chest, so Kimberley decided to interject the awkward silence that was amounting and spoke up on behalf of her best friend.

"Yeah, we got told this morning," she replied dejectedly whilst Brianna imitated that of a nodding dog.

"Aww, that sucks. I didn't make it into the football team this year. I found it disappointing at first, but it does get better pretty quickly. For one thing it's only the first year so we still have the chance to get into the team next year. Plus it gives us the opportunity to make some new friends when we don't have to concentrate so much on the one sport. Maybe it's a good opportunity to become involved in other clubs," Damien said in a hearting tone, but with something that maybe held more meaning than basic words of comfort.

"I agree," said Brianna in a voice that was much louder that what she had meant and felt herself blushing. Damien gave a small chuckle to her response, which made her blush even more furiously than the pale shade of red already blossoming on her face.

Heartened by Damien's views, Brianna soon found herself thinking about Damien and his kind words, picking out the way that his smile shone in the light and how his eyes looked into hers. Every word that he said sunk into her mind and etched onto her heart; in fact it drove away all thoughts on the news from earlier that day. It flew by in a rush of emotions and just as she looked to respond to him, he spoke again.

"Well, I suppose I should head back to my table," said Damien, turning very slowly back to Michael and Caleb with a look that seemed reluctant to leave.

"You can sit with us if you'd like," said Brianna quickly, keen not to let him out of her sight. She blurted it out in a slightly jumbled fashion but it seemed to make a bit of sense as Damien turned back to face her again.

"That sounds like a good idea to me," he beamed and he beckoned the boys over.

"Hello," said Michael and Caleb simultaneously as they sat down either side of Damien. Sitting in the row in front of the girls, they turned their chairs around and used the girl's table to put their books and pencil cases on. They spent a fair amount of time talking to one another with polite introductions; the conversation was fairly formal but nonetheless had a flow and degree of ease about it.

Realising that she had spent rather a lot of time talking, Brianna attempted to refocus her attention

back on her work. They sat researching the topic of the Salem witches for the next forty five minutes, but

every now and then Brianna could not stop herself from looking up towards Damien. She was pleasantly

surprised to see that he was looking up at her, his gaze fleeting and slightly shy when they looked at the same

time. She saw Kimberley nudge Madison lightly and the two of them looked at Brianna and grinned. She raised

her palm to her cheek and quickly realised that she must be blushing for they were fairly warm. She returned a

sheepish grin in their direction and attempted to refocus on her work.

As part of her research task, Brianna had decided to find out as much information as possible on Mary

Eastey. She wanted to see whether any facts on her could solve the potential family link. After trifling through

a few text books and newspaper articles Brianna had collected a few facts about her. She had found it

intriguing that Mary Eastey was a highly respectable figure in the Salem community. She was accused of

witchcraft after several members in the local community were seen to be under Mary's spell. She had been

found guilty of control and torture; targeting the young children in the village. It was hard to stomach the

stories told regarding the pain inflicted on young children. Brianna winced at the tales of paralysis and felt sick

at the thought that another child had been forced to feel the pain of a broken neck.

There was an incredibly sad ending to the horrific tale; Mary Eastey was cleared of all charges on all

accounts of witchcraft. However the notion came too late for poor Mary Eastey and she was hung before her

verdict was finalised. The family were still left to suffer in her absence; leaving a husband without a wife and

eleven children without a mother.

She started to research some of the other Salem witches, before being bought to attention by Miss

Ashdown. She hushed the class to be silent, with a clipboard in her arms held tightly in her arms.

"Well done in today's lesson," she said in her hushed tones, "By now you should have sunk your teeth

into your research project and have a plethora of interesting facts on the events surrounding 1692. Make sure

that you all find one topic that is of particular interest to you.

"I do hope that you have found some exciting tales about the trials of Salem, they are indeed most fascinating. You will have two more lessons in which you can truly develop your understanding of the Witches of Salem.

"Now, I have a short list of students that I would like to speak to at the end of the lesson. If I call out your name could you please stay behind?

"Kimberley Aldridge, Xavier Prince, Rose Bishop, Michael Proctor, Damien Quests, Caleb Williams, Madison Count and Brianna Eastey."

Everyone seated around Brianna looked around enquiringly towards one another, while Xavier came over to join the rest of the group. Brianna couldn't help but notice that Rose remained resolutely in her seat, ignoring the other seven students and looking idly in the direction of Miss Ashdown. The rest of the class left slowly, chatting without much concern about the remaining students, whilst Miss Ashdown waited by the door to usher them out. She closed it behind the last student before returning to her front desk and turning to face them all.

"Juniors of Merlin, I have a small proposition for each and every one of you in this room," began Miss Ashdown, looking at each student in turn, "But first of all it must begin with a confession and an apology.

"I am aware that some of you in this group recently received some bad news. Some of you didn't quite make it into one of the school clubs for one reason or another and for that I am truly sorry. Maybe even more so as I had to stress my wishes against your selection in the school teams"

The apology came swiftly and Brianna had not considered for a moment that strange Miss Ashdown would have anything to do with the school outside of her beloved history classroom. She turned to look around at the rest of the group who were equally looking at one another to decide on an appropriate response to the revelation. Some, like Damien, looked annoyed at the news that their history teacher had stunted their chances of making the football team.

"It is imperative that you were not a part of the school teams, but the reason for my meddling will be revealed in due course. For now, you need only know that I am starting an after school club. You are my selection of Merlin students that will be a part of the club.

"It is a club that I start up every year and it is available to all four houses. It is an exclusive club and only by my permission are you allowed to join; you cannot invite others to be a part of it. Your first task will be based around event organising. For the most part, the club is designed create bonds with the other houses of this school and realise your strengths in the school."

Miss Ashdown then bent down and retrieved a folder from her desk. Brianna was surprised that the book did not crumble in her hands as she lifted it up. The faded and crackled golden tome looked incredibly ancient and careworn. The letters on the front cover were similarly cracked and slightly peeling. Before Brianna had the chance to read the writing Miss Ashdown opened the dusty book and turned its blank face to show to the rest of the group.

"I like to use this book as something similar to that of a contract. The contract demonstrates a keen and willing attitude to commit to the club and keep it a secret between the members of the group. If you decide to sign up to the club it is a matter that should not be taken lightly as you cannot idly wish to forfeit from the group. If at any point you do decide to leave the club, like some have done before, you have no chance to re-join the club.

"If you still wish to join, please sign the book. I can say no more about the club until I know who wishes to be a part of it" finished Miss Ashdown.

Brianna considered Miss Ashdown's terms. Her warning did not scare her; on the contrary an immediate level of intrigue sprouted, desperate to know why a club was so particularly secret. A strange feeling formulated from her chest as she felt an immediate and inextricable attachment to the club; she couldn't see herself belonging to anything else. This was a feeling that she could not shake off.

Her mind was made up in a matter of seconds and in doing so trifled through her bag, retrieving a pen from the bottom with which to write her name in the book. She was the first to rise from her seat and walked over to the large book to sign her name.

She hovered over the page to see some names of students from the previous year. She was still not familiar with the names of the older students, so was unable to familiarise any faces with the names jotted down in front of her.

She went to put pen to paper, but as she did so Miss Ashdown intervened and gave her a quill to write her name down in the book.

"I prefer if you use this," Miss Ashdown said.

The quill, Brianna noticed, was the same colour as the gold covering of the book. She felt the soft feathers run through her fingertips and placed pen to paper. As she signed the book a warm tingle flowed down her arm to the tips of her fingers and Brianna thought she saw a golden glow shine out from the letters on her name. She blinked and the writing looked just as normal and she shook the strange feeling from her. She dropped the quill alongside the book and felt a small weight lift off of her shoulders, another strange feeling for such a basic task. It did puzzle her, but didn't question it to Miss Ashdown. Everyone in the group followed suit after Brianna, including a reluctant Rose Bishop and all too soon there were eight new additions to the history after school club.

Miss Ashdown looked to the clock on the wall before turning back to the juniors.

"Okay juniors, you are running late for your next lesson so I am afraid I cannot keep you here any longer. If you can come back to this classroom after school on Thursday I will introduce you to the rest of the group and then we can start our first exciting project of the year," she finished.

As the group filed out Brianna realised that she had left her planner on her desk and went back to the table to retrieve it. Picking it up off the table, she was surprised to notice that Miss Ashdown had vanished from the classroom. She hadn't left the room as far as Brianna was aware and she left the history

classroom even more puzzled by the mysterious nature of her history teacher.

Chapter 5

Thursday seemed awfully distant for the students of Miss Ashdown's club. Brianna and the other students of Merlin impatiently counted down the days as they waited to start up this mysterious club. Brianna soon found out the names of the other selected students from the other houses that had been included in the history club. To her dismay, one of the selected few was the extremely rude Zoe Cole.

They had overheard Zoe and some of the other Medusa students bragging about how they had been selected to be a part of such an exclusive history club; they had clearly ignored Miss Ashdown's policy on privacy regarding the club. Zoe looked down her nose at Brianna, believing that she was somehow superior to her.

"It must be such a shame that some students don't get selected for anything when they try so hard to be a part of something," Zoe declared particularly loudly. "Some of us are chosen because we have something particularly special that is above and beyond all others that try."

Her friends snickered at the unkindly remark, but Brianna wasn't particularly fussed. Zoe clearly didn't know that Brianna had already been selected for the history club. Well, thought Brianna, Zoe was soon going to be in for a shock.

The girls left a cackling Zoe and her cronies to their own devices and headed outside to meet up with Damien, Caleb and Michael.

A new friendship had begun to blossom for the six of them. Since the after school club, they had found themselves congregating together during their lunch breaks and the boys had also moved to work with the girls in their Maths and English lessons. They all got on exceptionally well; their vibrant mix of personalities complimented each other and created an overall positive atmosphere. Caleb was not as quiet as Brianna had first thought. Instead he showcased more of a comical individual when he had finally relaxed around the three girls and was often found to be the main cause of a few laughs in their lessons. Michael was the most reserved of the three boys, but very kind hearted and gentlemanly. However, in Brianna's eyes there was only one boy who truly captured her attention.

Brianna had tried not to become too attached to Damien or show him how much she liked him. This wasn't as easy as she had wished, as her feelings seemed to constantly simmer under the surface of her skin, leading to a number of clumsy actions and a permanent blush affixed to her cheeks. Her initial attraction had escalated as she had got know him more and more over the past week which made her quickly realise that her affections were far greater than a flying fancy.

There was only one problem that Brianna had to contend with. She was neither blind nor naive and soon she had come to realise that Damien was rather popular with a fair number of the female students at Witchcraft Heights. The majority of the juniors and some of the older students did a double take when they passed him in the corridor and a select few had actually blushed if he spoke to them. What amazed Brianna during these occasions was that Damien genuinely seemed oblivious to the effect that he had on the girls.

She tried to shut off her mind from these disheartening thoughts that threatened to incense her as the group sat together in their English lesson. Soon they were back to discussing their favourite topic of the week; Miss Ashdown and the history club.

"I wonder how many students will be attending the club this evening?" pondered Madison.

"Do you reckon Miss Ashdown will have invited any of the older students?" queried Caleb. "Maybe we will have the chance to meet some of the other students within the school."

"That would be a first," retorted Damien, who was correct in a manner of speaking. It had soon come to Brianna's attention that the number of older students roaming the castle seemed exceptionally depleted. Other than the prefects and head of the sporting teams, the corridors and rooms of Witchcraft Heights did not seem to carry the load of students above their own year.

The English lesson itself went along without an interesting or particularly exciting moment passing by. Miss Lotty set them the simple task of writing a newspaper report with reference to the list of events that they had read from the Wizard of Oz earlier on in the week. Brianna set at her seat, busily scribbling away at a topic that she truly enjoyed. Most of the class seemed equally as focused; the only exception was Damien. As she looked up and saw him, she couldn't help notice the furrow of concentration lining his brow, she wondered what it was that he seemed so intent on.

When the bell rang for lunch time the three boys went off to play some American football on the back fields; leaving the girls to sit by the benches behind the Merlin building. Kimberley and Madison sat discussing the amount of homework that seemed to be piling up and the sorrowing matter that their free time was being slowly stolen from them. Brianna was dipping in and out of the conversation, nodding and saying an offhand yes every now and then.

"Brianna," Kimberley chuckled as she waved her hand in front of Brianna's face.

"Yes," replied Brianna automatically, before realising that she hadn't really paid any attention to the other two for at least five minutes.

"We were have a girly chit chat and went to ask you a question, but you were definitely on a different planet," said Madison with a grin on her face.

"Well we know what planet she was on. Planet Damien," giggled Kimberley.

"Ah, knock it off you two," said Brianna blushing bright red, batting away their teasing with her hands.

"Don't worry. We saw that he touched your hand today in class and you went a deeper shade of red then what you are now," said Kimberley, "not that I blame you, he is definitely one of the good looking guys."

"What do you think of him then?" asked Brianna with a slight defensive tone to her voice.

"Oh I don't fancy him; I just can see why you like him. I can see why most of the female population at Witchcraft Heights like him too," noted Kimberley wisely.

"You've noticed the Damien fan club then," she answered Kimberley dejectedly.

"Well, yes, but in case you haven't realised, you're one of the only girls that he actually talks to and most definitely the only person that he has touched the hand of. You should feel extremely privileged" teased Madison.

Brianna kept her remaining thoughts to herself and thought about what her friends had just said. As it started to sink in she was somewhat reassured and secretly pleased at the truth of their words. It was true that she and Damien got on exceptionally well, even if he didn't see her quite in same the way that she did.

Their last lesson of the day was one that all the juniors greatly looked forward to as it was their only free of the week. The students could use this time to play sport, relax in the common room, or as was the case with the three girls; start doing their homework in the school library.

One of Brianna's favourite parts of the school was undoubtedly the library. It was situated in the middle of the Morgana building and occupied the majority of its bottom floor. She had always loved to read books and had done so from a very young age. Nothing could harness her interest and imagination more than the page turning escapades of dragons and stories of far off exotic places. Sometimes she would even dream of taking the place of characters in some of the books; from creatures as strange and wonderful as a mermaid to princesses locked up in a high tower by a wicked stepmother.

Back in Jacksonville she would happily spend her whole weekend in the library, with her nose in a book for hours on end. That library seemed an insult to its purpose in comparison to the beauty of the Witchcraft Height's library. Its cavernous contents stretched off for what seemed miles in the Morgana building. Like the rest of the school, it was incredibly old fashioned with rows of oaken shelves that were distinguishable only by the flickering orange glow set off from the lamps. All the shelves were labelled categorically to books related to a wide array of subjects in the school as well as books of fiction and non-fiction. The shelves that lined the walls pertained moving ladders that allowed the schools librarian Mr Flounder to fly along the walls, helping out students to find a particular book and placing each book back in its rightful home.

Mr Flounder was a kind natured elderly man who was always useful for an array of information and knew where every single book resided in the library. He did have his stern moments due to a fond affection for his collection and therefore greatly detested seeing any book being mistreated. She had not seen anyone suffer the consequences of flouting the rules, but she had been told that failing to meet the library standards could result from a harsh telling off to a sentenced ban from the library. The cane that he used to walk with was also told of in tales. It had been said by the prefects that he would cautiously whip the table of misbehaving pupils within his supporting stick.

They walked quietly into the library and soon Brianna, Kimberley and Madison managed to find an empty spot in one of the corners of the library. They set themselves down by some squashy maroon armchairs and Brianna went to remove her history project from the depths of her bag. Whenever she thought of something to do, it was her Salem Witches project, which seemed to reach out to her, wanting to be completed and pushing her to learn more about the local history.

One of the many things that she wanted to know more about was the tales regarding her own ancestral lineage. Resolving to find out more information regarding Mary Eastey within the depths of the library, Brianna got up from her plush seat and soon set out searching the hundreds of thousands of books to sate her hunger.

She managed to find the history section of the library, where after searching for only a fraction of minute she found herself picking out a particularly old looking book. It seemed almost weird in a way as it had seemed almost as if the book had called out to Brianna. Its front cover held some faded letters and Brianna took a good minute or so to distinguish what it said; 'Historia de Celatum Coed'.

Although she could not cipher any meaning from its title she tucked the book tightly under her arm. She continued to scan the rest of the shelf, but didn't find anything of interest. She unfathomably decided that her first choice was all that she needed and therefore went back to sit with the other girls. Whilst Kimberley and Madison dithered between the rows of the library, Brianna sat engrossed in her book, poring over pages and pages of information regarding the witch trials. She sat flicking through the pages before she stopped her finger at a point that explained a detailed account regarding Mary Eastey. It contained details regarding the trial just before she was led to the gallows.

As she read all the way to the bottom of the page, drinking in the notes from the sort event, she noticed a small scrawling had been placed in the bottom hand corner of the page; 'The Witches of Salem stay true. The ROS is a secret I will hold close to my heart'.

Brianna reread the sentence and the pace of her heart quickened. What did this mean? What was ROS? She flicked through the rest of the book but found no other hand written scrawling's hiding amongst the pages.

The bell for the end of the day chimed and the girls put their things back into their bags. Brianna looked around and noticed that Mr Flounder was currently occupied with two students and for some reason unbeknown to her, she snuck the library book into her bag before following the other two girls outside.

They led the way out of the library and walked back to the Merlin lockers to the drop off their books from the lessons of the day. As they turned the corner that led to their lockers Caleb, Michael and Damien were approaching the girls from the other end of the corridor. Michael was sporting a mud-splattered pair of shorts and Caleb had a slight resemblance to a scarecrow from the turbulent wind that had swept up his hair.

"It's really starting to blow a gale out there. I feel like I'm in Kansas rather than Salem," said Caleb.

"I can tell," giggled Madison, "I didn't realise the scarecrow had come to join us. I don't suppose you two are the tin man and the cowardly lion?"

Caleb returned a sarcastic laugh as he ruffled his hair back into submission. The girls opened their lockers and deposited their items. Brianna raked around in her bag and her hand stopped on the library book. As her fingertips brushed the spine she thought whether she was going to leave the book behind as well. She decided she didn't want to leave it behind and her hand left her bag as she closed the door of her locker, leaving the new found treasure in her bag.

"We best head off to the history classroom then for our history club," informed Kimberley, who had become something of the self-elected group leader. They all agreed and the six of them walked back down the locker corridor. They made their exit out of the western edge of the Merlin building and headed over to the Medusa building.

They passed the grassed courtyard where a few of the older years were sitting down in the unusually mild autumnal air, before heading into the Medusa building. They walked apprehensively into the history classroom, not too sure what to expect from the club they were about to become a part of. They were not the first ones in the room; Rose was sat with her arms folded by one of the seats at the side. Xavier, the other selected Merlin student was already seated at the front of the classroom and Kimberley led the group's way to sit with Xavier.

Over the course of the next five minutes the other selected juniors of Witchcraft Heights entered the classroom. When Zoe entered with the rest of the Medusa juniors she sat directly in the seat in front of Brianna and the rest of her group spread out along the row. As she turned to sit in her chair, Zoe flashed a Cheshire cat grin in Damien's direction. He did not return the favour and instead gave a glance in Brianna's direction. An angry blush blossomed on her pale cheeks and Zoe turned her smile quickly to one of her contemptuous glares directly towards Brianna, swinging herself back around in a windswept whirl as she faced the front.

Miss Ashdown crept out from among the shadows yet again to greet the class and Brianna found herself wondering where Miss Ashdown's hid during the times that she wasn't teaching. If she kept creeping out from the shadows what else could possibly be lurking in the dark corners of the classroom?

"Hello juniors, welcome to your history club. This club isn't a lesson so we can forget most of the formalities. For one thing, I am not the person that leads the sessions and I do not expect you to listen to every word that I say," she said making her way to the middle of the classroom so that she could centre herself amidst the group.

She perched herself on the desk next to Brianna and beckoned for everyone to look her way.

"It requires a lot of time and commitment to be a part of this club. From today you will be tested to develop and demonstrate a very important trait; the effective use of time management. The first event that you will need to organise is the schools annual Halloween Dance Spectacle, scheduled to take place at the end of October. This event is solely organised by the juniors of this club for the juniors; helping to encourage communication between the four houses," she explained and a murmur of interested quickly started to spread its way around the room. Brianna could already feel the excitement welling up inside of her; she loved to attend parties and dances and was thrilled at the idea that she was going to be able organise the event itself.

After her brief introduction Miss Ashdown proceeded to one of the cabinets in her classroom. The students faced one another and decided, as they were spending so much of their time together, that they should know the names of one another. One of them was Logan, the boy that had also attended the cheerleading trials. The other boys in the group were Riley, Emmanuel, Xavier and Nelson. There were a few more girls that joined the throng including the obnoxious girl named Rose. Zoe's cronies were also a part of the group; Regina, Cynthia and Alexis sat surrounding their queen bee. The only other person that they had not properly met before was a girl named Isabella, who was in the same house as Logan.

Miss Ashdown finished her rummaging and started to make her way back to the newly acquainted group. She allowed the class to quieten down before continuing. "The event that you are taking into your own hands is a particularly special moment in the school calendar as it is not only accessible for the students of Witchcraft Heights. We will also be sending out invitations to the juniors of Eastwick Grammar, Goodwin High and Salem Sisters; they are the other high schools based within the town of Salem."

At this news the class started discussing the inclusion of other schools whilst Miss Ashdown headed back up to her desk and looked onto the rest of the group. For those who had grown up in the area of Salem, they gave the rest of the group as much information as possible as to what they knew about the different

schools. Zoe was the first in the group to allow her voice to be heard by the whole class,

"I don't know why we would want to include some of the juniors from the other schools. It's not as if

we need or want to talk to students from the other schools," she said, placing a strong emphasis on the word

others.

"What's wrong with the other schools?" piped up Logan in response, "my older brother goes to

Goodwin High and it was the school had originally planned to attend."

Zoe turned a deep shade of red for the second time during this club meeting and muttered something

incomprehensible as she turned back to her group of cronies. Brianna quickly looked down the row to

Kimberley who gave a smile at Zoe's continuing humiliation. Brianna could not help but allow a grin to creep

up over her face.

Once more Miss Ashdown walked over to the group of juniors, oblivious to the conversation that had

just occurred between Zoe and Logan. She instructed the class that they would spend the remainder of the

session completing a brainstorming task. They needed to come up with as many ideas for a Halloween school

dance as possible on the piece of paper that she was giving out to each member in the group. Isabella and

Logan came to join Brianna and her group, with Xavier, the only other boy from Merlin.

"Hi," said Isabella to the group, "can me and Logan come and sit with you?"

"Yeah, sure," said Kimberley, and the rest of the group gave warming nods of acceptance at the three

new members to the group.

Just as Brianna instinctively knew she would, Kimberley took immediate charge of the group. She

started by writing a heading in the middle of paper where she carefully centred the writing, wanting to make

everything look neat and precise. They penned out ideas of what they thought suggested the theme of

Halloween. Images of ghouls and vampires, zombies and mummies crossed the groups mind and sent them off into a creative spiral of ideas. Brianna kept thinking of witches as an idea, but she thought that too obvious

an idea, no matter how much it plagued her mind.

The hour seemed vanish and in no time at all Miss Ashdown called the club to a close. She set them off

the task of finalising ideas for the spectacle for the next group meeting. She told them that it was not an easy

task; it would require a huge portion of their free time. As they all filed out they quickly agreed that the strain

would be worth the result; they would put in as much effort as was necessary to make it the best Halloween

Dance Spectacle that Witchcraft Heights had ever hosted.

*

As the fourth week at Witchcraft Heights begun, the members of the history club started their

countdown to the Halloween Dance Spectacle. They had less than three weeks in which to get the Halloween

dance spectacle organised. This meant that the planning of the event needed quick completion and approval

from the moment they had left the history club on the Thursday. Brianna had invited Kimberley and Madison

to her house over the weekend to set the wheels of the event in motion.

One revelation that she had recently discovered was that Madison was secretly a very creative person.

Since they had left the club meeting she had thought of some amazing ideas for the dance spectacle. She

suggested that they could serve pumpkin juice punch in carved out pumpkins and even had the time to sketch

her ideas down for Kimberley and Brianna to see. Another idea that she had come up with over the weekend

was to project spooky images depicting visions such as skeletons and witches on brooms across the sports hall

walls. When they had been in their first meeting Madison had kept all thoughts to herself, her shy demeanour

taking over her ability to present some truly original ideas. When it came to the second meeting the following

Thursday, Kimberley spoke on her behalf, staying true to Madison's ideas and never taking credit for them.

Xavier started to sit with the group for a lot of their lessons, particularly when they were sent off to do

their own tasks, and he helped to formulate ideas with the rest of the group during some of the more

lacklustre moments. Isabella and Logan also tried to meet up with Brianna and the rest of the group from

Merlin as often as possible. When they found themselves discussing ideas for the spectacle it had been a surprisingly stressful yet satisfying affair. They were springing out so many ideas that they were soon deciding on some of the bigger aspects of the event such as sorting out the musical arrangement for the dance spectacle.

Most of Brianna's week seemed to pass by without much excitement, as the majority of her attention was put to the planning behind Halloween dance. When her thoughts weren't planning another part of the dance, her mind averted to something completely non-academic.

Damien Quests flowed in and out of her thoughts every single day. He seemed to become a more frequent train of thought now that they spent every Thursday together in the history club. She often replayed every conversation that they had had together in her mind; whether she was at home or in sitting in class. Every smile that they shared or any time that his hand had brushed against hers had sent the familiar butterfly fluttering around her stomach. Although Damien seemed oblivious to her affections, Kimberley continued to reassure Brianna that he gave no level of attention to any other girl like he did to her.

As well as attempting to develop her relationship with Damien, Brianna had an altogether different sort of relationship to contend with during her sessions at the history club. Three sessions of the club had passed and three sessions later Zoe Cole continued to look down her nose at Brianna. Whenever they had a group discussion, Zoe always sniggered or disapproved of Brianna's ideas. She never showed one kind courtesy and since Damien and Logan had publicly humiliated her, Zoe had vented out her vehemence on Brianna to an even greater extent.

*

With less than two weeks to go till the Halloween dance spectacle, the planning had finished and the group were finalising the bookings for most of the necessary items for the dance. It was during their second to last session when they were sat in the history classroom printing off tickets for the event that Zoe decided to conduct a fresh wave of malice towards Brianna.

Brianna sat among the group; busily explaining the ticket selling process when Zoe chose to stand behind Brianna's back, imitating Brianna in an overly authoritative and crude fashion. Brianna turned around as she heard a continued torrent of tittering behind and saw Zoe flailing her arms around and continuing her unkind imitation. Angry tears sparked her eyes as she understood what her enemy was up to but she turned back to face the rest of the group. She did not wanting to give Zoe any satisfaction in the knowledge that she had successfully upset her.

The group tried to ignore the malicious act from Zoe and contented to finish printing the tickets, giving each person an equal number of tickets to sell before saying their farewells and exiting the history classroom.

"I think it's all going rather well," said Kimberley, who had been off to the printers a couple of rooms down from the classroom and as such was unaware of the vindictive nature of Zoe.

"Well it would be even better without certain people in it," Brianna commented gloomily.

"I'm sure Miss Ashdown had her reasons for selecting each member of the group," answered Kimberley in a diplomatic fashion.

"But, Zoe... really?" asked Brianna with tremendous disbelief at her friends words. "I had her again, being rude, trying to make me look stupid and uncomfortable."

"What did she do this time?" questioned Kimberley.

"She kept being rude whenever Brianna spoke," Madison said, contributing to the conversation. "I saw her at it, flailing her arms and being downright malicious. I agree with Brianna, it certainly is strange as to why Miss Ashdown has selected some people to be part of the group. Zoe and her clones don't contribute in the sessions and try to claim all the credit when the teacher comes in. I'd love for Miss Ashdown to see her being horrible. In fact I would love to deal with her myself, turn her into a toad or something; she's ugly enough to suit a toad."

Brianna chuckled and wiped the lingering tear from her eye, grateful for Madison's supportive words. They left the school, walking back to Brianna's home, which was becoming something of a routine. Her home was quite an easy route from Witchcraft Heights; they could cut through the local park and down past the

towns favourite bakery to bring them out onto her avenue. Within twenty five minutes the girls had made it

back to Brianna's home and went to park themselves on the stools' in the kitchen.

"Hi girls," called out Gretchen as she came through the front door, her arms laden with shopping bags,

"did you have a nice time at school today?"

"Yes," replied a smiling Kimberley, "it was a good day apart from…" she started before Brianna nudged

her and gave her a look that told her explicitly that Brianna did not want her mom to know about the incident

with Zoe.

"Apart from what?" asked Gretchen inquisitively, looking between the three girls for some sort of

explanation.

"Only that we had to put up with Mr Downswood first lesson which nearly sent us back to sleep,"

replied Madison quickly, coming into the rescue.

"Oh. Brianna has mentioned him before," said Gretchen, still looking doubtfully towards the three girls,

unsure as to what was really going on between them.

"Okay mom, we're going up to my room now if that's alright?" asked Brianna.

"Of course sweetie, I'll bring up some snacks for you in a bit. Dinner will be served around seven if

that's not too late for you girls?"

The girls said that seven would be fine and Kimberley and Madison thanked Gretchen for allowing

them to stay for dinner. The three girls then left the kitchen, walking back into the grand entrance hall and

heading up the stairs to Brianna's room. This was one of the only rooms to have been decorated since the

move. Her mom and Dad decided that it would help Brianna to settle into a new area if her room was a place

that she had designed herself.

Brianna had decided to have her room decorated very simply. The walls were painted a light cream

with pale blue flowers sprinkled onto the walls in a delicate fashion. The floor was of real oak floorboards with a woven rug in the centre, which matched the walls. The furniture was panelled in white, creating a sense

of space and tranquillity, which was aided by the reflective light cast from the antique mirror that they had

bought up from Jacksonville. This was Brianna's haven; somewhere that she could escape from the busy life

that she had experienced thus far in Salem.

As Kimberley and Madison went to sit on the bed, Brianna went to put on some music, tuning into the

local radio station for background noise.

"Brianna, why did you stop me telling your mom about Zoe today?" Kimberley asked with a

disapproving frown.

"I don't want to worry her," replied Brianna shortly, averting Kimberley's gaze.

"Your mom would want to know about it."

"Well, I don't want her to know."

A short silence descended among the group, but it was abruptly cut as a new song came onto the

radio. They began planning their outfits for the Halloween dance spectacle, deciding that they wanted to do

something as a group. They sat there listing the names of different beasts and creatures most associated with

Halloween; ghosts, vampires, zombies, werewolves. None of these however seemed an attractive idea to any

of the girls and Brianna thought that she wanted to wear something that would at least attract Damien's

attention for the right reasons. As they contemplated a bit longer, Brianna's mind wandered around the room

and then her eyes fell onto her school bag. A light sparked in her eyes and she tore open her bag, reaching for

the library book; the 'Historia de Celatum Coed'.

"What about the Salem witches?" she exclaimed excitedly. "Wouldn't that be the most fitting idea for

the occasion?"

"But surely every other girl will think up that idea?" questioned Kimberley doubtfully.

"We don't have to be witches in the old fashioned sense though," thought Brianna, almost as much to herself as to the other girls. "I mean, we could look in this book for inspiration and then put our own personal twist on our costumes."

"That does sound like quite an interesting idea, I could sketch up some ideas if you'd like?" suggested Madison.

Brianna flicked through the book and stopped at some of the artist's drawings. She was a little shocked as she saw another scrawling on the left of the page.

'A witch must always wear a dress; the girls of Merlin say sleek dresses and a flowered headband suits us best. ROS forever'

Her puzzlement began to settle in again, she had flicked through this book a few times since taking it from the library and she was sure there had only been one previous note. Yet here, in black ink, was another scribbling. What did ROS mean? She looked doubtfully at the book, before returning her attention to the girls. She couldn't explain why, but yet again she said nothing to Kimberley or Madison about the mystical book and flicked to another page of pictures where there was pertained no hand written scrawling's.

"We could take inspiration from these pictures, but put our own modern twist on them. What do you think about long, slender cut dresses and flowered headbands?" she asked Kimberley and Madison as casually as possible.

"The dresses sound like a really good idea, but are flowers very witch like?"

"Think about the stories of witches though. Didn't witches in stories often use a lot of herbs and plants for their spells and potions? I think it would just symbolise the link that witches have to nature," she said, not quite sure why she had made the link, but sure that what she had said was true.

"I think she's right you know," added in Madison, "I always thought that they used herbs and elements of nature for their magic. Why don't we add the elements to our dresses then? We could have blue for the water, gold for the sun and green for the earth?"

"Yes! That's perfect," proclaimed Brianna, her imagination running away with her at the thought of the new creations.

"Okay, supposing we do this. How are we going to even get the outfits?" enquired Kimberley.

"Tomorrow, after school, we'll go into town and look around the shops. We can either buy the dresses or we can make them. Mom has made loads of outfits for me in the past, so I'm sure she would be able to help us," replied Brianna, the answers coming from her quickly and with conviction.

The girls had their dinner with Gretchen and Brianna's dad Harry. When they had cleared their plates they returned back to Brianna's bedroom for another hour with cookies laden in their arms as a treat bought by Gretchen, drawing designs for their perfect dress. Kimberley and Madison managed to perfect their dress designs before being picked up by their own parents and heading home.

Brianna got ready for bed and then reached for her library book, fanning through the book to read over the hand written line once more, believing that maybe Salem was not as it all seemed.

Chapter 6

The replies from the other schools fortunately came in thick and fast. This was extremely helpful for the members of the history club as the spectacle was a mere week and four days away. From the sheer number of replies the members of the club could only stand to believe that all the juniors from the neighbouring schools were attending.

The students of Merlin sat in their history lesson during their second period on Friday. Miss Ashdown she went over to Brianna and the rest of the members of her club in Merlin to congratulate them on their big success.

"Hello juniors," she whispered to the group as if trying to exclude all others from the classroom. "Please could you attend the final club meeting before the spectacle? There will be plenty of things to go through, so it's best to make sure that everyone is prepared."

She turned away with an encouraging grin on her face. Although everything seemed to be running smoothly, the pressure of getting the event fully prepared was starting to affect some members of the selective club. Even Kimberley, who was a highly organised individual, was feeling drained and stretched as she tried to manage organising the event at the same time as keeping up with the mounting level of school work.

A main priority for the girl's revolved around the creation of the costumes for the dance. The girls had gone into town at the end of the school week, the day after they had decided on their costumes, to look for three dresses. Unfortunately for them the task at hand was not easy as they had no such luck in finding their desired outfits. Instead they had had to settle in making the dresses from scratch, using bought materials from one of the arts and crafts shops. The girls thought that they could take full control of their dress wishes and hoped that that it would be an exciting and fairly simplistic task. Much to their dismay they soon discovered that making a dress was not as easy as it seemed.

They had been over Brianna's for most of the weekend trying to make their dresses. It had been the best place for them to all work together as they were able to enlist the help of Brianna's mom Gretchen in order to complete the dresses. They were becoming increasingly frustrated as the dresses started to take shape. The designs that they had carefully drawn out on paper were certainly not translating into the creations that were being produced before them. In fact, it felt as if they were having a moment from Sleeping Beauty; they were the three fairies working away to get the dresses ready. They had the designs laid out in front of them and could see what they wanted to make, but no amount of time, love or patience could seem transform their pictured designs into a reality. Brianna even thought that the use of a magic wand or a fairy godmother would be highly useful as she slaved away, attempting to smarten up the neckline on her creation.

They hadn't asked around to see what the rest of the group had planned to dress as for the spectacle. Brianna believed that everyone wanted to keep their outfits a secret as nobody wished for their ideas to be replicated.

Although Zoe didn't tell anyone what she was coming as, she kept bragging about the development of her costume during the course of the week leading up to the dance.

"Well mommy and daddy have said that I only deserve the best," she declared loudly on the Friday, "Daddy has paid for a world famous costume designer to make my one of a kind dress. He's been told to use only the finest materials that daddy has had personally imported from Paris. I suppose for others they don't get the same treatment because they clearly aren't as deserving."

Her friends were equally as pleased as Zoe as they were also being given the same treatment, courtesy of Zoe's dad's extensive bank account.

Even Damien, Caleb and Michael had gone into what Brianna called their stealth mode. They had said nothing to Brianna, Kimberley or Madison on what they were coming as, whispering to one another rather than including the girls in the conversation. Brianna noticed during lunchtime in the canteen, whilst Zoe was once commenting on how pearls were being selected fresh from the oysters for the neckline of her outfit, that the boys sat sniggering away in a corner pointing at something laid out in front of them. Brianna was slightly intrigued, but thought it best to leave them to it.

Although she couldn't change their attitude, Brianna had found it increasingly difficult to deal with as she sat there in one of their classes on the Wednesday, two days before the event. Brianna's mind went into a worrying frenzy, as she feared that the lack of conversation hinted at a deeper issue. Maybe Damien wasn't interested in her at all and did only see her as a friend. At that moment, maybe only by coincidence or rather fate, Damien noticed Brianna looking in his direction and responded with a beaming smile and vigorous wave. Her mood lifted and once again she set to her mind to the worry of finishing her dress.

*

Brianna, Kimberley and Madison had gone over to Brianna's once again after the last history club before the Halloween dance. With only one day to go till the actual dance, they all sat in silence actively adding the finishing touches to their dresses and making their flowery headbands to go with it. Brianna had made the blue dress, using a silk like material to create a beautiful flowing quality. To complement the dress she had made a headband with little blue violets and bluebells strung together with light green twine. The dress wasn't bad, she thought to herself, but it didn't translate the flowing and sparkling quality that she had hoped to achieve to represent the water element of her drawn design. Kimberley's green dress was a similarly good effort, but it wasn't the right shade of green. She had hoped for a jade coloured dress, where the jewels that were sewn onto the dress could have hung on like flowers sparkling in the sunlight. Madison was equally as distressed as her dress didn't have the warming glow that she had envisaged; it looked more mustard yellow than a golden sunrise.

Still they had made a valiant effort, which Gretchen was quick to point out. She thought they were good dresses, especially given the amount of time that they had been given to complete them.

As the girls resigned the inevitability that their efforts could not be changed anymore, they said their goodbyes to one another and were once again picked up by their parents from Brianna's home. Brianna hung up the completed dresses in the spare room, leaving the door ajar as she went back to her bedroom to get

some beauty sleep before the event.

She soon drifted off, but it was a highly uncomfortable sleep. A state where one is halfway between

sleeping and waking as her mind was too full to completely switch off. It was in the early hours of the morning,

when she felt more awake than asleep, that something rather peculiar happened.

A faint buzzing sound permeated her ears, irritating her so much that she opened her eyes in the

looming darkness to identify the source of the noise. The overwhelming blackness engulfed her. Suddenly, a

light glow seemed to emulate from the spare room with the dresses. Odd trails of sparkling dust floating past

the crack in the door that seemed to glitter a hundred different colours in the dancing light. She also thought

she heard the sound of wings, but as her mind struggled to bring her imagination into the reality, the pillow

was too soft for her to fight against the onslaught of a deep sleep.

When she awoke the next morning she struggled putting the pieces of her night together. She tried to

network the smallest bit of information, but as she came to her senses the incident regarding the peculiar light

and sparkling dust seemed to slip out of her mind.

She hastened to get ready, as she needed to get school earlier than normal. As well as their lessons of

the day, the members of the history club had the task to design the sports hall for the evening's event. She sat

downstairs and wolfed down her breakfast, while her mom dotingly looked after her.

"I do hope things slow down for you sweetie," she said with concern, "You were up all night pacing,

because of all the added stresses they are giving you. I have a good mind to ring up the school."

"Mom, what are you on about?" Brianna asked in a confused manner, "I wasn't out of bed last night."

"Maybe I was hearing things then," she answered with a doubtful glance, "but I was sure that I heard

shuffling and other noises on the landing."

Brianna let out a false chuckle and attempted to let the mysterious events pass her by. Today she only

had the time to concentrate on one matter; the Halloween Dance Spectacle.

Brianna got to school just as the sun was beginning to rise, hopping off an empty bus and walking up to the front doors of the Merlin building. In the dim morning light she made her way directly to the sports hall. It was an eerie environment to be in when the school housed no other students. Every step echoed around her as she made her way across the entrance hall and through to the main corridor that led to the back of Merlin. The weak autumn rays cast meagre shadows in the circled courtyard.

All of a sudden, she felt the hair prickle on the back of her neck as she heard the fluttering of tiny wings. She looked around for the source of the noise but could see nothing in such a dim light. Picking her feet up she quickly paced across to the Morgana building, with the unshakeable feeling that she was being watched.

"Hello, Brianna," called out a voice and as Brianna looked around she saw Kimberley approaching her from the direction of the sports hall. "Hey, are you alright?" she asked when she saw the fretful worry that Brianna carried.

"Oh yes," she replied falsely, trying her hardest to shake off her feelings of worry, "how long have you been here?"

"Only about twenty minutes," Kimberley answered, "some of the boys are already here. They have been moving the tables from the canteen to the hall. I've just got to head off to the common room to get the candles for the tables. Do you want to come with me?"

"I think I'll go straight to the hall, they will need me more in there," she replied, not wanting to pass back through the disturbing courtyard.

As she left Kimberley behind, she once more quickened her pace and reached the sports hall in record time. She saw that some of the banners needed hanging up and decided to set her mind to that particular task. It was an excellent choice for Brianna as it required both physical and mental strength which helped her to push the fears set by the events from the courtyard to the back of her mind.

Throughout the rest of the day, the students of the history club flitted in and out of the sports hall to set up the hall. They managed to gain some lesson time as some of the more lenient teachers excused them from their own lessons. Only Mr Shrewsborough, the head of Morgana and their science teacher, insisted that they remained for the entirety of the lesson. He claimed that their lesson on the lifecycle of a frog was far too important to be missed.

By the time the clock struck three, every member of the history club was amazed that the hall was finished. As exhausted as they were they had no time to dawdle or linger to admire their hard work. They busily rushed home to transform themselves into their costumes, with the intent to be back at the school as soon as possible so that they could greet all the students that were attending.

As the dresses were at Brianna's, Kimberley and Madison once again headed over to Brianna's house. They ran for the majority of the journey and only paused for breath once on the way back. When they crossed the threshold of Brianna's home they ended up crawling up the stairs from their combined hard day of working and running.

"That hall looks amazing, the other schools are not going to believe that they are in a school hall!" said Kimberley in low breaths as they sat in Brianna's room.

"Yes, I hope they like it. I can't believe it," Brianna began, "we have successfully completed our first planned event. I think we will need a break before another event though, I have so much work to catch up on."

"Hi girls," said Gretchen who had walked across the landing to Brianna's room, "are you excited for your evening? Are you feeling a little bit better, Brianna? I can't wait to see what you girls are going to look like. I've got my camera ready."

"Oh mom, do we have to have pictures, I'd rather not remember our failed dresses," said Brianna somewhat reluctantly.

"Of course you do Brianna; it's the first main event in your new school. It's something that you will want to look back on," Gretchen stated.

"Sure mom," Brianna resigned to agree for she was too tired to put up an argument against her mom, "Well we'd better starting getting ready, we've got to be there before the other parties arrive."

Brianna left the other two girls in her room as she headed over to the spare room to retrieve the three dresses. As she pushed the door wide open her eyes looked towards the three dresses hanging up.

"Kimberley, Madison, quick, come here," Brianna exclaimed, "Come look at our dresses."

The excitement that emulated from Brianna made Kimberley and Madison sprint across the landing to the spare room. They raced to the spare room and Madison clung onto Brianna to stop herself from falling into the dresses.

The girls couldn't believe their eyes. Their dresses were hanging up just as they had left them the night before. Only they weren't the dresses that they had made, not exactly. They were the dresses that each one of them had envisioned when they had drawn up the designs of their dresses. Kimberley and Madison looked towards Brianna with grateful expressions.

"Believe me girls, it wasn't me," she said to them. They looked towards her and shared her expression of bewilderment. Brianna thought for a second and remembered that her Mom had been at home all day. She headed out to the top of the stairs.

"Mom, thanks," she called down the stairs into the silence, not sure as to where her mom had wandered off to.

"What's that for sweetheart?" called up Gretchen, the sound of her voice coming up from the living room.

"For finishing off our dresses, they're amazing."

"Brianna, I haven't touched your dresses. We said last night that they were fine as they were," she called back.

"Umm, okay Mom, never mind then. I must have made a mistake."

Slightly confused, Brianna went back to the other girls and started getting ready for the dance. She fashioned her long hair into waves, sweeping her bangs away with her flowery headband. She put on a light layer of makeup, wanting to look as naturally pretty as possible. Luckily for Brianna this was a look that came quite easily to her.

For three girls, they got ready in a remarkably fast time and all too soon the girls made their way back downstairs with their three new beautiful dresses on. The girls went down to the living room to get their pictures taken by Gretchen. As Brianna's mom led the girls out into the garden to pose for their photos, her dad got the car out from the garage to drive them to the school.

"You look beautiful ladies," said Gretchen, wiping away a tear from the corner of her eye as she welled up with emotion, "you should be very proud of what you made."

In her daddy's speedy Dodge, the girls were escorted to the school in record time. Within ten minutes they found themselves driving through the wrought iron gates and up the winding, tree lined drive that led to the entrance of Witchcraft Heights. Brianna's Dad stopped directly outside the stairs that led up to the front of the Merlin building and the girls clambered out of the car.

"Have a nice time girls," he called out of the car, "I'll pick you girls up from here at eleven, no later." He gave them a small wave and a beep of his horn as he drove back around the fountain towards the winding drive.

The girls turned back to face the school once her dad's car had vanished and they proceeded to hold up their dresses as they climbed the steps to the front doors of Merlin. They followed their hand made signs, which led to them to the recreated sports hall.

As they opened the doors to the sports hall and entered the transformed room the lights were the last things to be adjusted so that they could cast eerie shadows of all things dark and scary on the walls. The images moved in a fashion that looked like a slow dance was being orchestrated across the walls. The girls looked at one another with sheer delight and Brianna felt a sense of accomplishment as she drank in every corner of the transformed sports hall. They spotted Miss Ashdown and the rest of the history club and slowly made their way over to join them.

"Wow," exclaimed Isabella as the three girls' approached the group, "those outfits are beautiful. Where did you get them?"

"We made them ourselves," stated Kimberley, with a small grin directed towards the two girls.

"Really?" said Isabella with shock, "that's incredible. I'd never be able to make something as brilliant as that. What Halloween characters are you?"

"The greatest of course," replied Brianna with a chuckle, waving her arms in a dramatic fashion, "the Witches of Salem. Descendants of our ancestors. With an added modern twist."

"Well isn't that just touching," said a voice sarcastically behind Brianna. Brianna made a quick assumption as to who had just spoke and turned around to see if her bet was correct. Sure enough Zoe was right behind her and as usual she had her lip raised towards her nostrils for her signature sneering glance.

"Well what are you supposed to be," replied Brianna scathingly, she was not going to be bullied around by Zoe anymore. "I can't tell what you are other than a beast with horns; your face is the only scary thing that seems to fit the occasion."

"How dare you speak to me like that, you better watch your back," stated Zoe in a threateningly quiet manner, not wanting to be overheard by Miss Ashdown, "You can keep hiding behind others in your group but it will make no difference. No one insults me and gets away with it."

Zoe stormed off to the direction of the girls' toilets with her cronies in tow. As she passed down the hall a blackened shadow seemed to engulf the direction that she had just walked down, as if the anger was being projected out from Zoe herself.

Kimberley patted Brianna reassuringly on the back, but as she turned to face Madison she noticed that Madison looked frightened at what Zoe had just said to Brianna.

Once again Miss Ashdown came over to where the commotion had been; she was never there when the students actually needed her. Once again she seemed oblivious to any potential conflict between members in her group. It was as if the trivial matters of teenage arguing weren't something that she needed to be involved in or question. In fact, Brianna had come to notice that Miss Ashdown was always rather distant from the group. She was their club teacher, but she had never shown any sense of attachment to any of the students. Instead she tended to gaze at a member of the history club every lesson with that continuing look as if her mind was focused on some other element of their character.

"Well first of all I must congratulate you juniors, yes indeed," declared Miss Ashdown, "this is one of the best events that Witchcraft Heights has ever hosted. Your dedication to this task has proven that you are a very promising year, full of talent and imagination. Congratulations!"

"I will proceed to the main doors and welcome our guests. By my clock they should be five, no seven minutes away," and with that Miss Ashdown led her way out of the sports hall. Brianna noticed that Miss Ashdown did not look for the time on any clock or watch and pondered as to how she knew that the guests were only seven minutes away. It must be teacher's intuition.

The power of teacher intuition seemed unquestionable as seven minutes later to the very second, Miss Ashdown re-entered the sports hall with the students from the other schools in tow. The sheer number of students was overwhelming as they cascaded through the entrance with a wide array of costumes. It was hard to distinguish students by the schools that they went to, but the costumes that they wore almost signified a certain personality trait. Some dressed in depths of dark colour like the blackened corridors of Medusa while others were bright and light like the walls of Medea. Brianna noticed that there were several girls from the other schools also dressed as witches. Some had gone for a more traditional representation, with cloaks and pointed hats. Others, like Brianna had taken a modern twist on their witch like costumes; with stars and sparkling glitter over dresses or robes.

As well as the witches there were warlocks, vampires, ghosts, mummies, werewolves, and a wide variety of other different creatures. One costume that Brianna found particularly amusing to behold was a boy who had fashioned his outfit to resemble a gigantic spider.

The band that had been booked for the first part of the evening started to play as the students filed in, playing an eerie mystical musical piece. They had fashioned themselves as a group of zombies and gave an overly dramatic performance as they played.

During the first part of the evening the members of the history club resembled waiters as they directed the students of Eastwick grammar, Goodwin high and the Salem sisters in to an enormous table laden with food and drink. The spread that had been laid out was all-themed for Halloween; with pumpkin cupcakes, spider web lollipops, bat shaped sandwiches and an assortment of other treats that all surrounded the gravestone cake centrepiece.

Brianna, Kimberley and Madison helped themselves each to a wand shaped carrot cake and grabbed a glass of the ice-cold cream-mist soda, which had vapours of white mist pumping out from the surface. They sat sipping the cream-mist soda's, watching the other students take to the dance floor in the centre.

"Hi girls," Michael called out from among the crowd and Brianna saw the boys making their way across the dance floor towards them. Brianna couldn't help but chuckle as she looked at them in their costumes. They had decided to come in as three superheroes, or at least that was what Brianna could gather. Their lycra outfits and shiny coloured pants suggested a league of superheroes, but they did not resemble any that she knew.

"Whoosh!" exclaimed Caleb dramatically, "We are the anti-calamity league! Fighting danger using comedy and daring wit! I am Captain Nonsense, leader of the squadron. I can send out silly string from my shoulders to trap the enemy."

"And I am Numpty Trapper, catching foes through my inability to remain standing," chipped in Damien, "My cloud of trapping dust does not allow for escape. When I start tumbling; the tough get rumbling!"

"And I am Doctor Wit," declared Michael, "using poor one liners and jokes to crush the enemies. They would rather be in prison than listening to what I have to say!"

They finished their introductions and stood in a huddle with Caleb standing tall in the middle and Damien and Michael on either side holding up large pistols. They pressed the triggers and silly string shot out from the ends. The girls burst into laughter and applauded the boy's imaginative, if not peculiar, efforts.

"You are truly the strangest people we have seen tonight, but I'm sure glad you're here," said Brianna, "you have definitely brightened up our evening!"

The group stood their talking to one another, forgetting the absence of conversation for the past few days and falling back into their normal friendship troupe.

The evening was going extremely well; the band had finished their set and the hired DJ was now playing some more current music. One of the songs caught Brianna's attention and her feet started to itch; wanting to get up and dance along to the catchy song. She turned to Kimberley and tugged her on the arm. Kimberley, being a good dance was quite happy to get up and the two of them beckoned for Madison to join them. Madison however, was far more reluctant than Kimberley to get up and dance. Luckily, Caleb went to sit next to Madison and she was quite contented to sit and talk to him for a while.

The other two boys were happy to join Kimberley and Brianna and soon enough the two witches and superheroes made their way into the middle of the floor and started to dance to the music. Brianna found it entertaining to watch the boys perform their silly dance moves; she and Kimberley were very able dancers who knew how to keep in time with the music. The boys on the other hand were a completely different story; their arms were flailing around in a propeller fashion and they were jumping around in such a comical fashion that it made Brianna laugh out loud.

They continued to bop around in an erratic fashion for quite some time as the music elated to an even faster crescendo. Brianna got so carried away that she began to join in with the boys jumping around, which was fine as the music was still kept at the fast tempo. She turned around and spotted Madison in the corner happily chatting away to Caleb and decided to carry spinning around and round until the crowd were

nothing more than a blur.

The DJ quickly changed the song and Brianna found herself spinning around to a romantic slow dance. Kimberley bolted off the dance floor without a backward glance, pointing towards the food table with Michael following in her wake. Brianna and Damien were left on the dance floor as they looked awkwardly towards one another. Everything slowed down to a near standstill for Brianna as she failed to notice anything that was going on around her. Damien didn't drop his gaze from her and she found her feet making small steps in his direction. A small grin caught his mouth and she found herself smiling in return; their hands started to extend towards one another and it looked to Brianna that Damien was just about to hold onto Brianna's waist when there was almighty eruption of laughter.

Brianna blushed violently, thinking that the laughter was directed towards her and tried to look around to where the laughter was coming from. She instantly pinpointed where the laughter was, but she noticed that they all had their backs turned away from her and were laughing at someone else.

Brianna looked quizzically at Damien, the previous emotions and plan of events cut sharply by the tumultuous laughter. They sidled over to join the crowd and snaked their way to the front of the group.

Zoe was lying flat on the floor with her long charcoal cape draped across her face. Brianna went to take another step forward, but was met by a seemingly invisible wall. She couldn't physically move any further towards Zoe. As she looked around she noticed that the group, which had students from all the four schools, were stood around Zoe in a perfect circle.

Zoe could not seem to move as she struggled in the wrappings of her cape. She struggled for a full minute before the cape fell from her face to reveal a very purple complexion with tears staining her face.

"What happened?" Brianna asked to a girl standing on her right who was still pointedly laughing.

"Oh, well..." the girl began to say as she tried to control her laughter," well someone bumped into this girl, it was someone from my school and she became really aggressive. We thought that she was about to strike the girl. Some of the students turned around when we heard that horrible girl shouting and then…

well I'm not entirely sure. It was almost as if a wind came and swept the girl from under her feet. It was such a

quick torrent that we weren't sure where it came from; she has been struggling to get up ever since then."

Brianna walked back out of the circle and went to find Kimberley and Madison to see whether they had

seen any of the events that had just unfolded.

"Hi, Madison," she called out as she caught up with the other four standing by the front door, "did any

of you just see what happened?"

Both Kimberley and Madison shook their heads, so Brianna quickly recited what she had just been told

by the girl. By the end of it Madison and Kimberley looked questioningly back towards Brianna and all the

group seemed at a complete loss as to what could explain such a strange incident. They were all fairly tired by

this point, so when Damien made his way back to the rest of the group they all decided to head to the front

entrance. Fortunately for the girls, the clock was soon to strike eleven so they did not have to wait long before

Harry came to pick the girls up.

They waved goodbye to the boys, Brianna giving an awkward smile in Damien's direction as thoughts

of the slow dance resurfaced, before they were driven back down the drive and the boys were out of sight.

The girls were staying over Brianna's, walking tiredly up the stairs to her bedroom. Gretchen had set up

two little camp beds for Kimberley and Madison and the three girls got changed quickly and curled up in their

beds. They mumbled their goodnights and Brianna smiled at the idea that Damien had shown a genuine

interest in her. What a shame for her that her perfect moment had been disrupted by such an ambiguous

event.

Chapter 7

The success of the Halloween dance echoed through the school for the next few days. The juniors that had attended were busily talking of their thoughts regarding the evening; what songs they had enjoyed, the quality of the food and the amazing transformation of the sports hall itself. It had been a great way for the students to really get to know one another and some had even made contact with the other schools. They chatted in their groups about their newfound friends, deciding when they were going to meet up with them.

For Brianna, her thoughts on the Halloween dance were of an extremely mixed bag. On the one hand she felt a grim sense of satisfaction, when Zoe had fallen into a heap in the middle of the dance floor by an unfathomable circumstance. From that event, Zoe had changed her attitude ever so slightly as she walked down the corridors. Usually she was one to parade down the corridors, but since the embarrassing event she now tried to make herself unnoticeable as she passed other students who were quick to point and laugh at her.

However the event that had resulted in Zoe's humility had interrupted a potential romantic circumstance between her and Damien. She was extremely disappointed since the aftermath of the event as Damien had shown no sign that he remembered what had gone on during the slow dance and he had reverted back to his usual friendly self.

As the dance was over and done with, Brianna and the rest of the history club could no longer excuse themselves from the homework that was set. They also had to suffer the consequences of not completing the homework that had been set during the time prior to the event. Every assignment, essay and project that the other teachers had set had to be completed and there were to be no excuses as to why a single student could not hand in the work. The spirit within the history club was heavily dampened as they set to work on the mountainous task before them. Miss Collier had set them a particularly strenuous art project on water and Miss Lotty had asked for them to write an essay on the threat and danger associated with magic in the Wizard of Oz. All in all, Witchcraft Heights had definitely lost some of its sparkle for Brianna. She felt connected to

Merlin and the students within the group and even felt a part of the history club, but for some strange

reason she could not settle her heart into Witchcraft Heights. She almost felt herself wishing for something

more, something that could excite and challenge her in new and enchanting ways.

Maybe it was because she had centred her whole world on such an extravagant event, but for Brianna

the week had definitely suffered from a slow start. She was greatly relieved when Monday finally came to a

close and she was able to head back to the haven that was her bedroom.

She crossed the threshold of her home and called out to see if anyone else was in. There was no

response except for the echoing tones of her solitary voice in the empty house. She grabbed a chocolate bar

before plodding up the stairs and dropping down onto her bed. She couldn't understand how things could

have taken such a sudden turn at Witchcraft Heights. She had previously been involved in such a vibrant

atmosphere and now it felt as if she was wrapped up in a wet weekend.

At this moment in time her whole world seemed to relate back to her school and she desperately

didn't wish to feel trapped in a life consumed by Witchcraft Heights. She tried to think of something that could

distract her for just one evening. Strangely enough there only seemed to be one comfort that Brianna that she

could really convert to at the moment; her new library book. She was still very much intrigued by the book and

flicked through it pages, pausing every now and then in the hope of finding another handwritten scribble. She

didn't know what she was looking for specifically, but she almost believed that the all the strange or

unexplainable events that had occurred so far this year could be explained within the pages of this absorbing

text.

Brianna continued to read the book even as the light faded outside to give way to the darkness. When

she awoke the following morning, she looked down and found that the library book was still lying across her

chest and she was still wearing the clothes from the day before. She hadn't realised how exhausted she had

actually been, the dance had taken all her energy out of her. The weekend had clearly not given enough time for her to recover and she must have fallen asleep and woken with a slightly sore neck from sleeping in a rather peculiar fashion.

As she attempted to gather all her things together in a sluggish manner, her mind was also struggling to process at its normal rate. Although she felt as if time itself was spinning backwards due to her seeming lack of productivity, Brianna still managed to catch the school bus and made her way successfully to the first lesson.

She only managed to recognise Madison and Kimberley due to her stupor, when they were eventually seated at their table for their English lesson. She gave them a weak smile and they replied in a similar fashion. In a way it was a relief that they were all suffering the same torpor. It was very clear that it was best to leave each other to their own devices for the English lesson and continue scribbling down notes for their mini essay.

At the end of the lesson a figure entered the classroom, a figure that immediately caused Brianna to wake herself to a more alert manner. Miss Ashdown entered the classroom and was standing in the doorway. Miss Lotty took a while longer than the students of the history club to realise that Miss Ashdown was standing in the doorway; she clearly was unable to detect her art of secrecy like the entire student body.

"Hello, Miss Ashdown, is there something I can help you with?" Miss Lotty asked uncertainly, as Miss Ashdown continued to stand by the doorway in silence. It was slightly eerie to see Miss Ashdown interact with other members of staff; for a long while she simply stood there with a slight sway and her eyes looking wildly around the classroom. "Miss Ashdown?"

"Ah yes," Miss Ashdown finally answered, coming out of her reverie, "I need to see the members of my club after school today in the usual place. Thank you very much, Miss Lotty for allowing me to present this notice during the course of your lesson."

Brianna looked towards Madison and Kimberley with curiosity in her eyes. Miss Ashdown had never been one to give an impromptu meeting; even in the times when the club had an immense pressure to organise the dance, she had only made sure that there was ample meeting time with fair warning. As she looked back in the direction of Miss Ashdown, she had vanished as quickly as she had appeared. As they filed out of the classroom the girls went to talk to the boys on the journey to their science lesson. They all succumbed to the same conclusion and proceeded to ask one another the same question.

What was their next club task going to be?

The time sifted in the walls of Witchcraft Heights and soon enough the bell for the end of the day reverberated loudly in Brianna's ears. They packed away their books and supplies in their lockers before slowly walking back to their ever-familiar classroom for another after school history club. They were curious as what to expect and as such went into the classroom with a slight level of anticipation.

The boys followed in a little while after the girls, laughing and joking amongst one another with Damien at the front of the group. He waved over to the girls, but as he looked in Brianna's direction he held more of a sheepish smile and averted his eyes to the floor. She felt her stomach flutter as she saw him, but was soon bought back to earth at the thought that he was now unable to look at her in quite the same way. He was embarrassed to look at her, and she feared that it was not as a fanciful sort of embarrassment. She gloomily thought that he had seen her true feelings, of which he did not reciprocate. Maybe he didn't wish to put her under a false sense of hope anymore as she had clearly got the wrong idea.

Love was a very cruel game Brianna thought to herself as the boys proceeded to join them at the table. They waited in silence for Miss Ashdown to appear as the rest of the juniors quietly entered the classroom.

"Well done, juniors," Miss Ashdown said all of a sudden, once more creeping out from her undetectable hiding place "you have completed what I like to call the induction to the club. The dance was a test for each and every one of you; to prove to me that you can manage the demands of such a time consuming and challenging club. We must now keep the pace going as I already have another project that we must get started on at once."

The group looked around at each other, some looked curious and some looked rather downcast at the thought of having to start another project so soon after their last exhausting event. Brianna noticed that Zoe was looking less than pleased at the idea of hosting another school event, but then again she had fallen

over in front of everyone during the last one. This improved Brianna's mood; maybe she would suffer a similar

fate once again and take another peg off of her evil manner.

"We, or rather you, are going to host a small gathering for a select number of students. In past years it

has been something of a red carpet event in which we hold a banquet for certain juniors that attend

Witchcraft Heights and select students from the three neighbouring schools.

"Half the battle has already been done for you. I have already handpicked the students that are to

attend the banquet," she said as the class looked around questioningly. Brianna contemplated as to what the

criteria could possibly be to receive an invitation; it was the same question she had thought of when she

considered the reason when she had first been selected to join the history club.

"When and where will this event be held then?" asked one of Zoe's friends, Regina, with a sincere lack

of enthusiasm in her voice.

"Here of course," replied Miss Ashdown as if that were the most obvious of facts regarding the event.

"We will need to get ourselves organised quickly, as I have already sent out invitations and the event

will take place next Thursday, instead of our club meeting. Events are taking place at the moment that cannot

be stopped and we must make sure that we meet them at the correct moment," she finished, turning away

from the group to allow their creativity to be unperturbed.

Most of the group settled off into their own little groups, busily scribbling away at ideas for the feast.

Kimberley, however quickly turned to face Brianna and Madison with a look of puzzlement spread across her

face.

"What did she mean events are taking place?"

"I have no idea," replied Brianna, "I don't think she knows what she is talking about most of the time. If

you ask me, it was just another one of her strange comments; in their last meeting she was going on about

hidden qualities that will shape the fate of the worlds. She is really just a very strange lady."

"Strange isn't the word for it," Madison stated.

"The only thing is that, compared to some of the other strange events that are happening at this school, Miss Ashdown actually seems to fit into what would be classed as normal here."

"What do you mean Brianna?" asked Kimberley.

"I'm not too sure myself, but since I have moved here things have been happening. Events that aren't completely out of the ordinary but certainly are unexplainable," she answered; then continuing in a voice that was directed more as a personal thought, "I just want to know what it all means."

As she finished her sentence the boy's decided to face the girls, wanting to listen into their conversation. The girls had managed to rekindle their friendship with the boys during the dance, but the incident with the near kiss had caused a certain level of discomfort within the group. Brianna feared as to how Damien could have possibly explained the detail of events; she felt completely innocent in terms of her involvement in the affair. Nothing had happened after all; much to her secret dismay. They all looked towards one another and it was Michael who decided to break the ice with his customary jovial manner.

"Does Miss Ashdown remember we're at school and not her members of staff?"

The two groups relaxed as they laughed at this statement, melting back into their original group of six. They went into a large discussion regarding the amount of time they had to devote to this club while piles of homework kept creeping up on them.

"I'm still about two weeks behind in my Maths homework. Mr Downswood doesn't register that he is teaching a class half the time so I don't think you could go to ask him for help. He would be shocked to realise that there are students in his actual lesson," reasoned Michael.

"I know what you mean. I am so behind in my art project and I certainly do not want to get into trouble with Miss Collier. I wonder if the other teachers know about what we actually are involved in and how much it affects our school work?" quizzed Kimberley.

"They must do," chorused Damien and Brianna, which made her blush as they simultaneously shared the same opinion.

"I mean, it's not the first year that she's set up the group. They must know the commitment that the club is subjected to make. They've seen the pictures and been to the events in the past," concluded Damien.

"I'm not too sure about that," Madison replied knowledgeably, "I've never seen pictures around the school of past events, I don't think I even saw one flash of a camera that night. Plus none of the teachers attended the spectacle. In fact I can't recall seeing any other adults apart from Miss Ashdown that night."

"Well it's hard not to tell when a big event is going on; all of the juniors were talking about it last week. Plus they did let us out of lessons to set up the school hall."

"But never in lesson." retorted Madison, "We were told by Miss Ashdown not to draw attention to the event in case the older years tried to sneak in an invitation. Maybe the teachers just forget about the event completely, they've got their own lessons to worry about after all. The teachers didn't know what we had to set up the school hall for, no one said what it was being changed into and none of the teachers went to see the finisher product."

Brianna sat there, drinking in the discussion that was happening before her. She agreed with what Madison was saying and thought that it was rather strange that none of the teachers actually got involved with the event. Surely they would want to see how different students from separate houses cooperated. After all wasn't cooperation and unity elements often strived for in a schooling community?

By the end of the hour, the group had managed to agree with a theme for the dinner and they also managed to plan the different dishes that would be laid out for the evening. They had selected a wide range of classic American dishes from across the states in order to bring the 50 states to Salem. They thought it was a good idea to offer as much variety as possible, as they weren't sure on the students preferences from the other schools and this menu most definitely improved the chances of the new students picking up something of fancy. Brianna, Kimberley and Madison used their creative minds to effect within the session and had come up with some amazing ideas for the deserts including a profiterole tower that would become the centrepiece for the desert section of the evening.

*

By the time that the following Thursday had arrived, the history club were well and truly exhausted. They had worked nonstop since the event had been set in motion. Arduous tasks had included getting the caterers to agree with a menu, getting a number of workers that were happy to help with being waiters and waitresses for the evening, making the table favours and redesigning the canteen so that it looked like a medieval castle banquet hall.

Brianna and Kimberley had suggested that the students dress in casual wear to attempt to save on time and effort. They therefore arrived in school wearing what they deemed appropriate for the evening.

Oddly enough, Brianna had made more of an effort in picking clothes for the event that evening and selected something slightly more formal than her usual attire. She had looked long and hard through her wardrobe and finally plucked out a flattering pleated red dress that was ruched in at the waist. She selected a woven golden belt to compliment the dress and wore a pair of golden wedges on her feet to compliment the belt. Both Kimberley and Madison had stated how lovely she looked in her dress and Brianna gave a very grateful thank you in return. She knew why she had decided to make such an effort, but it still embarrassed her nonetheless. She was reaching the point of desperation in an attempt to grab Damien's attention and considered a stunning outfit may at least catch his attention for one moment in the evening. Brianna couldn't help but think that he had become ever more distant since the Halloween Dance spectacle, he continued to act a little awkwardly if the two of them were left alone and he rarely sparked a conversation between the two of them. She still didn't fully understand what she could have possibly said or done to have caused the level of hostility between the two of them. It had seemed that there was a wall being built rapidly between the two of them and she was struggling to climb over it.

When three o'clock finally arrived the Merlin juniors went to settle in the common room for a little break, needing some time to rest between the lessons and the banquet, which was to start in the evening. Brianna took a seat in one of the squishy armchairs, grabbed one of the books from the shelves and began reading the first chapter. As she looked around the common room she realised once again that they were the only students in the room. It was rather odd that the number of older students seemed a lot lower than the amount of juniors at Witchcraft Heights. She tried to think of an explanation to the mystery, but could come up with no resolution, so she decided to ask a question that she had often pondered.

"Why is it that the juniors are the biggest group of students at Witchcraft Heights?" she enquired to both Kimberley and Madison, her voice echoing around the empty common room.

"I'm not too sure," replied Kimberley offhandedly, "I've been too busy to give it too much thought."

"I know we've been busy, but it just seems rather odd that we hardly ever see other students. Even when we have lunch together, we never struggle to get a seat and I never see many older students walking around the school or heading into class," pursued Brianna.

"Maybe they move around to different schools. I heard one of the juniors from Goodwin High say that they were considering moving to Witchcraft Heights; maybe it's a common thing to do in Salem," said Madison.

"Hmmm, maybe," Brianna replied slowly, thinking that something else must explain as to why almost a third of the school was missing on a daily basis. She had even noticed that some of the older years that she had seen arrive on the bus at the start of the year had not been on the bus since the initial day.

She tried and failed to focus on the book so she returned it back to the shelf, her mind was too full of questions to really focus on reading. As she looked down at her watch she decided that it was time to get the final pieces ready for the evening's events and rose up from her seat. With Madison and Kimberley in her wake the girls walked over to the Medea building where the school canteen resided and saw that the students of Medea and Morgana were already putting out the party favours at intervals along the long tables. They had decided that they were going to fashion the tables in the style of an old medieval banquet, where everyone would sit on a long lined tabled that stretched across the length of the canteen. The table had a white tablecloth with golden crescent moons and stars dotted on the cloth like glitter.

Brianna went to fetch the goblets from which the students would be drinking from and Kimberley went with Madison to fetch some of the real silver plates, to really present an element of medieval authenticity to their evening. As Brianna stood up with a crate of goblets in her arms, she turned on her heel and almost collided into Damien who had come to collect a box containing some of the plates.

"Hello," said Brianna feebly, avoiding direct eye contact with Damien.

"Hello Brianna, you all right?" replied Damien in a slightly puzzled tone.

Brianna chanced a look at Damien and saw that he looked utterly perplexed at her awkward greeting. It was weird that he should seem confused by her awkward approach when he himself had been causing the rift during the last week or so. She questioned his expression and thought that maybe he saw nothing different in their friendship. The only other possible explanation was that he was very good at hiding his true feelings towards Brianna. His flippant behaviour almost put her on edge, when she considered after a small thought, that he had not registered her existence since the Halloween spectacle.

"Yeah I'm fine, just got to put these goblets out," she said, talking down to her crate as she tried to sidle past Damien. He didn't say anything in response so she carried on walking away from him. When she was further from him, so that he couldn't really recognise the painful expression in her face, she did chance a quick look back and saw that the usual sparkle in his eyes had vanished; it was as if his behaviour had once again changed, as unfathomable as ever. Maybe he did notice the change in their relationship after all.

"What's up with you?" asked Madison as Brianna went back to the two girls.

"Nothing," responded Brianna in a sullen voice, her eyes continually averting back to where Damien had just been.

"It's Damien," stated Kimberley knowledgeably, "Brianna has been acting strange towards him ever since the dance and Damien doesn't know quite how to act around her anymore. He's stumped as to what to do or what to say."

"What would make you say that?" asked Brianna, slightly shocked and a little hurt that Kimberley had been so blunt when she was explaining her best friends emotions.

"Well, I've been talking to Michael and Caleb," she confessed. "They noticed that something odd has happened between you two. They said that Damien hadn't noticed any change in your friendship until the day after the dance. They said that he was shocked that you seemed so distant with him and he couldn't understand why you had changed. Boys see things a lot more simply than us girls, he didn't and still doesn't know that you like him more than anything but a friend. Caleb said to me that Damien thinks you don't want to hang around with him anymore."

"Why didn't you tell me this before?" she asked incredulously. She was stunned that Kimberley had retained so much information from her, information that Brianna thought would have been vital for her to know. "It's been his behaviour that has affected my manner around him; every glance at him seems to offend him. I have tried to be friendly, but his mood is so erratic that it's hard to keep up with how he is feeling at any one point."

"You don't often tell us an awful lot Brianna. You keep looking wistfully at him, but you don't actually express your true emotions. I can't help you out unless you tell me and Madison what is going on inside your head," responded Kimberley.

Brianna's anger subsided as she thought the comment over and realised that Kimberley was completely right. She didn't talk to them enough about Damien, but she had never normally been one to worry about boys, so it was a completely new territory for her to be a part of. "I'm sorry girls," she said sheepishly.

"Its fine," Kimberley comforted Brianna, "just remember; if your girlfriends can't help you out then nobody can."

They continued to set up the rest of the canteen area and at the stroke of five they were finished. The juniors took a moment to take in all of their efforts as they acknowledged the fact that all their hard labour had once again paid off and they had set themselves for a well prepared banquet. The Morgana students were then instructed to make their way to the Merlin entrance hall to welcome their external guests.

Within ten minutes they had returned with the students from the neighbouring schools. Brianna looked towards the other students and wondered what criteria they had had to present at the Halloween Spectacle that would to merit an invitation this evening. The students of Medea, Merlin and Medusa helped guests as they directed them to their named seats.

Brianna waited for a person to direct her to her seat. A girl escorted Madison to her seat and as Brianna looked over her shoulder her attendant came to greet her; a tall, athletic boy with wavy blond hair that fell around his hazel brown eyes. He gave her a warming smile, which showed off a perfect set of dazzling white teeth. He was a quite attractive boy, but with a heart set upon another she found it remarkably easy to talk to the striking young man.

"Hello, my name is Taylor," he said to Brianna in a polite and warming voice to match his smile, "may I ask for your name?"

Brianna was so stunned at his polite formality she just about managed to stammer out her own name. She was shocked at the effect that Taylor had on her as he addressed her, but she put the stammer down to his level of confidence.

"Ermm... Br-Brianna."

"That's a lovely name," he said with a smile, his smile reaching his hazel brown eyes as he continued to gaze directly into hers.

"Thank you," she replied and despite her lack of attraction toward Taylor she couldn't help herself from blushing. She turned and directed him to his seat and as she did her gaze fell to Damien, as it always did. She couldn't help but notice that Damien was eyeing Taylor with a slightly ill favoured look.

As the students of Witchcraft heights became more acquainted with the students from Goodwin High, Salem Sisters and Eastwick Grammar, trays and trays of food were bought out to the table.

The waiters, who had been recommended by Miss Ashdown, were wearing slightly strange attire; long red robes, with hoods that covered their heads and ears. They went in and out of the kitchen, one after the other, so that it was almost impossible to pick out particular faces or count the number of waiters that were actually there. When the table seemed to bough in the middle with the sheer weight of the food, the students started to pick out their favourite dishes, wolfing down their meals whilst chatting animatedly towards one another. Brianna tucked into a slice of turkey and pork with roast potatoes and a heaped helping of lasagne.

"So," whispered Kimberley in Brianna's ear as the noise built up around them when everyone had managed to get their hands on a sizeable portion, "who's the new guy?"

"Sorry, who?" asked Brianna bemused by Kimberley's question.

"Jeez Brianna, how bad is your memory," she said a little bit louder, "you did lead him to his seat."

"Oh," she said as realisation came to her mind, "his name's Taylor. He was very polite."

"Polite!" exclaimed Kimberley, "that's all you can say about him. He's polite! I do worry about you sometimes Brianna, you never know what to say about boys. Couldn't you see that he is probably one of the hottest guys in this room this evening?"

"I hadn't actually," said Brianna defensively, averting her gaze and holding a wistful gaze in Damien's direction.

"Leave her alone Kimberley," chipped in Madison, once again helping out Brianna, "she is more interested in what Damien thinks of her for her to be interested in any other guy this evening.

"Even if he is drop dead gorgeous," she added as an afterthought.

They continued finishing off their main dishes; Brianna having a little more than food for thought to contend with. She looked back to Taylor again, who immediately gave her another one of his dazzling smiles and she began to question her own thoughts and sensibilities. He was extremely good looking and he was showing interest to Brianna in an almost obvious manner. Why was she so hung up on Damien when Taylor had shown her more interest in five minutes than what Damien had done in nearly two months? Slightly disheartened to defend her own questions, she kept her eyes from looking at either Damien or Taylor as the debris of main dishes were carted off to the kitchens.

"You are spoilt at Witchcraft Heights," stated one of the students from the other schools, "we never receive this level of service at Eastwick Grammar."

"It's a one off," Isabella answered, "Only special occasions merit the silver service!"

"So how did you manage an invitation?" pried Damien.

"Damien!" the rest of the group, a bit shocked at his blunt attitude and intrusive manner.

"I was just asking," he retorted.

"I'm not too sure," the girl responded thoughtfully, "I have been thinking it over in my mind myself. There are only a group of us that were selected. The only link that I can fathom is our link to Salem. The teachers at our school looked down a piece of paper and called us out. It was headed from Witchcraft heights so I assumed that the list came via your school."

"That happened for us as well," chipped in Taylor. "There are only a few of us from Goodwin High. We didn't understand why we had been chosen to attend either."

The conversation came to a halt as the puddings were soon brought out I wafts of delight; a vast array of mouth-watering desserts spread out amongst the juniors, each looking as delectable as the next. Brianna immediately reached over and gathered a piece of chocolate and peanut butter brownie, a peach tartlet and hefty slice of apple pie; accompanying the dish with a generous dollop of vanilla ice cream.

The desserts vanished far more quickly than the mains and not a crumb was left. Some of the boys, being slightly less well mannered, had proceeded to scrape the crumbs off plates so that nothing was missed.

As the waiters came to collect the dishes, Brianna looked up into one of the faces. She was quite startled as she saw a pair of purple eyes gleaming in her direction. The hat had hidden the faces of the waiters for most of the evening and the rest of the event had been far too indulging for Brianna to allow anytime averting her attention to one of the waiters. However when she saw the purple gleam she did a double take; the waiter winked at her with his purple eye drawing her in, before turning sharply on his heel and exiting back into the kitchen. Her eyes swept the room to see if she could look into the faces of the other waiters, but they had vanished along with their winking companion.

Brianna turned to tell Kimberley and Madison about the peculiar looking waiters, when a chink of glass rung from the far end of the canteen. Miss Ashdown had appeared, once again from nowhere. None of the Witchcraft Heights juniors knew that she would be attending the event, causing a great level of surprise to most of the students.

"Welcome one and all," her voice rang out clear and loud for all to hear. "For those of you that don't know who I am, my name is Miss Ashdown, one of the teachers of Witchcraft heights and founder of the history club."

The students from the other schools looked questioningly towards the Witchcraft Heights students. They didn't know anything about the 'history club' so it didn't make an awful lot of sense to them why she was here; it was not an everyday occurrence for a history club to formulate a string of events. Brianna also thought that Miss Ashdown had dressed in rather strange attire, which was that of a blue powered robe. Brianna couldn't help notice that some of the external students were shifting in their seats as if they felt uncomfortable by this peculiar woman.

"I'm so glad that you have all come to this occasion," she continued, seemingly unaware that many of the students were doubtful of her presence. "The selection of Salem's finest students is something that I have dealt with for quite some time now. Every single person who sits before me fits into that my criteria to meet that magical quality."

Brianna began to question Miss Ashdown's real reason for them hosting the event as the waiters returned to the edges of the hall and started guarding all entrances. They surrounded the students like a bordered perimeter, trapping their prey within the school walls.

"We must first thank our waiters for their efforts this evening. They help out every year to ensure that you receive a superb level of service, which often goes unnoticed," she stated; bowing to the waiters in gratitude.

"But now the time has come when we must turn our attention to a more important. I must reveal the primary reason for this event. If you could follow me back to my classroom I will introduce you to something, or should I say somewhere most spectacular."

The students rose slowly from their seats; each face showed either utter confusion or questioning doubt. Brianna noticed that Zoe's usual sneer had vanished to be replaced by a far more hungry expression. She could see the element of superiority that shone on her face as she felt exclusively involved in something secret. Brianna thought to herself that Zoe would be eager to find out anything that would regard her as someone special. She found it rather humorous that Brianna took her seriously; as far as she was concerned Miss Ashdown was just a barmy history teacher with a head full of eccentric ideas. She continued to look around the room but no other student shared that sense of superiority and as she looked towards her friends Kimberley who merely shrugged her shoulders in response.

"I wonder what this is about. Did you know she would be turning up?" someone questioned Brianna suddenly, making her jump with surprise. Turning around she saw that the good looking boy Taylor had caught up with her.

"No she doesn't really talk to us an awful lot in our meetings. She set up the history club for a group of selected students, but it's mainly the students that do the actual work. She usually sets us our project and then she seems to vanish for the remainder of the time. Even in class she creeps out from the shadows. She's a bit weird," Brianna finished somewhat lamely, stunted as how to explain the peculiar activities of her bizarre teacher.

The students finally made it across to the Medusa building and began filing into the classroom, finding seats or hovering around the edge of the room. Brianna was the last student in, closing the door behind her and taking a saved seat at the front with Kimberley, Madison and Taylor.

Searching around once more, Brianna noticed that Miss Ashdown had disappeared along with all the waiters except one. She hadn't even realised that any of the waiters had joined the procession of students, but then her attention had been plagued with questions surrounding the reasons as to what Miss Ashdown actually wanted with the students. This concluded her reasoning that it wasn't a huge surprise that she had managed to miss one of the waiters walking alongside the group. The waiter was lingering on the edge of the lighted corner at the far right back of the classroom, before the blackness swallowed the waiter whole. It was one of the areas of the classroom that was never seen, always cast in shadow, and often-intrigued Brianna as to what lurked among the darker corners of the room. Right now, her curiosity was boiling under the surface of the skin.

Miss Ashdown suddenly stepped out from the darkened corner that the waiter had been guarding, her robe powerfully billowing behind her in a non-existent breeze. A few of the students from the other schools jumped as she presented herself. The students of Witchcraft Heights had become accustomed to this entrance from their erratic teacher, so it was no longer a shock as to where she appeared; it was more a case of when she would appear.

"Juniors," Miss Ashdown began in an overly pronounced fashion, "it is a wondrous thing to be a teacher. We often see the potential that students have to offer; talents that they themselves are sometimes are quite oblivious to. For some there are other talents that are buried deep within the very heart and soul.

"All of you who sit here before me have been specially selected. You share a rare talent or should I say a rare gift. It is a gift that I can see flowing and glowing around you but it is something that you are not aware of yourselves."

Brianna felt unsure about what Miss Ashdown was implying and resolved to look around at the rest of the group. Some scoffed at Miss Ashdown's status, quite sure that this teacher had not an inkling as to who they were or any sort knowledge with regard to a talent that they may have. Others like Isabella and Logan showed intrigue at being selected for something special. Her eyes finally settled on Damien who looked doubtful and without presuming him to be dramatic, somewhat downhearted as if he didn't believe Miss Ashdown had correctly picked him for possessing a special talent.

"I will explain myself further, but for that you need to follow me on a short journey for I doubt that any of you will believe what I have to say until you see it with your own eyes," she said, only giving mystical clues to the group.

The students of the four schools raised slowly from their seats; each one somewhat reluctant to make the first move. In usual Kimberley fashion, she decided to make the first step towards Miss Ashdown who gave a gratifying smile. Miss Ashdown turned to the shadowy corner and disappeared.

Brianna followed Kimberley at the head of the group and they began to follow the sound of Miss Ashdown's footsteps. The dark corner led onto a completely pitch black area; they could see nothing in front of them, not another person, a wall, ceiling or floor. Brianna held her arms up to the side and felt a rough wall, which was cool due to the absence of any source of heat or light. After walking in the pitch black for a minute she realised that they were walking downhill. It was only a slight slope at first and not a downhill degree that they registered, but the tunnel soon dropped to more of a steep decline and the group had the feeling that their path was taking them below the ground level of the school.

After a further couple of minutes Brianna spotted a faint light growing brighter and brighter with each step. Kimberley's outline came into focus before her eyes and the wall on either side of her became steadily more visible, revealing the rough grey stonewall on either side. As she started to see ahead of her the dim

glowing light revealed something that she had not quite expected; a most peculiar chamber. Built into the

walls were four large archways, each pertaining to the name of one of the four schoolhouses that had been

scribed across the keystone of the archways'. The lettering was peeling, peeling away like the front cover of

the textbook she had been given in her first history lesson and the book that she had signed to sign onto the

history club. In the middle of it the entire floor raised onto a small mound. On top of the mound was another

arch that was covered by a black silken cloth. The students filed around the middle arch so that they could

look onto Miss Ashdown who was positioned on a small plinth.

"Enough of the mysteries," began Miss Ashdown as the last student entered the room, "it is time to tell

you the true meaning for the history club, why I set it up every year and why you have been bought together

for the banquet this evening.

"I have been in this post for the past twenty four years, looking for students who possess something

beyond the ordinary. Each year they have been identified and sent to a place that they could never dream of;

a place where they can harness and develop their talents."

"What do you mean?" enquired Madison. Brianna and Kimberley looked at Madison in surprise, who in

their knowledge, had never spoken to a teacher.

"Magic," proclaimed Miss Ashdown, "every single one of you has the aura and the ability to perform

the gift of magic."

The students looked around to one another and a unanimous realisation sunk in. Miss Ashdown was

stark raving mad. They looked disbelievingly towards one another, some of them even giggled openly at Miss

Ashdown's proclamation. There were a few, however, such as Zoe who seemed to be drinking in every word

that she had said.

It was quite a comic scene, Brianna thought, as she saw the reactions of all the students. She sat their

thinking through the statement to herself. True, magic was a completely barmy concept, something quite unrealistic. On the other hand, a lot of strange things had occurred since she had moved to Salem. Maybe this was the real reason for the move; maybe the whole family had been moved for this revelation to occur. She looked up to Miss Ashdown with interest, waiting for any further clarity from her teacher.

"Since the start of this year I have been watching the juniors of Witchcraft Heights, selecting students who have a magical aura around them. I'm known as a sensor in the magical community, able to pick out people who have raw magic within themselves.

"Magic itself leaves a trace behind you and around you. For a sensor this aura is physically visible. Imagine, sparkling dust being drawn towards a human. It's a matter that I can visibly see and when I perceive that I see that aura I know that I have a witch or wizard in my midst."

Within a small fraction of a moment, a sparkling glow lit the air above all of the students. It was brief and soon faded away to nothing and Brianna wondered if it was her mind playing tricks.

"After I have discovered the magical students are within my school I seek to find out other potential witches or wizards in the area. That's why I start up the history club. The students of Witchcraft Heights organised the Halloween spectacle. Their combined unbeknown powers enabled them to successfully organise an event and circulate the magical powers within the four schools of Salem under one roof. The event enabled me to whittle the number students to the witches and wizards that preside within Salem to the group I now see in front of me.

"Tonight this party has allowed me to bring you all together so that I could escort you here; to the transporting chamber. We are at the gateway to the Realm of Salem."

And with that, she swept to the middle of the room and pulled the black draping cloth that was stood on top of the mound. It had covered an ornate old mirror, but it was the strangest mirror that Brianna had ever looked upon. Where the glass should have been there was none. Instead it was filled with an odd sort of swirling mist; a combination of silk and water flowing in a nonsensical fashion but never escaping the constraints of the silver gilded frame.

"I possess no magical powers," she told the group, "so this mirror allows me to communicate with those that reside within the Realm of Salem. The Salem of the Realm world is similar to our fair town, but it is a place where magic can be taught without the mortal world having any knowledge of its existence. You can pass into the realm through one of these four doors placed around the edges of this chamber. The four houses of Witchcraft Heights are named after four completely different schools within the realm world."

Brianna was starting to become extremely baffled by this point. The mirror was something she had never witnessed before and the speech that Miss Ashdown was presenting to the class was almost too convincing and intricate to be a simple fabricated extension of her eccentric mind. Maybe there was some truth in what she was saying after all.

"To shake off any last resounding doubts in this class," claimed Miss Ashdown dramatically, "I will ask one of you to come and touch the mirror. The magic that flows within you will bring out one of the more spectacular powers that this mirror possesses.

"Do I have any volunteers?" she asked the group, peering around, trying to find a single face that held an expression that didn't scream reluctance or continuing disbelief.

Brianna stepped bravely forward from the crowd, "I volunteer," she said nervously, not too sure what she was letting herself in for.

She gingerly walked through a group of students that were crowding in front of her and came to stand on the other side of the mirror. She looked once more to the cascading portents of the mirror before extending her index finger and edging her arm towards the gilded frame.

Her finger met the frame and sudden rushing warmth spread up her arm before a great wind whipped around the entire group. Ribbons of colour shot out from the mirror and rose in high flowing circles above the students.

The colours and air suddenly withdrew back into the portents of the mirror and Brianna felt as if she were being pushed into the mirror itself as the colours and wind moved rapidly before her eyes. The ribbons of colour swirled on the silken like mist, swirling faster and faster before shapes started to form.

Two black dots centred themselves in the mirror and pools of a sparkling topaz soon surrounded them. Silky Auburn curtains fell either side of the now framed eyes and a prominent chin held the base of the face. A thin-lipped line formed the mouth and slightly rosy cheeks filled the gaps either side of a slightly pointed nose. The neck extended itself from the chin, like fast racing water droplets before stopping to be held by a dark blue robe, which covered the shoulders.

A man was now looking out from both sides of the mirror to all the students; a real man, breathing in and out. He blinked every now and then and as the eyes registered the new shocked faces that filled the chamber, the corners of his mouth began to curl into a warming smile.

"Welcome," announced the man in the mirror, "to the gateway to the Realm of Salem." The shocking revelation that a mirror could talk caused a fair few of the students to squeal and jump in exclamation. The man in the mirror chuckled, a rich warming chuckle that relaxed the group almost immediately.

"My name is Professor Allard and I am the headmaster of Merlin, one of the four schools within the Realm of Salem," he continued once the room were silent once more. "As Miss Ashdown has rightly explained, you are extraordinary people with a rare gift. Magic. It has always been around, passing through generations unnoticed in the mortal world. Fortunately, we have been lucky enough to have someone sense the power you have in and around you. We wish for you to enter to our world in order to train to be the witch or wizard you should rightly be; learning and honing the mysterious and astounding elements that magic holds for every one of you.

"Well, that's enough of me waffling. I will leave you with Miss Ashdown and allow her to inform you of the final formalities. I hope to see you all very soon on the other side," he finished off and with his last remark the kindly face of Professor Allard swirled until the mirror returned to its former state.

Once the face of Professor Allard disappeared the chamber erupted. Students could not hide the excitement and shock of what they had just seen. Hearing Miss Ashdown talk didn't really seem to address the issue at hand, nor had it made it seem truly believable. It wasn't until they had been engulfed in colour and addressed by a person in a mirror that they fully understood their lives were no longer going to be normal.

Brianna and Kimberley babbled on about what they had just seen; talking about the connection that they had felt towards Salem from the beginning. Brianna now understood why she had selected the library book; it had chosen her, drawn by her magical prowess. She could feel the power emanating from the people in the chamber, the same power that had been around after Zoe's fall. Everything had been set up from the start, from when she had moved to Salem or maybe even before that.

She waited for the noise to die down, eager for Miss Ashdown to give them the last instructions before they were to head off into the mysterious portents of the Realm of Salem.

"Juniors, it is a simple task that I must carry out now," Miss Ashdown said as the noise finally gave way, "I must now send you off to your new school.

"There are a few rules by which you must be bound. Most of the rules will be addressed when you arrive at your chosen school, for every school sets slightly different standards."

Brianna had only a second question as to how different the schools could be within the Realm World before Miss Ashdown continued.

"Firstly, if you are a student of Witchcraft Heights can you please go and stand by the labelled archway which has the name of your corresponding house. You're fresh and youthful magic has already suited your personal attributes to the house that you are most likened to. In time you will discover more about the qualities that link you closely to your school."

Brianna took Kimberley and Madison by the hands and led the way over to the archway labelled Merlin. They greeted Damien, Michael and Ethan as they stopped outside the archway and turned back to the plinth to receive further instructions from Miss Ashdown.

"I will now give out the list of students from the other schools that are also to attend Merlin. When the last name has been called out please proceed through the door behind you. The door will only open to the students who I call out; it helps to keep the secrets of each school from the other schools as well as from the mortal world.

"Ivy Pristine, Taylor Presley and Orlando Tucker. Please could you join the rest of the Merlin group by the door, and place one palm on the door. It will remember your magical aura and will therefore only admit you into the school from this day forth."

Miss Ashdown had finished her speech and the group turned around, Brianna the first to touch the door. The rest of them followed and as the last hand touched the door it emulated to a warm golden yellow. Brianna pushed on the door and she along with Kimberley and Madison stepped through the door of Merlin and made their way through to the start of an altogether different adventure.

Chapter 8

A light breeze whistled in Brianna's ears as she stepped into the unknown, not quite sure what to expect as she walked through the door into a new world.

At first Brianna had to look behind her to check that she had just walked through a door. The room that she had stepped was identical to the one she had just been in. As she scanned the walls she noticed there was only one difference to the room that she had just stood in and that was that there were no other doors leading off to the different schools of Witching Salem.

All the students of Merlin filed in behind Brianna, Kimberley and Madison with a handful of students from the other schools following in behind. Taylor was last in and stepped around the back of the queue to catch up with Brianna.

"This is totally crazy," was the first thing that Taylor said as he stepped to stand right next to Brianna. "I mean, I know this is happening, but how can it be happening. Everything about it just doesn't make sense," he continued in utter disbelief.

"Well, we will just have to find out what this place is all about. There must be someone in this place who can give us some guidance," Brianna replied.

"Indeed there is Miss Eastey," said a squeaky voice that Brianna was not familiar with. The students all turned their heads and some members of the party squealed with shock when they noticed who had just spoken.

It was a person, Brianna supposed, for they were human in looks. However, there were two main differences. One main difference was that the person seemed to be somewhat scaled down, for although they looked about sixty years of age they could have been no larger than the frame of a two year old child. The other main difference, which probably explained the squeals of fright, was that the person was floating above the ground as the wings on his back flapped vigorously.

"Welcome everyone," chortled the winged man, "I am Professor Merrydew one of the teachers of the school of Merlin. Oh and I also happen to be a fairy, if that's not too shocking a revelation. If it is, I'm sure you are going to be in for quite a few surprises.

Now I would all like you to follow me please; we have a lot of things to be getting on with."

Professor Merrydew twirled in mid-air before leading the students back out of the chamber. Unlike the tunnel of Witchcraft Heights, the tunnel that led up from the chamber in Merlin was well lit. Brianna supposed that this tunnel didn't need to be hidden like the one back home because everyone this side of the door knew about magic and mortals; they didn't need to keep witches away from a world they were already aware of.

As they walked back up a slope they found that tunnel ended with a large wooden door. Professor Merrydew placed his palm on the door where it glowed a faint golden hue. He whispered a couple of indefinable words and the door swung forward admitting the group out of the tunnel.

The students did not step into a classroom such as they did back at Witchcraft Heights; instead they found themselves halfway down a wide corridor. The first noticeable thing about the corridor that they had entered was that it was exactly like the corridors of within the Merlin building back in Witchcraft Heights. In fact, if Brianna weren't following a man with wings she would have believed that she was back in her Merlin building walking in around the school walls of her mortal school.

They followed in silence looking at their surroundings and Brianna wondered how magic could reside in such a normal looking place. Taylor continued to follow Brianna and it seemed that this result had caused Damien to fall far behind to the back of the group. Eventually they reached the entrance hall and Brianna furthered agreed with her previous assumption. This school was exactly the same lay out as her school back home. The grand staircase was at the back of the hall; a small marbled reception desk lay in the far back corner. Even the drapes hung from the ceiling to the walls in the same extravagant fashion.

She was not the only student to recognise the resemblance, as the other students from Witchcraft heights were pointing out the various similarities between the two schools. There was one difference however as they gathered in the entrance hall and that was that they were greeted by a man who was standing at the bottom of the staircase. It was the same man that they had seen in the mirror, with his auburn hair and pointed nose. The dark blue material they had seen around his shoulders were in fact robes that cascaded down to the floor.

"Welcome to Merlin," proclaimed the man with his arms held out in an open embrace. "I am so pleased to see so many new faces, with potential beaming out of each one of you. There is no doubt in my mind that you will make a great contribution to this prestigious school.

"I am Professor Allard the headmaster of Merlin, one of the four schools within the Realm of Salem. I am sure that your other friends of Salem are busy settling into their schools and we must do the same. There is much to discuss so I will permit you to follow me to the conference room."

They followed Professor Allard to the room they had used to be sorted into their houses on the first day at Witchcraft heights. It even had the similar rows of wooden benches that they had sat at whilst they had eagerly awaited their fate on the first day.

Professor Allard waited patiently for the students to sit themselves down, gave them a welcoming smile and addressed them all.

"I must first say well done and congratulations to you all. It has been a long while since this great a number of students from the other world has made their way into the Realm. For many of you this is a huge shock and I we wish to make this journey as comfortable as possible. I myself was born in dear Salem and found it a most beautiful place, but the Realm of Salem also has a magical beauty that will hopefully entice all of your hearts.

"I permit you to let me speak for a little while and then I will happily ask any questions that you may have. If there are none I will be highly surprised, so I welcome anyone to speak no matter how odd you may think the question is.

"The first main point that I will need to address and will most definitely reiterate is that the Realm of Salem and everything around you is real. The art of magic is real and everything that exists within the Realm of Salem and beyond is real. The people, buildings, lakes, creatures, sky and sea are all real. There is nothing false to this land and by understanding that overwhelming matter you will find that the transition period is a far easier process to deal with.

"Magic has always been around. It has been addressed in stories and myths in the foundations of mortal history. Miss Ashdown has taught you a small portion our history, but she barely scratched the surface as its roots go far deeper than a simple questionable uprising. The two worlds have always lived side by side and we have strived to keep it that way for many an age. Laws have allowed the wizarding community to exist without the need to worry about mortal intrusion as well as keeping the mortal world away from the influence of magic.

"This school will train you, if you so wish, to become a witch or wizard. There are choices that you must make along the way, choices that can be made by no one other than yourself. Previous students from mortal beginnings have thrived and flourished in this world, realising their true potential and fitting into a society more so than the place that they originally called home. But to come to this school must be of your own doing; for only your own heart will tell you where you truly belong within the two worlds."

Professor Allard waved a wooden stick high above his head pointing to the door to his right. It was the same door that the juniors had been led through to their tour of the school back in Witchcraft Heights. In stepped a variety of men and women. Some had wings like Professor Merrydew whilst others were dressed in robes like Professor Allard. As the last four entered the room a few of the students gasped, for they were only half human if they could be called human at all. They had the torso of a human, with human heads and hair that swept down their backs in a long ponytail. However, at the waist there was simply no waist, but the large body of a horse. Brianna had read of such creatures before in a fantasy novel of hers. From what she could recall they were known as Centaurs. Brianna rubbed her eyes to check that they were not cheating her, but when she refocused her gaze they were still standing there on their four legs, smiling with slightly

humorous grins to the students' reactions.

"I would like to introduce you to the teachers of Merlin," he said waving his arm without the wooden

stick at the ensemble that had just entered the room. "You will be meeting them all at some point in the

coming weeks, either through attending lessons or other means. At this school we enlist the help of witches

and wizards, as well as fairies and centaurs who know the magical world in terms of its natural resources and

powers."

They all nodded in approval before exiting back out of the room. Although the introductions were over

and the students managed to familiarise themselves with some of the teacher's faces Brianna was attempting

to come to terms with the existence of fairies and centaurs. Brianna watched the centaurs as they trotted

back out of the room swishing their tails from left to right. She thought it was now a good time to ask

Professor Allard some questions and being one of the braver ones in the group she decided to put up her hand

first.

"Professor Allard, I have a question," she asked tentatively.

"Yes of course Miss...?" questioned Professor Allard.

"Miss Eastey, Brianna Eastey," she replied. "How is it possible for people like us with no knowledge of

magic or witches or wizards in their family history to suddenly possess magical powers?"

"Ah well, for you Miss Eastey and for some others of you in the group your surname actually suggests

that you have a witch or wizard ancestor from a direct bloodline. You were told by Miss Ashdown that you

shared the same name as that of one of the witches of Salem from the persecutions of 1692, were you not?"

"Well yes, but sorry Professor," she said in a slightly apologetic tone, not wanting to sound demanding,

"but how can I have a witching ancestor and no other sign of magic since then?

"Sometimes witches don't pass on their magical powers to their children but the magical essence is still

contained with the bloodline. It can sometimes be awakened for a number of different reasons; that reason is not always known at first but I'm sure in time it will. Of course there are many witches and wizards that live in this world. This shows that magic can be passed directly down and present itself to each generation."

Kimberley was next to raise her hand "But Professor, when would we have time to learn all our magical studies when we have school work to be getting on with back home?"

"Well for your first year you will only be requested to attend school in this world after your day of studying back in the mortal realm. You shall be timetabled to learn two lessons an evening, leaving this establishment at six every evening."

"Professor," called one of the boys in the group. Brianna turned and noticed that it was Damien that had spoken before turning her head back to the front. "What is that in your hand?"

"That's an easy one to answer," chortled Professor Allard, "that is my wand. Unlike fairies and centaurs, Wizards and Witches cannot draw the power of the elements to their fingertips .We require the use of a wand as the connecting point to generate our power. You will all get a wand on your first day of lessons."

"And when will that be?" piped up Caleb who looked as interested in the wooden stick as Damien was.

"That will be discussed between Miss Ashdown and myself. For now I believe it is time for you to be heading back, as we must prepare for another day and you must all make a decision. Do you wish to become a witch or wizard?" finished Professor Allard in a rhetorical fashion. He stepped down from the stage and exited the room.

Professor Merrydew opened the door that they had entered through and called out for them to follow him back to the gateway to mortal Salem.

They followed the all too familiar corridors to the chamber that would lead them back home. Brianna followed in Professor Merrydew's shadow and after deliberating for a couple of minutes, proceeded to ask him a question.

"Professor?" she started.

"Yes Miss Eastey," replied Professor Merrydew.

"How is it that you knew my name without me even telling you?" was the first of the million questions that zoomed out of her mouth.

"Well that's easy," he said as if the answer should be an obvious one, "firstly it is one of my rare gifts. I can use the auras that you have around you to gather information about who you are. The essence of a witch or wizard flows from within and out of the body, which is one of the other reasons why you have to use wands. You are extremely volatile creatures; you cannot permanently control or contain the powers that you have. This isn't always a bad thing, but it isn't always a good thing if you don't know how to control and focus your energy. Secondly, you look so much like the other Easteys' that have attended this school and you did state your name to Professor Allard."

"There's more of my family here?" asked Brianna who was astonished to find she already had relatives in this world.

"Why of course. Mary Eastey had several children and that bloodline has spread farther and farther over time. You will find that you have family all over the world both mortal and magic alike, its remarkable really," explained Professor Merrydew.

"Yes," agreed Brianna, "I also have one other question if that's not too much to ask."

"Ask away Miss Eastey. If you have but two questions to ask me at the moment you are taking this revelation rather well."

"Well, it's about this school actually. How is it that it looks exactly the same as the Merlin building at Witchcraft Heights?"

"Ah yes, that little conundrum," said Professor Merrydew in a rather amused tone. "That is one invention of the wizards doing. The schools in the world of the realms were built long before Witchcraft Heights was erected. A wizard by the name of Merlin, a name of which you are probably familiar with and for a good reason as well was one of the most influential and powerful wizards to ever have existed. Merlin was exceptionally bright and during his education he learnt many new and wondrous things. He came from the world of the realms, but somehow came into the knowledge regarding the existence of the other world; your world. He grew very curious about this undiscovered world and as such managed to find a way to use magic in order to transport him from one realm to the other. Over time people surrounded his abilities through a belief of an advanced and far superior magic.

"He found it incredibly easy for him to transport between the two worlds, but he could not transport a mortal in this way. For reasons still unbeknown to us, mortals cannot pass through the vacuum that magic can create between worlds. Therefore he created the first ever gateway that allowed safe passage between the two worlds; a most advanced piece of magic if I do say so myself. He built one in England for him to meet with Arthur, you know of the tale of Merlin and Arthur, of course. He could travel to the mortal world, but had the powerful insight to know that Arthur would thrive and learn a great deal from the Realm world. He would gain a great level of knowledge and wisdom in which to rule the country like no predecessor had ere done before. He therefore decided to build a gateway that would connect the mortal world to the world of realms.

"The main problem was that in the mortal realm a single chamber would amount suspicion. If people kept vanishing and reappearing from the same spot, least of all the king, it could lead to a greater epidemic and entice mortals entering without consent into the world of realms. Merlin knew in his heart that not all mortals could act with civility and be as wanting of the world of magic as Arthur had been. He therefore used his love of education to design the first two schools in the mortal world so that he could hide the transporting chambers in places spread across the globe. The first one was built in London and as he could foresee the integral link between the magical and mortal Salem he decided that the second gateway should be erected in your fair town of Salem.

"Brilliant though he was he was not fully aware of how the mortals envisioned neither the layout nor the ambience of a school. He therefore decided to replicate the schools to their realm duplicates. From these humble foundations more linking chambers have been constructed over the course of time. You will find that all over the world there are mortal schools with hidden chambers that lead to realm schools that look like their realm counterparts. Although if I may permit, the extravagance of schools in the mortal world are surpassed by our schools and there are always some differences which can be pleasurably discovered."

"With that in mind, Professor," Brianna probed, "does that mean that all the schools relate to the name of an old witch or wizard?"

"No, not every school," he answered, "in fact it is only in Salem that the four schools were in fact led by the witches or wizards after who it was named. Unlike Merlin they were not always the person who you would associate it to. Medusa's descendent built the gateway for the Medusa school to the building in Witchcraft Heights. That probably explains why all your school buildings are so different from one another; for different witches and wizards had different ideas about how to design a school."

They had finally reached the chamber that led them back home, only Brianna was feeling somewhat reluctant to return. She still has so many burning questions to ask and she didn't want to leave this world behind for fear that she may forget about its existence once she had crossed the gateway. She looked to Kimberley with a glum expression on her face to show her reluctance to leave and Kimberley returned the favour. Brianna then looked in the direction of Madison who had been quiet since the first moment that they had stepped into the Realm of Salem and was surprised to see that she was looking as what could only be described as frightened. This puzzled Brianna and she nodded at Kimberley to look over at their friend, who looked so alienated within the group of excited students.

Professor Merrydew, cleared his throat and the students turned their attention once more to the fairy in the middle of the room.

"It is now time for us to part," he said sadly, "But we shall meet again very soon, which is very exciting news. Miss Ashdown will be waiting for you on the other side. She will instruct you as to what will be the next step now that you have been welcomed into the world of the Realms.

"Farewell and fair fortunes!" he finished before flying to the door and touching it with the palm of his hand so as to open it for the students.

They walked back through the gateway to see that all the other students from the other schools had returned. Miss Ashdown was waiting at the entrance of the chamber and with a simple wave of her hand she beckoned them to follow her back to her classroom.

They all seated themselves back down and waited for her to start talking again; to say something that would reassure them that what had just happened was true and that it was indeed the start of a wonderful adventure.

"Well done my new found witches and wizards," she began, "for now the time of talking has met an end. I will ask that you all come to the after school club next Thursday. It will be the end of the clubs, but the start of your new adventure. Thank you kindly and good evening."

At this brief and almost less than helpful consolation, the students rose from their seats and exited the school, heading back home or waiting for a parent to come and collect them. Brianna caught Madison by the arm before she could jump in her dad's car.

"Madison, are you alright?" she asked with concern.

"Yeah," Madison replied in a slightly strained tone, "I'm tired Brianna, I think I just need to go home and have a nice long sleep."

"Ermm, okay," Brianna was not convinced, "we can talk about it tomorrow then."

"Yeah, sure," Madison returned in the same strained tone.

Brianna walked home, deciding that some fresh air on her face would help to clear her head. She bid farewell to Kimberley halfway along the walk back home and allowed her thoughts to collect from the events of the evening. She couldn't quite believe that the small yet peculiar situations that had happened since her move to Salem had been due to something after all; she was a witch!

She tried to digest those words, but it was too extraordinary an idea to make any real sense. She couldn't believe that this morning she had gone to school worrying about how a dinner party was going to go or how Damien was acting towards her. Now she had a much greater revelation to deal with, she was a witch!

She couldn't stop thinking those four words and as she entered her home she walked quickly upstairs and got changed for bed straight away. She wasn't sure if she could even tell her Mom and Dad, which was another question that she decided to put to the back of her mind.

Instead she resolved to go straight to sleep and attempted to relax as her heart pounded with excitement at the prospect of what a new day would bring.

Chapter 9

It was a very long week for Brianna who was keen to get back to the Realm of Salem. She had only seen the corridors and rooms within Merlin that were identical to those at Witchcraft Heights and was yearning to see what the rest of the world had to hold. She wondered whether every part of the world was the same, replicas of the mortal world placed side by side. She considered the possibilities of other worlds yet to be found, or had they been found within the Realm of Salem.

She had tried to talk to the others in regard to their newfound discovery. Kimberley was equally as excited as Brianna, her intelligent mind being blown away by revelation of a completely new world. They sat discussing all the burning questions they were going to ask Miss Ashdown and the Professors of Merlin. They came up with ideas about what magic really meant and what branches of magic they would learn. They created lists of items that they would need in a school of magic, thinking of books and potions and considering what other equipment would serve a purpose. They designed how they would want a wand to look along and Kimberley even started to design outfits that a witch may want to wear, focusing largely on the idea of a black hat and a long billowing black cape.

There was one member of the group who had still not said a word during the excitable conversation. It seemed as if she was growing steadily quieter as the days had passed since they had journeyed through the doors to the Realm world. It seemed the silence was a way to tackle anyone from bombarding her with a question about the other world; a poor attempt at some new diagnosis of deafness to block out all the conversations around her.

Madison had distanced herself from Brianna and Kimberley a great deal since they had returned from the Realm of Salem. She had sat and only talked in lessons where magic could not be discussed, but at lunch she had recently decided to sit with some other students in their classes like Xavier and Casey. Madison had not met up with Brianna and Kimberley after school all week and she had even cancelled on a lunch that they had organised to have at the weekend in the old Salem village. Brianna was worried about her friend's reluctance to discuss what she had been made aware of, but as she was refusing to talk to them there was not an awful lot that she could do.

Madison was not the only person who had been acting strangely since the events of last Thursday. Damien's constantly changing, if not peculiar behaviour towards Brianna was still prominent and after her interaction with Taylor the feeling of animosity between the two had only intensified. Michael and Caleb continued to talk to the girls, but as it had been Damien that made most of the effort in the first place, the conversations were usually short and often during lesson time.

As such, the promising culmination of a group of six strong friends had fizzled out over time, which Brianna for one saw as a great shame. She desperately wanted to patch things up with both Damien and Madison. Seeing that Madison was the greater problem, as her alienation from the group was affecting her in class as well as out of class, she resolved to corner Madison after their English class the day before the next after school club.

She went through to the Medea building and sat next to Madison just as she always did, waiting for Miss Lotty to enter the classroom. The English lesson was an enjoyable affair as usual; Brianna loved to read the tales of Dorothy in Oz as it was such a riveting read. They were currently scouring through the part of the story where Dorothy steps out of her house into the world of Oz. Brianna thought it almost a strange coincidence that they had reached this part of the story just after she had found the new world, the Realm of Salem. It seemed an almost side by side symbolic link. They spent the lesson reading the chapter out loud before being set their task for the lesson. They sat in silence, which suited Brianna as it gave her the chance to plan the best way to get Madison to talk.

Luckily for Brianna, she didn't need to think of a way to keep Madison behind. Madison had classroom duty; meaning that she was the student that checked the classroom was left in a tidy manner after all other students had left.

"Hi Madison," Brianna said making herself aware to Madison. She had let Kimberley go, deciding

that her abrupt nature may not be helpful for this occasion.

"Oh hello," Madison replied in a wary fashion, looking around and noticing that she it was only the two

of them left in the classroom.

"Madison, it's only me." Brianna felt hurt that her friend seemed frightened of her. She felt hurt that

her friend seemed repulsed by her; she couldn't fathom a reason why.

"I only want to see how you're doing. I'm really worried about you and so is Kimberley," she continued,

"You haven't spoken to us since the dinner last Thursday," she was careful not to mention the Realm of Salem

as she was concerned that Madison would escape the classroom.

"I'm fine Brianna, honestly," she retorted in short clipped tones, a tone of voice that had never

escaped Madison's lips before "I've just had a lot of work to catch up on so I've been trying to focus on that.

My parents are worried that I am falling behind in my studies,"

"But can't you just tell them what you have had to do recently? Can't you tell them that you've had

extra work to do because of the demands of the history club? Surely they will be pleased with the progress

you've made here and how much you have been helping out," Brianna said to Madison, trying to make sense

of why she was acting so reserved.

"It's not as easy as that. They wouldn't really understand. My Dad went to Harvard and my Mom went

to Dartmouth. Grades mean everything to them, so they wouldn't think it a good idea for me to be involved in

a club that distracts me from my academic progression. It's always been their dream and mine to go to one of

the Ivy League schools, so I really have to get things back on track and sort out my priorities."

"But why have you been avoiding me and Kimberley?"

"Because, well, because you two are so happy about everything that has happened. You don't want

things to things to go back to normal and I know you want to tell me that what we... saw... was amazing and a good thing," she rambled out, as her true feelings had that had been pent up for so long cascaded from

her lips.

"I don't want to be part of...that. I want to be normal, be concerned about normal things. It isn't where

I belong and I just don't know how we can be friends if you feel differently."

"Why would that stop us being friends? I don't mind if you don't want to carry on with the after school

clubs, but we can still talk when we're here. You know that we still have normal days at school, it would be

near impossible not to see each other."

"I don't know if we can Brianna. I don't agree with your choices, if you agree to stay on. I don't believe

that what you would be learning is right, it's not normal or even real for that matter."

Madison's words stung Brianna. Brianna thought that she was just being quiet because she was

overwhelmed by what they had been told recently, but it wasn't. Madison didn't want to be friends with her

or Kimberley because they were pleased to be Witches.

"Oh, I guess that I better leave you to clear up then," she struggled to say as the tears began to choke

at her throat.

"That would probably be best," Madison replied in a finalised manner.

Brianna exited the classroom and headed straight back to the Merlin common room where she knew

Kimberley would be waiting. She rushed back, not wanting to process the hurtful words that Madison had just

said; she would wait to discuss them with Kimberley.

She stepped through the Merlin front door, looking at the wizened old wizard with a new found level

of interest and respect. She spotted Kimberley seated down by one of the seats by the stained glass windows

and was very surprised to see that Caleb and Michael were also sat down with her.

"Oh, hi," started Kimberley, "Caleb and Michael wanted to talk about tomorrow, when we go back to

the Realm of Salem." She stopped suddenly when saw the saddened expression that covered Brianna's face.

"What's the matter?"

"Ermm, I just spoke to Madison," Brianna replied.

Kimberley saw that there was something more than the short blunt words that Brianna was echoing.

"Brianna, I really fancy getting a drink from the canteen, do you mind coming with me?"

"Yeah sure," Brianna said and the two girls left Caleb and Michael sitting in the common room.

"That was nice that the boys' came to sit with you," started Brianna.

"Well, they came to apologise if truth be told. They noticed that we haven't been talking to them an awful lot. They know things were strained between you and Damien, but they said that they didn't want that to interfere with our friendships," she said this all rather quickly, wanting to skim over any details regarding Damien.

"Well I guess that's good news."

"Yeah, they said that maybe we could all go out as group and get Madison and Damien involved resolving any broken bridges. They are keen for our group to go back to the way it was and I completely agree with them, it's been too long since we have properly spoken."

"You might have a bit more trouble in bringing Madison along for the ride. I spoke to her at the end of class when she was left on classroom duty."

"Oh, well what did she say? Have you managed to talk to her properly," Kimberley asked eagerly.

"She doesn't agree with what we want to be. She doesn't want to be a part of the other world. She said that it means she can't be friends with us any longer," Brianna ended with a great bitterness and sadness.

"Are you joking?" exclaimed Kimberley. "She is turning her back on us for being Witches, when she is a witch as well?"

"Pretty much."

"But what's so wrong about being a Witch. What's so bad about the other world? She's not even given it a chance."

"She said that she wants to follow her parents dream and they want her to attend one of the Ivy League schools. She believes that what we're choosing isn't normal or real and she doesn't want to understand it. She didn't give me any sort of chance to explain," Brianna finished, with the hurt rising once more in her voice.

Luckily for Brianna, Kimberley decided that this was not the moment to speak her opinion and instead she settled with putting her arm around Brianna and walking back to their lockers off of the Merlin corridor. They decided to spend their free period in the library completing some of the maths homework that had been set from the previous week, not talking to one another so that they could just appreciate one another's company for what it was.

*

"Welcome everyone," said by Miss Ashdown as the Witches and Wizards of Witchcraft Heights', Goodwin high, Salem Sisters and Eastwick Grammar sat in the history classroom.

All the students had returned to the afterschool club. Even Madison had come along which was a great surprise to both Brianna and Kimberley. They hadn't spoken to her and she didn't show any sign that she had seen the two of them as she passed them to take a seat against the wall furthest from the corridor. Zoe was sat with a small group at the back of the classroom, with her hungry expression back on her face. Brianna saw that it expressed her desperate desire to go back to the school of Medusa. This was one part of the other world that Brianna was extremely pleased about; that Zoe was no longer a part of her school and therefore couldn't bully her across the two worlds.

"Today you will be venturing to your respective schools where you will be inducted to the next part of the school transfer. There are some delicate rules and laws that need to be addressed before you can become a fully-fledged trainee witch or wizard, yes indeed.

"If you would all follow me to the chamber we can quickly get the final task underway."

Once again the students stumbled their way in the dark to the chamber that linked the two worlds together. As they were walking down Brianna tripped and fell into the person in front who gave a low echoing 'oh' of exclamation as they were hit.

"Oops, sorry!" she said with a great feeling of embarrassment.

"Don't worry about it," replied a voice that Brianna was quite familiar with after having many conversations with them before.

"Damien is that you?" Brianna enquired, more so to keep the conversation flowing.

"Yes, don't worry I'm not hurt," he replied shortly.

"That's good to hear. Ermm," Brianna struggled to think of something to say to Damien and so her next question came out as a low mumble, "what do you think about all this then?"

"Sorry, what did you say?"

"I said what do you think about all this? I mean what are your thoughts on the realm of Salem and all the other crazy bits and pieces that we have found out?"

"I'm not too sure," he replied in a manner that seemed almost surprised as he engaged himself in a conversation with Brianna, "It's pretty cool I guess, but I'm still trying to get my head around the fact that it's all real."

In Brianna's head, Madison's words echoed 'it's not normal or even real for that matter' and it made her think that maybe Damien was suffering from the same doubtful thoughts as her old friend. They remained in silence as the light brightened before her eyes and she stepped into the chamber, shuffling around to the door that led to Merlin.

Miss Ashdown went to stand back on her plinth so that she could see all of the students in the chamber. They slowly filtered in. Brianna watched as the students walked into the chamber, looking at the plethora of people that entered and stood waiting. She could see faces that ranged from ecstasy to doubt, fear to reluctance. Brianna felt hopeful, hopeful and joyous step in her life. As the last few filed in, Miss

Ashdown saw fit to address the students before her.

"Welcome back, you have all remembered your way to the transporting chamber. This is the last time

that I will need to give you instructions; anything else about the other world is hidden from me to keep it safe.

You will go through your respective doors to your school. There is one more stage to induct you to the Realm

world, of which you shall learn when you are back in school. You will need to come to this room every day to

go through to your respective school and the exciting lessons that they have lined up for you. If you come

from one of the neighbouring schools you must make your way to Witchcraft Heights as soon as you have

finished the school day. There is only one portal that can transport you to the Realm of Salem.

"You can never tell any of the other teachers or students where you are going. A mortal is never

allowed to enter the Realm world. If they were to find out about this connecting chamber I'm sure that

common curiosity would lead a few down this path and it is a path that they must never take. The realm world

is a dangerous place for a mortal and you would do well to consider the safety of those that you have been

associated to up until now."

Kimberley and Brianna simultaneously looked to Madison, who went a light shade of green at Miss

Ashdown's words. Brianna wondered if she had already told her parents everything about the afterschool

club, or if Madison felt ill because she had no one to talk to.

Trying not to let the query cloud her mind, Brianna focused on going back to the Realm of Salem. The

bubbles of excitement welled beneath her skin as she thought of returning to the new found exciting world.

She stepped in line behind Damien and followed him through the door that led to the school of Merlin.

As she walked into the chamber she saw that Professor Merrydew once again greeted them.

Immediately, Brianna felt elated and comforted by his presence. He seemed to emulate a warm and kindly

nature that was infectious to all.

"Welcome back juniors of the mortal world," he said in a delighted tone, "it is so nice to see all of you back here with us today. I have a couple of announcements to make today before you are truly inducted into the Realm world."

The combined students of the four Salem schools all looked eagerly to one another wondering what would be the final element so as to be inducted into the school and by extension, the world of magic.

"Firstly I must address a matter which is most serious as it flouts our most sacred of laws. It is this; you must never use magic when you are in the mortal world. By using it in the mortal world you could upset the balance of nature and potentially exposing our world to those, which we have hidden our secrets from since the Second great Battle of the Realm.

"Another thing is this; if, for any reason you decide that this is not the path you wish to go down you must let us know. A doubtful witch or wizard can become extremely volatile. If you keep unwanted magic pent up inside of yourself it will ultimately lead to erratic magical occurrences which are often dangerous or lead to the breaking of Wizarding laws.

"If you choose to leave the world of magic behind you, it comes at a price. Your memory shall be wiped clean, cleared of all matters and days regarding your time spent in this world. As well as erasing your memory of your own power, you will also forget any friends who are witches and wizards. It would not do well for you to remember other students who possess the power of magic. Again this would flout Wizarding law and place the associated witch or wizard before a magical court for exposure to the mortal world.

"There is but one more piece of information that I must divulge. You will now come to Merlin everyday under the illusion that you are attending the history club that Miss Ashdown formed. This will be something that you should uphold every single day after school for the rest of the academic year. It is a way to excuse your constant presence within the walls Witchcraft Heights. By the end of this year you will need to make a decision, but the options will be told in due course."

After Professor Merrydew had finished he went to unlock the door and led them out of the chamber. They reached the entrance hall and headed out in the direction of the north doors, which Brianna remembered led to the seated courtyard back in Salem. As Professor Merrydew opened the door they were shocked to be looking onto another corridor that wound its way out of view. Brianna looked back over shoulder into the entrance hall. She had always known that the entrance hall was huge, but now she thought about it more she realised that it was much smaller in comparison to the vast hall that she saw behind her. She saw Professor Merrydew floating at the head of the group and she remembered him telling her that the schools in the Realm World surpassed the mortal counterparts and now she understood why he had been inclined to say so.

It was rather peculiar as they walked down the corridors; although they had shifted their location the surroundings still seemed all too familiar. As they were taken along their silent tour of Merlin, Brianna began to notice some more distinct differences between the two worlds. For one thing, they were walking down corridors and doors that were definitely not in the Merlin building back in Salem. She also felt that the building in the Realm world felt older and richer in knowledge, as if the magic of the ages filtered through the walls. Brianna noticed that there were a number of portraits and marble busts of people dotted along the corridors and around the walls of a few passing atriums. She saw men and women, both old and young as she tried to read the descriptions placed beneath each picture. Below each marble bust were plaques with words and dates, so Brianna presumed they must have been notable figures.

Professor Merrydew stopped the tour in a vast expansive hall. A golden light streamed into the hallway, lit by a most beautiful glow that filtered in from archaic windows before her. Professor Merrydew took the group through the door between the windows and the group found that they were being led outside. As she stepped her first foot onto the stone path, Brianna couldn't quite believe her eyes. Although it was only one week till December you would have thought it to be mid-July. The sunlight was raining down and there were bright coloured flowers and trees in bloom everywhere. Brianna looked up, shielding her eyes against the bright sunlight. Or was it sunlight? There were yellow rays filtering down and feeding the plants, but red rays, blue rays and a whole other array of colours that Brianna couldn't quite distinguish.

"Students, I would like to welcome you into one of my most treasured parts within the school. This is the school's Viridian Flos, or as you would know it, a greenhouse," Professor Merrydew proudly informed the students. "It is most unlike the greenhouse that you would think of; a small green house shaped building with a few small plants. You won't have a Viridian Flos back in Salem because most of the plants in here are magical and the conditions created in here provide the best environment for them to grow and thrive. They need magical rays; the different colours provide the plants with all their essential needs. This helps to keep them fed throughout the year, so that they may be used in the student's remedies lessons throughout the year. You will be taught in here as well and if I may be so bold to make a claim I do believe that we are the only school in the Realm World to house such a magnificent Viridian Flos."

The Viridian Flos was only the start of the tour around the school, which Brianna soon realised, was far more in touch with nature than Witchcraft Heights. Passing through the wondrous plants that filled this enormous glass dome, Professor Merrydew led them to the other side and exited the dome out onto a forest, which was almost trying to climb its way into the warmth and light of the Viridian Flos. It was far colder out here, much more like the November climate back in the mortal world and Brianna felt her teeth begin to chatter as they all filed out into the cold winter air. It was already dark outside so Professor Merrydew pointed at various points with his finger in the distance and a series of small lights highlighted a path for them to tread. They walked in deeper and deeper into the forest until they eventually came to a circular clearing deep in its middle.

The group were highly puzzled as to why they had been bought here, where the clearing seemed to almost be guarded by a wide variety of both familiar and unfamiliar looking trees. As the light had faded from the day, Professor Merrydew once again proceeded to light up the area with tiny floating balls of light. This time he hung balls of silvery light around the clearing, making the area seem almost ethereal where the rays fell onto the branches of the trees and dotted spots of light on the floor. She soon realised that they were not alone as she looked around and noticed a few older people patrolling the clearing; Brianna assumed that they were the Professors of Merlin.

Professor Allard was also there, standing at the opposite side of the clearing to where they had entered and it was he who Professor Merrydew was leading the group over to.

"Witches and Wizards to be," began Professor Allard when all the students were close to him. "I am so pleased that you are all here for one of the most exciting parts of your magical life.

"The Aura and the Wand ceremony; all Witches and Wizards receive their own wand when they first arrive at their destined school. Every student must receive a wand from one of the schools wand trees as every school has its own personal ceremony with sacred trees apt only for a select few. It is an extremely special occasion as your wand is the most defining piece of the equipment that connects you to the world of magic. Your wand will become something of a best friend; by your side for all your needs and endeavours."

Brianna was still wondering why they needed to be brought into the woods to receive a wand, wouldn't they buy a wand? She had at least considered the possibility that the wands would be kept up at the school; it was a huge school where surely a small stack of wands could be contained.

"We will at ask you to come and stand in the middle of the circle one at a time. There are a number of different wooded trees lining this area. They include ash, willow, oak, cedar and walnut. All the trees your see before you are wand trees, meaning that they have magic within them. The auras that you have are connected to the magical essence within one of the trees here. The wand will enable you to translate the magic within you to help you to cast the spells that you shall learn in time. Your chosen wand will only ever work for you; it can do no good to anyone else as they will not be compatible with its properties."

Excitement flooded Brianna once Professor Allard had finished the introductions. She stood shivering in the clearing where it seemed as if she was only one step away from truly becoming a witch.

It was a simple notion to say that one was a witch, but that had only been a word with no sense of reality behind it. By receiving a wand she now felt that it created a true link to becoming a witch. She would have a way to unearth powers that she was unable to truly feel and would now develop something amazing where she considered herself so ordinary. However that was all about to change, she felt that now she was really about to become connected with the Realm World.

"Brianna Eastey," called out Professor Allard.

Brianna felt as if she were back in cheerleading trials. The anticipation welled up inside of her as she felt all eyes turn towards her. She gave Kimberley a smile, before turning her head and making slow and faltering steps to the middle part of the clearing.

She stopped in the centre and Professor Allard began to speak:

"Of woodland trees,

We call to thee,

Great boughs and leaves abound.

We say to pine

And ash divine

Gather once, and eternally sound.

And you will find

In heart and mind

Your wand to you is found."

With that, Professor Allard swished his wand high in the air and bought it down where it made a ring, racing around in fast circles of reds and oranges to form a fiery glowing ring around Brianna.

"The attraction spell is now complete. Once Brianna has been drawn to her wand you must follow suit when called and enter the glowing ring. The attraction spell will hold out and help you to locate your wand tree.

"Brianna I must now ask you to close your eyes, free your mind and allow your magical essence to guide you to your wand."

Brianna did as she was instructed and closed her eyes. The strangest sensation was warming in her heart, whispers danced around her and little lights shadowed across her closed eyes. She saw the lights form a trail, a guiding line and her heart was telling her to follow it. She picked up her feet, which felt so very light and purposeful, following the trail up a small hill out of the circle in the middle.

Whispers spoke softly to open her eyes and so she did, setting her eyes on a reddish tree. The whispers spoke again, to touch the trees bark and as she did the trailing lights formed a square around her hand. The whole square glowed a brilliant golden sun yellow and she felt the square moving into the tree. There it remained for what could have only been a second before she withdrew her hand.

She looked down and opened up her palm. In her hand there it was a beautiful reddish brown wand. It had a ringlet a fifth of the way from the thicker end to present the gripping end. From the tip to the ringlet swirling engraved lines flowed up and down, connecting and branching off in an ornate fashion. Brianna was overwhelmed at the gift she had received and found herself bowing to the tree before remembering she was in a clearing with other students and teachers. They were all clapping and she held her wand aloft as overwhelming joy and pride stretched a smile from ear to ear.

"Our first scarlet oak wand, a great wand for brilliant minds and destined for great deeds, this is truly a special wand," explained Professor Merrydew, who was of course knowledgeable in trees as much as flowers and herbs.

The rest of the class were treated to the same experience. As Brianna watched her friends go up to collect their wands she saw how wonderful an experience it was. She felt immensely overjoyed as she saw her friends go up to collect their wands; Taylors's northern white cedar wand; Caleb's silver linden wand; Damien's black walnut wand. Tears of pride collected in her eyes as Kimberley collected her yellow pine wand and she went to embrace her as she returned.

It was hard to watch Madison go to collect her wand on two accounts. One, it was painful to see the anguish that she held in her eyes as she forced herself to collect a wand from the weeping willow tree. Brianna also found it hard, though she couldn't think as to why, that she felt sorry that the wand may not remain with its owner for very long.

The ceremony came quickly and sadly to a close. It was the first time that the class had been involved in something magical and Brianna for one did not want it to end.

"That was a beautiful thing to see, dear students," said Professor Allard wiping a tear from his eye, "the union of wand and its owner is something that we as teachers are blessed to see. You must keep your wands safe and hidden as you re-enter the mortal world. I look forward to your return next week where the hard work will really start; farewell all."

His speech had ended and Professor Merrydew collected all of the students up, leading them back through the Viridian Flos and the much larger school of Merlin. Brianna and most of the group followed reluctantly behind, talking to one another and comparing each other's wands. Madison remained at the back of the group in silence; Kimberley and Brianna didn't make much effort in going to talk to her as her comments had still left deep painful welts in their old friendship.

All too soon they found themselves back in the chamber and were filing through the door one by one. Miss Ashdown greeted them on the other side, where the day had now changed to the dark of night as they walked through to the mortal world.

It wasn't until she got into bed in the evening that she crept over to her bag, pulled out her wand and looked at it from every possible angle. She looked from both ends and turned it over and over again in her hands, admiring its beauty and taking in every line that she had seen from earlier and new ones that seemed to have etched since she had taken it home.

Her last thought before she placed the wand carefully in her top drawer and went to turn her light

out was a sheer sense of completeness. It was as if she had been waiting all her life to be united something

that had always meant to be a part of her; her beautiful scarlet oak wand.

Chapter 10

The mortal world had never looked the same to Brianna Eastey since the day she discovered she was a witch. The streets of Salem were no longer laden with luscious trees, their foliage seemed plain and inferior compared to the trees in the Merlin woods. The sky didn't sparkle and shine with rays of a thousand colours, capturing the world in a wondrous array of beauty like the lights of the Viridian Flos.

The Realm of Salem had captured her imagination and her heart longed to return back to the extraordinary school of Merlin. Kimberley had been out with her family for the weekend, so Brianna had been left to occupy herself at home. She couldn't tell her parents what she was, as they were mortals and it was against Wizarding law to inform any mortal of the existence of magic. She had flittered around the house, being unable to stay in one place for too long as she attempted to retain her sworn secrecy. She had tidied up her room, sorted through her books and tried to make space for a new set of studies soon to be taken. She had gone out to the garden and looked at the different flowers, wondering what ones were held in the Merlin Viridian Flos, if any.

"Brianna, sweetie, what on earth has got into you this weekend?" asked Brianna's dad, Harry. Brianna did not reply to her pop's question as she was once again daydreaming about the realm of Salem and her eagerness to return.

"Brianna," said Gretchen a little louder, "your dad just asked you a question."

"Sorry Daddy, what did you say?" answered Brianna, a little embarrassed at being caught daydreaming.

"I asked you what has got into you this weekend. You have been acting rather peculiarly, cleaning and staring at plants and daydreaming. You haven't spoken to us once since you got back from school. It's not like you at all. Is there something you need to tell us? Are you struggling with school? Are you not getting on with the people at school?" he asked with concern.

"Oh no, daddy," she replied quickly, trying to pluck a little white lie from the air. "I've just had a really busy week and I'm just giving my brain a mini vacation, that's all."

"Okay," Harry said in a manner that suggested he was not entirely convinced. "Well, you know you can tell us anything sweetie pie, we will help you anyway that we can."

"I know daddy," she said, but her words were saddened. She never had been in the situation where she couldn't tell her parents about something; as a family never had the need to hide anything from one another. Keeping a secret as big as this from them was very difficult and she had to keep shoving the guilt to the back of her mind to stop herself from spilling the beans and breaking the biggest and most important of laws.

When it was time for bed, Brianna was extremely relieved, for it meant she could escape the growing suspicions of her parents. She closed the door as she got into her room and went over to her bedside chest of drawers. She looked cautiously over her shoulder before turning back and opening her top drawer. She felt her hand to the back of the drawer and pulled on the carefully placed silken scarf that wrapped her newest treasure. She dropped the scarf and held on tightly to her scarlet oak wand, turning it over and over in her fingertips before sleep finally overcame her in waves of dreamlessness.

*

At last, Monday had arrived and Brianna had never been more excited to attend school in her life. She rushed out of the house, nearly forgetting her lunch and sports kit, which she had to double back and retrieve. In her mad rush she just about made it onto the bus and went to join Kimberley who had found a couple of seats at the back of the bus. A small pang of sadness hit Brianna as she noticed the ever-present absence of Madison.

"Hi…Kimberley," panted Brianna, "how…was…your weekend?"

"Really good thanks, it was nice to spend time with the family. It was quite hard though, not being able to tell them anything."

"I know what you mean," Brianna said, her breathing back to normal, "Mom and Dad were asking far too many questions for my liking. It was like they knew that I was hiding something from them. It wasn't the interrogation that I found so hard though, it's the fact that I have never had to lie to them before. I hated it."

As they carried on the remainder of the journey they chatted away discussing their weekends. They kept the conversation light as they did not want anyone to hear their conversations and did not want to run the risk of exposing their secret to some unknown listener. Brianna thought that it would be near impossible to talk about the realm of Salem anywhere in the mortal world as there were always people bustling around and she didn't want to face the consequences of breaking any of the rules.

When they reached the front entrance of Witchcraft Heights they headed straight to their lockers. They slipped their wands stealthily from their bags as they stashed them carefully at the back of their locker, with books piled high in front to protect their treasure. Brianna felt a pain all day, almost as if she was being pulled against her will as she continued to be separated from her wand. She kept strong against the current of loneliness that threatened to consume her and enticed her to retrieve her wand as she knew in her heart of hearts that it wasn't worth risking exposure of her wand to the mortal world.

The day went slowly and without much excitement. Zoe was her usual ghastly self in games. Since they had completed their initial fitness tests the girls and boys had been split up. For the past four weeks the girls had been indoors doing gymnastics. Brianna liked that they were doing a sport that she really enjoyed, but it came at the cost of having to deal with Zoe. She knew why Zoe was been buoyant today, but she didn't see the reason as to why it had translated to such a vile attitude.

Since Zoe had discovered that she was a witch her necessity to demonstrate a state of superiority had intensified along with her daily amount of bullying; she had gone back and intensified her evil personality since the embarrassing fall that she endured at the Halloween dance. It was no longer simple snide comments or evil glances; it had now led to a combination of pushing and shoving as well as making nasty vindictive comments at other students. She still made sure to focus the majority of her hatred towards Brianna who didn't care. Another target was Madison; a person whom she seemed to find disgusting pleasure in inflicting torment towards. Madison was not as tough as Brianna and that was plain to see. In their games lesson, Zoe had ran over the mats and pretended to stumble right into Madison who was attempting a handstand. She carried on twirling around and left Madison to sit in a crumpled heap. Brianna could see the tears sparking her old friend's eyes, but as Madison didn't want to talk to her, she felt powerless to do anything.

In history Miss Ashdown reverted to her normal self during lesson time, trying to detach herself from any particular group and certainly not drawing attention to those that were a witch or wizard. Their lessons still revolved around the Salem Witch Trials, which put Brianna on edge as her mind escalated with an irrational fear that mortals in the room would believe Miss Ashdown and discover that wizards and witches really did exist.

Their lessons had now changed focus; they were being educated on past members of the Salem village committee, with a focus on those who sentenced the witches of Salem to prison or death. A couple of the students in the school, after looking at school records, shared the same surname as with those on the original Salem committee. There were two brothers who shared their surname with Francis Nurse and another girl who shared her surname with Joseph Putnam. Miss Ashdown informed them that the current mayor of Salem was called Joseph Porter, thereby sharing his name with original Joseph Porter of the Salem committee during 1692. Brianna was once again bowled over by how connected this little town was to its magical history and the reality behind all of the legend. Miss Ashdown soon set them to task and Brianna rifled through the textbooks to discover more information regarding the committee of 1692.

A thought fluttered into her mind as she sat in the lesson. So many of her ancestors had been persecuted for being witches and wizards back in 1692. Could mortals ever hold the same belief that they once had for magic? What would her parents think if she revealed her magical quality? Would magic be regarded as evil in a modern world? Could magic be a possible concept in a rather cynical and fact based world where magic found its place in movies and fictional books?

Then another, less pleasing thought crossed her mind. Could magic itself be an evil? She thought of those that she had met thus far; Professor Merrydew and Professor Allard. They did not seem like servants to dark magic, from what she could tell.

How could magic, be perceived as evil then? As she read through the past and filed through case after case of the 'dark magic' and 'evil bewitchment' she wondered why they saw magic in that way. Was it all passed down from a mere escalation regarding the crisis of war that had plagued America at the time? Was it possible that a group of narrow minded people were simply trying to discover a way to blame people that they did not understand? It shivered down her spine at the thought of being subjected to a magic that was wreathed in darkness, but she knew that she would never want to learn dark magic. There must surely be light where there is dark, the realm world could not be pure evil. The old world could have been completely mistaken, their naivety thwarting their understanding. The thought kept firmly in her mind and she decided that she would find out as much as possible about the Realm world before she made any further decision on her future. She knew that there must be some resource that could divulge some more information for her.

The end of the history lesson had dampened her excitement and a steady build of worry grew in her heart, plagued by the stories from the past. She feared the idea of working with dark magic and began to wonder if the world of magic was shrouded in evil. She wouldn't practice dark magic; she was resolute in that belief, it was not in her nature with a heart that only ever strived to be kind and caring. She had never once felt so much as a single horrid thought towards anyone, not even Zoe when she had been at her worst.

For the rest of the day Brianna was marred with doubt of what she would face, wondering whether anyone else had put as much thought into what being a witch or wizard actually entailed.

Her worry caused the frames of time to change completely. Time was a horrible matter and when one craved for a certain event to arrive, time would drag on. If time was visual it would be like watching every single grain of sand fall through an hourglass. Now that she didn't want the time to pass her by, it of

course did, cascading past in seamless hours, without any warning or possibility of slowing down and before

long the bell rung for the end of the school day.

Before long Brianna found herself sitting their last lesson of the day, music, with Miss Arietta. Brianna

decided to slowly put her flute away in an overly reluctant fashion, pushing other instruments aside as she

found its place in the store cupboard, before dragging herself back to meet Kimberley who was practically

dancing on the balls of her feet. She attempted a half-hearted smile, but it crumpled to a grimace and she

resolved to lower her head.

"What's the matter?" Kimberley asked, confused with Brianna's less than frivolous attitude.

"It's nothing," Brianna tried in her best effort to sound cheerful.

"Come on, don't you shut out on me as well, what is it?"

"I can't really tell you here, but let's just say that what we learn in history sure does play on my mind. I

don't feel so certain about things as I once did."

"Do you mean when you felt the breeze in our first lesson?" They had gone over their lessons so many

times that Kimberley was easily able to recall key moments from their first couple of months.

"Not exactly, we can talk about it later."

The finality in Brianna's tone shocked Kimberley somewhat and fortunately she decided to drop the

subject and leave Brianna in her own thoughts as they returned to their lockers.

They met Caleb, Michael and Damien at the lockers and asked if they wanted to walk with them to

Miss Ashdown's classroom. Damien was the most subdued of the group. He remained at the back of the group

as they made their way out of the Merlin building and towards the history classroom. They didn't speak to one

another as the nerves settled in; Caleb kept twiddling his thumbs as they walked around the stone courtyard

and had to pull his interlocking fingers apart in order to open the side door that led to the Medusa building

entrance. Brianna briefly thought whether the Medusa school in the Realm World was a replica of this building like it was at Merlin in the Realm World. This however fuelled her previous admonitions regarding the

prominence of dark magic within the Realm World. The Medusa building of the mortal world was fairly sinister

looking and only hinted towards the notion that the darkness would consume and fuel the Medusa school in

Realm World.

She blocked the thoughts out of her mind as they entered the history classroom. As nobody else was in

the room they made the joint decision to walk down the pitch black corridor hoping to find the rest of the

students down in the transporting chamber. As they stepped closer and closer to the chamber a noise began

to steadily grow within its depths and Brianna guessed that most of the students had collated there already.

She was not surprised when she arrived as the chamber was indeed teeming with the students of

Witchcraft heights as well as students from Goodwin High, Eastwick Grammar and the Salem Sisters. The black

cloth had once more been removed from the mirror in the centre of the room, so as they all reached their

respective door they resolutely turned to face the entrancing cascading mist.

"Miss Ashdown has already been down here to remove the cover. She said that the doors to the

schools will open when everybody is in here. Do you know if there were any following behind you?" said a

voice in Brianna's ear.

Spinning around Brianna saw that it was Taylor who had just spoken, his eyes gleaming and his smile

bright as he engaged his attention securely on Brianna. Brianna warmed immediately to his approach, it was

almost like a comfort to her but she couldn't explain how that was so. She quickly glanced over to Damien and

noticed that he was once again carrying the sour expression that seemed to cross his face whenever Taylor

was near to her.

"Ermm..," she began, but soon stopped as the mirror in the middle chimed and sent four streams of

light to the four doors, weaving around the students on its way. On the lights impact the doors swung inwards,

opening the gateways to the Realm of Salem.

The students of Merlin followed the trailing light through to the Merlin school, the warmth of the beam guiding them through to the other world. It was a strange sensation to pass through to the other world; it was as if nothing and everything was visible at the same time. As if the black abyss was complete with the combination of a prism of light and colour. A vacuum and a ranging tornado played in her ears as the millisecond of time passed through her, but at the same time it seemed to take an eternity.

Professor Merrydew was once again waiting for them in the identical transporting chamber and for some peculiar reason the sight of him allowed Brianna to completely relax. It was an overwhelming torrent of ease that passed from one crinkle in his eye to the curl by the crown of his hair. As she looked into her Professor's kind face she saw that each feature could not contain any portents of malevolent practises and she immediately believed that here, in this school, they would never be taught or practice dark magic. The school flowed with a warm, pleasant energy; the portraits that she passed held true pleasing smiles or the echoes of jubilant laughs. This was a bright place, a place of love, light and laughter.

Professor Merrydew led them on another walk, but it was far shorter this time and as Professor Merrydew halted in mid-air they found themselves looking on an all too familiar door. It was a door where a picture that pertained an old man with long hair and a matching long beard. He wore a hat with crescent moons and stars atop his head. They had been taken to the merlin common room. Professor Merrydew flew into the room and they followed in behind him.

"This is the Merlin common room," he stated as he addressed the students. "Many of our students gather here so I am sure in time you will meet many new faces. There are a number of different common rooms, one for each year group, but they are all associated to Merlin. Your common room door shows a fairly old looking portrait of Merlin, but the other engravings for different year groups denote other various ages within his life. There are a lot of students in one year group so it may take longer than you think to become acquainted with them all.

"One of the key rules that you must obey is the curfew law that apply to the mortal based witches and wizards. We are happy for you to remain in the Realm of Salem till the clock tolls six. Your lessons will normally finish at five so you are free to use the common room, library or other parts of the school if you wish. You are free to study or perform magic, but I must stress that you must return to the mortal world when the bell tolls six. When you are back in the mortal world you are not allowed to practice magic, it could easily expose you and our kind to those we desperately shy away from."

"Professor, what should happen if we didn't get through the door? How will we know when to return to the mortal world?" Kimberley asked.

"Miss Aldridge, we must get you back before the last stroke of six for that is when the portal closes. If you do not get back in time the door will seal itself shut and you must stay here till the next day. We have to set times to return or it can cause suspicion to arise in the mortal world. Miss Ashdown will help you to manoeuvre to and from the mortal world, she will make a conscious effort to help out each and every one of you. Although she will remain distant and unaware, when asked a question by a magical being her locked in knowledge will surface to answer any lingering inquires," he said in an informative tone, "I will take you back to and from the transporting chamber for the rest of the week in order for you to become accustomed with the school's system, but then you must think for yourself and get yourself to and from your schools. The way to do this shall be taught in due course."

He held open his arms and a stirring occurred from the chairs at the back of the room. Two students in matching attire stood up and joined Professor Merrydew at the front of the group. One was a girl and the other a boy. They looked older in Brianna's opinion and she noticed that they had badge with a golden letter H pinned onto their jumpers. Brianna thought that they looked somewhat similar to the P badges that were pinned to the Prefects tops back in Witchcraft Heights.

"When students reach their final year at Merlin they hope to reach the position that these two students have attained. We have here the Head boy and Head Girl of Merlin whose duty it is to look out for the welfare of all our students and set an example towards our expectations as practioners of magic. They

are the next step up from what you call Prefects in the schools from the mortal world," explained Professor

Merrydew "Head boy and Head girl are both highly sought out positions and this year we were very fortunate

to have such a talented pair of students that could inspire the younger years.

"We have Penelope Fleece and Duran Whitmore here. I will leave you in their company; they will take

you to your lessons, as I am afraid I have to go off and educate young minds myself. I will come to collect you

at the end of your second lesson," he said, finishing his speech and flying back out of the common room.

"Hello, junior witches and wizards. As Professor Merrydew has already kindly pointed out I am

Penelope Fleece," said Penelope, once Professor Merrydew had left them to look after the juniors. "If you

could follow me across the common room to the locker chamber, we can dump your school bags in your

selected locker.

"The common room was one of the first rooms to be built when the school was erected," Duran

commented in a tour guide manner as they led the way over to the locker chamber, "although the mortal

duplicate is similar to its original counterpart it misses a few key elements. If you can spot these differences

they will add onto your student score."

"Excuse me, what did you mean by student score?" asked Taylor. Brianna noticed as she looked at him

that he showcased a rather athletic build. The idea of a competition would obviously intrigue him.

"Oh, each student can collect points throughout the year. In the trophy room you will see one trophy

that is dedicated to the student that collects the most points throughout the course of the year."

"How do you receive student points?" he asked, even more interested at the idea of having his name

engraved on a trophy.

"It can be for a number of things," Duran began to explain, "but only a teacher or the head boy or girl

can credit student with any points. They can be given during lessons, when competing in a sporting event or

by completing challenges that are noted on the notice boards throughout the course of the year. There are several notice boards in the school and the challenges aren't always placed on every board so you have to keep your eyes peeled at all times."

Although Taylor was the only person to question Duran about the student points, Brianna was equally as eager to collect some student points and get her name embossed on a trophy.

They reached their lockers and Penelope the head girl informed the students what the number of their locker was. Brianna's was 9135/2809 in one of the middle rows of the chamber, so that her locker was back to back with another student's. She was intrigued by the number, for there were most definitely not over nine thousand lockers in this chamber, so she wondered whether the number meant something special or personal to her.

Brianna turned the handle to open her locker and was extremely shocked by the portents within. The locker held no sense of dimensions and stretched on and on for a length that seemed untouchable. She edged around to the other side, to see what lay behind. The other locker still remained on the other side, to her knowledge, thereby showing that the locker was charmed in some spectacular way or another. She edged back to her locker and felt inside to see whether the illusion contained any actual boundaries, but as she stretched her arm to the furthest possible point, her finger tips still didn't reach any back wall. As she went to close the door she noticed a pouch holding a key and a piece of paper hanging from the inside of the door, which she removed from the locker.

"The lockers are bewitched with an extension charm," explained Penelope as many of the other students looked from around their lockers in states of confusion. "You will find that you will collate a huge number of belongings over time and you will therefore need a lot of space in which to secure the items. You may keep your wand here if you wish, but it is hard to keep a distance from your wand as it is now a part of your being and existence. It's a rather painful feeling that most wizards and witches cannot endure.

"Make sure you have your timetables with you, you will need them for your first lesson. I will take you to your first lesson; you will find that the layout of the school and the goings on within the school are highly intriguing. We are probably a little late, but I'm sure Professor Tabitha will forgive you this one time."

Duran raised his hand to stop the students from moving after Penelope's speech, "I need to add that you need to make sure that you check which Professor you have each day. There are a few main subjects that are taught here, but within the main areas there are a number of different branches, which are taught by one teacher that holds that particular specialism. In your charms lesson you will be taught by Professors' Tabitha and Petra in your junior year."

They followed Penelope and Duran out of the locker chamber, back through the common room and out to the western quarter of the school. They went up at least four flights of stairs in a tightly spiralling stairwell where portraits of different witches, wizards and other creatures were clustered on the walls. This was one of the other notable differences between the two schools as the buildings back in the mortal realm were only two storeys high. The school of Merlin in the Salem Realm seemed to keep reaching higher and higher into the clouds.

At the top of the stairwell they ventured their way along a crimson carpeted corridor. It was lit by bracketed candles and looked an awful lot like the other corridors that they had ventured through with Professor Merrydew. They were stopped about halfway down and Penelope beckoned the juniors into a door on their left.

A lady was waiting for them in the room. She was standing on a small raised stage, which split the room in half. Steps led up to the stage from the door and the stage linked onto a high arching window at the other end of the classroom which looked out onto the a part of the forest grounds. Raised pews went up either side of the stage where a few unknown faces were already seated. The juniors filed silently along to the empty seats, sitting to face the lady in the centre.

"You must be the new students," stated Professor Tabitha matter-of-factly, "for those of you who aren't sure as to who I am, I am Professor Tabitha, teacher of rhythmic charms.

"You are fortunate as you have only missed out on three practical sessions, of which you will need to catch up. On the downside, my subject requires a lot of theoretical knowledge and as such you will have to catch up on the theoretical notes in your own time."

Brianna looked over to Kimberley and they shared the same expression. Brianna could feel the worry coursing through her as an ever amounting pile of homework crept up on her once more; now from this realm as well as the last. Brianna decided it best to push the concern to the back of her mind; she would deal with that matter when she didn't have to concentrate all of her attention on something so especially important. Her attention turned back to her Professor with wand in hand waiting for her to carry on with her instructions.

"For your lesson today you will be practising the concealment charm," informed Professor Tabitha. "It is a simplistic spell, designed to hide whatever you deem necessary to be hidden or important to yourself. You can use this spell to erase words off a page, keep items from prying eyes and by extension you can even learn to conceal living objects.

"We will begin at the most basic level of this charm and your primary aim will be an attempt to erase the words on your timetables. Juniors from the other world, this will be highly beneficial for you as you can keep your timetable safe from prying mortal eyes."

Brianna retrieved her timetable out of her back pocket and laid it out flat on the desk in front of her. The other juniors from the mortal realm were following suit, looking eagerly towards one another at the prospect of actually using their wands. Brianna for one, had not expected to cast magical spells on her first day in the new world.

"You will need to recite the incantation with the correct inflections in order for rhythmic charms to be successful. These lessons draw their main source of power from the way the words are said. It is therefore imperative that you use your inner magical source to be able to correctly annunciate the words or pattern

of words. Listen carefully to the spell that I will now recite and then you may begin your attempt:

'Celare secretum'

Brianna looked down at her timetable and began to recite the incantation, "Okay, celery secrets… no,

clarity senses…," she tried, getting more and more frustrated as she realised she couldn't remember the two

words that at first had seemed so simple. She was so nervous about the idea of using her wand, scared that

she might do something dangerous as it was still new to her, that the incantation had sifted clear out of her

head.

"Kimberley," she muttered under her breath, "what did Professor Tabitha say?"

"Calm yourself, Miss…" replied a different voice to Kimberley's. Looking up Brianna saw that Professor

Tabitha had made her way over to her.

"I can see the doubt and confusion in your mind," she said serenely, "you need to believe that you are

capable of magic. It lives within you; the words are their somewhere, once you are more confident they will

come back to you."

"But how do I use this wand Professor?"

"You don't *use* the wand; it's a part of you. You merely use it as an extension of your magical power,

allowing you to focus your attention to one object or force at one time," she said a little louder and Brianna

soon realised that the speech was not for her benefit alone.

"Newcomers, remember you all have power inside of you and we are teaching you how to use it

properly," Professor Tabitha reassured the group, for they were also looking doubtfully from wand to paper.

Brianna decided that it would help if she closed her eyes in order to block out all the distractions

around her and so she did. She then focused all of her attention onto the wand in her hand; feeling the

engravings on the wood, feeling them flow past her fingertips and as the sensation consumed her she knew

where she wanted all of her energy to go. The sensation that was bought about from the concentration felt strange, like a warming glow and for some self-assuring reason Brianna knew that she was correctly

channelling her energy.

She and Kimberley both spent the rest of the lesson becoming accustomed to the feel of the wand,

trying to push the warming glow further down to the tip of the wand; to really get a feeling of the entire

length of the wood. By the end of the lesson none of the juniors from the Mortal Realm had been successful in

erasing the words on their timetables, but Caleb had advanced the most and managed to change the tint of

the ink to a paler hue. For this feat, Professor Tabitha praised Caleb and provided him with his first point on

his student score.

Penelope and Duran waited for them at the end of the lesson and took them to another quarter of the

school where the students stepped out from the building onto a viewing balcony. From there they headed

down to a courtyard that was reminded Brianna of the link between Merlin and Medusa back at Witchcraft

heights. Brianna walked along with Kimberley, Caleb and Michael. She looked around for Damien and saw that

he was keeping himself away from the rest of them. She was fairly puzzled as to why he wasn't walking with

the two boys, hoping that might bring him and her closer for a while, but then she realised that Taylor was

also walking along with them and that soon resolved the mini mystery.

She didn't see what was so wrong about Taylor; in fact he had been nothing but nice to Brianna since

their first meeting. He didn't keep blowing hot and cold on her like Damien did. She was fully resolved in the

idea that she would continue the friendship that was blooming between the two of them. She would not stop

talking to such a lovely person purely because Damien was sulking. Secretly, she was pleased that Damien was

sulking because at least it showed that he was more interested in her than she had initially thought.

"This is the quickest way to remedies by cutting out the winding path of the northern section,"

informed Penelope, pointing out the path that linked one part of the merlin building to another side. "The

remedies classrooms are well known within the school for their loud noises and the smells that can permeate

beneath the classroom doors."

"What is that we learn in remedies?" asked Kimberley, once again demonstrating her commanding tone and eagerness to find out as much as possible.

"Well, normally a class would be required to collect herbs and plants in their flora studies and then use the collected ingredients in order to concoct magical draughts. Of course you have not yet had a flora studies lesson yet so the other juniors of Merlin have kindly collected your ingredients for you. Professor   Vita is one of the few elves that work within the school and he is of a highly important race. Elves are one of the most sacred races within our world and blessed with long life. Professor Vita has lived through many lifetimes and as such his knowledge will provide you with rich and plentiful information whenever you should need it."

They entered the remedies classroom where Brianna was immediately greeted by a light honey like odour. The classroom was at first not easy to see. Slowly but surely her eyes adjusted in the dim classroom as the musty, dusty particles shifted. Shapes began to form and Brianna was able to see a series of round tables dotted around the room. Bottles and phials stood on shelves of varying colours with things in jars that Brianna could not distinguish. The honey like odour was protruding from a large black cauldron placed in the centre of the classroom. A tall, thin man stood over the cauldron commanding a ladle to stir using a long thin silvery wand. As Brianna approached the cauldron in the middle she was able to study the man's face more carefully. It was strange; he did not look decaying or old, but the few lines that were etched on his face seemed to present a sense of great wisdom.

He addressed the class in slow tones, "To newcomers, welcome. Today you will come to grips with what is required of a remedies lesson. I would ask you to collect one of the textbooks from the front and turn to page ninety six and read the instructions on creating the potion for elated calm. You will instruct the students who live within this realm to concoct the potion. By the end of the hour it should look similar to the potion that I have formulated with its honey like odour being its most distinguishable feature."

Brianna soon set off to collect a textbook, gathering another one up for Kimberley and they crowded around two free cauldrons. Fortunately, the ingredients had already been laid before them and they busily set to work, instructing two students named Fortuna and Melody to place the ingredients in the cauldron at

the correct moment and stir the concoction the correct number of times. By the end of the lesson Brianna had

managed to tutor Fortuna and Melody to create a fairly accurate potion of elated calm. Brianna placed some

of the potion into a phial and handed it into Professor Vita.

As they filed out of the classroom at the end of the hour it was Professor Merrydew who was waiting

to collect them. He led them along another mind-boggling pathway and they ended up outside of two large,

thick wooden doors. With a shocking amount of strength he opened the door and the students were amazed

as they looked onto the library.

"This is one of my favourite places after the Viridian Flos. This is the library of Merlin. Its extensive

collection is second to none in the area with some of the books dating back to the days of Merlin; some of you

may be fortunate enough in your time here to even discover a book written by Merlin himself. The basic

booklist that you will find left in your lockers will bring you up to the same level as the other witches and

wizards in your year," he explained, his voice echoing around the expansive library which was enormous in

comparison to the library back in the Mortal world.

He allowed them the opportunity to explore the library themselves. They filtered into their own groups

and walked off in different directions down the many corridors within the library. The shelves looked fit to

explode with the sheer volume of books that crammed up each row. Brianna and Kimberley walked down one

aisle and stumbled upon two most peculiar creatures. They looked like people only they were no taller than a

two year old toddler, with white tufty beards and matching sets of green dungarees over a white shirt.

They were talking to each other in a sound that was nothing more distinguishable than a series of low

grunts to Brianna's ears, but they must have made sense to the two short men as they were nodding to one

another in a vigorous fashion.

"What do you suppose those were?" Kimberley asked Brianna quietly when they had turned down the

next aisle, leaving the smaller gentlemen behind.

"They looked like dwarves, but that's nonsense," Brianna said.

"In a world full of centaurs, fairies and wizards you think that dwarves are nonsense," Kimberley giggled which made Brianna laugh as well.

They meandered their way back among the shelves to Professor Merrydew who was patiently waiting among an area of desks planted in the centre of the cavernous library. They sat there and Brianna began to think about all the secrets and fascinating information that she could discover. She was mildly disgruntled that she could only spend an hour when she knew she could spend a day comfortably in here without suffering from any real boredom.

Shortly after their return Caleb, Michael and Damien came and sat down with Kimberley and Brianna. Caleb and Michael both gave encouraging smiles to the girls and even Damien gave somewhat of a weak grin, which was something of an improvement thought Brianna. They sat quietly talking to one another as the rest of the class began to slowly return to Professor Merrydew.

Madison was the last in the group to return, who had the look of someone that had been hiding away from everyone else rather than exploring the library like the other students had done. She screened herself at the back of the group and followed the troupe back out of the library to the travelling chamber.

The end of the first day at Witchcraft heights had finally come to an end. For most of the students it was had come too soon and they reluctantly followed Professor Merrydew's extended arm to the door that connected the two worlds. Brianna was silent as they walked back through the empty corridors of Witchcraft Heights, holding on to every little memory that she had gained from her time in Merlin. She could not wait to return once again to the Realm World and knew that what she would discover in the unforeseen future would be both spectacular and life changing. Her last lingering view of the Realm world was to see Professor Merrydew's fluttering wings lead him further back into the school and a place that she was quickly growing to love herself.

Chapter 11

After being introduced to charms with Professor Tabitha and remedies with Professor Vita on their first day, they had attended number of other weird and wonderful lessons for the remainder of the week. Brianna was amazed at the many different branches of magic that they were being introduced to; it was not a mere wave of the wand but involved a whole host of other disciplines. She studied her timetable by night to remember all of the different subjects; charms, remedies, wand lore, magical history, remedies, duelling, flora studies, fauna and mystical creature's studies and sports.

She had found herself engrossed in her fauna and mystical creature's lessons with Professor Autumnleaves, where they had been immediately immersed in the many varieties of magical creatures and beings that walk the realm world. Professor Autumnleaves had spent the first lesson introducing the class to mermaids, a creature half human and half sea serpent that aims to send sailors to their doom. To show the new witches and wizards the first creatures, the Professor waved his wand and out came a floating portal that held its position in the middle of the room. In its portal it contained what seemed a real life mermaid. As it spun around in mid-air Brianna wondered if it was in fact real, it seemed aware of all those looking in on it.

Although the pictures from the mortal world had often identified the beauty of these creatures, Brianna noticed that some of their actual features had been smoothed over. Their faces seemed were more pointed and a grey tinge plastered their face in a dark shadow. Their hair looked quite unkempt and their fingernails were dirty and jagged. As it spun around in its watery globe it bared its fangs and its piercing eyes flashed dangerously at the students in the classroom.

They had also had one lesson a week with the ever jubilant Professor Merrydew who presented his love for plants in such an infectious manner that the whole class made sure to fully apply themselves and show as much enthusiasm for the subject as he did.

They did use their wands and the lessons that required the use of a wand were again part of an extending branch of different concepts. They had been introduced to another branch of the charms subject with Professor Petra, which centralised around elemental magic. They were introduced to the most basic

of elements this term, Earth, which they would be focusing on for a large portion of the year. As well as

charms they had also duelling lessons with Professor Rubesco, a practical discipline, but one that the students

from the Mortal world were not yet ready to participate in.

They had to learn wand lore from an old warlock named Professor Eldridge. The main purpose of the

lesson was to appreciate and understand the full power of their most prized possession. It was one of the

hardest lessons to come to grips with. In the very first lesson Professor Eldridge introduced the topic of trees.

They were to spend the first term studying the different properties attributed to different wand trees. Their

first lesson focused on wands created from the elm tree. The tree was said to exhume great powerful

properties and was particularly good at sending powerful shooting spells. It was great for needs of accuracy

and helped the caster by finding the greatest point from which to draw magical power.

As well as learning the use of the magical wand and the spells under the different branches of magic, the

students of Merlin were also taught the history regarding magic with Professor Benethon, one of the centaurs

that taught in the school and sports with Professor Llewellyn. Brianna was highly excited at the idea of playing

sports in the Realm world, wondering what could possibly be played in a world with infinite possibilities. They

had spent the first lesson being introduced to the sports facilities, both indoor and outdoor, but Professor

Llewellyn had remained fairly secretive about the names and nature of the sports in this world. He informed

the class that their sports lessons would commence after the Christmas break as they already had enough

information to digest.

It was a struggle enough, even if it was an exciting and unimaginable struggle, to merely get her head

around the new world that she was now a part of, but that was unfortunately not all that she had to deal with.

She was still a student within the mortal world and as such she was still required to attend lessons at

Witchcraft Heights by day. Her day was constantly full to the brim with schoolwork and catching up on

homework until the school bell rung for the end of the day.

When the bell finally struck at the stroke of three she and Kimberley made their way over to the travelling chamber and took part in the lessons in the Realm World. The students that they had met in Merlin pleasantly surprised the students from the Mortal world. They had only met a handful of new students from the Realm World but they were all particularly friendly and accommodating. The students that they had met had mainly been those that they had shared their classes with and it had seemed to Brianna that a select number students had been placed in their class to provide help and support so that the mortal students to get up to the necessary level with lecturing from the teachers.

Brianna had become well acquainted with a couple of the female witches who attended the majority of their classes to support them. When they first met Serena and Alleyen they seemed very similar to most of the female students from the mortal world. When they began to know each other a little better Brianna couldn't help but notice a couple of key differences between those in the mortal and those in the Realm world. For one thing, their dress and cosmetic design was far more eccentric than what they were used to back in the mortal world. They fashioned brightly coloured streaks in their hair and clothing that had never been seen before in the mortal world. Brianna also found that the way in which they spoke was of a rather peculiar fashion; it was old fashioned and in a strange way seemed almost British as it was so precise and rather slow.

The four girls found it easy to be friends and surprisingly for Brianna, Serena and Alleyen found the mortal world just as interesting as they did about Realm world. Brianna had questioned and questioned the two girls on anything that had popped in her head. She wanted to know about the magical artefacts that laced the school and how doors seemed to move across the school. She asked about the different plants that lived in the viridian flos and wanted to know more about the forest at the back of the school. She had noticed that colours bounced around more freely, making patterns through the corridors and in areas of the Viridian Flos. She had seen the sparkling glow of magic flitter around the school as students learnt the magic of the ages.

One of the most exciting pieces of news that Serena and Alleyen had told Brianna and Kimberley was that Merlin was to hold a Winter Ball. According to Serena it was one of the most memorable and anticipated events of the school year. All the school attended and it was an excellent chance for the juniors of the

Mortal world to grasp how magic thrived and shaped the Realm world. They kept most of the details a secret,

claiming that they didn't want spoil the surprise, but instead informed the group that they would find out

more information later on in the term.

*

As their second week came to a close at Merlin, Brianna found herself at the front of her history class

with Professor Benethon lecturing to the rest of the group. As a Centaur, Benethon's history classroom was

situated on the ground floor of Merlin. Brianna found his presence very commanding and his manner of

teaching highly absorbing. During their first lesson they were amazed to find out that the topics of archived

history were pertained in orbs that floated around the classroom. As well as these light-casting orbs, timelines

of key Wizarding events were annotated on scrolls, where the images moved and flowed in a seemingly

endless sequence across the parchment scrolls.

Professor Benethon explained that the first few lessons would introduce the class to the fundamental

Wizarding laws that the realm world abided by. It allowed the students from the mortal world an insight into

the way that magic has been controlled and conditioned over time as well as giving them information into the

rules that they would need to address and adhere to as members of the magical society. Brianna sat staring in

the direction of Professor Benethon as he taught the group the declaration of the first Wizarding law. She

studied her teacher more closely, noting the change from the olive coloured human torso to short chestnut

coloured horsehair. The chestnut tone was well groomed and his dark brown tail swished lightly from left to

right. His long hair went down in a plait, intertwining closely to his back in dark brown tones with flecks of

chestnut woven in. His hooves were well polished to an onyx shine that matched the onyx depth of his eyes.

His tones rolled off his tongue with French inflections as he started to inform them of the first law. It

was a simple law that all magical beings must follow; to keep mortals hidden from the world of the Realms.

Given a greater amount of liberty than in the Mortal world, the students were given the freedom to research the impact of the first Wizarding law by leaving the classroom environment and looking through the extensive number of books held in the school library. The easiest way for the students to access the school library was through a small piece of genius. The school placed a door in every classroom that held a connecting portal spell. It was similar to the one that connected the mortal world to the real world but this one connected each classroom to the school library.

Brianna and Kimberley were one of the first two students to walk through the door to the library, with Serena and Alleyen in their wake. They had created something of a quartet that it had distracted Brianna from the progress that other students in their class had made. For one thing she had not given much thought towards Madison since they had started their schooling at Merlin. However, as she opened the door and noticed Madison following behind she chanced a quick glance in the direction of her old friend.

Madison was darting her eyes between Brianna and Kimberley, but it was in a slight tone of fear and disgust. It was as if she was angry and frightened that they were choosing to immerse themselves further and further into the magical world by the assistance of their new found realm based friends. Brianna turned her head back around, determined not to let Madison's manner disturb her feelings of sheer happiness.

The four girls, once in the library, went searching among the many shelves to find books that pertained books on Wizarding law. As she searched through the books in the library Brianna found herself skating her fingers along a line, which surprisingly held a common theme. The books all held titles on dragons; 'A Happy Owner makes a Happy Dragon' and 'The best dragon flyers in Britain: A Definitive Guide' were traced against her fingertips. She stopped and removed the last book from the shelf and opened it out, quite sure that dragon meant something quite different to the fire-breathing creature she was thinking about.

As she opened the first page her jaw dropped, for as plain as the nose on her face she was looking directly at a photograph of a real dragon. The photograph depicted a huge fire breathing red and purple scaled dragon with a rider seated on its back. The beast was poised in a way that allowed the rider to sit comfortably while its wings spread wide across the page. The rider's eyes were intent and focused on something or somewhere that the photo did not show. A name 'Dilly Burbank' was signed in gold lettering along the top

corner. If it wasn't for the fact that many of the students had peculiar names in the school of Merlin, Brianna

may have thought that Dilly Burbank was the name of the dragon. She knew better though and read

underneath the photo to find out that Dilly Burbank was the number one dragon rider of 1982, as seen here

with her Quebec Claw dragon.

Just as she remembered that she was in a lesson, a shower of pearlescent periwinkle blue sparks shot

above the topmost shelves of the library, a little locating spell that they had learnt in their rhythmic charms

lesson with Professor Tabitha. She knew that it was Kimberley who had cast the showering sparks as they had

discovered that the colour of the sparks was a different colour or hue for every student.

She found Kimberley seated in the middle of a circle of books. She had been far more successful in her

searching quest in the library and had managed to find a number of books regarding Wizarding law. Brianna

thought it best not to abandon her friends on the task at hand so she took a wide step over the ring of books

and sat next to Kimberley. Alleyen and Serena soon found the two girls with a few more books laden in their

arms. They dumped their pile of books on top of the large collection that had already been gathered. Brianna

picked up one of the books from her pile and began to read a paragraph that looked promising,

' ... what had started out as a promising coexistence between the magic and the mortal was soon to be

altered.

'Through many an age, witches and wizards had resided in the realm world, flittering across to the

mortal world at their own leisure to enjoy the differences that the two worlds had to offer. They performed

magic in the presence of mortals, who applauded and were in awe of the magical displays set before their

eyes. The witches and wizards found that they could return back to the realm world, where the mortals could

not follow and work harmoniously with the other magic folk, telling stories of the adventures that they had

experienced in the mortal world.

'The coalition between the two worlds was sadly not to last forever. An old witch by the name of Medusa was a being of a most unusual and unique appearance. Unlike most witches and wizards who looked similar to mortals, Medusa held a greenish tinge to her face with snakes protruding from her scalp instead of strands of hair. She was not the only magical being to look different from most of the Wizarding population; A Witch in a far off Western Quandary also favoured the greenish hue on her face and Felucifa was a renowned fairy, similarly cursed with the face of green.

'They were laughed and jeered at for being so different; witches and wizards pointed at them and made ill favoured comments to these witches that looked so freakishly odd. As time passed they grew resentful of both their kind and the people of the mortal world who also shared the same face and look of most that resided in the Realm world.

'Fuelled by their hatred of those that scorned and shunted them, the three beings formulated a plot. It was their mission to control both worlds under a tirade of pain and suffering, controlling all of those that opposed their will to dominate. They created creatures of the dark, with a pure essence of evil pulsing through their blood. Medusa was famed for her relationship with snakes and created gigantic cobras and fierce adders that possessed dark powers and venomous fangs. The witch of Western Quandary created demons that resembled skeletal winged dogs, believing that their intelligence would allow them to plan attacks and fight those that opposed them. Felucifa created a wide range of evil creatures that followed her command. Creatures such as black dogs and ravens are creatures that Felucifca used for her evil doings; creatures that are often associated in this day and age superstitiously associated as servants to dark witches and wizards.

'They successfully combined their powers and created their mass army of darkness in secret. Their alliance went unknown until a war erupted, known as the Dark War that persisted for many years. Its main aim was to wreak revenge on those that had shunted and humiliated them. Their tyrannous efforts led to a near domination of the realm based world, had they not been defeated by a gathered collection of good witches and wizards that fought tirelessly against the dark magic till it was vanquished.

'The three witches were defeated by none other than Merlin himself. They were sent to the gallows for the crimes that they had committed on both the magical and the mortal world. When they exhaled their last breath they were set up in flames, for that is only way to truly kill creatures consumed by pure evil.

'This first rebellion of the three green witches sparked a resistance supported by future generations of witches and wizards for a many centuries since the first rebellion, hiding among the shadows but fuelled by the beliefs and thoughts of Medusa, the Witch of Western Quandry and Felucifa. The secrets of the green resistance and those that believed in the dark ways continued to lie low and passed down their knowledge regarding the forces and spells of darkness.

'The next major rebellion occurred in the middle ages, 1692 to be exact, when witches and wizards of the green resistance wanted to be more open about their powers, believing that they had the right to rule and control. They started to abuse the two portals that Merlin had created and practiced magic in the mortal world, but then the mortals grew afraid. They saw magic as the work of the devil and sought to rid the magic that they believed plagued and damned their world. Once more the evil magic was stunted in 1692, but with the help of those in the Wizarding community as well as the town council in Salem.

'From 1693, the first Wizarding council was formed and from the council came the law that that magic was to remain a secret from the mortal world. After the events of 1692 witches and wizards were forbidden to enter the mortal world and no mortal was to enter the world of the realms to keep the witches and wizards safe'

Brianna sat engrossed in her book, amazed at how little she truly knew about the Realm world. There had truly been evil that had plagued both the realm and mortal world; a dark magic, a magic that had fuelled a certain fear within her. There was also a Wizarding council, presiding somewhere within the Realm World, keeping the people safe and controlling the forces of magic.

These revelations made her question what she really knew about the world that she had now become a part of. She had been so narrow-minded and had only ever thought of magic residing within the school walls.

She had never considered, incredulously, that the incredible idea of magic and the world that she had become a part of had been referred to as a world. Of course there would be rules and laws to govern it. Of course magic would stretch farther than that of her beloved Merlin.

She wanted to ask either Serena or Alleyen more questions on the topic. As she looked up she was surprised to find herself looking up into the eyes of Damien who was hovering very close to her, with a leaning stance over her and the book.

"Can I help you?" Brianna asked him a little standoffishly, feeling slightly annoyed at his inconsistent and unpredictable manner.

"I just wanted to see how you were getting on with your work," said Damien, "it's been a while since we last spoke," he finished in a manner which threw Brianna off completely. He was acting so calmly, as if his odd manner and slightly reluctant attitude towards her were a mere figment of her imagination.

"I'm getting on fine thank you," she replied somewhat cautiously, if not a little blunt.

"Good to hear. What do you think of our new school?" he continued to question Brianna.

"It's nice," she said still unable to give a normal reply, shocked as she was to be speaking to him. For some reason however, she felt that an inability to relay too much information to him, and preferred to keep her thoughts to herself.

"Well I better head back to Caleb and Michael, I said I would only be gone for five minutes," Damien said with a boyish grin. He sauntered away from Brianna as if the conversation had gone swimmingly well.

Brianna could not help but return the smile as Damien turned back to the boys, sadly taken once more by his undeniable charm. Her heart fluttered, which she knew was not a good sign. It was not fair that a boy who was so unpredictable could affect her in such a predictable manner.

"I wonder what has bought on his change of tune?" enquired Kimberley when Damien was far enough from the four girls. She had walked over the second he had left and Brianna could not help but think that Kimberley had been keeping an eye on her throughout the whole conversation.

"I don't know," Brianna said as she they walked back to join Serena and Alleyen and tried to settle herself into a composed manner, "he was acting just the way he used to when we first started talking."

Secretly, Brianna was just happy that Damien was talking to her again, so she didn't really think about a reason behind Damien's desire to rekindle their conversation and consented to believe that things were once again going in the right direction.

She looked down at her watch to see how much longer was left of their time in the library; it was the first time that they had had to govern their own lesson time. She was surprised to see that her watch was not reading past 3 o'clock; the time that she had ventured through to Merlin.

"Kimberley, what's the time? My watch needs a new battery."

"Oh that's not the reason why it has stopped," said Alleyen taking her nose out of one of the books she was busily reading.

"Huh?"

"All things that operate without magic in this world don't work in the Realm World. That thing that you use in your world… technology, is it?"

"Yes."

"Yes, well technology isn't needed in this world so it doesn't exist. Anything you bring into here tends to stop working if it can't be controlled by magical means."

"Couldn't I make my watch magical?"

"Of course you could, but that requires more advanced magic. For now you will be best to rely on one of the tick tock clocks. You will definitely need to keep an eye on the time so that you get back home in time."

They decided to collect their things, walking to the library desk to loan out the books they thought would help them the most.

They went back through the transporting door to the classroom and found that some of the other students had already returned and were sitting facing Professor Benethon who was poised at the front.

Madison had not seemed to move from her seat; her arms remained folded and a scowl still plastered on her face. Taylor was also sitting with a couple of the other students, whose cheeks turned crimson red as he spotted Brianna. His friends turned in their seat to see who had affected their friend and they smirked as their eyes fell on Brianna.

The girls sat back in their seats, where Brianna carefully positioned herself with her back to Taylor.

"You've upset him," teased Kimberley.

"Who have I upset?"

"As if you don't know," she replied, "I personally don't understand your train of thought. Taylor is incredibly good looking and is showing you a lot more attention than Damien. I know Damien is probably a little bit more gorgeous than Taylor, but close to perfection would be good enough for me."

"I know Taylor is good looking," she replied somewhat stubbornly.

"Well, why don't you start paying some more attention to him then? Forget about Damien, he's more trouble than he's worth."

"I know me and Damien have something worth fighting for. I can't completely explain it. All I know is that my heart wants Damien, even if my head says Taylor is the wiser option."

Kimberley was going to retaliate but by then all of the other students had re-entered the classroom and Damien was only in the row in front of them.

As Professor Benethon dismissed the class, Brianna and Kimberley followed Serena and Alleyen back to the Merlin first year common room, still not sure on their bearings of the school. Brianna secretly believed that the school had a mind of its own and changed its layout from time to time. Sometimes when she went through a door it would lead to a corridor, but the next day that same door could lead to a bathroom. One time she even thought that she heard a door giggle as a student opened it to reveal a brick wall.

Kimberley and Brianna opened their history books to start on their work again, with Serena and Alleyen sat in the chairs opposite them, having a quiet natter and helping out when they could.

"...and I still need to find a necklace that suits my dress," Brianna overheard Serena saying as her concentration on her work slipped.

"What do you need a necklace for?" Brianna couldn't help but ask.

"Oh of course, we haven't told you," exclaimed Serena as she clapped a hand to her forehead.

"We have our Winter Ball at the school in three weeks' time," explained Alleyen, "It's a tradition that has been held for centuries in the Realm world. It allows the teachers to reward the students for all their hard work in their first term. My sister told me that it's one of the best events of the year. All school years' attend and the school takes care of all the planning."

"How come we haven't been told about it before now?" asked Kimberley who hated to be unprepared for anything.

"Well I think they tell you about it when you go back to the mortal world, but most people will know about it by then. I think Professor Merrydew will tell you the details as you are led back to the transporting chamber."

"But what do you wear? A witches hat and cloak?" asked Kimberley somewhat sceptically.

"Ha-ha, very funny. We have moved on from the dark ages a little bit. We have managed to be a bit more up to date with our fashion sense since then. All the boys tend to wear a very pretty version of a suit, but all the suits are hidden beneath a cloak. I guess that's in homage to the witches and wizards of old.

"We get the better end of the deal and get to wear any dress that we want. Most students wear full length dresses, our fashion sense is a little older than some of the designs that you might wear over in the Mortal world, far more regal and classic some would say."

The work lay abandoned as the four girls talked about the Winter Ball. Kimberley thought it a wise idea to wear the dresses they had made for their Halloween dance spectacle and after explaining their creations to the girls, they were eager to see them.

"There was something rather odd about those dresses," said Brianna, "something in my dreams almost played a part in the transformation; they were exactly what we created. In fact, if it wasn't for the fact that none of it made sense, I would have said I wasn't dreaming at all."

She went on to explain to the girls about her evening when the dresses had been changed dramatically. As she finished her story Serena and Alleyen looked as puzzled as she was, which was fairly disappointing. Brianna had almost expected them to give some form of revelation to the transforming mystery. The tick tock clock rang in the common room as the time chimed six. The four girls reluctantly stopped their conversation and collected all their things together, heading to the locker chamber at the back of the common room.

Once they had stowed away their belongings the quartet said their goodbyes and Brianna and Kimberley headed back to the transporting chamber where Professor Merrydew was already waiting for them. Taylor was up ahead and still held the crimson tone to his cheeks at the sight of Brianna. The conversation that she had had with Kimberley echoed in her mind and she made it her mission to go over and approach him.

"Hi Taylor," she said rather sheepishly, "I didn't realise it was you that I had my back turned to. It was a bit awkward for me to fit in the room without doing so." She thought that telling a little white lie was not the worst thing that she could do in the current situation.

It seemed to have the desired effect as his mood seemed to become immediately uplifted. She had been rather wrapped up in this whole new world and realised that she still needed to be the teenager that she was. Damien, although showing her more interest, seemed to have an unknown motive. She needed to be careful with regard to his erratic emotions, unless she wished to be sucked into a torrent of highs and lows. Taylor was steadfast and still remained true, so when he gave her that smile of absolute contentment she felt a wriggling sensation nestling around in the pit of her stomach.

"That's okay," he stated. It was simple, but she knew that he meant it completely. As he brushed his hand against her arm she smiled warmly in return and headed back towards Kimberley. The group patiently stood in the transporting chamber as they waited for the next instruction from Professor Merrydew.

"Juniors this is the last time I will need to greet you," Professor Merrydew informed the group as he floated before the students. "You have been taught the school motto and through the combination of rhythmic charms and the words of the school motto you shall be able to open this magical door to this school. You can go through in a group, but the incantation must be repeated if the door is shut and you wish to use the door again. This obviously keeps our world safe from those that could stumble upon on a transporting door.

"We are passing over a great sense of responsibility and trust to everyone in this chamber; you cannot tell anyone the motto in the mortal world nor can you bring any mortal with you into this world. This is against not only the school rules but also it is against the law. As you were bought up in the mortal world, a violation of these laws will result in your powers being stripped from you."

Professor Merrydew shuddered at the thought of having his magical powers stripped from him and Brianna understood why he would shudder. Magic was in her blood, it was a part of her soul and having her magic taken from her would be like having part of her soul stripped from her body.

Professor Merrydew waved his hand up and down in a straight line and a white stick, an imitation wand, filled the space. He needed no wand, for his fairy body allowed a more natural form of magic. Instead, this prop was required for demonstrational purposes and he waved it in a simple figure of eight fashion. He said the words of the school motto, 'superbis ac veraciter de concordia iunctis' and touched the door with the tip of the wand. The door glowed in the same way and opened, just as it usually did when Professor Merrydew touched it with his finger. He closed it again and stood beside the door as he waited for the students to come up one by one and perform the spell, making sure that they could successfully manage it.

Brianna was the first to attempt the tricky spell. Holding her wand and declaring the school motto she bought the wand down in a straight line, where she smiled brightly when the golden glow shone to show that she had cast the spell. As she headed back into the mortal world again she took a while to reflect on what she had learnt so far. The subjects were mind-blowingly fascinating, but she knew that would not be the case without one clear factor that rang loud and true for every moment that she had spent learning.

The teachers that Brianna had met so far had captured her imagination and enthusiasm in a way that no other teacher had ever managed to do before. All of the teachers had been extremely welcoming to the new students, from the likes of Professor Benethon to Professor Tabitha. They had been a rock for the mortal based students, providing them with a calm and warming environment and doing their utmost to ensure that the students had a smooth transition. As she turned to look at Kimberley she made sure to look at Professor Merrydew.

"Thank you sir," she said with sincerity, "thank you for everything."

Chapter 12

With only three weeks left to the end of term, Brianna and the rest of the newfound witches and wizards were set an impossible task. They had to, through sheer determination and hard work, catch up with their fellow students in the first year of Merlin. Being weeks behind in her work was not a new phenomenon as she was still struggling to catch up with the work set by the teachers of Witchcraft Heights. Her main issue was that she was being educated in something that she had not even known had existed a few weeks ago.

She had imagined that she would be turning toads into toadstools or extracting a rabbit from a hat. On the contrary, her lessons at Merlin were becoming far more intense as the weeks progressed. Although she was starting to remember the names of the Professors and the subjects that she attended, her capacity to retain all the information she was being given was proving to put even her acute knowledge to the test.

In lessons such as Professor Autumnleave's fauna and magical creature's studies, her brain and understanding of the world had taken a huge U-turn. Creatures of myth and legend were notably real in this world. After they had been educated on Mermaids, they had moved on to learn about fluffapods and hobgoblins. She had noticed that the creatures of this world seemed much more human than the creatures of the mortal world. A lot of them had voices of their own, thus allowing them to communicate with the witch and wizard kind.

One of the other lessons she found mind-boggling was history where her time involved absorbing knowledge and information from Professor Benethon. He filled the minds of the young students with fantastical facts about a world that seemed all too spectacular to be true. Long off battles and tales of woe; triumph and love; disaster and new found discoveries told in impeccable detail and encased in a rich plethora from the books that they could access through the portal doors.

They had hardly anytime free time to be sociable with their friends and Brianna's parents were constantly questioning her on her workload. They had even gone as far as to threaten ringing the school and ask why the students were being loaded with so much work. Of course Brianna objected to this as it would only bring attention to the work that she was meant to be completing without all the extra work that she

was now set.

*

It was Saturday evening and Brianna had decided to take a small break from the mountainous pile of

work that was spread out around her. As she lay on her bed she retrieved her treasured wand from her top

draw and with wand in hand waved it in the unlocking figure of eight shape. She did not cast the spell, she

simply wanted to feel the simple touch and the retrace the pattern that could help cast the spell.

She had spent the last hour frying her brain as she had attempted to complete the research project

that Professor Tabitha had set them, looking into the reasons for creating inflections when wand waving. Each

spell created some new difficulty; each spell required a great degree of concentration, but for the first time in

what seemed forever she just wanted to switch her brain off from the whirlwind that seemed to be her

current lifestyle.

She knew that hiding wouldn't rid herself of her problem so Brianna reluctantly rolled off her bed and

decided to return to the impending pile of homework that lingered in the corner of her eye. One of the major

benefits gained from learning the theoretical side of magic was that it helped her to understand how to

perform spells in their practical lessons.

It was annoying that in the mortal world when you were trying to practise magic the wand rendered

useless. Underage witches and wizards were only permitted to use their powers in Realm world; magic

performed in the mortal world would strip the witch or wizard of their powers. Once you had become a fully-

fledged witch or wizard you could perform magic wherever you wished, but until then the Wizards Council

saw this measure as a necessary precaution to retain their levels of secrecy.

She found all of her books from the Realm world extremely interesting, but there was still one book in

her possession from the mortal world that she found impossible to ignore. 'Historia de Celatum Coed'; the

book that she had collected from the Witchcraft Heights library was a comfort to her for some unknown reason. She had not yet learned the true secrets of the book and wished to know why it has chosen her.

Since her discovery of being a witch she understood now that the book held notes from the Realm world, having managed to cleverly decipher the cryptic 'ROS' to mean Realm of Salem. This led her to the conclusion that the book had some sort of link to the students in the realm world. However, the mechanics behind its operation and its purpose were still something that Brianna was looking to explore. It seemed almost too coincidental that it had fallen into her hands. As a consequence she kept it ever in her possession, not wanting it to fall out of her sight and into the hands of someone that could also see its mystical qualities. She quickly flicked through its parchment pages, finding nothing new, before falling into a deep and dreamless sleep.

*

The following morning Brianna headed sluggishly to her English lesson at Witchcraft Heights. Madison, although no longer talking to Brianna and Kimberley anymore, still chose to sit next to the two of them. Brianna was not entirely sure as to why someone with a clear dislike towards two people would want to be near them. Madison's presence merely seemed to set an extremely awkward mood for the three ex-best friends.

In fact, as Brianna thought about her dwindling interactions with Madison, she also noticed that her personal involvement with Witchcraft Heights had taken a dramatic decline. She no longer looked wistfully towards the cheerleading squad and in fact had no great desire to participate in cheerleading or any other school club at all. The other students, including the other houses in the history club were now nothing more than old acquaintances; people who they only really saw in passing on their way down to the transporting chamber.

Zoe had also decided to ignore both Brianna and Kimberley; Brianna had noticed that Zoe still retained her contemptuous manner but it was now held in a way that suggested herself as above all that dwelled within the moral world. On their way down to the Realm World Brianna had found herself walking behind Zoe.

She was keen not to be noticed by Zoe and Zoe gave no inclination that she had even noticed Brianna and Kimberley approaching from behind. Her voice was loudly echoing off of the walls in the narrow corridor and Brianna was able to catch onto the conversation that Zoe was having with her cronies.

"Well, I don't know about you girls, but I certainly won't be taking this pointless trip for much longer," stated Zoe.

"What do you mean? Aren't you going to come to Medusa anymore?" replied Tanya, her questioning voice hissing up the corridor.

"It's not so much the trip there that I won't be doing, it's the trip back."

"I'm definitely not following you."

"Well if you haven't had time to talk to the older students like I have then I am afraid I cannot tell you anything. I've found them a very interesting and inspiring group of girls," she said and Brianna could tell the Zoe felt of high importance to be mingling with the older students of Medusa.

Brianna and Kimberley gave each other a quizzical glance, but could hear no more of Zoe's conversation as they entered the dimly lit travelling chamber.

They headed directly towards the Merlin door; a smile crept up Brianna's face as it always did when she knew she was going home. She couldn't describe why it felt that way; she had always thought that home was where you grew up and where your family resided. However, in the short time since she had attended Merlin she had never felt as at home as she did back in the Realm World. She wondered how long they would have to keep travelling to and from the two worlds and if she could in fact reside in the Realm World permanently.

The two girls walked through the door on their own, with no fellow Merlin student in front or behind them. They stepped across into the transporting chamber in the Realm world and as instructed by Professor Merrydew, Brianna performed the magical figure of eight and bought the wand tip to the door reciting the school motto. She knew that the magic was working as the familiar warming sensation stretched from her head to the tip of her fingers where the wand seemed merely to extend to the door, with no sense of

separation.

"It worked," Brianna said in surprise, amazed at successful her first piece of magic. It was even

more incredible that she was successful without the presence of a teacher to guide her in her first attempt.

"Come on lets head up to wand lore with Professor Eldridge. Did you manage to complete his work on

the properties of the elm wood?"

"Hey, wait up you two," interrupted a male voice as Brianna and Kimberley felt the door closing behind

them. Kimberley turned nimbly on the spot and grabbed the handle of the door to keep it open to the

approaching voices. As Kimberley opened it wider they found that Damien, Caleb and Michael were jogging

across from the transporting door over to them.

"Oh hello boys, did you have a nice weekend?" asked Kimberley.

"Well I tried to, but there was too much work to be getting on with," said Michael.

"Yeah, I've left most of my Witchcraft Heights homework and concentrated on building up my magical

ability," added in Caleb, "if I want to become a qualified wizard I won't need to get my qualifications in the

mortal world."

"But, you would have spent all those years in the Mortal world for nothing," said Kimberley, who was

slightly shocked at the idea of completely abandoning years of hard work, "Besides, if anyone is unsuccessful

in their time here, surely it would be ideal to have good mortal qualifications to fall back on."

"It would be helpful, I guess, but this is what I really need. My past school life built up my ability to

cope with the idea of the new and now my true self is being discovered and pushed through magical

propriety."

They continued to discuss the pros and cons of their proposed education routes until the time they

reached the north-eastern quarter of the school for their remedies lesson with Professor Vita. Brianna kept her thoughts to herself; chancing the odd glance in Damien's direction, secretly hoping that his talkative demeanour from Friday would continue today.

"Hello girls," Serena called over to Brianna and Kimberley and they went to sit down in their seats alongside their two friends who lived in the Realm of Salem. As Brianna walked over to meet them a sudden thought occurred to her; Alleyen and Serena had given them bits and pieces of information regarding their lessons or the layout of the school, but Brianna had never asked about life in the Realm World.

What did it look like outside the school walls? How far away were the other schools? How big was the Realm World? What did witches and wizards do out of school?

As the questions zoomed around in Brianna's head she tried to keep them locked in her mind as she started her remedies lesson.

Professor Vita had spent the first couple of weeks as any other teacher had done; educating the newer students in the theoretical background of the magical fundamentals associated to remedies. Brianna still found it extraordinary that the witches and wizards who had already learnt the fundamentals were willing to learn it again to benefit the newcomers. Perhaps that was why they got along so well with those students, because they were genuinely nice people. Another question popped into Brianna's head as she wondered how much schooling the students had already had before the mortal based juniors joined; how was the school day structured for Alleyen and Serena?

"Today, we finally start to put theory to practice, "said Professor Vita, "you will be trying to concoct a basic cold curing potion. Its medicinal properties saps away the drained feeling one often gets with a cold and allows one to carry on with the days task without the sniffles, inability to breathe or nasty sore throat. You should have the collected the ingredients and instructions can be found in your workbooks. If you do need any help, the other students will be able to assist you as they have already successfully made this potion."

Professor Vita set down his crocodile clock, which walked around in circles, ticking away. Brianna loved this little contraption as it seemed to teem with life and with every single step the clinking of the china scales could just be heard underneath the tick tock noise. She went to the store cupboard, retrieving some of the basic ingredients that they didn't need to collect for their potion and then began to start placing the first items into the cauldron. Taylor came and placed his ingredients near to Brianna, with a small smile in her direction.

"How are you?" he asked in his usual polite fashion, sweeping a strand of hair away from his eyes.

"Not too bad." Her warm feeling that she had not felt for a while returned to her stomach and settled there; calmed almost as soon as he spoke to her.

"Did you have a nice weekend?"

"It wasn't too bad," she said, "I've just being doing work most of the time. I reckon I sound like the most boring teenager alive."

"You and me both! I tried to play a bit of American football at the weekend, but there just never seems to be any free time. Dad keeps moaning at me and saying that my scholarship to a college will never happen if I don't apply myself now."

"Do you want to go to college?" she asked, the warm feeling wriggling uncomfortably for some strange reason.

"I'm not entirely sure," he said, "I'm still processing the fact that I'm half a wizard."

"I've never thought about it like that before," she said with keen interest, "what do you mean by half?"

"Well if both of my parents were magical beings, I would have been bought up in the realm world. Even if both have magical lineage, I have still been bought up in a mortal community which would suggest that I am half mortal." His wisdom seemed so advanced for a young person, she was quite overwhelmed by his prowess and his ability to understand a world so well when it was all so new to them. She drunk in his words and couldn't help but remain a little transfixed on his deep _ eyes.

"Ahem," coughed Professor Vita behind the two of them. Brianna realised that they had spent their time talking when everyone else in the group had already started to mix their potion. With Taylor's words echoing around in her head; Brianna decided that she had better start catching up with her work.

Alleyen and Serena stood in the background as Brianna and Kimberley busily worked through the list of instructions, adding eucalyptus leaves and stirring the potion in a clockwise direction. One of the many notes that they had collected as part of their homework stated the importance of stirring; a reversal of the direction altered the potion completely as energy was drawn from the air to formulate the potion. As they stood around their cauldron they began to breathe in the menthol and eucalyptus fumes that clouded the air above them and gave a slight greenish tinge to the atmosphere.

Brianna smiled a little as she looked over to the three boys and witnessed a small purple cloud engulf Caleb. He coughed and spluttered as Michael and Damien laughed at their friend's mistake. Professor Vita swept across the classroom and cleared the air with a wave of his wand.

As the rest of the lesson passed other students suffered different mishaps; Logan had managed to cause his cauldron to splutter out gold droplets and Reece had managed to change the actual colour of her cauldron.

The cold curing potion was meant to be a mint green colour by the time they placed it into glass phials to be tested. Brianna ladled the almost perfect potion into a phial and labelled it with a quill and yellowing piece of parchment.

"That looks pretty good," said Kimberley as she deposited a similar looking sample into her phial.

"Same to you," Brianna replied encouragingly.

"Time is up," declared Professor Vita amid the fumes and smells that permeated the classroom, "if you could please place your phial in one of the holders, clear away any unused ingredients and clean out your cauldrons before you leave."

They busily did as they were told; most of the students were slightly afraid of Professor Vita and didn't want to be placed into his bad books. Michael and Damien were still sniggering about Caleb's mishap, but Brianna couldn't help but notice that their phials contained substances that were almost as poor as Caleb's failed attempt.

As the last unused ingredient was placed back into the remedies cupboard the students filed out of the lesson and walked back to the direction of the common room. Brianna found that they often had to retreat back to their lockers due to a small piece of genius that Professor Allard had designed. This was because homework assignments were often transcribed on pieces of parchment and pinned on the door of each locker. It was a good method for the Professors to contact the students so that they could meet deadlines, but it was always slightly stressful to find another piece of homework sprung unexpectedly on their return.

Students from Witchcraft Heights didn't complete the other lessons with the rest of the students from Merlin. The other students spent their school day during the hours that they were stuck in the mortal world. One of the shocks that the mortal students received more than their realm acquaintances was the higher amount of notes pinned to their lockers as they were still expected to complete work that they had set during the day. Even though it was only theoretical homework tasks, unlike some of the practical tasks that Alleyen and Serena had to complete, it was still more work added on to that of the homework they were given in Witchcraft heights and after school lessons at Merlin.

Brianna and Kimberley went back to their common room; Alleyen and Serena had duties to fulfil, which included reporting back to the Professors with information regarding the progress students from the mortal world.

They went to collect their '1001 Creatures to astound, amaze and astonish' book, thinking it best to start their fauna and mystical creature's homework that Professor Merrydew had set them. They had started to create a scrapbook of information regarding the creatures in the realm world with Professor Merrydew, even if it only scratched the surface. Sometimes Brianna found herself questioning whether such creatures could exist, the true peculiarity and wonder of the creatures seemed too amazing to be true in a manner. After the initial lessons where they had seen them in a bubble, Professor Merrydew informed the students that they would now meet some of the creatures in real life. It was imperative to research the creatures before being introduced to them. Apparently, most creatures could sense knowledge from the students and would not be comfortable showing themselves if the student wasn't aware of their existence or their habits.

They were now coming to terms with the shocking revelation that griffins, a creature that was half eagle and half lion, actually existed. Their task at hand was to research Selkies; seals that could shed their seal skin to become beautiful women. The Selkie needed to be sure that the witches and wizards wouldn't steal their skin, thus preventing them from returning to the seal form.

Brianna reached into her locker and felt around for her books. As she opened the door she noticed a new homework note pinned to the inside of her locker. She sighed a little in frustration at the thought of more homework.

'Collect dill and barleyfurn from the Viridian Flos, to be bought to Remedies next week – Professor Vita'

"Hey, Kimberley," Brianna called out, "we've been given more."

Kimberley groaned in response, immediately understanding what Brianna meant.

"It's not too bad; we get to go to the Viridian Flos to collect some ingredients, which means we will have another practical. Shall we go and do it now; we can leave Professor Merrydew's assignment and do it back at mine."

"Will we be able to find our way without Alleyen or Serena? I am still way too confused about this place, I think it's amazing that anyone can work their way around this maze."

"I've got a good idea where it is," reassured Brianna, quite eager at the idea of going on a walk around the school as always, even if she didn't have a real idea of the location of the Viridan Flos.

Kimberley conceded and the two of them retrieved their remedies carrying kit. It was a small leather bound set of pouches that the school had provided every student with to keep their ingredients safely in.

They decided to take a left turn out of the common room, hoping that it would lead them in a northerly direction. They knew that it was at the back of the school, but that was a long way off from where they were currently situated.

They noticed that they school had started to get into the spirit of Christmas and Brianna saw the smallest of decorations starting to fill the corridors. On every window ledge, ornate ice skating figures were pirouetting on an everlasting ice rink. They way that they moved so profusely and elegantly cheated the eye to believing that the figures were actually real. As well as this, holly and ivy had been hung from the ceiling and small snow flurries passed up and down the corridor to unsuspecting students. A few snowmen were dotted around the school, held in a whirlwind of colourful sparkles. Brianna was extremely excited to see what the sparkles would do to the snowmen in the days and weeks to come.

As well as admiring all the new decorations, Brianna tried to look at the everyday items that were plastered on the walls or covered the floor, to create a mental map of her school. The doors sometimes moved up and down the walls they resided, which was not particularly helpful, but highly entertaining for those that watched students walking into a brick wall or down the wrong corridor.

The lights that hung in glass baubles lighted the corridors in the winter, for it seemed that the Realm World suffered the extremities of weather to a far greater degree than its mortal counterpart. As such, a thick white wall of snow largely blocked the windows.

They turned left and right along some of the more twisting corridors, feeling no sense of knowing whether they were any closer or farther away from their final destination. As they turned another corridor and Brianna started to completely lose hope, they found that the way was barred a small way ahead by a group of five older male students. They were busily chatting away to one another, unaware of Brianna and Kimberley approaching from the other end of the corridor.

As Brianna and Kimberley tried to shyly edge past the boys by scraping along the wall, one of them noticed them and stepped aside.

"Sorry girls, we were being extremely rude weren't we?" said one of the boys presenting a warming smile to both girls.

Brianna noticed Kimberley blush quite profoundly and she tried to conceal a little smile. She had never noticed Kimberley to act, so… well… girly. Her eyelids were fluttering and her gaze was at the floor, as if she couldn't physically lift her head up to meet the new appealing face.

"My name's Truesdale," he continued, "this is Blutain, Ethan and Landon. I don't think we've ever met before." His comment, Brianna noticed, directed more in the direction of Kimberley.

"Ermm… ," Kimberley tried to reply, but found that her voice was lost somewhere in her throat.

"I'm Brianna and this is Kimberley," said Brianna, jumping in to save Kimberley, "we're new to Merlin."

"That's cool, what part of Salem do you come from?" he politely returned to Brianna, but couldn't help from focusing his attention back to Kimberley.

"We're not from this part of Salem exactly," Brianna said hesitantly, not sure how everyone responded to people from her world.

The rest of the group started to show some interest and Blutain looked quizzically at the two of them.

"Oh, it's nothing bad. We're from the other world so we've only been here for the last couple of weeks," she explained. Kimberley continued to avert her eyes from Truesdale, even though he was barely showing any acknowledgement of anyone other than her. He snapped back into reality as he realised none of his friends were continuing the conversation.

"Oh… well there's nothing wrong with that," Truesdale said with a warm smile, bringing the conversation back up to speed. "Ethan is from the other world as well. Wasn't it Boston that you moved from originally before you landed in Salem? It was a shock for him when he found out that the Realm world had had him purposefully relocated so that he could train to be a wizard!"

His friend Ethan nodded in response. Brianna was pleased that someone else in this school had shared a similar experience. It wasn't just her then; Kimberley always moved around from place to place anyway, but she had not yet met someone who had moved for a singular purpose.

"I had exactly the same thing happen to me. I relocated from Jacksonville in the summer. How far do people come from to transfer to this school?" she questioned Truesdale with extreme interest.

"Ermm... I think there are about fifteen areas in the USA, which have schools that link to communities in the realm world. It's a bit different over here to your world. This world tends to draw schooling communities to areas where magic has a link to its realm counterpart. Salem is an obvious choice based on its Wizarding history, but places like Enchanted Rock in Texas and Jasper in Arkansas also have a great magical link. Magic and the wizarding council pull students from nearby communities to those particular towns that contain the linking portals.

"There are usually quite a few schools in one realm area, like the four that we have in Salem. This allows different magical personalities and qualities to be carefully catered for." He looked down at his wrist and Brianna saw a flash of colour and whirling patterns dance before her. She could make neither head nor tail of what it was, but Truesdale certainly did.

"Sorry girls, we need to head off now. Hopefully we will see each other again?" he looked hopefully in Kimberley's direction.

Brianna nudged Kimberley in the rib and Kimberley gave a small nod in return.

The two groups separated before Brianna had a quick idea,

"Sorry, but are we going the right way to the Viridian Flos? We were rather lost when we found you!"

"Yep, it's just one turn right, two turns left and a final right and you'll be there. Hope that helps," Truesdale said over his shoulder. Brianna gave Truesdale a thumb's up and a nod to show that she understood before the girls continued their walk to the Viridian Flos.

They walked along the winding corridors, nearly stepping through a trick door that would lead them to the main entrance, before remembering that Truesdale had not informed them that they needed to head through any door. In the northern end of the school the corridors had been decorated with thousands of twinkling fairy lights that cast dancing rays of lights that bounced along the walls of the passing corridors. The girls followed the lights as they made their second left around the back of the school in the hope of following the directions to the Viridian Flos.

After a good ten minutes, they saw a pale blue glow and knew that the Viridian Flos was near. The grandeur of the entrance hall that opened out onto the northern corridor and it allowed for the light to flood in to the rest of the school from the huge dome. It was seen as one of the most spectacular parts of the school and one that always caused a sense of awe on its initial glance. It looked like an ice palace that had been placed on the back of a school; the ceiling looked chiselled and pieced together in the most intrinsic design. The crystal clear colour was visible from the outside view, but once inside it was unidentifiable under all the brightly dancing beams of colour.

Brianna was looking up at the sky, where the snowflakes from the chill winter air fluttered down and melted as they landed on the domes ceiling. She didn't look where she was going and received a shock as she collided into someone.

"Oops, sorry," she began, and as she looked in front of her she could feel herself beginning to blush.

It was an awkward moment as she realised that it was Damien that she had walked straight into, not for the fact that she had bumped into him, but that above their heads was placed a bundle of mistletoe. It was similar to the mistletoe that she knew of back in the mortal world; the only main difference was that it the berries sparkled with silver glitter.

"Don't worry about it," said Damien, trying to break the tension, "what are you doing in this part of the school?"

"We're doing Professor Vita's homework. There are a couple of ingredients that we need for next lesson."

"You and Kimberley are way too organised," Caleb said, catching up with Damien.

"Well what are you three doing up round this way then?" implored Kimberley as Michael also made his way round the corner of the corridor and joined the other two boys.

"We're here to do a little bit of exploring," Damien said in a mischievous manner, "there's so much of this school we don't know about. We... well more me decided that we are taking touring the school into our own hands.

"Why don't you join us?"

The curiosity immediately welled up inside of Brianna; she had wanted to explore more of the school, wanting to answer the questions that she had about the Realm world. The narrow view that she had be given of the Realm world was not enough for her; she needed to find out more. It did not take long to make a decision.

"Sure, where are you three going?" she looked meaningfully towards Kimberley, but Kimberley merely resigned to the knowledge that she would be following whatever Brianna had decided on doing anyway.

"Well, why don't we take a look around this dome a little more," said Damien mischievously.

They walked through the small tunnel that led to the entrance of the Viridian Flos and helped the transition between climates possible. As they looked around she noticed that the flowers were still a vibrant array of colours, even in the middle of winter when the entire surrounding world was a white flurry.

Brianna thought it would be a good idea to collect the necessary ingredients for their next remedies lesson. She went off in her own direction to locate the plants, but in a way she wanted to take in the surroundings on her own accord. Since they had arrived in the Realm World they had never been given the chance to be alone, to take it in at ones leisure or sit and reflect on the new world.

The beauty surrounded her and flared her curiosity as she spotted plants that seemed at first to be rather ordinary. She walked slowly down an isle that was teeming with little pink flowers. They floated away from their stem before revolving back to their original place. As she passed down the aisle some started to follow her before returning; others changed colour as a ray of coloured light hit their petals. She turned down another channel, but soon turned on her heel. The plants had feelers with ends that resembled snapping heads. They were reaching out to the middle of the path, biting at one another, and Brianna did not want to run the risk of her being the new target.

Instead she turned down another where she thought another ingredient was situated; she kept hearing a lot of sneezing. As she looked at one of the trumpet shaped flowers she realised that it was in fact the flowers that were sneezing. As she carried on walking and looking intently around she was met by small blasts of air that whipped her hair from left to right. Some of the sneezes also sprouted a small amount of water that splattered droplets across her face. She met the edge of the dome and noticed the stringy plants that rustled in a rhythmic fashion. Brianna noticed that the flowers of the rhythmic strings were the flowers that she needed for her class so she approached it carefully and went to pick five of the little vanilla scented flowers.

"This place is incredible," exclaimed Brianna, as she plucked the flowers delicately from their stems and pocketed them in the remedies carrying case. The magical world was a place that seemed to constantly amaze her. She went to fetch a few of the necessary water droplets that replenished and strengthened the flowers once taken from their source. She placed them carefully into a water droplet shaped phial and then went off to find Kimberley or one of the boys.

She heard a sudden shuffling and saw the boys and Kimberley all approaching as one group

"Why don't we go outside?" enticed Damien as they joined up with Brianna. The students from the mortal world had not been outside since the wand sorting ceremony. As all their lessons had been based in the classroom on either a theoretical or practical note they had not been taken back out into the woods of Merlin.

"Do you think we are allowed to leave the building without consent?" questioned Kimberley, doubt clouding her excitement, as she was not one to go against the rules.

"Well they haven said that we aren't allowed to," reasoned Damien.

"Neither have we been told we are allowed outside," responded Kimberley, "Alleyen and Serena haven't taken us outside since we started. Don't you think that suggests the boundaries to which we must remain in?"

"Well, it's not exactly a new revelation for them so they may not be so bothered about the school to the extent that we are."

"I agree with Damien, Kimberley," Brianna said with a tone of pleading. Kimberley just gave her an exhaustively resigned look. Brianna knew the real reason she was siding with Damien, but Kimberley had to understand her reason for doing it. She and Damien were finally on good terms and she would do whatever was necessary to keep it a strong relationship. Surely Kimberley would understand the importance of this.

"Fine," snapped Kimberley, "let's go outside. That's if we can even find the exit of this cryptic dome."

The five of them walked down a number of paths, scanning the outskirts of the dome, some of them becoming very familiar as they recognised they were retracing their steps. Surely there had to be some sort of spell that could help them out, but until then they were limited to the power of memory.

"Hey guys," called out Michael, "I think I might have found something."

They followed behind Michael in a huddled fashion and were halted before a canvas of green ivy.

"It's just another plant," said Damien disappointedly.

"Look closer," Michael said, taking Kimberley by the arm and pointing at a part on the ivy canvas.

Kimberley gasped as she looked at where Michael was pointing. Brianna looked in the same direction and saw that there was a yellow knocker intertwined among the green ivy. The ivy wasn't covering the wall; it was a door itself.

Michael tried to pull open the door but it stayed locked. He pulled a couple more times; unsure as to whether he had used enough force.

"Maybe it's like the door to our world," suggested Kimberley.

"That's an excellent idea," Damien said excitedly and he drew out his wand. He bought down the wand in the rhythmic fashion that they had been taught, muttering the small incantation under his breath. Brianna was amazed by the extra energy that seemed to surround Damien as he cast the spell.

The handle glowed momentarily and the door slowly swung open, allowing the students to step outside.

It was a winter wonderland, just like a picturesque Christmas card. The snow was densely packed, pearlescent white and sparkling on the ground. Brianna placed her foot on the snow and received the gratifying crunching sound as the snow crystals were compressed. The trees had sprinklings of snow on the tips of their branches and outermost leaves, but as she looked closely she noticed that some of them seemed to shiver as they shed the snow from their skin. The light snow fell in sparkling forms and for the first time ever, Brianna could actually see the individual flakes fall delicately onto the palm of her hand. There they rested with their intricate patterns of diamonds, circles and web like lace for a moment before they melted away to nothing.

The forest loomed in front of them and stretched out to the east and to the west. Back at Witchcraft heights there had been trees at the back of the school which were thinly lined to demonstrate the mere boundaries of the school but as Brianna looked onto the forest in front of her she could not tell how far back the forest went. It seemed as if this forest was far more mysterious and steeped in majesty than Witchcraft heights.

The boys didn't go towards the forest; instead they led the way around the side of the school. As they trampled through the snow around the edge of the Viridian Flos they found themselves walking towards the most north-westerly part of the school. It was a beautiful building, very medieval with aged stone and steeped roofs that reached so high it seemed that they would be able to climb to its highest peak and touch the sky itself.

They carried on walking around and Brianna felt slightly nervous, worrying what would happen if one of the teachers caught them walking around the back of the school. There was so much snow that they couldn't identify any sort of clear path, so Damien as the designated quest leader led a trail that the others all followed behind in a uniform fashion.

The snow started to fall again as the five reached some bushes, which were clumped in a jumbled huddle. Brianna was starting to wonder if they were going to turn back at any point when they heard a crunching noise behind them.

They hid behind the one of the bushes as they realised that the noise was the crunching sound of two other people walking in their direction. Brianna sneaked around the side and was horrified to see that two of the Professors were walking directly towards the bush that they were hiding behind.

"...Well the cold does affect their flame," said Professor Merrydew.

"Yes, we need to make sure that their enclosure is protected with a flaming hearth charm. If they get too cold it can affect their mood," agreed Professor Llewellyn.

The Professor's passed the five students and as they heard the volume of the Professors' voices dwindling away, Brianna stepped out from the bush to check that they were truly gone. She saw that their tracks had gone around the corner and slowly started to follow their path.

"What do you think that was about?" asked Caleb.

"No idea. Let's follow their tracks and see where they've been," said Damien, in sync with Brianna's thoughts it seemed.

"How long do you think we have got before we need to get back to the portal?" asked Kimberley in an attempt to bring the other four back into some sort of practicality.

"I'm sure we have plenty of time," said Damien offhandedly, "besides, if we don't follow their tracks today they might be gone tomorrow."

Brianna turned to face Damien, wanting to side by him again and proclaiming wordlessly that she too wished to follow Damien's track of thought. Damien noticed Brianna and gave her a warm smile. She felt herself blush and was at least satisfied that he could not see the warm glowing feeling inside of her.

They followed the Professor's footsteps, intrigued to where they heading.

"What was that noise?" asked Brianna as they turned another corner and heard a low combination of growling and snorting. She saw Damien look at her with a grin on his face before she realised that she had grabbed onto Damien's arm.

"Don't be frightened Brianna, I'll look after you," reassured Damien. She had to look away quickly so that he didn't notice the massive smile that was plastered across her face.

They edged around the corner to where the noise was coming from. Brianna was not prepared for what she now saw in front of her.

It was an animal enclosure, which was a surprise in itself, as the students hadn't been informed that animals lived within the school grounds. The other surprise was that the enclosure housed eight live dragons. Brianna tried to tell herself that she shouldn't be surprised. Dragons should come part of the magical package they were probably one of the most well associated creatures to the idea of magic and its existence.

One thing she Brianna hadn't thought was that they would look so normal to her; as if she encountered dragons on a daily basis. She looked into the eyes of one of the enormous beasts; its fangs were bared and its eyes were balls of flaming orange. It was one of the largest animals, if it could be called an animal that she had ever seen. It was covered in small scales of purple and pink hues. The scales seemed to glimmer even in the dimming light. Its belly was the only colour that was different; it was a blood red sheen with a swirling pattern underneath. It had two small horns on top of its head that curved in to the apex of the beast's head. Brianna stood frozen as the dragon held its gaze, taking one step forward with a purple scaly claw and all that Brianna could do was to stand there with all the breath seeming to leave her body.

"Brianna, move!" called a far off distant voice as she saw in slow motion a ball of fire making its way in her direction.

"Brianna!" the voice shouted towards her and Brianna felt a colliding strike as she was pushed to the floor. The ball of fire sailed past her and hit a solid wall behind her, where it disintegrated and vanished into nothing than black ash.

She looked above and saw that Damien was pinning her to the floor with a look of panic in his eyes. It took a moment before she realised that the jet of fire was heading straight for her and she had done nothing to move out of its way. Damien had come to her rescue; Damien had saved her life.

"Thanks," as her life sped back up to a normal speed. Kimberley rushed over and comforted her friend and looked accusingly towards Damien, as if it was his fault that she had nearly been burned.

"How could you be so reckless," Kimberley said out loud.

"I'm sorry!" Brianna responded, shocked with the manner in which her best friend was talking to her, "I didn't ask for a dragon to turn me into dust and ash."

"I'm not talking to you," Kimberley stated with a scathing tone, "I am asking how he could have let this happen."

"Who?"

"Him," Kimberley pointed towards Damien. "If it wasn't for him you wouldn't needed saving. It's his stupid idea to go exploring the castle when we have no idea about this world. It's his stupid idea that we go off by ourselves without knowing what could happen to us."

"Kimberley, how could you say things like this? Its not his fault, we all wanted to explore the school," Brianna answered back.

"No," she replied, "it was Damien that wanted to go gallivanting around the school. You just want to please Damien by agreeing to his every command and for what? So that you could get yourself killed? We are no longer going anywhere with someone that doesn't know the world that we are a part of."

"It wasn't his fault," Brianna said, defending Damien. "I think you need to calm things down a little bit Kimberley; no harm has been done so just leave it at that."

The atmosphere had reached a very tense level between the group and Brianna could think of doing nothing other than turning and walking back to the school. The end of the tour had taken a turn for the worse and Brianna resolved to try and talk to Kimberley when they weren't with Damien.

She felt a pang of guilt rising in her stomach as she realised Kimberley simply cared about her and that was the only reason as to her outburst and fury at Damien. Even if she liked Damien she couldn't abandon the unwavering loyalty from her best friend; even she knew that no boy was worth that amount of trouble.

They walked back as a group towards the transporting chamber and were pleased to see Logan and Isabella up ahead, knowing that they had returned before the portal had closed. Damien had not spoken a word since Kimberley had shouted at him, but he looked in a foul mood rather than showing any sense of regret or concern for what could have happened.

They left the front of Witchcraft Heights in silence and only until they parted ways did they decide to communicate with one another. The goodbye said between friends was extremely strained and most definitely not the way that Brianna had wanted to end such an adventurous albeit dangerous day. She left Kimberley with a hug and tried to convey an apology in the way that she looked at her best friend. Kimberley gave a weak smile and Brianna knew that all she needed was time to get over the shock of her best friend becoming a piece of charcoal. She turned away and thought quietly to herself of the adventure she had had and the adventures that were sure to come.

Chapter 13

It wasn't until Wednesday afternoon that Kimberley and Brianna had a chance to sit in the first year

common room. Due to their wandering antics at the start of the week they had fallen slightly behind in one of

their research topics for Professor Petra. It was a follow up from their flora studies lesson where they had

attempted to take the colour from a petal and create a ball of light from its essence. It was the hardest spell

that they had tried to master so far in their practical sessions. After straining her mind to concentrate on the

yellow petal in front of her they had not managed to produce even a wisp of magic from their wand. Professor

Petra had told them that the magical presence that they had, although helping them to draw magic to them,

did not automatically mean that they could brandish their wands and call out different spells all the time. This

was a lesson that most of the Professors had drummed into the students' minds; once again reiterating the

importance of the theoretical lessons. From this lesson, Professor Petra had informed them to research the

theory of drawing magical power from plants.

They had managed to get started on their homework but Damien, Caleb and Michael entered the room

and chose to join the girls. This soon stopped the progress in their work as they sat with the girls and spent

their time discussing dragons. The books that they had found to help their research on transferring spells got

left on the floor by the table to make way for books on dragons. 'A definitive guide to Dragons in Great Britain'

and 'Dragons: Riders of the Sky' were skimmed through by the five of them. Brianna stopped on a few pages

where pictured dragons were captured on the page.

As she looked at a blue and green scaled 'Hornbeam Dragon' she found the word 'hornbeam' captured

her attention. She had looked at her secret book after their run in with the dragons and was sure she had seen

the hornbeam mentioned somewhere in it. She picked it out of her bag and flicked through its pages. She

found one of the scrawling's that had formulated itself on the page, 'Hornbeam is a riders dream'.

Today, she looked again at her book. She opened it at the page she had found the dragon scrawling.

She had spent a lot of time looking for scribbling's in the past that she hadn't really focused on the contents of the book itself. It was therefore a surprise that 'Dragon rearing and looking after your own dragon' was a heading at the top of the page 130. It was as if the book was writing itself, creating the life that Brianna was fast becoming a part of as she found out about each new revelation in her life. She started to read the first paragraph, when Alleyen and Serena entered the common room and she decided to avert her attention to those instead. They had been off once again on Freshman Prefect duties.

"Hi girls," said Serena, "what did you two get up to after the lesson on Monday then? I completely forgot to ask you yesterday."

"Oh, nowhere really, we just browsed around the school. We really want to get to know more about our surroundings."

Brianna wasn't entirely sure why, but she didn't want to disclose her antics with Alleyen or Serena. They had been so good to them and helped them to get used to the school. She was still not entirely sure that what they had done on Monday was allowed. She knew that her decision had been swayed by Damien's presence but this did not mean that what they had done was right; he wasn't exactly aware of the rules himself.

"What have you got there?" asked Alleyen looking at Brianna's book.

"Oh nothing," she tried to say offhandedly, attempting slyly to place the book back in her bag. Serena swiped the book from her hand as she had been looking at Alleyen and fanned through the pages.

"What book is this?" she questioned Brianna.

"Oh, it's just something from the other world," she tried to say without real interest in the topic.

"Cool," said Serena who was keen to learn about the other school as much as Brianna was eager to learn about the Realm World.

"Wait a second," she paused as her eyes saw the scrawling on page 130 where Brianna saw her read the lines, which had changed to the topic on dragons from its original text, "What is this book?"

Kimberley looked up at this point, wondering why Serena was so interested in.

"I don't know exactly what it is," she began sheepishly, "it sort of called out to me."

"Alleyen come here," she called over the other freshman prefect urgently, "you don't suppose it is a Magia Animabus?"

"Brianna, where did you get this from?" Alleyen asked with an incredulous tone.

"I found it in the school library when I was at Witchcraft Heights. It sort of found me... I think," Brianna tried to explain. "As soon as I had it in my fingertips I had an instinctive feeling that I was meant to find it."

"Well I would agree with you there," Serena faintly responded, "I am just amazed that it has finally been found after so many centuries."

"Centuries?" Brianna repeated, completely confused.

"Yes," answered Serena, "one of the books' of Lost Magia Animabus have been the thing of myths for centuries. It is said to provide the information necessary to its owner, to help keep the realm world at peace and protect the mortal world in times of great need. It holds all of the secrets to the world that we live in and identifies the ways in which peace can exist. No one truly knows where the source of information derives from, only that its answers to the aid of its owner. The information is meant to create a great power, a power that only the owner of the book can control; the book chooses the person it wishes to use that power."

"The book has a name," was the first thing that Brianna could say. Its faded cover had never revealed anything to suggest its contents.

"Of course it does, take a look yourself." Brianna closed the book and there in front of her she saw a looping scrawling covering the front cover. 'The Book Estas Orientem Magia Animabus.'

"Wow," she said as the book slowly started to reveal more of its purpose. "What else do you know about the book?"

"Not a lot other than the purpose. It's been lost for such a long time that the secrets of the book have been long forgotten. Have you noticed anything strange about the book?"

Brianna once again felt protective of the book, should she say anything to the others? As she looked into the faces of her three friends she quickly shook away the doubts, realising it was stupid to question the intentions of her friends.

"Before I came to the realm world it was as if the book was talking to me. Notes kept popping up on random pages; as if other people, students I guessed, were writing in the book. When I first came across the realm world I supposed that people in the realm world might use books as method of communication between this world and the mortal world. In the days since my arrival in this world, the pages started to change and now sections have been replaced by my own magical experiences; almost as if the book is writing a narrative of my experiences."

"Hmmm..." Serena said, looking questioningly at Brianna and the book. "Well this book is a rare relic. I'm pretty sure that other students from wouldn't be able to write comments in it."

"Well that doesn't make a lot of sense then. I wonder how the writing made its way into the book," Brianna contemplated as she scratched her head in thought.

They all sat in silence, trying to make sense of the revelation. Brianna felt relieved that she finally understood something more about the book, but as some answers surfaced she couldn't help but think that there were a lot more questions that needed answering and that there was a lot more to the book than she had first anticipated.

"So going back to what I just saw... where did the two of you really head off to the other day?" said Alleyen with her hands placed firmly on her hips, "because this book clearly shows that you had a run in with some dragons."

"Okay, so we may have gone on a little tour of the outside of the school," confessed Brianna. "We haven't seen the world outside these walls. I just wanted to be able to see what the world was like. Can you understand that?"

"Well, yeah, but why didn't you ask us to show you around? If you didn't get back in time you could have been in serious trouble."

"But we did, so there's no harm done."

"You need to be much more responsible than that Brianna. The consequences of you being in the realm world after your curfew is bad news and not just for you. The Professors' of this school will blame us for failing to looking after you and will most likely strip us from our prefect duties. Plus it could also lead to an inquisition as to your whereabouts from your loved ones and threaten to expose our world to the Mortals."

Brianna hadn't thought of the how her antics could affect others and she felt extremely guilty for putting her friends at risk about it. She looked up to apologise to Alleyen but her eyes caught Damien sitting in the corner of the room and she knew that she would not and could not change what she would do when Damien was the one calling the shots.

"Sorry," she tried to say convincingly and it seemed to work as Alleyen gave her a forgiving smile.

"Okay, we have lectured you two enough. We might as well tell you why we have dragons in our school.

"You haven't met Professor Llewellyn yet. He's our Sport Professor who will teach you how to play all of the main sports hosted in the Realm World. There are three popular sports in our school that most of the students follow. Witch hunt, Hurdlekurl and for the necessity of our dragons; dragon riding."

"You ride dragons?" asked Kimberley incredulously, finding her voice once again.

"Yeah," chuckled Serena, "it's the best sport in our world by far. The dragons that we have at the school cater for all the needs from rookie to national champions. Championship riders usually have their own dragon that they search for, or they call for them. It's a weird connection and one that is pretty much unbreakable."

"You'll find it out for yourself pretty soon," stated Alleyen teasingly.

"What do you mean?" enquired Brianna.

"Well most dragon riders start their training at school," said Serena informatively, "so you will be taught after Christmas how to ride the dragons. We didn't want to spoil the surprise, but I suppose the wands out of the woods now and spoiled it anyway."

Brianna took her book back from Serena and opened it once more to page 130. It was now covered in detailed information regarding dragons that stretched over to page 132. It was true then; the book was revealing the world to her as she discovered it herself. Her one of a kind, own personal journal was becoming something of a personal magical relic. Brianna felt that there was a great deal more to the book than just this information-providing quirk, but she decided not to press the subject and soon Kimberley and Brianna packed all their things back in the locker room and went back to the Mortal world for another day.

*

With all the excitement that had procured from the revelation of the dragons, Brianna had forgotten about most of her worries. Madison was a friend long forgotten and had now merely become a reluctant student in the world of magic. Her distant attitude and disapproval towards Kimberley and Brianna remained strong. Brianna tried to talk to Kimberley about it, but Kimberley did not wish to hear the name of someone that was not kind or caring towards her.

"She has made her choice and we have made ours," was all that Kimberley wished to denounce regarding the matter. Brianna, although torn by her need to make everything right, knew in her heart that her friend was a lost cause. No one could be forced to choose the path of magic.

Another matter that she had also forgotten about was the Winter Ball, being swamped by everything else around her in her life. Only when flying banners declaring its commencement and changes to the dining hall in the last week of term did Brianna start to contemplate the looming date itself.

Taylor, who had shied away from Brianna since she had rekindled her friendship with Damien, approached her cautiously on their way down to the transporting chamber.

"Brianna," he called out, jogging to catch up with her before they went through the door.

"Oh, hi Taylor," she said as she turned to face him. A twinge of guilt rumbled in her stomach as she struggled to think of the last time that she had properly spoken to Taylor. The past week or so since their encounter with the dragons had been some of Brianna's best times in Salem. Damien hardly left Brianna's side and they had since been on other adventures around the school, sometimes with Serena and Alleyen to get a basic understanding of the school.

They had also used the girls as an inexhaustible source of knowledge, and sometimes Damien was found pandering to the girls when he wanted to find out more information. His innocent demeanour was often underlined with an impish glint as he used the material given by Serena and Alleyen to go off to further flung corners of the school. As he only took Brianna with him, she felt less guilty at using her friends for their own desirable purpose.

They had managed to find the head boy and girls chamber and had also seen the outside of the kitchens. Their ventures into the forest had had a rather eye opening impact on their understanding of the natures of the world, as they discovered a few of the smaller creatures that presided in the realm world. They had encountered strange Salamanders, Cats that could converse with them and banshees that squealed with fright. When they had stumbled upon a small pool of water Asrai, small aquatic fairies that danced lightly on the surface of the water and darted around the Dard's, met them; lazy creatures that were part lizard, part cat and sported the mane of a horse.

They knew that they had only managed to scratch the surface of the secrets pertained in the school walls, but they found that with every discovery their link to their beloved school grew stronger and stronger. Brianna also liked the change in Damien; it seemed to hold a level of confidence. His need and drive to learn more, like that of an excitable child discovering their first place to build a fort.

However, as she looked towards Taylor she realised how she had really left him out of the group since this time. Taylor was a decent guy and it made her guilt settle further as she knew that she had not given him a single thought. It was particularly hard to stomach when he had been so supportive and kind since their

first meeting. She didn't want him to get the wrong impression that she was attracted to him. At least that is

what she kept trying to tell herself, attempting to justify why she would disregard a good-looking boy that was

clearly interested in her. She knew she was covering up her own voice in her head, the little voice called

reason and guilt when she knew she had just forgotten all about him as her head and heart were clouded in

thoughts of Damien.

"How have you been?" he asked, giving the best attempt at keeping a cheery and light manner in his

voice. Brianna couldn't fail to notice that he looked slightly nervous than what he normally did when speaking

to her and she decided to carefully answer his question, wondering what his real motive was to spark a

conversation. For some unknown reason she felt a sudden warning noise sounding off in her mind.

"Really good thanks," she began, "still trying to keep on top of all the work from the two schools which

makes no change. I don't know how you manage to keep on track with it all when you have to spend time

commuting between three schools as well as playing football at the weekend. I thought they would have had a

portal at the different schools."

She wanted to keep the questions pointed towards him and it seemed to work.

"I spoke to Miss Ashdown about that a couple of days into our first week from finding out about the

realm world. She said it was too risky to have too many portals into the Realm world."

"Risky?"

"Well, I guess that if there are more portals into this world it could increase the chances of a mortal

stumbling across a door that could carry them through to the Realm world. She also said that a school that

holds portals' needs to have a magi-seeker that is designated to controlling who passes through the portal.

Part of her job is to remain attuned to the chamber room and recognise when a mortal is at a high risk of

finding the chamber."

"I never really thought about that before. In fact I haven't really given much thought about Miss Ashdown after the history club had come to an end."

"I find that I miss that club, which is an oddity I suppose, as I was never really a part of it. Don't you?" he said with a touch of nostalgia showing in his eyes.

"I guess so," she said, not really understanding why Taylor would really miss the club, he hadn't been involved in it an awful lot. Taylor had been invited as a guest to the two events, but he had never been involved in the planning and preparation of the events.

"We had so much fun, talking all the time," he said rather sheepishly, "I just miss that connection and ease of conversation."

'Ahh' she thought to herself, it was a better time for him because they had spoken a great deal more when they were in the history club. They had sat together at the banquet and spent a fair amount of time together when they had first ventured through into the Realm world.

"So... anyway," he carried on with a slow manner. "I actually have a question that I've been meaning to ask you for quite some time."

"Oh, what's that?" she asked warily.

"Well... the Winter Ball is coming up soon and I was wondering if you had anyone to go with?"

"Ermm... no one has asked me actually," she said truthfully.

"Oh," he said and he cheered up immediately, "well, would you like to go with me?"

He flashed her one of his smiles, looking hopefully towards Brianna. She didn't know what to say or what to think. She didn't want to upset Taylor, but she had completely forgotten about the ball and to be asked out of the blue was a complete shock. Now that he had asked her she also immediately thought of Damien.

"I need to speak to Kimberley first," she blurted out.

"Why?" he asked slightly suspiciously.

"Well I need to see whether she has a date, I can't go with a date if she hasn't got anyone," she stated, formulating an explanation along the way. "It's a girl thing, so could I get back to you maybe tomorrow?"

She didn't want to give him a definite answer and it seemed to satisfy his doubt as the crease that had formed across his forehead smoothed out a little. He nodded in agreement, saw someone ahead, and quickly rushed over to greet them. Brianna was sure he wasn't a great friend to Emmett, one of the students that had come from Goodwin High, but it gave both him and her chance to process what had just gone on.

She sat through elemental charms with Professor Petra. They were still focusing on using the most basic of elements to assist with their magic; the earth. She tried her best to stay on task but her mind refused to remain focused on the lesson. Professor Petra was quick to notice this as the stool that Brianna was meant to be creating from a pile of earth had shown no sign of transformation.

"Miss Eastey, you need to concentrate much more on your rubble. The 'Umbreyting' spell requires all of your being to focus on the item that you desire to change," she said sternly before whipping her cloak around and walking over to Madison who was similarly doing nothing.

Kimberley eyed Brianna suspiciously, but Brianna just shook her head in her direction and tried to refocus her attention. Getting told off by Professor Petra was not considered a wise move and could often land you in detention. Caleb had lost one of his free hours last week because he had tried to charm one of the teapots on the side of the room instead of the button that he had in front of him.

When the end of the lesson final arrived, the four girls headed back to the common room. Alleyen and Serena were busily chatting about a couple of the Prefect duties they had been set for the evening, for which Brianna was thankful. This meant she wasn't highlighted as the central topic of conversation. It also gave her the chance to think things over. What was she going to do about Taylor? On the one hand she didn't want to say yes to Taylor just in case Damien asked her out. On the other hand if she said no to Taylor that would crush his heart and spirit, and he didn't deserve that. What if Damien didn't ask her to the dance? Would that suggest that he wasn't interested in Brianna, contrary to her hopeful wishes and level of progress that they

had seemed to make in the short space of time.

She tried to distract her spinning thoughts by thinking back over the course of the first term and

attempting to start remembering the number of spells that they had been taught in their different subjects.

The spells that they had learnt were meant to be basic, but the mortal students found them exciting, if not

extremely challenging most of the time. The two girls sat together in the common room before Damien, Caleb

and Michael went to join them. Serena and Alleyen followed behind where they soon found themselves under

a hot seat spotlight as they were continually questioned on different aspects surrounding the realm world.

"What's the trickiest spell that we shall ever learn?" Caleb asked the two girls.

"Well, that's a very subjective question," Serena answered, "one person will find one area of magic

easier than another. It is entirely dependent on your strengths and personality. For example, I am particularly

good at rhythmic charms, whereas Alleyen is far more suited to remedies. You will soon pick on what you are

particularly good at."

"That's all fair enough, but when will we learn to do something like flying?" asked the ever-inquisitive

Damien.

Serena and Alleyen both started to laugh simultaneously.

"What?" he questioned the laughter, "what's so funny?"

"People can't fly!" Serena exclaimed, clutching at her side as she laughed so profusely.

"Well, I thought you could do anything with magic." His face flushed red as the girls laughed at him as

he seemed embarrassed and a bit angered at their mockery. Brianna almost sensed his attitude and quickly

set to remedy, if not support his embarrassed companion.

"Well, I can see were you are coming from Damien. We have come into a world where everything

seems possible, so a thing like flying would not seem so farfetched."

"In a world with seemingly endless possibility there obviously has to be some restrictions and things that cannot be achieved by magic. We cannot fly through the wave of a wand, but I suppose there are other ways. There is no spell to turn us into something different permanently or a spell to make someone fall in love with you. It's the basic principal law, that all things are put on the Realm earth for a purpose; it is not natural to change by the use of magic. The elements will return to things as they once were in a long or short amount of time, for nature overrules the real power that magic holds."

"Are there not ways to overrule the basic rules though?" Damien questioned, "surely there must be witches and wizards in the world who are not who they once were or have forced someone to love them."

Alleyen looked at Damien almost in a horrified way and Brianna couldn't fathom what he had said that was so wrong.

"What you are speaking of is something that I will not answer. There is no point sparking the flame of temptation in the minds of those who know nothing about the darker elements of this world."

The group fell silent as the mortal students realised they had bought up a topic of conversation that had crossed the point of comfort. It was not through their fault, but nonetheless the mortal students knew that they did not need to pursue the topic any further. After a couple of slightly awkward glances towards one another Damien got up and the two boys joined him and headed over to their favourite seats in the common room.

The boys started to talk amongst one another, every now and then stealing glances over in the direction of the girls. Brianna secretly hoped that they were talking about who they would select as their dates for the Winter Ball, even though she doubted boys would really talk about that sort of topic.

"So, what's on your mind?" asked Kimberley as Alleyen and Serena left the common room to commence their prefect duties that they had been assigned to complete for the remaining hour.

"Taylor came and spoke to me," she said in a voice that carried across the common room. She wanted Damien to hear what she was saying as she hoped it would spur him on to ask her to be his date to the ball.

"Well what did he say to make you so worked up? Was he horrible to you?"

"No, nothing like that he was as sweet as ever," the compliment seemed the right thing to add and sure enough it gained Damien's attention. His eye's narrowed so she decided to carefully pick out her next words.

"Actually, he asked me out to the Winter Ball," she said, "as a date."

"What did you say?" Kimberley asked in an interested manner, unaware of what Brianna was actually up to.

"I said I'd think it through," she looked meaningfully towards Damien who immediately dropped his gaze as he noticed her looking in his direction. She dropped her voice a little, "I said it would depend on whether you had a date actually. Sorry, it was the best reason I could think of."

Kimberley looked around the room and spied Damien sitting in the corner; by the fireplace. As the wind whistled through the cracks in the common room windows, Brianna decided it was an opportune moment to get up and head over to Damien. She went and sat opposite Damien who was looking pensive. They had been around the school and the two of them looked through some books in the school library, trying to find out some information on the Realm world. He had spent an awful lot of time searching, taking out a black notebook that he had bought to write a small note every now and then.

"How far spread do you think the families are within the Realm world?" Damien asked suddenly.

"I'm not too sure if I'm completely honest, a lot of my family seem to reside in the Salem area. What about your family?"

Damien looked to the ground, a rosy complexion rising in his cheeks.

"I don't know," he said in a hollow voice.

"What do you mean Damien?"

"I don't know who my family are. I was bought up in an orphanage and I have been shifted from foster home to foster home my whole life. Some families, when they managed to have a child of their own decided they no longer wished for me to be a part of my family. Other families seemed to be doubtful towards me; they had me removed from their family. I moved to Salem about two years ago and I have been living in the care of an old lady; I'm more of her carer than she is my foster parent."

"I'm sorry to hear that," Brianna replied, "It must awful not to know who your family are."

"At first it used to bother me, but then I got used to the idea of not having anyone to depend on." He spoke without bitterness or sadness, which came across as rather odd, if not a little worrying to Brianna. "Knowing that I am a wizard gave me an identity; it allowed me to know that I have family somewhere because everyone has to have magical ancestry."

They continued to sit in silence as the wind whistled through and Brianna was left to feel sad about Damien's life. She went back to sit with Kimberley, feeling guilty that she had bought up the subject and decided that she would wait until he cheered up before hoping to be asked to the Winter ball.

Brianna could see Kimberley putting the pieces of the puzzle together, even if she did not approve of her choices. Kimberley had not truly forgiven Damien since their first interaction with the dragons. She gave Kimberley a pleading look to not respond to the last comment, which Kimberley did obligingly if not a little begrudgingly. Her best friend didn't understand her crazy obsession with Damien but as her best friend she knew that Kimberley would not want to ruin any opportunity that she could possibly have with him.

After a good forty-five minutes Serena and Alleyen were relieved of their duties and they sat together as a group of four. With work finally pushed to the back of their mind, the girls started a flow conversation about the winter ball, with not so much as a peep of the previous conversation that had been exchanged between Brianna and Kimberley. They discussed the matters of what they believed of greatest importance. Questions about accessories, what the older students would be like and food choices seemed to be the key topics of conversation. As the questions floated around Brianna started to think about her date options again. She considered confronting Damien; it would at least put her mind at rest as to whether they would be going together. On the other hand, she saw that it would be an awful thing to do if Taylor was to discover that he was her back up option. She shouldn't lead on Taylor, this she knew, but for some inexplicable reason she could not bring herself to refuse him.

She turned back to the girls who were now considering whether to have their hair up or down for the occasion; a trivial matter in Brianna's opinion as she would simply wash her hair and let nature set a design.

It was as she dropped back out of focus that she saw Madison. True, they were no longer friends and this was completely of Madison's doing with her cold callous behaviour towards both herself and Kimberley. She couldn't talk to Kimberley about Madison; as far as she was concerned Madison had made her choice and she was making hers.

Unfortunately, Brianna was too compassionate for her own good and she couldn't fail but let her emotions affect her. She looked over to the glum face of her old friend and for the smallest moment in time she felt sympathy towards Madison. Here she was with a group of three girls in a whirlwind of excitement at the prospect of another school dance and yet she couldn't help but notice Madison alone, with nothing to do or anybody to talk to. Brianna was saddened when she remembered that just a short while ago it was Madison who was excitedly chatting away about the upcoming dance at Witchcraft Heights. Maybe she should approach her, not in front of everyone else, but she was sure that she could get Madison by herself, she was alone all the time anyway.

With so many unresolved issues, it was with a rather subdued set of emotions with which Brianna left Merlin as the bell rang for six, thinking that it was only a mere twenty four hours before the infamous ball.

*

"Wake up sweetie; you're going to be late for school."

Huh? Brianna tried to compose her thoughts and realise what was going on. It took a good minute before she realised she had been having a vivid dream about flying dragons that breathed ice instead of fire. It had seemed so real that she hadn't realised that she had been actually been asleep.

"Come on Brianna, it's your last day of school today," called out the voice again and as Brianna decided she needed to open her eyes she saw that her mom, Gretchen was standing in the doorway with her hands on her hips.

"You were talking in your sleep, sweetheart. Is everything okay?"

"Yeah Mom, just last day jitters I suppose," Brianna answered sleepily, slightly worried what she had been saying in her sleep if she had been dreaming about dragons.

"You have had a lot on this term. I can't believe the amount of work that they have given you. If I didn't know better I would say that you are getting extra work from outside of school."

Brianna gave an attempt of a cheeky smile; her Mom was often insightful on Brianna's antics, which wasn't any help to her when she was attempting to conceal her magical secret. Gretchen shut the door on Brianna and gave her opportunity to spring from her bed, rush around her room and stow her dress in her school bag. She didn't want her mom or dad seeing that she was taking her Halloween dance dress in case it bought up some more probing questions.

As she tucked the last corner of material into her bag she cascaded down the stairs and out of the door. She didn't think that her face could hide her excitement from her parents and instead of arousing suspicion she decided that avoidance was the safer option.

She arrived in record time to the front gates of Witchcraft Heights and made her way to the Merlin common room. The weak morning rays had not yet entered the walls of the Merlin building so she made her way slowly and blindly through the dark, feeling slightly jumpy and nervous with the sense of unknowing before her.

She pushed lightly on the face of Merlin, but the door still seemed to echo as she made her way to the comfort of an armchair and rested herself for just a few minutes before the busy day was about to commence. As she waited for Kimberley and the boys she tried to recollect the dream that she had been having so vividly last night.

She remembered the dragons had taken her on a journey. Her feet had landed on an echoing paving stone path and as she looked up an image flashed before her eyes of a row of odd shaped buildings on her left hand side; individual and situated at different distances and angles to the path. The image blacked and was replaced by a quick image of a gravestone. She squealed in fright as Eastey came to focus from the depths of her unconsciousness. She tried to bring to the surface any other telling from the dream but none occurred and she tried to calm herself and wait in the lightening common room...

"Brianna," called out an echoing voice and Brianna turned her head to see a darkened shadow cloud her view.

"Brianna!" it called louder and Brianna realised that her eyes were shut. She must have dozed off in the common room.

She opened her eyes and saw Kimberley standing over her with a hand on her hip. Brianna could not help but chuckle as she saw the image of her mother from this morning mirrored in her friends greeting.

"How long have you been here?" Kimberley asked, "You were practically snoring when I came in!"

"I don't snore!" she replied, hoping that Damien hadn't seen her in this manner, "I had to leave early before mom and dad started questioning me. It was still dark when I came and sat in here so I guess I have been here quite a while."

Kimberley chuckled in response and the two of them went to stow their things in their locker. The last day of term seemed almost pointless at Witchcraft Heights; there were no lessons to attend and there was no special event to commemorate a term of hard work. They sat and endured the school assembly; where they were lectured on how to be safe during the Christmas vacation and that they were not to neglect their studies over the festive period.

Brianna has switched off at this point and instead contented to think about the ball that she was to attend later that evening.

When the bell finally rang to signal the end of the day the students of the Realm World dawdled as the rest of the crowd dispersed and said their farewells to their friends. As everyone headed in the direction of the front entrance, Brianna and Kimberley made their way back to their lockers to retrieve their things fro the evening and made their way to the portal chamber.

Brianna performed the unlocking charm that allowed them to step through the portal and stepped back into what she liked to think of as home. Unsure as to where the other juniors were, Brianna and Kimberley decided it was best to head to the first year common room. Brianna couldn't help but notice that Kimberley seemed to be very interested in her surroundings and although the decorations were exquisitely beautiful, she knew that the decorations weren't what her best friend was so interested in.

They arrived at the common room and Kimberley pushed on the door.

At first Brianna believed that they had gone through the wrong door and that they had miscalculated their sense of direction. The common room had completely vanished and in its place there was a room that could only be described as a large vanity studio. There were a various number of partitions that housed mirrors and stools seated before a large desk.

Brianna nodded to Kimberley and they stepped forward. As they crossed the threshold a most extraordinary sight immediately greeted them. Brianna had come across fairies in her time at Merlin, Professor Merrydew for one was a fairy, but these small sprightly creatures were not like the fairies she had thus far encountered.

They were no more than the size of her hand and were a sparkling jade green in complexion. She blinked and they changed to resemble a rose pink and as Brianna forced her eyes to stay open she saw their colours change in dazzling shades of electric blue, glittering gold and vivacious violet. Their clothes seemed to fall like water over their changing skin, where there seemed to be no end and no beginning to the material. Their hair was cropped and framed their petite faces, which were dimpled, were softened with warming smiles and sparkling eyes.

They didn't speak but beckoned with tiny fingers to come and sit at one of the units. Brianna did so

obligingly and went to retrieve her dress out of her bag, but as she felt around there was no feel of a silken

fabric against her fingers.

One of the fairies shook her head as she pointed at the bag. As they placed a surprisingly strong grip on

her shoulders and seated her down she noticed a dress floating and twirling in the air. It was not the dress that

she had bought along; it was far more beautiful than anything she could of have imagined. As it twirled a

ribbon appeared around the belly and she saw her name stream along the silken material. It had been

designed especially for her!

The fairies gave no more time to look at its sparkling front with crystals cascading down in different

shades of pink as they span her to face the mirror and started working busily away at her hair and face. They

used an assortment of different bottles and boxes that were laid before her and somehow managed to wash

her hair without a drop of water in sight.

The dedication and precision that the fairies put into their work made Brianna sit in the most

statuesque manner so that she did not disturb what could only be described as their newest project. She lost

track of time, but all too soon it seemed they were done. They fluttered away so that she could see their work

for herself and she was gobsmacked. Her hair had been fashioned into an intricate woven plait with a woven

headband and tiny sparkling gems dotted in and among her hair. Her makeup was light with a small blush that

highlighted her rosy cheeks and eyes that dazzled with the subtle hint of mascara and a small sweeping line of

black eyeliner.

The fairies fluttered back over with the dress and slipped it over her head where it fell so easily and

fitted against her body to perfection. She looked back up and saw a strange princess looking back at her. She

could only ever imagine that a princess could ever feel like the way that she now felt.

Looking around to find her friend, she noticed a face beaming back at her and realised that it was

Kimberley looking back at her equally as beautiful in a turquoise dress that resembled the element of water.

They giggled at one another and reached simultaneously for a friendly hand. Now they were truly ready for the ball.

They meandered their way through the altered common room, directed by more fairies that seemed to point their attention to an area obscured by the high vanity units. They arrived at a door that had been fashioned out of nowhere; it had certainly not belonged to the room before. Tentatively, they stepped through the door where they were greeted by the most amazing sight they had yet seen in the Realm World.

The dining hall had been completely altered to resemble a Christmas wonderland, a place where Santa himself could proudly reside. The floor was like ice with glitter speckled into its swirling patterns; a long table moulded itself around the edge of the hall covered in a red and golden cloth. Real life snowmen were walking around the hall with trays of fruit punch in arm and swirling skating figures danced gaily on platforms that were situated in the sills of each window. She couldn't count the number of baubles and pinecones that littered the huge Christmas tree, proudly standing at the far end of the hall and as she looked up high she noticed the angel on the top of the tree singing merry Christmas songs.

"Isn't it just wonderful," said an approaching voice and Brianna turned to see Taylor walking her way with a broad smile on his face. Brianna couldn't help but take in a sharp breath as she looked upon him. He was wearing a tailored navy suit, crisp cut with a light blue cravat, which matched his piercingly blue eyes. His smile continued and made a small bow to both the girls before holding out his arms in a gentlemanly fashion and leading the way for Brianna and Kimberley to find their seats.

"Hello girls," called out Michael as Taylor parked the girls among their friends. Caleb was there as well, with Damien sitting next to Caleb. Damien gave a beaming smile up to Brianna, but it soon became a rather strained grimace as he noticed Taylor.

"Welcome all," a loud voice called out suddenly, breaking the brief tension in the group and Brianna turned towards the Christmas tree where Professor Allard stood in a green robe. It was a rare sight to see their headmaster, but it was always a pleasant meeting with the most content of wizards they had met thus far.

"Welcome to the Christmas ball. It's a chance for you all to celebrate your achievements for this term. Please enjoy all the entertainment, food and good company that we have to offer."

There was a generous applause as Professor Allard took a seat and the food was whisked into the hall. Brianna had never seen such a vast assortment of dishes set before her eyes. There were mounds of turkey, goose, ham and chicken; piles of potatoes that had been mashed, roasted and sautéed. The vegetables nearly rolled out of the bowls and cascaded down onto the tables. As well as the staple parts of the meal there were pyramids of stuffing balls, stacks of Yorkshire puddings and hundreds of sausages wrapped in bacon.

She placed as much food as her plate could hold and the table fell silent as they all focused on the meals set before them. When the tables had been wiped clear of all the food set before them, they were quickly replaced with the desserts.

The Christmas puddings all proceeded valiantly on floating trays; with pretty flames that changed colour from red to green to purple trailing behind as it made its procession towards the table. As well as the scrumptious Christmas puddings, there were a wide assortment of other desserts that included the likes of pecan pie, trails of chocolate brownie bites and another number of deserts that Brianna was just dying to try out.

When the desserts had finally been cleared Professor Allard stood up and addressed an ensemble of people who were standing at the entrance to the hall. They obligingly stepped forward and made their way towards a stage that Brianna had not noticed. It held a number of ice-sculptured instruments that didn't look at all playable. She was therefore greatly surprised when a gentleman placed his fingertips on the keyboard, at which point his whole body turned progressively to a shade of electric blue, and began to play a tuneful melody.

The rest of the band found their positions on the stage and turned similar shades of electric blue as they touched their musical instrument to which the music commenced. The first piece was a vibrant, catchy tune that got a lot of people onto their feet and onto the dance floor in the middle of the room. Brianna was led up by Kimberley and they started to bop and twirl around on the floor. As she turned around she spotted Taylor looking over in her direction. She gave a polite smile in his direction and he nodded and smiled in return.

The girls danced and danced until their feet seemed ready to fall off; the music had maintained its upbeat tempo for a good hour and this had encouraged most of the people to leave the comfort of their chair. Even Caleb and Michael got up to join the girls; they weren't good dancers by any measure but they certainly made up for their lack in dancing skills by a good level of enthusiasm.

They continued dancing until the tempo changed and the song became a slower and more of a romantic tone. Brianna sensed that she was being watched on more than one account and sure enough she saw two sets of eyes looking on her. One was Damien watching sullenly from the table. He had not gone up to join the party; maybe it was something to do with Kimberley's less than positive opinion of him or maybe he didn't want to clown with his friends tonight. His eyes flickered across the room and as Brianna followed their direction she found another reason for his sullen expression.

Taylor was making his way over to the group and she couldn't help but notice that his eyes were locked on her. She panicked as the pieces of the puzzle fitted together; the slow music, Damien's miserable demeanour, Taylor's level of focus. She didn't want to make things awkward; true her opinion of Taylor had grown, but she wasn't ready for a proclamation of his fancies.

She therefore did the only thing that she saw as possible and made a cowardly escape, making a gesture to Kimberley that she needed to go and get a drink. Kimberley, who was usually able to pick up on all of Brianna's moods, seemed oblivious to her friend's current situation. Brianna only had to take one look at why Kimberley had turned misty eyed and saw Truesdale walking towards Kimberley, taking a small bow and holding out his hand in a gentlemanly fashion so as to invite her to a dance.

As she had made an escape, she had no other choice than to go over for a drink. As she stood at the drinks counter she looked across the floor she noticed Madison looking extremely uncomfortable. In a dull plum gown that seemed to wilt for her body, Brianna seriously doubted whether such an outfit would attract any sort of attention. Perhaps the fairies had an insight to the emotions of the students and knew instinctively how to dress them to suit their mood. She felt the pang of guilt and sadness wash over her as her friend sat there alone among the crowded room.

Whether out of pity or odd interest, Brianna couldn't help but watch Madison; like a strange species that Brianna was observing and making behavioural notes on. Every time she moved her position Brianna monitored how she looked and then Brianna realised that Madison was in fact looking at Professor Allard and watching him rather intently.

When Professor Allard made his exit from the hall Madison, for some strange reason, followed Professor Allard out into the hall. Curiosity took a hold of her and she decided to follow Madison and find out what she was up to. The door that they had exited through opened onto one of the main corridors of the school.

She looked left and right for and listened intently for any sign of movement. She waited and waited until at last she saw the flicker of a candle in the corner of her right eye, so she proceeded in that direction. As she met the candle there was the sound of footsteps making their way up the circling stone stairwell. Taking her shoes off so that the heel didn't echo on the hard stone steps, she followed the pattering sound of feet to the top and heard the echoing sound trail off around the right hand corner at the far end of the corridor.

She approached cautiously and noticed that there was a stream of light ahead. A slit of light and a low level of murmuring were protruding from a door that had been left slightly ajar. As she made her approach to the door she realised that there was a plaque on the wall beside the door.

'Professor Allard, Headmaster of Merlin.'

She was standing outside the headmaster's office; so she had only managed to follow the sounds of Professor Allard roaming the school. She turned to leave and seek out Madison when she heard a voice from inside the office and realised that Professor Allard was not alone.

"Are you sure that this is what you want?" Professor Allard responded to the previous murmur.

"I am absolutely sure. I have never wanted this...this burden; I don't want to deal with it anymore."

Brianna stifled a gasp as she realised it she recognised the voice of Madison communicating with the headmaster. What on earth could she possibly want to talk to the headmaster for?

"Miss Count, this is a decision that should not be taken lightly," he said soberly, "once it has happened there is no going back."

"Have you not been listening to me," she said sounding half mad as her voice got louder and to some degree, angrier. "I do not want to be a part of this... this freak show. It is not natural and I will not go around disappointing those who are closest to me."

"But Miss Count, you must realise your importance within our world. Your ancestry is so vital to the balance of our world and the sanctity that it presents."

"I'm not the only one from those stupid witch hunts," she responded with an acidic tone, "find others that actually care about this place. You will find no solace from me."

"Well, I cannot force a student against their will," he responded and Brianna could sense the level of pain that the Professor had in his heart. "If you wish it, I will obligingly grant you what you desire."

A sudden energy seemed to pulsate from inside the room. The gathering dust swirled with a golden glow that seemed to suck into one particular point in the room. Brianna could not chance to open the door and instead resolved to look at the slither of light that was glowing brighter and brighter. Her hair began to move towards the crack in the door and she held onto it tight. The drawing power become greater and greater still, until it felt as if she would fall through the door itself. The noise of the blowing wind and the light intensified to such a climatic point that Brianna feared as to what was occurring on the other side of the door.

All of a sudden a sure blackness consumed the room and everything that was once light was lost. Doubt rose within her heart and she began to question what had happened to her friend. At the moment that she was about to burst into the door it swung inwards and Brianna dashed to flatten herself against the wall.

Madison walked slowly but surely back down the corridor; the door closed behind her as she left. Brianna followed in her wake once more, wondering where her old friend was heading. They meandered through the many corridors of Merlin until they finally reached a corridor that Brianna was familiar with. She had been led to the corridor that linked the school to the transporting chamber.

"Madison," Brianna called out. She wanted to make sure her friend was content before she headed back to the mortal world. Madison didn't respond so Brianna called out even louder than the first time.

"Madison!"

Still Madison did not turn around. At first Brianna though this was rather rude, but surely Madison would at least turn around to identify who it was that was calling out to her. Brianna decided to catch up with Madison and get a response from her, even if she didn't want to give her one.

"Madison, are you alright," she said tapping Madison on the shoulder. She didn't stop or even turn so Brianna grabbed her firmly by the shoulders and looked directly into her face. The strangest of looks seemed to pass over Madison's face, it was if she was in a sort of trance and she was looking straight through Brianna. Stranger still, Brianna looked down and realised that Madison's feet were still walking even though Brianna was holding onto her steadfast.

The shock of this made Brianna release her grip and Madison walked through the door and down to the transporting chamber. Panicked, Brianna made a dash back to the main hall, searching frantically to find Kimberley.

She spotted her cuddled up with Truesdale and decided she would have to speak to her another day.

"Is everything alright?" asked a voice tapping Brianna lightly on the shoulder.

Taylor, the ever-present Taylor, was there to check on Brianna. It was oddly as if he was in tune with her and knew exactly when she needed someone to talk to.

"Ermm…," she couldn't think of a way to explain what she had just witnessed because she could not fully understand it herself. "I think I am just a bit worn out."

"You've been gone quite a while." So he had noticed her absence, "What have you been up to?"

"I've just been looking around at all the decorations," she spun a story, "I'm ready to head home now though. It must be time to go now."

He looked doubtingly at her, but did not push the subject. He kept a hold on her as they left and headed back to get changed before they exited through the transporting chamber.

As she finally stepped through to the mortal world Brianna could only think of one thing. Madison. She wondered what had happened to Madison, what had possibly overcome her old friend and what it was that Professor Allard had reluctantly agreed to do.

Chapter 14

Brianna had tried to forget about the world of magic and the Realm of Salem over the Christmas

vacation. It had given Brianna the chance to sit with her Mom and Dad like a normal family, playing card

games and eating far too much Christmas dinner so that her stomach pushed uncomfortably against her jeans.

All thoughts outside of her home were pushed to the back of her mind as they sat watching Christmas movies,

with a bowl of sweets placed precariously on each lap.

The only glitch to the perfect family Christmas in Salem was when Brianna had sat down to open her

presents from her mom and dad. She had been spoiled this year, as a way for her parents to congratulate

Brianna for taking the move so well, but as she opened her presents of endless DVD's, clothes, make up and

jewellery she felt something was missing. She said thank you in an overly enthusiastic manner and retreated

to her room to put all her new things away from the Christmas clutter in the living room. She piled the

presents on her bed and went straight for her drawer, taking out her wand from its inconspicuous necklace

case.

Magic; no matter how she carried on living her life in the mortal world she always found the same

emptiness in the pit of her stomach. She was most grateful for her presents this year, but she would have

loved to open a spell book or book on magical history, something that reminded her that the last few weeks

had really happened.

*

When Brianna awoke for her first day back at school she was greeted by a large mound of snow piled

all the way up to her front door. The snow, which had fallen persistently over the last couple of weeks, had

reached such a height that it had crept up the steps from the garden to the front porch. It was white and crisp,

but once again she found herself comparing the quality of the snow to the snow she had seen in the Realm of

Salem. Like everything else in the mortal world, it just didn't hold the same quality of awe and wonder as it did in the Realm World. Brianna had thought that the snow in the Realm World glistened and bounced off in a million shots of beams, resembling rainbow lights in an everlasting glow.

The buses couldn't run in this weather so that meant that it was a cold walk to school. She trudged through the snow, the damp cold ice melting through her shoes and socks until her feet began to feel numb. So it was that as she walked down the winding driveway that led to the front entrance of Witchcraft Heights that she was in a slightly disgruntled mood. She walked to the Merlin common room to fetch her books for the day. As it was a Monday, she knew that she would have to suffer Mr Downswood and his dulcet tones in Maths, which was probably the last thing that any student would want if they wanted to try and get back into the swing of the school day.

"Brianna, wait up," a voice shouted behind her and Brianna turned around to see Kimberley running to catch up with her.

"I've been trying to get your attention for the last five minutes. Didn't you hear me shouting after you along the corridor? I looked so silly."

"Sorry, I must have been consumed in my own thoughts. I'm absolutely itching to return to Merlin. I know we have gone through this before, but I just don't feel the need to carry on at Witchcraft heights. I have been thinking more and more about it over the Christmas period."

Kimberley looked understandingly at her friend before she responded. "Brianna, you know that we need to carry on with our education here. We have no idea what the future holds for us in the Realm world. They always seem so secretive; we still don't know anything about the world outside." Kimberley was like the voice of reason in her mind, it stabilised her desires and understood that although she wished to become a witch, shoe couldn't merely abandon her mortal duties.

"But we know that there is more. We've met people that exist in that world. We just need to be given the opportunity to explore the world for ourselves."

"And what if they don't let us out of the school because we were not bought up in the Realm World? You would have no other back up plan, no other form of education."

Brianna knew that Kimberley made sense, but it didn't change her opinion on the matter. She knew where she wanted to be and it was not in Salem or anywhere in the mortal world for that matter.

The two girls went to sit in their maths class, feeling a bit odd without the presence of Serena and Alleyen as they seemed such a natural element of their friendship. She saw Madison sitting at a table with Rose and Daisy, who for the first time in forever seemed content instead of brooding around. Brianna couldn't quite believe the change in Madison's manner during her first lesson; she seemed so content and happy. They were two emotions she had not seen from Madison for quite a while. The last time Brianna had seen Madison she had resembled a zombie, unable to communicate with Brianna but set on a purpose or destination of some sort. Yet there she was, happily chatting away to other students in her class with a big smile across her face; there was no sense of impending doom that she used to hold whenever she knew she had Merlin to attend to at the end of the school day.

Their games lesson with Coach Williams managed to bring back a little bit of life to the students. He decided to wake them up with an indoor volleyball tournament, which contrasted completely to the weather outside; personally Brianna had thought cross-country skiing would have been a better option. They were split according to gender and the Merlin and Medusa teams got up to play the first game. The boys all decided to take off their tops, perhaps to keen the authenticity of the sport alive or for the mere fact that a lot of girls were in the room. Damien although previously shy and unaware of girl's attention took off his top and gave a direct smile in Brianna's direction. His athletic body stretched up and allowed for a nice smash shot down by the net. It was a rare opportunity to see Damien in action, but it suited him. Again he seemed like the boy that she had met before the revelation of the Realm World, a confident and lively boy with nothing more than a happy demeanour to pass along to the other students around him. The girls around him picked up his positive vibes and a lot of the old smiles were being flashed once more in his direction.

As Brianna watched the ball slam against the ground winning a point for the Merlin boy's she looked at the faces of the Medusa boys. It was as she looked around to the last boy that a revelation occurred to her, none of these boys were in the Medusa school in the Realm of Salem. Furthermore, she could not recall any boy entering through the secret door to the Realm World. Wizards did exist in the realm world, Damien was living proof of that, but why were there no boys in one school?

She felt preoccupied with her thoughts as she went to sit down in the canteen area with Kimberley. She allowed for Kimberley to take charge of entertaining their friends and asking the questions regarding their Christmas vacation. She scanned the canteen and noticed Madison sitting among a group of the first years; she was still smiling and looking as if she had not a care in the world. It vexed her as she wondered what could have caused such a change in her attitude. Why was she now so frivolous and full of content when she had seemed so downhearted before? She worried slightly as she thought about the condition she had seen Madison as she had left the headmasters office. How did the pieces link together?

As she scanned around she had to complete a double take. Sitting in one of the corners Zoe sat eating away at what appeared to be no more than a celery stick. What disturbed Brianna most was not the fact that she was essentially satisfying her hunger with water, but that she didn't seem to have any of her cronies crowding around her. She looked somewhat sullen and her body seemed to defend herself from the rest of the world. As Brianna focused more on Zoe she noticed that her hair was fairly lank and unkempt. Her face had a greyish tinge and her eyes seemed to be black, before she realised that there were massive dark circles around her eyes causing them to shadow away.

Her thoughts carried her through to the end of the day when they walked down the familiar path to the transporting chamber. Her heart pounded in her chest as the excitement flooded through her and her footsteps quickened as she made it closer to the link between worlds. The separation between her and the realm world had been surprisingly painful and she knew that for all Kimberley's efforts, there would be no way that she would be taught in Salem when she could learn and thrive in the Realm World. The new world held a sense of belonging that she had never had before; like a hook that scraped against her heart and became

painful and tight when she stepped into the mortal world and released as she went back through to Merlin,

back home.

Serena and Alleyen were waiting in the corridor outside the door that led to the chamber and they

shared a small embrace at the reunion of their quartet. They asked questions about Brianna and Kimberley's

Christmas all the way up to their lesson with Professor Llewellyn. It was their first lesson with the sports

Professor and Brianna for one was extremely excited at the idea of playing sport in the Realm world. Serena

and Alleyen had mentioned the names of the main sports, but she was still yet to discover the details

regarding them.

The girls led them to the north-western corner of the school, where trophies from the schools sporting

achievements preceded the entrance to the classroom. Some signed photographs hung on the wall and as

Brianna looked around she noticed several pictures of students with a stick that looked like an ice hockey stick.

She looked went past a photo of a girl named 'Batina Rupple' who had been placed up on the wall as the

'Hurdlekurl champion of 1973-1974' and stopped in her tracks. Before her were a row of pictures where

people were riding the beasts that they had seen back in the enclosure. Dragons. In the pictures, they looked

tamed, not wild like the ones that roamed around in the enclosure and it intrigued Brianna rather than

frightened her.

She walked into the classroom, guided by Serena and went to take a seat. Professor Llewellyn was

already standing at the front of the room. It was rather bare, with a few items that Brianna supposed were

sporting equipment, but none that were particularly recognisable. Professor Llewellyn was the exact opposite

to Coach Williams; he was rather short with a skinny build. His hair fell just short of his shoulders in waves,

now it was mainly grey save a short few speckles of black, which would have dominated his hair at one point.

He wore a blue robe, much like the other Professors, but his one was lined with a bright yellow line. As he passed by to shut the door she saw a large yellow dragon emblazoned on his back; its mouth open and fire spouting up towards his right shoulder.

"Welcome back everyone," greeted Professor Llewellyn with arms wide open as he proceeded back to the front of the room, "I have a quick start of term announcement and then we shall commence with the lesson.

"You will all need to report to the assembly hall as Professor Allard has a few start of term announcements that he wishes to discuss with all of you. Also, after school clubs are now available to the students from the mortal world. A list has been compiled of all the possible activities that you can join. They are pinned to the notice board in the first year common room for you to inspect.

"For the moment however, we must get on with todays' lesson. Last term, you were briefly introduced to a wide array of sports that witches and wizards take part in here in the Realm World. I believe that practice makes perfect so practical application will be the basis for the majority of your sports lessons."

An excited murmur spread around the classroom as the students from the mortal world wondered which would be the first sport that they would be taught. Professor Llewellyn led the students out of the theory based training room, taking them to the back of the school and out of an exit of the main building that Brianna was not familiar with. When they walked out she tried to gather her bearings. It wasn't until that they walked past a clustered set of bushes that she realised that they were following the path that led to the dragon enclosure.

They went past the caged area that had originally held the dragons, but which was now devoid of all dragons. Professor Llewellyn carried on his walk with the darkness becoming more complete as he walked on. He held his wand aloft, swinging it down in a blazing arc. Little blue lights shot onto the floor and did not extinguish against the snow-covered ground. Instead it lingered there and lighted a path among the trees that had enclosed around them.

The lights were beginning to get brighter as trees thinned before them. As she looked ahead, Brianna found herself looking onto a sight that she wasn't likely to forget. They were standing at the far end of an enormous stadium. How it had been hidden away from every window in the school Brianna could not figure out, but there it stood right before her eyes. Bright brackets burned along with the blue lights and flickering shadows were cast across the stadium highlighting the stands. The floor was not even, there were carefully placed walls of stone but the grassy areas had great brown slashes across their surfaces. It was a large rectangle; with areas of the stadium that resembled caves and wholes that made hissing noises and Brianna noticed jets of steam spurted from the holes at random intervals. Brianna wondered about the purpose of the stadium, it looked more like an outdoor recreation park rather than what she had thought a stadium should look like.

As she took in more of her surroundings, she started to take in the sound of grumbling and heavy stomping footsteps. Over on a platform, on opposite side of the stadium, Brianna espied four dragons tethered up to four huge poles. There were some other adults with the dragons, but Brianna couldn't make out their faces.

"This term we will be concentrating on dragon riding," stated Professor Llewellyn, but Brianna didn't really think he needed to state the obvious.

"Here we have the Medonna the Purple Firegazer, Derbin the Onyx Shooter, Gruellen the Azul Guster and Peabody the Kintly Welsh back. These are our four beginner's dragons; Gruellen is the linking dragon between the beginners and intermediate set. They can be used at a higher level, but they also have a slightly tamer element than some of our top class dragons. Our school houses a total of fifteen dragons, which is one of the biggest colonies within a school across the whole Realm world.

"There are several key safety points that you must follow when dealing with dragons. Never approach them head on, direct eye contact can startle the dragon and cause it to emit flames in defence. Approach the dragon slowly and raise one steady arm, it calms the dragon and shows the dragon that you are confident in approaching them. Lastly, when you climb on the dragons back make sure to place your foot just behind

the wing. Their wings are very delicate and any pain inflicted on them will lead to them using their tail to whip

off the sorry person that caused them any sort of pain."

That was the end of Professor Llewellyn's introduction to dragon riding, brief but memorable and one

that had Brianna immediately hooked. The class were led around the edge of the stadium to greet their new

topic for the term. Brianna felt slightly braver than some of the other students from the Mortal World and was

one of the first students to follow behind the students who lived in the Realm World.

"Do we have any volunteers to get us started with the basic approach and seating position?" asked

Professor Llewellyn looking around at the spectrum of different faces, some scared, others wary and some

excited.

"I will, Professor," Brianna said loudly stepping out from the group.

"Splendid Miss Eastey, if you would please make your way over here," he instructed, leading the way

to a purple scaled dragon flecked with gold on the wings. The dragon was breathing slow and heavy, as if

bored at the procession of students that had walked its way. Brianna almost sensed it was bored at the

prospect of not being challenged in the lesson, which she found strange, as she hadn't believed tuning to a

dragon's thoughts were possible.

"Okay Miss Eastey, approach slowly and see if you can make it up onto our Purple Firegazer's back."

She stepped purposefully, her hand stretched out high. She focused all her attention to make sure she

didn't allow any nerves to affect her approach. The dragon looked around in interest at the advancing student.

Their eyes connected and the class gasped in unison.

Brianna felt no fear and did not look away; trying to say to the dragon 'I want to try to be the best rider

and I mean to treat you with the utmost respect'. Surprisingly for Brianna it seemed that the Purple Firegazer

looked back into Brianna's eyes as if it was acknowledging her in agreement.

Her hand finally made contact with the dragon's scales, it was a rough surface and slightly warm as its flames simmering below the surface, flowed around its body. She lifted up her right leg keeping the left leg planted in the ground firmly and found the correct nook that she could use to hoist herself up onto the dragons back. She swung herself elegantly into the seat that was placed on the dragons back and held onto the reins that encompassed the dragon's head.

"Medonna up," called out Professor Llewellyn and as the dragon responded it rocked up to a standing position. Brianna was grateful that the reins were there to prevent her from sliding off of its back. She felt the slight awkward motion as she swayed atop the vast beast, but she was surprisingly unafraid as she rose higher and higher from the ground.   "Excellent Miss Eastey," called out Professor Llewellyn, and for some reason he sounded absolutely ecstatic. "You are a natural!"

She definitely couldn't understand how she was a natural as she had merely managed to sit on a standing dragon.

"Press your heels lightly just under the wings, Miss Eastey," instructed Professor Llewellyn from the ground, "That will tell Medonna that you want him to walk forward."

She followed the instructions and was amazed as the beast obeyed her. She instinctively tugged at the reins and the dragon walked in a large circle. She was wary for only the smallest second as they approached the trembling students, but she somehow knew that the dragon wouldn't hurt any of them.

She walked it back to where she mounted the beast and then stepped lightly down from its side. She was slightly confused as she met the rest of the class who were all applauding her.

"That was something that I haven't seen in all of my years of teaching," exclaimed Professor Llewellyn, "You're from the mortal realm aren't you?"

"Yes," said Brianna, slightly puzzled.

"Well that's all the more impressive," said the Professor with a wide smile across his face, "it usually takes a couple of weeks for any student to move the creatures, let alone sit on one so calmly. You have a natural gift with dragons; hold on to that gift."

Brianna felt stunned and very happy that she was naturally gifted at something in such a new world. They spent the rest of the lesson getting used to the dragons in the enclosure; those that felt confident could climb up and get used to seating themselves in the dragons seat. No one was able to get the dragons to walk like Brianna had and no one looked nearly as comfortable as she did on the back of the dragons.

By the end of the lesson Brianna felt truly elated by the progress she had made in the lesson and as they walked back into the school Caleb and Michael were talking about her accomplishments as if she was a famous athlete. Professor Llewellyn informed them that they needed to head back to the entrance hall. Professor Allard would be waiting for them before they moved onto their second lesson of the afternoon with his announcements.

As they rounded one of the corners of the intertwining corridors she noticed Kimberley's face suddenly light up. Brianna looked up and noticed that the boy, Truesdale, which they had bumped into the previous week, was walking in their direction.

"Hello," Truesdale said more to Kimberley than to anyone else, "fancy seeing you again. What have you just had?"

"Dragons," was all that Kimberley managed to mumble quietly.

"We just had dragon riding," Brianna said, coming to her friends rescue.

"Oh that's cool," Truesdale replied, "how did you all find it?"

"It was good," Kimberley mumbled, "Brianna is a natural."

"Is that so?" Truesdale looked questioningly in Brianna's direction.

"I wouldn't say a natural, but I definitely enjoyed it. Kimberley had a very promising first lesson," she said, trying to detain the conversation from focusing on her.

"Well that's very good to hear," he responded enthusiastically, "I'm the captain of the dragon riding team so it's good to know about the new and rising stars of our school."

"There's a team?" Brianna said with keen interest.

"Well, yeah. We compete against other schools; in fact I won't tell you too much today as I'm sure I will have to tell you of the news at some point in the near future. I suppose I shouldn't keep you any longer though, I hope we can see each other again some time soon."

Brianna had to give Kimberley a forceful nudge in the right direction and the group carried on walking towards the entrance hall. They had asked for a map, but Serena had explained that there was a constant movement of the schools doors and corridors. She further explained that it was important to use inner magic to guide you to your destination, rather than having a map to guide your route.

Brianna asked how everything could change, thinking back to Witchcraft Heights and thinking it would be almost impossible to move a whole section of the school to another building. Serena stated that the rooms stayed the same but the journey changed depending on the mood of the building and that magic, a constantly evolving and free spirit, was teeming within the walls to freely flow and shift certain parts of the school. The logic to this was almost there, but Brianna would still have preferred a simple map; particularly when she didn't know how to let her magic guide her blindly around.

They finally reached the entrance hall and found Professor Allard waiting patiently on the small plinth so that he could overlook all of the students. The noise subsided after a couple minutes, when the number of students became greater and it seemed that most of the school had arrived.

"Welcome back, my bright beams of magic," he proclaimed to the students in the hall with a wide smile across his face. "I hope you have all had the chance to recharge your thinking caps and are fully set for a new term at Merlin. For the older years, you will already be aware of this, but for the first years here is a small detail that may interest some of you.

"Clubs are now open to all mortal first years. Use the older students around the school for guidance and see the captains or chairperson of the club to give an insightful account of their club. I am sure Professor Llewellyn has rounded troops for his sporting clubs, but there is also a wide array of other clubs that are not related to sport. Use this opportunity to further develop your understanding of our world, but also identify who you are as an individual witch or wizard.

"There is a very important matter that you will need to start taking some thought or consideration for," Professor Allard informed the group of students, "the end of year exams.

"Testing your knowledge and understanding of magic is key for your own development. You will be tested in every single subject to make sure that you are showing relative progress throughout this year. It will also help to shape the decision that will need to be made at the end of this academic year. Start studying now and it will make your exam process a far easier experience."

"That is all for today, pip pip and scramble off to your next lesson!" he finished in his jubilant tone. He walked up the impressive staircase and out of sight. Serena beckoned for Brianna and Kimberley to follow her as they headed to their remedies lesson with Professor Vita.

The lesson was more of a reiteration on the rules that must be abided by when making potions, so Brianna found her attention waning and instead focusing on her previous lesson with the Purple Firegazer. She decided by the end of the lesson that she was going to track down Truesdale and find out more information on the dragon-riding club.

She left the classroom and quietly asked Kimberley if she would like to go and find Truesdale, hoping that she would agree, as she was pretty sure that Kimberley was interested in him.

"Yeah, of course," Kimberley said in a surprisingly wary tone, "why do you want to go and see him though?"

"To find out about the dragon riding club," Brianna stated, as this was the obvious answer.

Immediately, Kimberley's face softened and she felt happy to go in search of Truesdale with Brianna. They said their goodbyes to Serena and Alleyen, who had already been bombarded with Prefect duties on their first day back, and decided to head in the direction of the dragon-riding stadium.

Brianna tried to think of how to get to the Viridian Flos as she didn't think she stood a chance at remembering how to get to the dragon stadium from their lesson earlier today. After a good ten minutes, however, she felt no closer to reaching the back of the school.

"Why don't you think about dragons instead of the Viridian Flos,' suggested Kimberley, "as you're a natural at dragon riding you might have more of a magical sense of direction when you're thinking about a passion."

Brianna couldn't quite see how that would work as she had a passion for everything that came as a part of the knowledge of the Realm world. She didn't have much to lose in trying, so she refocused her mind instead to finding the dragon stadium.

She meandered among the corridors and felt the plan was soon becoming a fruitless one.

"Hey, I think I remember this door," she called out to Kimberley suddenly, with almost incredulous disbelief, "in fact I am almost certain that this is the door Professor Llewellyn led us out of earlier today."

She was amazed to find that it was in fact the correct door and as she opened it she recognised the familiar path to the stadium. She picked up the pace, following the blue lights that were still glowing strongly to guide their way. As she saw the façade of the stadium she heard an almighty roar and the furious beating of wings. As the two girls stepped into the stadium they spied Truesdale riding the onyx shooter dragon; its jaws snapping furiously at being controlled and directed around the stadium. Shockingly, he raised a hand and waved a hand in their direction as soon as they had stepped into the stadium, which was no easy task when fighting against a violent beast.

He took the beast to the landing point where it was immediately tethered up by magical chains that shot out from the ground and tightly gripped the dragon by the collar.

"To what do I owe this pleasure?" asked Truesdale.

"Well its mainly me that wanted to find you," stated Brianna matter-of-factly, "I would like to become a dragon rider and Professor Allard said it was good to talk to the captain of the clubs."

"Well that is brilliant news," Truesdale responded with a pleased grin, "We are always looking for new talent to represent the school. Would you consider joining the team, Kimberley?"

He looked over in her direction, but Kimberley was once again struck dumb by her attraction to Truesdale. He waited patiently, his smile remaining on his face the whole time.

"Ermm... I'm not sure that dragon riding is really my sport," she said in barely more than a whisper. She seemed almost a little downhearted at having to acknowledge this and Brianna felt a pang of sadness at her friend's lack of self-belief.

"I'm sure that's not the case," Truesdale said and he walked over to place a hand softly on Kimberley's shoulder. "Don't put your ability down when you have only just begun. I'm sure that in time you will be nothing short of brilliant. Come to the club and I will help you to build up your confidence in dragon riding."

She responded with a sheepish grin and nodded ever so slightly.

"So... when does training start?" Brianna decided to get the ball and asked some of the more practical questions out of the way. "What is involved with dragon riding? Do we ride with a specific dragon? Do some dragons work better with certain people?"

"Yes to one of the questions, and the others we would need more time to sit down and answer the specifics," Truesdale chortled, "I'm heading to the local village shop with some of the boys. You two could join us if you'd like and I would answer the questions."

"What's the village like?" said Brianna, immediately intrigued.

"Haven't you been into the village," Truesdale asked, he seemed a little confused for some reason. "Oh wait a minute... you two are from the mortal world. I completely forgot."

"Are we not allowed in the village then?" Brianna pursued, "No one has mentioned any of the places that exist outside of the school walls. We didn't even know that there was a village."

"Well the village is the main local point for a lot of the students of Merlin," he explained, "there are lot of areas outside of the village but the main places to go are in the centre of village. Can you go there... well yes and no. There is no rule to say that you cannot go into the village, but it's a bit of a journey so you don't want to risk going to the village and not getting back in time. What you would need is someone who can travel to and from the village in record time..." he finished with a cheeky grin.

"Well, maybe you could take us?" Kimberley piped up.

"I think that could be a brilliant plan," Truesdale said, "why don't you meet up with us after your lessons one day. I will take the two of you down to the village and show you more of our world; including the importance of the dragons."

"Thank you very much." Brianna said most gratefully, "We'll let you know when it's a good day to do so."

"Of course," Truesdale said, "I think you might want to head back now. Not that I want to get rid of you, but I think it's nearly time for you to go back to the mortal world."

Kimberley nodded reluctantly and Truesdale quickly said, "but I will most certainly look forward to seeing you tomorrow." This put a smile back on her face and the two girls left arm in arm, making their way back to the chamber.

As they made their way once again through the familiar route back to the mortal world Brianna thought excitedly about venturing into the Realm village. She wondered how long it would be before she could just remain in the Realm world and maybe even find a place to live. She couldn't help but notice the smile that seemed to be affixed to her face; at least someone was having a little luck in love.

Chapter 15

The lessons after Christmas were definitely more practical than what they had been learning at the start of their magical journey. They had still spent the majority of the time in the classrooms, but the layout of the most of the classrooms had taken a change in one way or another. In their duelling lessons the classroom, which had once been filled with lined tables to take notes on the basic defensive techniques, had been moved. Professor Rubesco had dissolved the tables on the walls so that wooden tables now formed the panels of the outer walls, which he said was useful in absorbing wayward spells.

Brianna soon came to realise was that the school was far more lenient with the students and allowed them to be far more independence than what they had originally been permitted. The prefects didn't chauffeur them anymore as the prefects had their own agendas to carry out. They were still friends in every sense of the word, but they were no longer their carer's. This suited Brianna to a far greater extent; she always felt as if she owed something to Serena and Alleyen, but for now they seemed on even terms. They challenged one another to a far greater extent, when it was soon realised that Brianna and Kimberley's magical ability nearly matched that of the Realm based students. They enjoyed the competitive edge and found that their relationship thrived on finding out the best in each of their classes.

One of the classes that Brianna most definitely excelled in was their sports lessons'. Although it was still the middle of winter and the snow lay thick on the ground, nearly all of their sports lessons had been moved outside. They had only one theoretical lesson in the week as Professor Llewellyn had explained that practical application was the best form of improvement. They had continued their dragon riding lessons and Brianna had been surprised at how easy she had found it to control the beasts. She had continued with Medonna, the purple Firegazer dragon, but after three weeks of lessons she was soon wanting a further challenge as the dragon she had perfected her skill on did not have the speed that could further test her abilities.

These practical lessons, though far more interesting, often left Brianna both physically and mentally drained. This didn't just result from a hard lesson of controlling a gigantic dragon as she still had the rest of the school day to contend with.

Even on days without sport or duelling she would tire herself out as she sat studying remedies or practicing charms, pushing herself to the limit so that she could improve her level of expertise in magic. One particularly difficult spell that they had been introduced to was the 'illicio' charm that cast light to the conjurer. No one in the group had managed to conjure so much as a glow from the wand tip, so it was tirelessly attempted when they had a moment to spare.

She soon found out that learning and practicing even the simplest spells was no easy task; the concentration that was needed to perform them sapped all of the energy out of her body.

Her adventures, that she had been so keen on before Christmas, seemed impossible to fit in with the sheer amount of work that they were now completing. Damien had hinted a little at wanting to explore more of Merlin and had even considered venturing outside of the school and into other areas in the Realm of Salem, but they were only feeble mutterings. He was often found slumped in a chair a few minutes after his newest plan, as exhausted as the rest of them.

*

They had finally reached the weekend, three weeks into the middle of January. Brianna, Kimberley and the three boys trudged slowly through the transporting chamber and back into the mortal world after suffering a particularly gruelling duelling session. They had suffered an hour of learning 'Icibus' the freezing charm, where their limbs turned to stone before the slow thawing sensation that loosened their stiff muscles and joints came into action. It had been painful work and they couldn't even summon enough energy to talk to one another about how much they had absorbed in such a short period of time.

As they headed out of the entrance of Witchcraft Heights, Brianna noticed movement approaching from the Eastern corridor. She panicked slightly, if it was a teacher of Witchcraft Heights they might question as to why they were still so late at school. As the person stepped out of the shadows Brianna realised that it was Madison that was standing by the main entrance.

"Oh hello," said Madison. The first thing that Brianna found strange was that Madison had just spoken to her and the others, when she had made a conscious effort to ignore them for such a long time. As Brianna looked to her she realised that it was the first time she had seen Madison leaving school after the Realm World since the Christmas vacation.

"Hi Madison," replied Brianna warily, "what are you doing here so late?"

"Oh, I'm really behind in a lot of my classes. For some reason I haven't finished a lot of my work so I'm staying extra hours to use the school library and computers," she explained. Her brow furrowed as if she was fighting to remember why she hadn't finished the work.

"So what are you guys doing here?" she asked without any sarcastic tendency or certain sense of disapproval.

"Ermm," Brianna was confused, surely Madison would know why they were late. She looked around to the rest of the group but they looked just as confused as she was. Then she thought it strange that she was having such a cheery conversation with a group of students whom she had previously sown great disdain.

"Pretty much the same," she continued, looking around and giving the others in the group a questionable frown.

"Oh, I didn't see you lot," she answered in an innocent but uncertain tone. Again confusion seemed to cloud her face. It was as the confusion left her face that a strange idea occurred to Brianna.

Maybe Madison didn't remember becoming a witch. Madison had still refused to carry on her education and pleaded her case to the headmaster. He had obliged to something that Madison had desperately wanted, but Brianna had never known the terms and conditions of her voluntary leave. Come to think of it, Brianna had never seen her in her lessons since the start of the spring term. Clearly something had changed so that Madison didn't have to return.

She stood there as Madison looked vacantly around; her vacant look sparked her memory as Brianna remembered the vacant expression that Madison held on the evening of the Winter Ball. A sudden idea occurred to Brianna; what if Madison had been trained to forget?

Now that she thought about it, it would be dangerous for a reformed mortal to remember their times in the Realm World. Professor Allard was also a kind man and memory modification would have rid of Madison's sadness. Maybe that was what had happened to Madison when she had pleaded with Professor Allard; she wished to forget about her time at Merlin.

Madison headed out with the group, but soon took a left turn at the entrance to the school with the boys as Brianna and Kimberley walked in the opposite direction to Madison' s home.

"Well that was weird," said Kimberley as soon as they were out of earshot from the rest of the group. They were heading back in the direction of Brianna's house, the two of them were trying to do their work together and it was quicker to get back to Brianna's house.

They entered through the entrance where a wave of warm air greeted them from the bitter cold that had surrounded them earlier. Brianna went to make the two of them a warming mug of hot chocolate before they headed upstairs.

Brianna jumped onto her bed, her bag swinging around so that it landed in front of her. She felt round in her bag for her duelling textbook and pulled out a book that she thought was the textbook. It turned out that it was in fact the 'Book Estas Orientem Magia Animabus', which she had not addressed since the revelation in regard to the dragons.

"I still don't understand that book," Kimberley said uncertainly.

"I've decided that it reads my thoughts," began Brianna, "it's like it wants me to think about the magical world and then it can fill in the missing pieces around my thoughts. Think of it as a definitive record of the history of the realm world based on my thoughts."

"Well that's just bizarre, what has it added in since you last looked at it?" Kimberley asked with a level of intrigue mingled with uncertainty.

"Well lets have a look, I can't really remember what I've been thinking of that would spark any additions within the book," she said as she flicked through the pages. As she fanned her way from front to back she stumbled on a scrawling that caught her eye. This was another new scrawling, in the same font as the older scrawling's, but newly formulated.

"Wait there's a new scribble and some information," she proclaimed excitedly and she read out the chapter titled Famous Witches of 1692 to Kimberley.

"The Witches of 1692 are notably some of the most famous witches in the history of the realm world. The likes of Mary Eastey and Evelyn Count, who settled in the mortal communities, were some of the first to trial life in another world. Mary Eastey was one of the first witches to marry and settle into a mortal family, producing eleven children before being sent to the gallows during the Witch Hunt of 1692.

'The great battle that linked the Realm Salem to its mortal counterpart in 1692 was led by Evelyn Count. The battle presided between those that wished to follow in the steps of the evil green witches and those that wanted to keep both worlds safe from persecution and the destruction of the mortal world. Evelyn Count, like Mary Eastey was a witch that strived for equality and wished for the chance to exist peacefully in the mortal world. Tibuta was a rebel leader at the time and a known descendent of Medusa. She was well known within the Salem council in the mortal world as a superstitious witch that dabbled with the dark powers and controlled members of the council. In the Realm World she was famously known as a witch of pure evil who lived in a pool of hatred to those that had condemned her ancestor. Tibuta tried to take control of the Salem community by enslaving the families of the powerful under the influence of dark magic.

'Mary Eastey, although hung for casting protective magic over the mortals, managed to defeat Tibuta and her tirade of witches who supported her in the Realm World. From that point it was proclaimed, by Wizarding law, that witches and wizards could only venture to the mortal world if they submitted their wand

and wished to live permanently as a mortal. Those that had parented half-blood children were forced to decide which world they would reside in.

"In the village of Salem in the Realm World, memorials can be found and visited to respect and commend the witches who laid their lives for the good of all mortal kind."

Next to this was scribbled, 'Escape and explore, a tide of change will come and preparation is key to fight the darkness.'

"What on earth do you suppose that scrawling means?" quizzed Kimberley.

"I'm not too sure," replied Brianna, "it's definitely a new note, which worries me slightly."

"Why?"

"I only thought that the writing happened back in the mortal world to help find out about the realm world. The new writing suggests that there are still others wishing to communicate with me," she stated, "unless it has been there for ages and I never seen it. I do hope it's the latter, but I suppose it has given us one useful tip."

"And what is that?" asked Kimberley.

"We need to find Truesdale and see if he can take us into the village," explained Brianna, "For one, I would like to see if I can find out more about Mary Eastey."

The two girls pondered over this information. Brianna had a reel of questions that she wanted to know. Who was Tibuta? Why did Professor Allard state that Madison's ancestral lineage so important? What did Mary Eastey truly fight for? The information that she had just found out was definitely a different sequence of events than the previous details that had been learnt in Miss Ashdown's class.

One piece of information that really sparked her interest was that there was a memorial that could be visited. She really wanted to read more about how her ancestor had made such a huge impact on the realm world. It would really explain the connection to the realm world and strengthen her association to the world that she strived to belong to.

"Brianna," called out Kimberley and once again Brianna realised she had been day dreaming, she really needed to stop doing that or people might start to think she was slightly strange.

"Brianna, we better get started on our homework," Kimberley said exasperatedly and Brianna tossed her Magia Animabus back into her bag, fetched her quill and textbook and set to work on their everlasting lanterns for Professor Petra.

*

Although a week had passed since Brianna and Kimberley had looked through 'The Book Estas Orientem Magia Animabus', Kimberley had made no further attempt to discuss what they had read.

She on the other hand could not get the new information out of her mind. She wanted to know more about her family, she had done since she had overheard Madison and Professor Allard at Christmas. The revelation that the answers to her questions resided a short distance away only strengthened that desire. She had planned a way to get down there, but she required the use of one important resource. She had looked for Truesdale to see if he could take them down to the village. He had not turned up the dragon riding training this week due to a spot of dragon fungitus; a serious case of dizziness and vomiting induced from a fungal infection on a dragons scale. Instead Landon had been taking the sessions and teaching them how to make their dragon loop in small or large circles. Brianna had been fortunate enough to take a ride on Gruellen, the Azul Guster, which was much faster and stronger than Medonna. She flew with ease, to the response of much applause and gasps of awe, which for the small part took her mind off the hunt for Truesdale. In fact, dragon riding was the only thing that kept her from diverting her attention back to her book or the desire to visit the local village.

She had spoken to Damien shortly after her evening with Kimberley, not drawing attention to the book, but trying to get his explorer bug back into gear. He was as eager as ever for an adventure, but Caleb and Michael were more interested in dragon riding now and refrained from joining in on the new venture.

"Come on Kimberley, please," pleaded Brianna once more, trying to get the last of her group on her desired trip. She wanted to go to the memorial, to get answers, but she didn't want to go without her best friend. She knew, not entirely as to why, but she knew that Kimberley needed to come along with her. She decided to question Kimberley as they moved away from the boys and headed in the direction of the library.

"I don't know Brianna," Kimberley responded rather slowly, "searching the school grounds was pushing the limit in my books, but going out into the village... I don't know."

"But why?" Brianna questioned further with slight incredulity, "What could be so wrong about going into the local village? We are part of the magical community now, we shouldn't have to shy away from every part of the world because they haven't shown it to us."

"The Professors have never told us of any visits to the village... Professor Merrydew hasn't told us we could go. I think that's a sign to tell us that we shouldn't take the risk."

"Yes, they may not have told us of visits to the village, but they haven't told us that we can't go to the village have they?" she reasoned with her friend, picking at loose strings to get some sort of sway in her opinion, "besides, Truesdale explained that mortal students don't often go because it takes too long to get there and back without some form of magical transport."

Kimberley just responded with a loud sigh and the two of them continued walking a particularly winding corridor to the library where they needed to research the 'Orachidous Dandie'; a love exemplifying plant that they were going to cover in their lesson tomorrow with Professor Merrydew.

As they turned the corner at the end of winding corridor, Kimberley, who had been purposefully avoiding eye contact with Brianna, bumped head first into something solid from the opposite direction.

"Oops! Sorry I didn't see you there, are you okay?" said a low masculine voice. Kimberley had managed to bump heads with Truesdale, the older student she had taken a shine to recently.

Every meeting that Kimberley had had with Truesdale thus far had resulted in her inability to hold a conversation around him and this encounter held no exception to the rule. Brianna could see the warm glow at her friend's cheeks and knew that she was extremely embarrassed at colliding with Truesdale. As the

silence got more and more awkward Brianna decided to save the day.

"Hi Truesdale," she started, "Kimberley was trying her best ignore me so she didn't see where she was

going. To be honest, you are just the person I was looking for as you may be able to sway her decision."

Kimberley shot a painfully embarrassed look in Brianna's direction.

Truesdale chuckled, "What did you say to her then to make her be so stubborn?"

"Well," she looked awkwardly towards Kimberley but a sudden thought struck her. Truesdale had

suggested he would take them to the village, but maybe he had forgotten. Well, she thought, now is the time

to jog his memory.

"I'm trying to stray off the path of righteousness, and she doesn't want to join the ride," she mused

with Truesdale, "I really wish to go to the village to see the memorial but Kimberley doesn't think we should

go."

"It would be cutting it fine for time," said Truesdale, with a thoughtful look across his face, "Most

students from the mortal world don't venture to the village until they start their second year because it's a

thirty minute walk there and back. Most students don't see the point in the journey at the risk of missing the

closing portal."

"Well there you go Brianna," said Kimberley, with a smug look across her face.

"Ah, wait a minute there precious; I said it's a thirty minute walk. It's only a ten minute all round trip

with other modes of transportation. I'd be happy to take you to the village on my Accipegus Carter."

"Well thank you!" Brianna exclaimed with a wide smile across her face, looking directly at Kimberley.

She had no idea what an Accipegus Carter was, but quite frankly, she didn't care. She had found a way down

to the village and that was the only thing that mattered.

"Would you come along as well?" he probed Kimberley.

"Well," Kimberley deliberated.

"You can't let Brianna go by herself," Truesdale reasoned with a speckle of teasing as he spoke, "plus… it would be nice to show you a little more of our world and what could be… well… your world."

"Oh," she said as her level of reluctance subsided, swayed by her attraction towards Truesdale, "I suppose there isn't a real harm in going to the village just one time."

"Well that settles it," Truesdale said rubbing his hands together in excitement, "We will have to take a couple of my boys with us as they always get the ride home with me. I will meet you outside the front of the school on Monday to take you into the village."

Brianna nodded at this, but a small pang of guilt hit the pit of her stomach. She knew that she still wanted to go, but Damien would not be able to join in the first venture outside of the school.

They said a small farewell to one another and the girls retrieved a couple of books from the library before heading home for the weekend. Brianna hoped that the weekend wouldn't drag and wished for Monday to come around in record time.

*

Truesdale pulled up outside the front of the school on the Monday as promised. The girls crept out the front of the school, looking around warily for any potential onlookers.   As they set eyes on the Accipegus carter both of them couldn't help but gape at what they were about to ride on. The vehicle itself looked like a rickety old carriage. The wooden frame was paling and slightly careworn; the purple curtains that hid away the inside of the carriage were slightly frayed at the bottom and the wheels looked as if their golden spokes would fall off as soon as they turned a corner. The carriage itself wasn't what intrigued the girls; it was the creatures known as the Accipegus that made them stare. Truesdale had informed the girls of the creatures that were part hawk and part flying horse, but they weren't entirely sure as what to expect. These creatures started with the feathery head and sharp beak and eyes of the hawk. Their feathers seamlessly linked to the sandy coloured hindquarters of the flying horse, a creature they believed only existed in mythology, well until now anyway. Kimberley looked at Brianna and although it was against her better judgement, Brianna could see

that she was excited at the prospect of spending more time with Truesdale.

The door opened before the girls as Blutain and Landon stepped down the appearing steps. Brianna

filed into the carriage with Blutain and Landon whilst Kimberley went to sit with Truesdale at the front.

Blutain closed the door and Truesdale kicked the Accipegus carter into life. Landon pulled back the

curtain so that Brianna could see the passing scenery. It was such a strange feeling as they dashed by quickly

without any forward or moving sensation at all. She could only compare it to the sheer brilliance of weightless

flight, like the one time that she had travelled in a hot air balloon across Tampa Bay.

They travelled through the woodland that shut off Merlin from the rest of the Realm world. As they

reached the clearing in the woodland Brianna felt as if her eyes were being opened to the Realm world for the

first time.

A vast green expanse stretched out left and right. Thick clumps of moss and heather dotted the green

fields over the rolling hills. In the far distance, among a slight haze in the afternoon sunshine, were great

mountains that circled the open plains. Brianna could see some small cottages and strange looking buildings

among the green fields.

"What are all those buildings out over the fields?" she questioned Blutain and Landon.

"They're homes," Blutain answered, "there are more homes in the village, but some of the magic folk

live in the countryside. The homes you see out here have more land and belong to some of the rich members

of the Salem community."

As she turned her attention to the direction that they were heading she saw that they were riding

down a snaking road that headed down into a valley. As they travelled further down the hill, more and more

habitual residences began to line the edges of the road until they started driving through a village.

For some reason Brianna had expected to see futuristic buildings where magic had advanced the living

conditions within the realm world. Instead it seemed as if the walls of Merlin had seeped into the village and devoured it to replicate that of an old eighteenth century village. The houses were of old light coloured

stone with quaint front lawns. Signs stood outside each residence, but the Accipegus carter was travelling too

fast for Brianna to read any of the words.

"Okay, we're here," Truesdale stated as he quickly applied the brakes and placed the Accipegus carter

into a space along the side of the road.

Brianna got out of the carriage and could do nothing more than stand and stare at her surroundings.

"Well, I suppose we should take you to the village square," Truesdale started. "You can really get a

flavour of the village's history and where a lot of the village life is centred," informed Truesdale and in the

fashion of a tour guide he led the first years to the village square.

She had always been amazed by Merlin, but the village was something else. It held a quintessential

beauty about it; the small cobbled stone upon which she stood combined together in a sporadic fashion. She

looked around to take in the sights where magic dwelled. They went past a number of quaint houses that

looked similar to the ones that they had passed on the way down the village. Each building was individual;

whether it was the colour of the door or the plants that laced the garden. She looked at some of the sign posts

that were now possible to read and saw some of the names that she supposed belonged to the families of the

properties.

"Megara Aldridge," she read out loud, "wait a minute… Kimberley, isn't that your surname?"

Kimberley stopped in her tracks and looked at the signpost that Brianna was now pointing at.

"Oh my god," Kimberley responded slowly, "is this my family?"

She turned to Truesdale, looking for some sort of answer.

"Well, Aldridge isn't an uncommon surname in the Realm World, but students that come over from the

mortal realm usually go to schools where their magical pull is greatest."

"Magical pull?" Kimberley responded, clearly unaware of what he meant.

"Magical pull relates to the link that you have to this world. The link literally pulls you towards the magical town that holds your greatest magical connection. That is usually a pull from magical ancestry or family that exists within the Realm world.

"Have you always lived in Salem in the mortal world?"

"No, we moved in the summer, it was a bit of a strange coincidence really, my mom has always moved around because of her jobs," stated Kimberley, "we've always moved around quite a lot. It wasn't until we arrived in Salem that I felt... well like I was home."

"Well that will be because your magical pull resides in the village of Salem. It isn't so strange a thing, in fact it happens to quite a few people. If you were in a non-magical area then your aura draws you closer to a town that has a magical portal. It must have been trying to pull you along for quite a while. I have also heard of situations where students have moved from one magical place to another because their aura is not linked to magical portal that they have been bought up around. They are transferred to another area where the magical pull is linked more so to the new witch or wizard. One reason why you have moved a lot may be because your magical aura was uncertain of its final resting spot," Truesdale explained knowledgably.

"Well, are you going to go and knock on the door?" asked Landon, with a small teasing nature.

"Oh yeah that would be a nice easy conversation!" she said with sarcasm on the tip of her tongue, "hello there, my name is Kimberley Aldridge. I think we might be related! Let's just move on to the village square."

They carried on walking until they arrived at the end of the street as it opened out onto Village Square. It was lined with a series of differently shaped buildings that made Brianna feel as if she had gone back even further in time. They had sandstone walls painted in an assortment of colours or slates of wood in crisp white or pale blue. Some of the shops had displays in the small circular or square windows and some looked more like a house than a shop. Signs swung from chains above the door, creaking in the cold winter chill. Truesdale pointed out the different shops that existed within the town square including the local tavern, the clothes store and a wand repair shop. Brianna's ear pricked up at the mention of a sweet shop and wanted to try out some of the delights held within.

A lawn was situated at the centre of the square, with benches that allowed for witches and wizards to sit and admire the old charm of their village. A couple of people were milling around the area, but no one stopped to look at the new comers or even addressed their existence. Brianna followed the track of two old wizards, watching them as they walked around the green, between a set of two poplar trees and towards an old tavern. The door swung open with a kind chuckle as it welcomed its new customers in and shut itself after they had entered its domain.

"Well, here is the centre of the village," stated Truesdale, "as you can see we have the main Salem records hall which is the focal point of the square. All past records of events and persons are pertained and cared for in the hall; you could find out pretty much anything in there. We also have the Whimpering Warlock, which is the local tavern. Students are allowed in it sometimes, but we have full access to Sipping Bucket, which is one of the local sweet and shake shops. Other than that there is the local library, a few tit for tat shops, a wand repair store and our little theatre."

"Ooh, what films are on at the moment?" asked Kimberley "I've been waiting to see 'Love is forever mine' for weeks!"

"Films?" Truesdale questioned the word as if he had never heard of such a thing before, "the theatre holds different forms of entertainment throughout the day. I'm not too sure what a film is though; sounds interesting."

"We'll explain another time," Brianna butted in; thinking the details of the film industry could wait another day. "I'd like to visit the Salem records hall if that's not too much trouble."

Truesdale nodded before he led Kimberley and Brianna to the other end of the square. They walked up the stone steps that led up to the Salem records hall. The doors swung open before them and groaned slightly as they widened to allow the students to enter, like the doors were ancient like the contents within.

It seemed at first a very plain looking room that they had walked into. As Brianna looked around she started to see shelves mould out from the walls as if the building registered it had company. Doors started to evolve before her eyes and some of the walls opened up and stretched backwards as corridors were made to head off in different directions.

"The hall can read the minds of those that enter the room," Truesdale informed the two girls, "there is too much information in the hall if you were to see it in its entirety, so it only gives you information on what it thinks you need or want to know. The layout is never quite the same, even if the same person walks through the door."

There were plaques lined around the hall and some of them shimmered in an attempt to attract the new visitors. Brianna noticed one gleaming particularly brightly and headed off in the direction to read what was on the plaque: 'Mary Eastey: A shining figure in the battle of 1692.'

Brianna looked as a book shifted slowly from the wall and floated down onto the plinth placed below the plaque. The book opened itself out onto a page that appeared to show a layout of something that looked similar to a graveyard which intrigued Brianna. Why would the hall decide to give her this piece of information?

Below the picture were written a long list of names. She scanned the list of names with her finger and stopped on a few that she recognised; Evelyn Count, Alberta and Tristan Alridge as well as the ever-recurring name of Mary Eastey. Underneath the heading was placed a small piece of writing;

'Of all the notable figures in the Realm world Mary Eastey has been identified as one of the bravest and most inspiring witches to have existed. She sacrificed an easy life in the mortal world with her darling husband and eleven children to fight in the battle of 1692. She assisted in the defeat of the evil witches that threatened to once more control the mortal world. She fought with the belief that all should have the chance to live as they choose and not to be controlled through cruel sadistic measures. Sadly those that she had sworn to protect believed her witchcraft was linked to the evil deeds that had been carried out and that the cruel deeds were of her doing. She was led to the gallows and hung in front of those that she had saved in the middle of the village square.

'What makes Mary a true martyr against the dark power was her strong belief that the mortal world held a decent race of people. Her steadfast belief that they should remain safe and void of the wizarding folk, even though they turned their backs on her, showed her unequivocal compassion and purity for good.'

She saw a caption on the side and read, 'The gravestones of famous witches and wizards can be found in the Salem Memorium, the memorial site for witches and wizards throughout the ages. Some memorials hold great significance, relating to the key historical moments throughout the course of Salem's history to celebrate the lives of those that have sought to do right and protect our beloved village.'

"Truesdale," she said, beckoning him over. "Where is the Salem Memorium?"

"It's not far from the village square," he answered as he walked over in her direction, moving away from a plaque about 'Onglish the dragon whisperer'. "It can't reside in the village or the spirits would be able to travel among the living and root themselves to things that could make them more human."

"What?" interjected Kimberley.

"Well, I don't want to spook you too much, but the spirits of the past sometimes linger in world of the living. Given the chance the will try to break through and stay permanently in this world. The distance allows us to pay our respects, without any attachment from occurring."

"Would it be possible for you to take us there?" she asked politely, without any real fear for the living past.

"Yes, it's a little dark but that shouldn't be too much of a problem," replied Truesdale. "We'll go right away as it's a little bit of a walk up to the Memorium."

The group headed back out of the county hall and Truesdale steered the group out of the square. They walked up a hill that took them out of the deepest part of the valley; where the main village square resided. It was a steep climb and as Brianna looked behind her she could see the network of streets that made up the village of Salem.

As they reached the peak of the hill it looked onto a steep downward slope of green fields. A thick line of trees obscured any further view, but Truesdale took them in the direction of the trees, drawing the group closer to an area that looked like a gap in the barrier.

As they stepped through the thick trees Brianna caught herself on one of the low lying branches. She turned to get herself free of the caught branch, untangling her top from the threatening looking twigs. As she turned herself back to the rest of the group she was suddenly alone; not a single soul could be seen among the dense dark wood. She decided to carry on walking and hoped that she would find the others on the other side.

The contrast between the village and the Memorium was remarkable. All the light had seemed to vanish and replaced instead with a low-lying mist. Thick black clouds consumed the graveyard and prevented any winter clouds from brightening up the area around them. Brianna looked down and realised that she was shaking violently as all of the warmth had been sucked out. She grabbed her arms tightly and held on tightly as she waited for the others with a small fear rising from the pit of her stomach.

A rustling noise sounded behind her and she panicked. Clutching at her heart, she relaxed a little as she saw Kimberley, Truesdale, Blutain and Landon walk out from the thicket of trees to join her in the desolate Memorium.

"Have a look around," said Truesdale, "I don't think that we have an awful lot of time left, so don't loiter too much when looking at the tombs and memorials."

Brianna nodded to show she understood Truesdale before she walked alone among the many tombs and headstones that filled the Memorium. Kimberley decided to remain behind with Truesdale, which allowed Brianna the freedom to find her ancestor and hopefully more of an insight into her history.

She walked among the granite tombstones, kicking small pebbles under her foot as her footing was slightly unstable on the uneven ground. She read the names of those that had been laid to rest not too long ago, not taking any sort of recognition to the names before her. She carried along pass the tombstones that eventually became more intricate in stone of marble and slate as well as greater in size. She supposed that the larger tombstones belonged to those of great importance as their headstones held more elaborate if not fading epitaphs.

Through the shrouded mist she noticed a particularly large memorial, protected by a border of bottlebrush buckeye plants. It stood six feet in height and the four sides were four feet wide. It reminded Brianna of the bushes that bordered her own home in the mortal world of Salem. She walked up to it and tried to, for the first time, use her wand outside the walls of Merlin. She imagined the light flowing from her mind, down her arm to the tip of the wand.

"Illicio," she said in a small whisper; she only needed a small glow to emit from the end of her wand so she knew that a whisper would suffice. A light glowed for a second before it dimmed again. She knew she was maybe expecting a little bit too much, but she didn't want to give up.

"Illicio," she whispered once more. The light shined and to her delight continued to do so. She kept the focus flowing down her arm as she waved her wand over the memorial, trying to see the names that had been placed so prestigiously in the Memorium.

She skimmed across the names of the witches and wizards; some of the names rang a bell as she recognised the surname from the students that she went to school with. Most of the students, such as the likes of Perrigrer Williams, Evelyn Count, Horace Pentucket and Elderfeld Parker were all ancestors of students that were current students of Merlin. Arthur Pentucket was one of the students from the mortal Salem, but surprisingly hadn't been selected to join the Realm World even though his ancestral lineage dictated a magical background.

She scanned around to see if Damien's ancestors were inscribed on the memorial, but after five minutes of searching she had no such luck in locating the family of the Quests. Instead she managed to find Mary Eastey, sparkling in the wand light at the top of the memorial. She noticed that a few of the letters were engraved in a different, more italic fashion than the majority of the lettering. She couldn't work out their

sporadic fashion and wasn't quite sure for this artistic difference.

She shifted her wand up past the names at the top of the long list and stopped on the larger writing at

the top; 'The Heroes of 1692- those that laid their lives for your freedom.' So this was the memorial that she

had read about in her book. Proudly it stood in its corner, on a small mound as if it were overlooking the rest

of the tombstones that filled the Memorium.

"This is pretty impressive," said a voice quietly behind her. Brianna nearly jumped out of her skin at the

shock of being addressed, when all of her focus lay on the memorial in front of her.

She turned around, clutching her chest, to see Kimberley standing directly behind her with Truesdale

walking up the small hill behind her. "This particular memorial is said to protect the rest of the tombstones

from harm. The power of the witches and wizards inscribed on the marble have an intense magical presence

that resides all the way to the woodland closure," Truesdale explained as he came to stand by them.

"But why is this memorial so much larger than the other ones?" asked Brianna inquisitively.

"The balance of our world is largely believed as a consequence of the sacrifices made from the names

that you see up on these four sides," he continued. "It has long been told that the ancestors of the witches

and wizards of 1692 created a balance for the future generations. As long as the descendants learnt and

practised magic, the mortal and realm world can coexist peacefully.

"This memorial signifies that balance and protects us all."

"What would happen if a descendant no longer wished to be a part of the realm world?" Brianna

questioned Truesdale further.

"The balance would be disrupted," he stated plainly, "the evil that we have set to thwart and quash

would be unleashed and cover the worlds in the second Dark Age. There is said to be a line of witches and

wizards who still support the likes of Medusa and Tibuta. If there is a weak link in the Salem witches the evil

witches will unleash their secret weapon to control the two worlds. The connecting portals would set free all the evil creatures and dark forces that hide in the deep corners of our world. Don't worry your young

minds though, the idea of that happening is superstitious nonsense and unlikely. Some descendants haven't

practiced magic without consequence."

"Is that true for all the descendants?" she asked with the worry unable to be masked in her voice.

"I haven't thought of that before," he responded pensively, "maybe some of the witches and wizards

have a greater impact on the balance and fate of our worlds. I would have to look more into the names that

hold the most importance to this prophecy.

"Brianna you have stumped me there!"

Brianna tried to process this information, looking at the names that filled up the marble. Kimberley

shuddered at the news and Truesdale quickly went to her rescue, placing an arm around her shoulder and

pulling her in tight.

They stood admiring the rest of the space below them for a minute or two before Truesdale walked

back among the headstones and beckoned the two girls to follow him. Kimberley rushed ahead, but Brianna

lingered back a little bit. As she turned to look back at the memorial she felt as if she was being watched. Out

of the corner of her eye she thought she saw the outline of a person and a pair of eyes watching her. As she

turned even more, the spot where she believed the person stood seemed to be nothing more than a pale blue

mist. She looked back towards the rest of the group and walked over in their direction, unable to shake the

feeling that someone was watching her.

"You ready to leave?" asked Truesdale when she finally met them by the trees that they had first

stepped through.

"Yes," Brianna said resolutely, "I think I have done enough exploring for one day. Thank you ever so

much for today; it was most definitely an eye opener."

Truesdale and the two boys escorted the two girls back to the school in the darkness. Kimberley had

become more talkative since today and Brianna for once was the quiet one. She was pleased that she had been down to the village, but she most certainly did not want it to be the last time that she visited it and

the many sights that it had to offer.

Chapter 16

The importance of so many surrounding her ancestry and the ancestors of those around had almost been too much to handle for Brianna Eastey. She hadn't been able to sleep for the past two nights and her fatigue was beginning to show. Truesdale had shown them the memorium that contained a memorial commemorating the witches and wizards from the trials of 1692, including the witches and wizards that suffered persecution during that time. That her ancestor had protected the people of the mortal world had filled her with pride, but she was almost met with great sadness as she realised the people that she had protected had sent her to the gallows as a result of their lack of knowledge and understanding.

On her first sleepless night she had gone over some of the names that had appeared on the memorial with one name popping up in particular. Evelyn Count, the infamous ancestor of Madison. Madison's ancestor held potentially a vital part to the balance between the realm world and the mortal world. When she awoke, it scared her somewhat that Madison had abandoned her responsibilities and she began to spin questions aimlessly around and around in her mind. The tales that Truesdale had told the two of them in the eerie graveyard, or Memorium as he called it scared her. What if the tales were true and the entire world was to change on the basis of one student's decision. She hadn't told Truesdale about Madison's abandonment; it felt as if she needed to protect her old friend's decision. She wondered whether the balance of witches could break the connection between the portals and set off a chain of events that could enslave the human and magical race to one powerful dark force.

How would they know when all this horror and destruction would take place, if it was to take place at all? The end of the second evening had bought no further revelation and she resolved that tales and stories gave neither reason nor rhyme to panic; they were merely stories to frighten those that believed in such superstitions. She did ponder at Truesdale's motives to telling the tale; it had certainly given him the chance to place his arm around Kimberley as she shuddered in fear. It was during these moments that she was slightly comforted; maybe he wanted to tell a ghost story to comfort the damsel in distress.

For it seemed things between Kimberley and Truesdale had certainly evolved since their last meeting. It was an odd sight for Brianna to see, but also one that filled her with joy at the happiness that had come over Kimberley. Before she had met Truesdale, Kimberley had shown no real interest in boys and had always chosen to spend her time completing her work or being the designated leader of the group.

Since their trip to the village, she had blossomed into a girl with a huge crush on a boy that was equally as taken with her. They had become well acquainted at the winter ball, but the Christmas break had reduced Kimberley back to her nervous demeanour. The visit to the village had built up the recent worries and allowed the two of them to be comfortable in one another's company. It was nice to see her friend show some true sense of contentment and Brianna had remained in the background for once as Kimberley received all the attention.

Over the following week Brianna had never seen such a change in Kimberley. Where she had been strict on her values on what she needed to do during the next couple of years, she had now swayed some of her opinions and considered something that Brianna had also thought. That maybe Witchcraft Heights wasn't the place for her.

"I mean, if we could stay in the Realm World it would be a much better move for us. Then we could fully concentrate on something we both love rather than struggle to keep up two facades," she reasoned with Brianna for about the tenth time in one week.

"Maybe this was how it was meant to be. You come to this world realise who you really want to be and how you see your life plans laid out," she tried to say rationally, using her most composed manner.

"Well you know I agree with you, but how do we know that they give us that option?" quizzed Brianna, "maybe they decide whether we get to stay; it might be a decision that is completely out of our hands."

"They must do, your book said about choosing between the two worlds didn't it?" replied Kimberley, "it stated that 'you' had to choose. That must mean that we get that choice for ourselves."

"Yes, but that was once a person is a fully fledged witch or wizard. It doesn't state what can happen when you're training to become a witch," Brianna said dejectedly, "I can't stand the idea of flitting between the two worlds for the next two years. That's a very big façade to keep up for three years without anyone noticing. I wonder if any of the older mortal based students could tell us."

"I could ask Truesdale," Kimberley suggested, trying to sound off hand , "one of his friends is from the mortal after all."

Brianna chuckled, "well that would be a perfect excuse to go over and talk to him yet again."

"Is it that obvious?" Kimberley replied blushingly.

"Well the big red love heart on your forehead with the name Truesdale does kind of give it away," teased Brianna, "but it's not a bad thing. I can tell he really likes you as well; it's good to have someone that shows explicitly where you stand with them."

"Are things not going well with you and Damien then?" Kimberley questioned her sympathetically.

Brianna hadn't realised that maybe the last comment had been pitched towards Damien, but she sat there and collected her thoughts that had been buried recently. She was happy for Kimberley, truly she was, but it only showed how dysfunctional her relationship was with Damien. It would be so much simpler if he could be as open with her as Truesdale was with Kimberley.

"Well things are going fine, if fine is remaining friends for the indefinite future. We sometimes have good conversations and I sometimes see a glimmer of something more in his eyes, but there only half thoughts. There not as obvious or strong as what you two have."

"Well, there are other options," Kimberley suggested.

"What do you mean? Plant a kiss on his lips and see how he responds?" she said incredulously, "I think I would die right there in front of him if he turned me away."

At that moment Taylor walked past Brianna and Kimberley, he looked up at Brianna with a sad expression on his face and continued on his way.

"You mean Taylor, don't you," stated Brianna with realisation, "we've gone through this before."

"But I can see that you like him. You change when you talk to him and your just blind sighted by feelings towards Damien," she reasoned, "I do like Damien, but there is something rather erratic about his behaviour. When has he stopped to have a real conversation with you apart from when he wants to go off gallivanting around the school? He started off as being polite and well mannered and now with the knowledge of magic he's become rebellious. Even Caleb and Michael have noticed something has changed in him and we all think you need to decide whether he is actually the good option. They don't talk to him as much as they used to; they have even started to talk to Taylor when Damien goes off on one of his strops. They have said that he keeps going off to the library, by himself, and won't really let them come with him."

"You make it sound like he's bad," retorted Brianna, "Kimberley, what aren't you telling me about Damien. It's hard for us to adjust to this lifestyle; look what it's done to the likes of Madison and Zoe. What if Damien is having a tough time? We can't simply leave him to wallow and panic alone."

"I don't think that that's the case Brianna. If he were feeling down it would be easy to see that. I mean it isn't as if he is particularly good at hiding his extreme emotions. The boys have noticed that he has a hungry expression on his face most of the time, as if he desperately wants something. They have mentioned it a couple of times when the two have been out on your adventures around the school me and the boys have sat down and had a good talk. They have been saying how he's not the same anymore, or at least he's a changed man to the one they met at Witchcraft Heights. In fact the two of them have become closer as a consequence and are now keeping an eye on him."

"But I've been with him and he's fine," Brianna tried to defend Damien as he had no voice to defend in front of Kimberley, "you lot don't have a clue; he's more vulnerable than you could possibly imagine, that's why he goes on adventures so that he can escape."

"You know why he's vulnerable? He's admitted to you that he needs to get away from everyone?" Kimberley asked with a sceptic line furrowed into her forehead.

"Well… no," she admitted with a sullen reluctance, "but it doesn't take a genius to figure out that he has an internal struggle. I can see his erratic behaviour, but you lot are making out that he has an evil scheme at hand. Everyone manages with things in a variety of ways, just let me deal with helping Damien and keep your judgemental thoughts to yourself."

Kimberley looked questioningly in Brianna's direction, if not a little hurt by Brianna's curt words, but did not pursue the subject any further.

Brianna knew that Kimberley was only concerned for her best friend, but her words towards Kimberley were a sort of defence mechanism. Brianna knew that Kimberley was probably right and Kimberley had managed to touch a nerve that she had wanted left well alone.

Brianna didn't fully understand it herself; her obsession to see the good in Damien and the long anticipated wait until he confessed his true feelings for her. She knew Taylor liked her, she had known that a thousand times over, but she just couldn't get past her feelings over Damien. She didn't want to abandon him like she had abandoned Madison.

The conversation had led them right to their elemental charms lesson in the enchanted forest with Professor Petra where they saw Alleyen and Serena waving enthusiastically in their direction. Although they saw them every day at school, it always seemed like ages since they spent the majority of their time in the mortal world; even with the students having a lesser dependence on the realm students and the ability to just be friends around them.

"How have you girls been?" asked Serena, "We didn't get to say goodbye to you on Friday. Did you get up to much at the weekend?"

Brianna felt slightly bad at keeping secrets from the girls, but she wasn't entirely sure that Alleyen and Serena would be impressed that they ventured out of the school without informing them. Instead she decided to change the track of thought to a more jovial topic.

"Not too bad thank you, Kimberley has been having the better time out of the two of us," teased Brianna.

"What's this all about? Kimberley? What haven't you told us," Alleyen asked in rapid succession. Out of the two girls, Alleyen definitely liked to hear the gossip within the school. She also resembled a sponge as she managed to retain an awful lot of information that she could recall back at any given moment.

"It's nothing really," Kimberley replied shyly.

"Apart from the fact that she's dating Truesdale!" exclaimed Brianna.

"No way!" shouted Alleyen gleefully, "He's in the year above and pretty much every girl in the school would love to be in your shoes! How on earth did this come about?"

"Oh, well we bumped into him a couple of times. He's helped us with our bearings of the school," Brianna said in a nonchalant manner.

"Well, congratulations Kimberley. He often likes to keep to himself and he only ever stays after school if there is a Dragon riding club on. It's fortunate you managed to bump into him, during the school day he likes to be surrounded by his close school mates and not really anyone else."

It looked like Alleyen had more questions to ask Kimberley but Professor Petra entered the opening in the forest and they set to work on their elemental charms. Today they were set the task to multiply an object that they had. Depending on the basic element of the object, they would need to gather the magic from that specific element. Professor Petra gave them a rock that they needed to multiply. As it was mainly an earthy material it was meant to be an easy spell to cast, drawing most of the power from the earthy floor around them.

Brianna sat in front of her rock, trying to cast the spell 'omnificus multiplus' on her rock. She was surprised to see that Damien was slowly making a move towards her, holding his rock in his hands. He placed it on the floor as he sat down next to her. For the first time, she found herself looking for Taylor. He had seen Damien's advance and was looking resolutely at the ground. Brianna wanted to mouth an apology and state that she didn't know Damien's intentions. Then she realised that what she was thinking was rather absurd and tried to clear her odd thoughts.

"How have you been?" Damien decided to start the conversation, "I see that you are getting along very well in your magical practice."

"Really?" she asked with a real level of doubt across her face. She hadn't considered her ability to be any greater than anyone else in the lesson. Normally she would feel elated at the idea of him giving her a lot of attention. Kimberley's words echoed in her head though and for some strange reason she actually felt a little cautious in his presence. Instead she tried to carry on with her rock and hoped that he would walk back over to Caleb and Michael.

"Yes," he said insistently, "we should try out some of our spells in the forest. It must be good to put all of our lesson time into practice."

"I used the illicio spell to look over a tombstone the other day," she said in a far off tone, before she realised what she said and clasped a hand to her mouth. She hadn't meant to tell anyone about the escapade.

"When did you go to a graveyard? Where was it?" he asked with a tone that made Brianna start to panic.

"Ermm... just the other day," she mumbled quietly, "it was nothing really."

"Brianna," he said sternly, "what are you keeping from me? Where did you go?" He finished the sentence and seemed to become angry towards her.

"Well," for the first time Brianna felt guarded towards Damien. She didn't like his tone of voice and felt slightly afraid of his persistent nature. She didn't want to drop Truesdale into the conversation but she felt trapped into a corner and was struggling to think of a way to dig out of the hole that she had made for herself.

"We were taken on to a trip into the local village," she rushed out, "we were lucky enough to know a couple of the students that took us into the town and back. He took us to the village square and a memorium to look as our ancestry."

"He, who was he?" he asked picking up on the male point straight away. He looked immediately over to Taylor and gave him a rather evil looking stare. It was a look she had never seen on his face before.

"No, no," she answered quickly to defer the accusation from Taylor, "it was one of the older students. We had a few questions and they said that they would be able to take us into the village to provide us with some answers."

"And you think that I don't have any questions?! Why didn't you think to take me with you after all of the times that I have invited you to come along with me? I introduced you to the idea of exploring and finding more about the world and this is how you repay me!" His words cut into Brianna and stung like an open wound, she had never thought Damien could react so cruelly to someone and she felt herself shrinking away from his unkind nature. She peered around and although it seemed he had been shouting at her no one else seemed to have heard, so he couldn't have raised his voice at all.

"I'm sorry," she pleaded, "If we go again I can ask if you can come along as well."

"Well… that's better Brianna," he responded, sounding somewhat controlling, "at least you have understood the error of your ways.

"God look at the time!" His change in attitude had changed in an extremely short length of time; it seemed almost scary in itself. "I better get some work done, can't fall behind on a spell. See you later and don't forget about me."

He turned and walked back to Caleb and Michael, leaving Brianna to sit with her rock and her woes. She spent the rest of the lesson focusing intently on her rock, trying fruitlessly to multiply its number.

At the end Professor Petra attracted the rocks to her with a wave and flick of her wand. The group left the clearing and headed back towards the warmth of the building. Brianna remained subdued and even when Kimberley tried to start a conversation Brianna continued to stay silent. Kimberley, with her excellent ability to understand the emotions of her best friend decided to leave Brianna to her own thoughts as they headed back through the transporting chamber and home for the evening.

*

The next morning Brianna woke up feeling fairly groggy. She had not had the best night's sleep and as she walked into Witchcraft Heights, Kimberley was there straight away to place a comforting arm around her best friends shoulder.

"Do you want to tell me what's up?" she asked sympathetically, "you don't look in the best of shape today... still beautiful of course... but far more tired."

"Well," she looked around to see if anyone was following them on the way to their maths lesson with Mr Downswood, "it was Damien. He came and spoke to me in our enchanted charms lesson."

"Yes I saw that he did," she answered, "I thought that would be a good thing, you both got to spend some time together. He seemed to have a nice long conversation with you."

"It wasn't one that I would want to repeat," she started and continued to explain what had happened the day before.

"He did what!" she exclaimed, "How dare he! That was nasty and controlling of him, I have a good mind to go and speak to him right now."

"No," Brianna panicked, quickly grabbing Kimberley's arm, "like I said I sorted it out. He's coming with us next time so that's the matter sorted out."

"He doesn't have to come along just because he threatened you," she insisted.

"Threatened," she tried to laugh it off light heartedly, "that's a bit extreme, I'm sure it will be fine from now on."

"From what you have told me it is a threatening manner and it's not something that you should have to deal with. Allow him to come one more time and then I think you need to consider cutting all ties with him, like I told you before he's changing."

They stopped the conversation as Mr Downswood entered the classroom and taught a house-building project based on angles and areas. The rest of the day flew by, without any real sight of Damien, for which

Brianna was rather grateful. Madison talked to Kimberley and Brianna during their lunchtime, still ignorant

to the matter of the past couple of months. She spoke in her original jovial manner, asking them about what

they had done with their evening. It was remarkable how normal she seemed, how much she had managed to

forget. Their friendship had not been rekindled, but they were not unkindly to her and didn't wish to act

cruelly for all the unkind things that Madison had said previously.

Brianna zoned in and out of the conversation, scanning around the canteen, worried that Damien

might come and speak to her again. Her eyes fell on Zoe instead, the gaunt Zoe, the Zoe who had lost all of her

previous lustre. Her hair looked lank, the circles beneath her eyes more hollowed. She resembled more a

ghost than a person and strangely enough she seemed to be staring intently at Madison. Although she looked

terrible, she seemed sound of mind and was focused on the one person for some reason.

The day finally came to an end and the students of Merlin walked to the transporting chamber. They

went to their remedies lesson with Professor Vita, discussing the qualities of the Moonflower, before making

the 'night before dawn potion'; a potion to recreate the night world. They then headed to their lesson with

Professor Merrydew where they were taught the difference between a basic begonia and the snap flywing

begonia. The subtle difference in the colour of the edge of the petals could lead to a sleep that lasted for

twenty years from the flywing or a mild perfumed scent on the fingers from the basic begonia.

The real motivation for Brianna that day surrounded the knowledge that she was to attend the dragon-

riding club after her lessons. When she entered the arena she was shocked and a little worried to see

Truesdale standing there. Brianna panicked that Damien would link Truesdale as the student that had taken

them to the village and she didn't want Truesdale to get it in the ear like she had done the day before.

"Welcome dragon riders, I have a small announcement to make. We will be hosting the dragon schools

challenge in three weeks' time. This is an event exclusively for first years so that they can try out dragon riding

in a competitive environment. It also gives my team and I the chance to see whether there are any candidates that are good enough to ride in the official school team. They compete against the other students in the

schools of Medea, Medusa and Morgana.

"The dragon schools challenge is a test to show off the skills that you have been taught so far this term. It will test your decision-making skills, your ability to manoeuvre the dragon and also develop an understanding of the importance of the relationship between dragon and rider. The prize for winning this tournament is no petty trophy. If you demonstrate a particularly astute talent for riding you are blessed with the prize of your own dragon. They have been kept hidden in the caves until they mature; the day that they mature is the day that a student becomes an accomplished rider. An accomplished rider will draw its power to one single dragon; not all of the dragon riders have won a dragon for their own but it has been seen over the ages. It will be the most loyal of companions and in this world dragons can be flown across the skies, for there is no fear of discovery.

"The other schools present a great challenge against the students of our own school. The juniors of Medusa always seem to have a particularly advanced understanding on dragon riding and will most certainly raise the expectations of our own students. Therefore we will be practising four times a week to make sure that all of our students have a fighting chance of winning the key prize."

Truesdale finished his speech and Landon took the majority of the students to the landing platform. This gave Truesdale the chance to run over to Kimberley and give her a tight squeeze around the waist while the rest of the students weren't looking.

"Hello Kimberley," he said delicately with a beaming smile that showed all of his attention and focus was entirely on Kimberley. This once again rendered Kimberley breathless and it took her a good minute to reply.

"Hello," she replied weakly and Truesdale chuckled merrily in response. "I didn't realise you had such a profound status within the school."

"Does that make me extra interesting then?" he replied with another small squeeze around the waist.

"Well she didn't really like you before, but I suppose your celebrity status might help," laughed Brianna which allowed Kimberley to relax and she joined in with the laughing as well.

"Well when do you girls want to come on another trip? I meant to ask Kimberley the other day but I completely forgot," enquired Truesdale innocently.

"What's this about?" asked Damien.

"Well I took the girls to the village last week, to the memorial," explained Truesdale without any concern about the matter.

"Oh this is the one that took you on a secret trip without bothering to invite me," Damien said scathingly.

"Oh sorry girls," apologized Truesdale, "I didn't think you would need to hide that. Unless you didn't want to tell anyone you had been seen with me," he added with a hint of sadness directed towards Kimberley.

"No, it wasn't that at all," Kimberley quickly interjected not wanting Truesdale to get the wrong idea about her feelings towards him. She shot Damien a disapproving look before continuing, "It's that we still aren't sure where our boundaries are and we don't want the Professor's finding out if we head into the village."

"And you think that we would tell on you? That's your excuse for not inviting us alone" answered Damien, dramatically pretending to be hurt.

"No. We did want to tell you," Brianna added in, still trying to defend herself even though he had upset her yesterday, "we just wanted to understand more about our ancestry. I read about a memorial in my book and Truesdale was kind enough to take us there. That was honestly all that there was to the matter."

"Well we can go again and this time we will come with you, help you find out a bit more on what you want to know. We don't want you to exclude us from your adventures; we are your friends after all," Damien spoke with an icily cool tone.

"Well, I think we will go on Friday," he answered curtly, "if that's alright with the two girls?"

"Yes," they both said at the same time, Kimberley holding a particularly large smile across their face as another time with Truesdale had been planned.

Truesdale left the situation with a slightly raised eyebrow. He looked somewhat confused by Damien's manner and left Brianna with Damien as Kimberley went off with Truesdale to select a dragon to ride.

"I'm sorry, yes I suppose that will be fine," she said turning to directly face Damien, "I'll ask Truesdale but I'm sure he will be able to fit you three in."

"Three?"

"Yes," she replied, "you, Caleb and Michael obviously."

"Oh yes, of course," he replied quickly covering up his confusion which once again unsettled Brianna somewhat. She wondered how he could forget to bring along his two best friends.

"Well when we know what time we are leaving I'll let you know. We don't really get a lot of time down there, so we need to make sure that the journey doesn't cut too much into our exploring," Brianna explained and the two of them proceeded down to the landing platform to start their afterschool club.

*

Brianna always noticed how strangely time would fashion itself; when you want to get to a certain time or day time travels slowly and for Brianna, Friday was coming around drip by drip. The long days at Witchcraft Heights did not help, especially with dull subjects such as geography and maths slowing down the hours that she wished to just brush away. The group were all anticipating the trip on Friday and the five from the mortal world spent their lunch times going through Brianna's book.

She had decided to show the boys the book as well. Although she felt slightly reluctant to show Damien, she trusted Caleb and Michael and wanted them to know about the contents of the book. Since they had been down to the village, information seemed to find its way into the book every single day. Some of it didn't seem to make an awful lot of sense so Brianna wrote down the notes on anything that she questioned. She hoped that another trip would help her to answer the questions that were mounting up.

As they sat in a huddle at lunchtime Madison crept over with a vacant expression on her face, it sadly seemed to be an expression that crossed her face until someone spoke to her. Brianna quickly stowed the book away in her bag.

"Was that an interesting read? I'm looking for a new book to bury my head in," she enquired.

"Oh, no it's just my planner, we were looking at a weekend to meet up in town," Brianna thought up quickly.

"Oh brilliant!' she said immediately "I have been meaning to go in town for quite a while. My mom's birthday is coming up so I'm trying to see what I can get."

Brianna felt uncomfortable as she tried to think of an exit strategy. It was extremely awkward lying to someone in the first place and now she had to think of a double lie to back her out of the situation.

"Well it's more of a family event," Brianna stated slowly, "but Kimberley has been invited along as well. I was checking a time that was good for her."

Madison looked questionably around the group as they all returned convincing nods of the head. Brianna sensed that Madison knew they were not completely telling the truth; she turned and walked away from the group with a sombre expression.

As she walked away, making an exit from the canteen, Brianna watched her with a guilty conscience. Once again she noticed Zoe watching Madison with the same hungry expression that she had showcased previously. Brianna wondered why Zoe seemed to have such a keen interest in Madison. Maybe Madison's link to the magical world had some sort of importance to Zoe, but she just couldn't fathom any particular reason why one student would be of such great attentiveness to another student. Brianna felt slightly nervous as Zoe left the canteen soon after Madison had made her exit and she panicked at the thought that Zoe had gone after Madison.

When Brianna returned her attention back to her group she found that the other four were already

back to planning their trip later this afternoon, unaware of the weird situation that had gone on between Zoe

and Madison, so it was a light hearted and welcoming conversation that Brianna returned her attention to.

The book had developed one very interesting element since its last use; a pull out map of the Salem

village. Since Truesdale had pointed out the different roads and dwellings in the village, the book had woven

itself its very own annotated version of the village. It didn't look like the Salem that they knew of back in the

mortal world. The streets were smaller and laid out in a completely different fashion. The homes were less

frequently dotted around the village and on the map you could pick out how every single building was

individual to the next. It was not a town set out in a criss cross grid fashion; instead they twisted and turned

around the page leading to many cul-de-sacs that led up from the centre of the valley.

The map also labelled the key parts of the village, parts that Truesdale had stated and other parts that

Truesdale had not. It pointed out the Salem records hall; the magical items repair shop, the local tailor shop

and an assortment of other shops. It was strange to look and compare the two different Salem's. The mortal

world and which had seemed so average, now seemed futuristic compared to the old world simplicity of the

Salem village in the Realm world.

After their last lesson of drama, one of Brianna's least favourite subjects, the group headed back to the

history classroom that linked up to the transporting chamber and onto their more exciting fauna and mystical

creatures lesson with Professor Autumnleaves.

Since they had begun practicing magic, Miss Ashdown had made no reference to their time at Merlin

or the other three magical schools. It was almost as if she had forgotten her involvement with the magical

world unless she had a duty to fulfil. Brianna could only consider that it was the best strategy to ensure the

utmost level of secrecy. Maybe Miss Ashdown had her memory wiped like Madison had had to maintain the

secret of the other world. Maybe Miss Ashdown knew, but she chose not to draw attention to the matter of

their magical ability. The other teachers didn't question that Miss Ashdown had stopped a club, when it had been so successful in its initial quarter. She must have been playing this façade for quite some time for this not to arouse suspicion.

When the five of them stepped into Merlin, Alleyen and Serena kindly greeted them at the other end. They were having their fauna and mystical creature's lesson outside today, as the snow pixies were out to begin the melting of the snow ritual. Professor Autumnleaves had said this was an occasion not be missed. It was an occasion that marked the end of long winter, where the realm world was encased in three months of thick snow. The snow pixies waited for no one so Serena and Alleyen decided to escort their friends so that they could get to the procession as quickly as possible. Serena was particularly good at remembering the shortcuts of the school and took the five of them through pretend walls and portal doors. Within ten minutes they were walking out of the northern end of Merlin, which compared to their normal twenty-minute walk, was an astounding achievement.

The lesson was highly entertaining; the snow pixies were clad in white furry robes, which resembled the edges of snow flakes, their hair was spiky and silver and contrasted beautifully to their pale peach faces. Their lips were blue and they whistled through their lips as the skipped around the snow covered ground. The students saw only a small number of them performing the ritual; laying their palms on different parts of the snow and allowing their power to absorb the cold frosty particles. By the end of the lesson the snow had been removed from the forest and Professor Autumnleaves informed the class that the snow pixies would join the rest of their kin and continue the melting process for the following few days in order for spring to officially start.

They walked back into the warmth of the school, knowing all too soon they would be out again in the bitter cold that had not yet completely vanished from the realm world.

They went out to the front entrance of the school to meet Truesdale. They were surprised to see two of his friends flanked on either side of him and Brianna wondered what was needed for this procession. The first years followed their tour guides and Brianna realised that the other two were taking another

Accipegus carter; she was a bit foolish to think they were to all pile into one vehicle.

She managed to scramble into one with Kimberley, but unfortunately Damien decided to jump into the

same one as the girls. Truesdale careered the Accipegus carter down to the village with Landon taking the rest

of the group in a second one. They arrived in good time and Truesdale was content to take them back to the

Salem records hall; one of the most historical sites within the whole town and one that the boys were keen to

see.

They followed the familiar path up the cobbled stone street and saw the looming Salem records hall

centred perfectly as the focal point of the village square.

"So where did you girls go the last time then?" Damien asked the two girls as soon as they stood at the

steps of the Salem records hall's entrance.

"Well we looked around the village square itself and then we were taken to a place where we could

find out more about our ancestry," informed Brianna.

"Well, where was that," he persisted in a tone that she was becoming less and less comfortable with. It

was similar to the tone that he had held in Professor Petra's lesson and Brianna couldn't help but regretting

bringing Damien with them on their venture. "Was it the graveyard that you had talked about before?"

"Yes. We went to the graveyard just over the brim of that hill," she pointed out the direction to the

right where they had been led the previous tie.

"Well I would very much like to go there," he stated with an almost unnatural grin.

"I was hoping to take the girls to the Whimpering Warlock, they have had such a busy day after all,"

interjected Truesdale at which Brianna gave a grateful nod. She didn't fancy going back to the graveyard, its

eerie atmosphere had frightened the living daylights out of her and she didn't fancy the nightmares that had

soon followed that evening.

"I insist that we go," Damien retorted, "besides, we can go to get a drink afterwards if we have to."

"Kimberley I think that might be a good idea," Brianna agreed. She wasn't entirely sure what made her agree to the conditions, but she did so nevertheless. Maybe if they got his wishes over with quickly they could get back to the tavern in a quicker time.

Damien smiled eagerly at Brianna before turning his attention to the direction that she had pointed towards beforehand. Truesdale pressed to the front of the group and Damien followed closely behind; the girls held back and gave each other a slightly worrying look before proceeding.

They walked and only paused as they reached the brow of the hill, where they were given the small chance to take in the unnerving quality that the graveyard possessed. They walked down to the outskirts of the graveyard before they had to pass through the dark and consuming wood. The trees scratched at their faces as they passed their thickset branches and dense leaves that separated the living from the dead.

As soon as they got out of the woods, Damien skirted off reading every single headstone and out of respect Brianna decided to make her way over to her ancestor's memorial once more. She looked at the other names that littered the memorial and paused as Madison's ancestor stuck out like a sore thumb.

Suddenly, a low glow seemed to dance in the corner of Brianna's eye and she turned to see what it was, but the glow vanished at the slightest movement of her head. It was similar to the low glow that she had seen on the former occasion.

"Kimberley, I think we should make our way back to the village," Brianna said with an element of caution to her voice. She tried to brush off her anxiety by adding, "I've been dying to try that lemon-treacle tea."

"What have you found?"

Brianna turned and was shocked to see Damien looking directly at her. His hungry expression had intensified to such a state that he looked almost hideous in the dying sun and for the first time Brianna felt truly scared of her old friend. Fortunately Michael walked up at the same point and looked questionably at the look of panic that must have been clearly etched on Brianna's face.

"It just looks like any other headstone doesn't it Brianna?" he said pointedly, "I think this cold air is giving me goose bumps. A cup of this famous lemon-treacle tea may just be what is in order."

Brianna nodded and gave a small smile of gratitude before walking back to the rest of the group and making their way out of the graveyard through the thickset trees. Damien followed somewhat reluctantly in their wake, after brushing his hand across the memorial of Brianna's ancestor.

They made their way back into the village with Truesdale leading the way to The Whimpering Warlock; the most popular tavern in the village of Salem. He pushed on the heavy wooden door and they were immediately greeted by the smell of roasted cinnamon and perfumed vanilla. The tantalising smell matched the equally appealing décor inside. It looked like an old fashioned cosy cottage home. It was filled with low squishy sofas, each centred around a number of round wooden tables. Everything was low to the ground and Truesdale had to duck under some of the beams as he made his way to the bar.

The girls went to find a seat with Damien while the rest of the group followed Truesdale to purchase the drinks. The girls sat in an awkward silence as Damien looked intensely at one of them and then shifted his gaze to the other.

"This... this really is a lovely place," Kimberley started, trying to break the awkward situation. Fortunately for them, the boys returned with the drinks of lemon-treacle tea at that point and the atmosphere seemed to ease up.

"This is a lovely village," stated Caleb, "I'm not so sure about your tour though Truesdale! Next time can you take us somewhere where I don't get the collywobbles?"

"Yeah, we can take you to the local theatre next time you come down. I think their playing the tale of the Mermaid and the Wizard of McKinley; it's one of the most famous stories of the Realm world.

"I'm sure that Morsensa is playing the part of the mermaid; she is one of the most talented merpeople in the acting industry and her voice is to die for."

"What?" Brianna blurted out, "mermaids are here in the village?!" Brianna had only ever heard of

the mermaid in her lesson, she had not for a single second believed that they would reside in the village of

Salem.

"Well yes of course," Truesdale answered, looking somewhat surprised by Brianna's response, "we

have to have a population that can maintain the laws within the ocean; how else could the creatures of the

sea and land coexist harmoniously."

"Truesdale," Kimberley said, "We have only heard about them in a lesson environment. There aren't

Merpeople in the mortal realm. For us they are as much a fantasy as witches and wizards to mortals."

"The mortal world is a very strange place," he responded, scratching his temple as if what they were

telling him was beyond comprehension.

They continued making conversation about the other residents in the Whimpering Warlock. Truesdale,

who was bought up in the realm world, saw nothing out of the ordinary but the rest of the group ogled and

gasped as new members entered through the heavy wooden doors.

Truesdale was happy to identify persons who didn't look quite so ordinary; he spotted a couple of

vampires whose faces looked strained as they breathed in what Brianna could only think of as a feast. A

Cyclops sat surreptitiously in the corner with a flagon that had a protruding green hand; Brianna didn't want to

think what was held within.

As well as the rather dangerous creatures, a pair of hobgoblins appeared to be deep in conversation

over a pile of rather odd looking pieces of metal and a trio of trolls seemed to be locked in the strangest three

way arm and leg wrestle that she had ever bared witness to.

It was as she turned to ask Truesdale about a gentleman that looked particularly off colour that she

saw the door open to a pair of people that she wished she had not seen.

It was Professor's Vita and Tabitha. Brianna had never thought that Professor's would have mingled in

the outside world, but there was no doubting the familiar faces of their Professors'. Brianna gave a quick terrified look towards Kimberley's direction and she bolted under the table, pulling on Caleb and Damien's leg as she did so. They followed and Kimberley bought Michael along with her so that only Truesdale remained above board and at the very least, occupied the table.

"What's with the sudden hiding place," asked Michael.

Brianna held a finger to her lips and whispered ever so softly, "our Professor's have come down for a drink."

Kimberley and Caleb gasped and Michael looked worriedly back at Brianna.

"What does that matter," Damien said in an unfamiliar drawling tone. "What would they seriously consider doing to us?"

Brianna couldn't believe how blaze Damien was being about the whole incident, "How could you be so calm?! We don't know if we're allowed down in the village. What it we get caught by the Professors; we don't know the punishment that they could give us!"

"They won't do anything. They're all too soft hearted and see the good in everyone," he said in his continued sarcastic tone.

"Don't be so stupid," Kimberley snapped back, "we will have to sneak back up to the school and hope that we don't run into anymore teachers."

The group nodded in agreement and spent the next few minutes formulating a plan to safety. Kimberley suggested that Truesdale should wait at the door and look as if he was waiting for a comrade, he would send out a quick whistle to signify it was safe to leave. They left in pairs and the fear was soon gone as the operation went ahead remarkably smoothly.

When they were all out of the tavern they sprinted back to the winding hill that led back to the school. They didn't dare to look back or stop running until they were safely out of sight from the eyes of anyone within the village. It was only when they felt safe within the shelter of the wood that separated the school from the village that Brianna plucked up the courage to speak out loud.

"I never want to deal with that again."

"I agree," panted Kimberley as she regained her breath. "I have never felt so scared in my life! Imagine if they had seen us; I shudder to think what would have been the consequence at being caught."

"Detention."

"A visit to Professor Allard's office."

"Losing our right to practice magic ever again."

"You lot can't be serious," Damien piped into the conversation, "They wouldn't want to lose valuable magical blood. They wouldn't let go of prestigious magical families."

"What would make you say that?" Brianna retorted, becoming more and more irritated with Damien's lack of compassion and disregard of any sense of boundaries. "We know nothing of our lineage. Why would that affect how we are treated as people?"

"Well Brianna, there you go again," he sniped back, "telling people what you want them to know, but never getting to the truth of things. You know that you know a lot more than you are letting on. My only concern is why you are less than happy at revealing what you already know to the rest of your so called friends."

"I don't know what you mean," she said falteringly. She worried whether he had found out about the situation with Madison; whether he had made the connection with the ancestors of Salem and their profound impact on the balance with the generations of now. Her conversation with Truesdale had sparked an extra level of information and she spent her time down in the village attempting to expand her knowledge. She had let Damien know a little about the book, but she had only allowed him to know more because the other boys were there at the same time. Brianna noticed Kimberley flash a fear of worry in her direction and guessed that more than one pair of ears was listening to the conversation.

"Fine, lie to us," he snapped, "You're alright learning about the Realm world if you're a step ahead, I don't know why I have bothered wasting my time getting to know you and helping you to adjust to this world.

"In fact, I don't need to be around any of you. Time wasters, that's all you are. All given this gift and you don't even know what to do with it, you think that living by the rules and being introduced to the world of magic is enough. Well if you lot aren't with me I'm going to go back to the school, alone. I'm going to find people that can really help me, those that truly understand my vision" and true to his word Damien sprinted off in to what was now the black of night, up the valley and supposedly back to school. The rest of the group were left in confusion as to what had just occurred.

Both Caleb and Michael put an arm around Brianna. She was a bit confused as to why at first, but then she realised that she was violently shaking and the boys were trying to comfort her. She pulled them in tight, thanking them without the use of words, as they were escorted back to the school in silence; coming to terms with the loss of what used to be a great friend.

Chapter 17

Since the near run in with the Professors of Merlin, most of the group had decided that they were quite happy to remain within the walls of Merlin. Truesdale had apologised a thousand times over to the group and they did not blame him at all for nearly landing in an awful amount of trouble. This stood in good stead for Kimberley as she didn't feel guilty for remaining close to Truesdale. The two of them spent their Monday during the free hour after remedies lesson to be alone; it was the first time for Kimberley so she felt nervously excited.

This wasn't the first time that Brianna had been separated from Kimberley, but that had been on her terms not Kimberley's. This time she was left behind and she went to sit with the boys to pass the time.

They sat and played fiery phoenixes, a game with live miniature phoenixes. It was similar to the game 'draughts' that they played back home but the phoenix's turned to ash if they were beat and renewed to new if they reached the other end of the board. All the while the three of them tried to ignore the obvious absence of Damien. He had kept his word from the ill-fated Friday and had resolutely decided not to be a part of their group for the past few weeks. They had reached Easter without one word from him. In an odd sort of way, Brianna felt that a small weight had been lifted from the group. She was still hurt by the way that he had spoken to her, but she couldn't pretend to ignore the fact that he had really changed and was much farther from the Damien that she had known at the start of the year.

They finished their game with five minutes to get back through the portal. The three of them made their way out of the common room. As they turned down the corridor that housed the door to the transporting chamber Kimberley came running towards them. Brianna watched her wave back to Truesdale as she caught up with the rest of the group.

"I've got really exciting news about tomorrow," Kimberley puffed as she tried to regain her breath. "Truesdale told me that we're to have the dragon challenge on the last Tuesday before the Easter break, next week. The trials to make the team are tomorrow."

The excitement immediately coursed through the group at the prospect of being selected to represent the school team. Brianna, as quite a talented rider was hoping to make the team. Professor Llewellyn had claimed her to be naturally talented and one of the few students to truly show a fast aptitude to dragon riding. As they exited back to the mortal world they discussed what they would do if they won a dragon and how they would feel belonging to schools dragon riding team.

*

"Are you ready?" Kimberley asked with a small nervous quaver in her voice.

"As I'll ever be," Brianna replied with the tension knotting her stomach. The tent that she stood in was filled with students. Students stood around her biting on their fingernails whilst others in the group paced around in small circles. Some were tracing patterns in the air as they waited with tense expressions for their name to be announced via the sound sonorous.

The day of the dragon riding selection had finally arrived and the first year students of Merlin were about to be put to the test. The test that was to be set before them was a test that they had not yet come across. The element of surprise was said to test their true understanding as a dragon rider. Brianna had felt ready to ride before today; now she was minutes away from riding she felt just as nervous as the rest of the people around her.

"Caleb Williams," sounded the sound sonorous, loud and clear. It was the voice of Truesdale ringing out clear in the stadium. As the captain of the dragon riding team he was the judge of all the potentials and had the final say into who would make the team. Even Kimberley was not given liberties to be automatically added to the team; she had to complete the challenge just like the rest of the first years. Caleb gave a small nod as he realised his name was called out and the two girls gave encouraging pats on the shoulder as he walked out to meet his own personal challenge. That was another thing about the challenge, every single student had been observed and they were to be tested against areas that they had struggled with and some areas that could show off their potential.

He closed the drapes on the tent as he exited and the remaining students were left in the tent that seemed to magically block out any sound other than the words called out on the sound sonorous.

After a few minutes had passed by the next name had been called out. As the tent emptied Brianna started to wonder if her name would ever be called out; what if in fact she had been forgotten about.

"Damien Quests," Truesdale called out for the next contender to step up to the contest. Brianna looked around the tent, although Damien hadn't come down with them to the tent, she had rather hoped that he would still be somewhere and ready to go. Brianna grew more worrisome about his constant absences and hoped that he was focused in something that he had professed to truly enjoy.

"Damien Quests," the voice called out once again. When the absence pursued the next name was called out.

"Brianna Eastey."

She froze for what seemed an eternity, when in reality it could have been nothing more than a second. She snapped out of her reverie when she realised she was being forcefully moved along by Kimberley. she started to move the blocks of lead that were in fact her legs towards the tent drapes and passed through.

The stadium blinded Brianna with the lights that filled the area, all pointing to the landing platform that she was currently standing on. The dragon stood tethered to its post as it waited for her to begin its course. The lights, she supposed, were light enough so that she couldn't see the magical course that had been set up for her.

"Miss Brianna Eastey," the sound sonorous called out, slightly quieter; perhaps the volume affected the distance or the material through which it could penetrate. "When the lights dim and reveal your course the timer will start. Your goal is to complete the course and reach the final ring in the quickest time possible. Follow the floating arrows that will tell you where the next ring is positioned. Good luck."

The voice stopped and the lights immediately dimmed. It had completely transformed from the training ground that she had been used to. There were high towering rock structures, pits that emitted lava bursts, dark circles that could only be seen from certain angles.

She could hear a sudden tick tocking noise and could see high in the sky a timer in bright yellow flames; timing her fate. She ran over to her dragon, it was the most challenging dragon that Merlin housed within its walls. It was the Yellow Snapfire, a ferocious beast with two sets of teeth and a long whipping tail. The claws curled and finished in dangerously piercing points. Its horns could break marble with one light brush and Brianna had to somehow control the monster.

She approached with confidence and found the accessible crook behind the wing that allowed the rider to climb up without the dragon snapping at its intruder. She took the reins in her hands and loosened the Elithier chain that held the dragon in place; it was the strongest metal in the realm world and the only one that the Yellow Snapfire couldn't penetrate with its brutal horns.

With one forceful kick she felt the forward thrust as the beast responded and took flight. At once everything around her had seemed to dissolve into nothing; she neither heard nor saw the crowd. She was imminently at one with her dragon who seemed no more difficult to manage than Medonna, the first dragon she had ever ridden.

She saw the first ring glowing brightly out the corner of her right eye and made an immediate advance in that direction. She flew straight and true, but had to swerve as a sudden jet of fire burst from a fissure in the rocky ground. She heard the swell ping as she became victor of the ring and spotted the arrow pointing her west as she passed through.

Creating a loop in the air she saw the next ring directly below her and made a fantastical dive towards the ground. The whistling sound of speed rushed through her ears as she drove the dragon to the ground, pulling out at the very last second to corkscrew through the ring. Quickly she darted left and right around some stalagmite threatening rocks that threatened to knock out a dragon on impact. The arrow at the end of the slalom caused her to complete an impressive flip turn and held her upside down as she passed through the next ring.

She could already see the following ring as she passed through the third. It seemed too easy as it lazily hung in mid-air. As she kicked the dragons crook in front of the ring it spouted some fire to show its understanding and streamlined its wings to propel itself forward.

Suddenly, five fireballs rocketed from the night air and rocketed themselves towards Brianna and the Yellow Snapfire. As they all found the centre point of contact and directed their focus Brianna cleverly pulled out the pirouette and raced straight up towards the sky. As the fireballs collided and made a horrendous booming noise that spouted sparks of flame Brianna nose-dived and went through the last ring.

The clock written into the sky stopped and magical firework like sparks emitted from the clock. She flew the beast back to the ground where the chains immediately tethered the dragon back to its post. It was only as she got down from the dragon that she could start to hear the cheers. The unified cheering and clapping from the crowd filled Brianna with pride. She had never received such a warm applause and she beamed and waved in response. They seemed particularly excited, but Brianna had considered her time to be rather slow as she had to make some fanciful moves in order to dodge the deadly spouts.

She had hoped for some sort of feedback, but Professor Llewellyn came out onto the landing platform and ushered her into another tent that had been erected on the opposite side of the platform.

Brianna stepped through to congratulatory claps from the other candidates. Caleb and Michael gave Brianna a tight squeeze and even Taylor gave a warming pat on the back. Everyone bar Kimberley had had their turn and all Brianna wanted to do now was to watch her friend complete the challenge.

Brianna was not sure how long she had to wait before Kimberley arrived; the postponement seemed to go on forever and as the tent still remained silent as everyone nervously waited for the verdict there minimal comfort to help pass the time. She thought maybe the crowd could be heard once the challenge was under way, but that was most definitely not the case.

When it seemed almost indefinite that she would ever return, Kimberley walked into the tent and Brianna rushed over to give a pat on the back and gave her plenty of warming applause.

All of the hopefuls had finally had their shot at making the team and now they had to play the waiting game. They slowly found the confidence to talk about their trial and figured how other people's trials differed from their own. Kimberley didn't have to dodge fire, but she was put up against water. Though not as lethal, water could still dampen the wings of the dragon and cause it to lose flight and speed. Caleb found that the stalagmite standing rocks protruding up and out at vicarious angles on the stadium moved so that they forced him to drag the dragon out of the main pathway.

Taylor was walking over to the direction to Brianna's group when the noise boomer was again sounded out.

"Would all candidates please make their way onto the landing platform," Truesdale said loudly and clearly. They all made their way out of the tent and now that the lights were dimmed they could see the full number of students that the school held. It wasn't a number that was a s big as Witchcraft Heights but it was still of a respectable size.

"First of all, as captain of the dragon riding club, I wish to congratulate every single one of you for the outstanding efforts that you have displayed today," announced Truesdale.

"I wish that I could select every single one of you, but I am afraid that is not the case. The members of the dragon riding club have come to a unanimous decision on will become a part of the Dragon Riding Club. Those that have been selected have so as they have demonstrated exemplary skill and an excellent relationship to control the dragon.

"As such these are the students that have made the mark. Caleb Williams, Kimberley Aldridge, Taylor Saunter, Michael Proctor, Danielle Clover and for a truly outstanding performance that has bettered the likes of Hubert Crackling, world riding champion for twenty years, Brianna Eastey."

Spotlights rained down on the successful members as the crowd roared, cheered and clapped as they congratulated them. Brianna and the rest of the group could do nothing more but beam brightly and wave to the crowd in thanks. A day had not passed that could beat the feeling she felt at this moment in time, even with all that had happened recently, her bright cheery disposition had once more returned.

*

Brianna had not before bumped into too many of the other students of Merlin; most of them were home by the time the students of Witchcraft Heights and the other schools of the mortal Salem crossed the transporting chamber into the Realm World. It was a different story now that the students were spending every after school session as a part of the dragon riding club. They had only been able to attend a club with the rest of the new riders in the beginning as the dragon riding team were always taking part in competitions so it seemed unfair to make them start from scratch.

When Brianna attended the training sessions she would often spot students with pieces of paper in the stadium, looking up and pointing to different students as they practised for the Dragon riding challenge. It was only after the second day that Kimberley asked Landon what they were doing and he informed her that they were making assumptions on who was the best representative for the school and who would win the competition itself. The competition between the four schools was still only for first years, but the riders could now gain expertise from the older students. Apparently bets were held on the day, trades for shop items such as sweets or items from the local shop in the village.

Brianna had found the time to practise a very useful tool as it had given her the chance to perform some more risky moves that she had read about whilst researching dragon riding in the local library. The books that she had pulled out demonstrated death defying acts that the likes of Truesdale deemed too risky for a first year, but left Brianna feeling exhilarated by the challenge.

She was trying to master the fleeting loop, which would help her to gain space between two different height hoops. It was too steep a slant to get through both hoops without the fleeting loop. She had managed to get the dragon to fly high up in the air, but her feet slipped and she lost balance which forced the dragon back towards the ground and found her hanging by the dragon's tail as she slid down its back.

Kimberley wasn't as adventurous as Brianna, but she was still very graceful as she sailed around the course. She carried a fear that her slow time would knock points against her score, but Truesdale explained that some judges looked for an aesthetically pleasing performance that would suit her performance perfectly. Brianna's performance still had the graceful edge, she knew that it needed to be included, but she held the advantage of speed and an astute understanding with the dragons.

By the end of Friday's practise session her inner thighs were sore and her arms felt heavy as she tried to maintain control of the great dragon. The pain of trying to control the dragon was also starting to affect the aesthetic quality of her routine and it was becoming a rather sloppy affair.

She jumped off of Zeberna after ten minutes of nursing her aches and then dragged herself over to Caleb, Michael and Kimberley.

"I can't do it anymore, I'm going to fail," she said despairingly and sat down to watch Taylor climb onto her dragon. He was also starting to show his fatigue as he flew around the course. The dragon could feel his fatigue and it resulted in an unresponsive lap around the stadium.

Brianna knew that her friends were being silent to avoid a relentless protest, where nothing they could say would make her feel better. She knew it was meant to help her, but she really wanted to have someone to bounce off in order to give her the opportunity to let off some steam.

"Where's Damien?" she asked Kimberley as they watched Caleb take his turn around the course. They no longer spent a great deal of time with him, but it almost seemed something of an automatic point of conversation.

"Ermm, I'm not too sure," she replied awkwardly her eyes darting quickly to Michael and back.

"Kimberley, what aren't you telling me. Do you know something about Damien that you have failed to mention?" Brianna questioned Kimberley directly. His prolonged absence with the girls had remained true, but Brianna had noticed that Caleb and Michael had maintained some level of contact with him.

"Well, he's in the library actually," she said vaguely.

"What's wrong with that? You can't seriously be avoiding the question if he is in the library. That's hardly the crime of the month."

Kimberley looked slyly left and right to check that no one was listening in on his or her conversation as they walked back to the first year common room.

"Okay, I'll tell you, but you can't tell him or he'll get mad at Michael and Caleb. Since his outrageous outburst they have been kind of spying on him. They figured out that he has been researching ways to travel to the village using magic, without the use of magical transportation. They haven't worked out his true motive, but he keeps loaning out historical books from the school library, but they have identified a key pattern for his research."

"But he knows that it is dangerous to go back to the village! He may hate me down to the bone, but he must surely see that it's dangerous to go back to the village after our near encounter with the Professors'. What possible reason would he have for wanting to go back?"

"I don't know, he told Michael and Caleb it's very important to him but he refuses to tell them anything more."

Brianna looked at Michael, who had joined in behind the girls after his ride and looked apologetically in her direction as he caught onto the end of the conversation. So Damien was keeping secrets from even his closest friends. It didn't make any sense to her and it made her ask the question that popped into her head so many times when it concerned Damien. Why did she still care about him so much? Why did she become bothered by his motives and apparently hidden agendas?

She decided that this information along with the poor last ride was enough to make her wish to return to the mortal world, away from the problems that were growing in the world of magic. She pretended that she needed to go back to her locker and said to Kimberley and the boys that she would meet them in the transporting chamber. She did need to return a couple of her books, but really all she wanted was to be left alone for a little while.

She stood there with her hands trembling as she attempted to open the locker door and it took a moment to realise that anger was burning from the inside out. It was the first time that she had felt angry at the magical world; it had changed Damien. For he was no longer a typical teenage boy, unaware of his appeal to most of the female population, he was now distant and manipulative. She sadly pondered his potential reasons for wanting to spend time together in the lead up to Christmas. Maybe he had only used her to find out more information regarding the school rather than purely going with her because he felt something between the two of them.

She managed to avoid contact with any other student and met with Kimberley and the boys back in the chamber. Whether Kimberley intuitively knew that something was bothering her or not, she was left to her own thoughts as the group walked back to the history classroom. As she stepped out the front of Witchcraft Heights she was left with only resentful thoughts towards Damien.

"Hello sweetie," called out her Mom when Brianna got in about twenty minutes later.

"Hey mom," Brianna called out with a false cheery disposition.

"I've got meatloaf in the oven if you fancy some?"

"I've already eaten in town; I think I'm just going to head upstairs for the evening."

She felt too tired and exhausted to be truly hungry and as she pushed her door shut and turned to her bed it gave her but ten seconds to reach her bed, place her head on her pillow before she fell into a deep sleep.

*

When the morning light glared through her window on the following Tuesday morning, Brianna woke up with a feeling of distress in the pit of her stomach. As she turned to face her clock she acknowledged the date and realised that her fear was associated with the realisation that today was the first year's paramount Dragon Riding challenge. All of her practising was about to be put to the test; now was the day when she would be tested and measured for her talents as a dragon rider.

As she sat on the bus to Witchcraft Heights she considered missing the lessons that day and sneaking through the transporting chamber to the Realm of Salem for a last minute practice. It was a very tempting idea, but she knew that it wouldn't be possible. For one thing Kimberley wouldn't condone skipping school and secondly there had to be a teacher present when a junior was with a dragon and she was sure that Professor Llewellyn would be teaching all day.

So, with a great reluctance she got off of the school bus and headed over to the Merlin common room to retrieve her books for her English and Science lesson. Kimberley met her in the English lesson, where they were now reading Shakespeare's 'Twelfth Night'. It wasn't too bad a read and for Brianna it gave her chance to take her mind away from the task that awaited her.

The rest of the day was fairly practical; in science they were conducting an experiment where they had to make a light bulb glow using a potato. She felt half tempted to use her wand and simply cast an enlightening enchantment over the potato to save her the time and effort. In geography they researched the plant life of the northern territories of America, but Brianna felt it atrocious that the Perfuming Water Flower and Chilli Dandeclouf were missing from their investigation. It almost seemed as if good fortune was on her side as the lessons continued to detract her attention from what she knew lay ahead later that day.

The free lesson after lunch was well used by both Kimberley and Brianna, who sat reading up on all the different moves that they could showcase in the challenge. They knew that the challenge would be similar to what they had previously faced, but this time it would not be individual to the rider's strengths and weaknesses. Damien was sitting over in a corner away from the girls. She couldn't help but notice the slightly light pallor to his complexion. Before it had almost an olive glow, but now it was reduced to a far fainter

shade of peach; if not verging to more of a ghostly white. It troubled her somewhat, but then she supposed

the constant miserable demeanour would surely take its toll after some time and affect the way that he

looked.

He was scribbling notes behind a propped up book looking craftily around the sides every now and

then as if to catch out those that were watching him. Michael and Caleb were letting off their pent up nerves

the only way they knew how; clowning around.

When the bell eventually sounded for the end of the day, Brianna and the rest of the group got up and

quickly headed to the locker area to put away their bags, they would only take their wand with them to the

Realm World, their items from the mortal world held little purpose in a teeming world of magic.

They headed down the blackened corridor to the chamber, where they were surprised to see everyone

else waiting. The mirror in the middle of the room had also had its cover removed to reveal the beauty of the

mirror itself as it had been so on their first meeting in the chamber was there.

They waited anxiously for a good five minutes, before the water like mist swirled and the face of

Professor Allard took shape.

"Hello, juniors of Merlin, Medusa, Morgana and Medea. For those of you that don't remember my

name, which I completely understand, it is Professor Allard," he began, taking a good look around at all of

those in the room before continuing.

"Students of Morgana, Medea and Medusa, you will be joining our school for today's magical event;

the four schools riding challenge. As the hosting school, students of Merlin will need to demonstrate their

impeccable level of hospitality of which I know will not be an issue. You will follow the students of Merlin and

proceed to the stadium where we will instruct you further."

As Professor Allard finished his speech the mist swirled once more and the cape, which they had never

seen move before, floated over to the dais and placed itself neatly over the mirror.

The door to the Merlin glowed and the students started to file through in groups. Brianna

meandered through the throng to find students that needed help. As she moved through the crowd she

bumped into a girl with her back turned to her.

"Watch where you're going," the girl scorned and Brianna returned a resentful glare as she realised

that it was Zoe that she had bumped into.

"Oh it's you," she jeered, "Well I don't need any help from you. Go and pester someone else with your

little house on the prairie attitude."

"I didn't come over to help you Zoe," she retorted, "I came over to help people that I consider worth

my time."

Brianna continued wending her way, inflamed by her run in with Zoe. As she looked for people to help,

her mind flitted quickly back to Zoe. She knew that Zoe wasn't an ugly girl, even if she did hold an ugly look,

but she could truly see the change in her features now that she had an up close encounter. Her skin was toned

more so to a pale sort of grey and her hair was lank and hung in thin tendrils. Her eyes were extremely heavy

lidded with deep purple marks that looked like bruises under each eye. Her lips were no longer full but thin,

cracked and taut. It concerned her a little bit and she wondered what could cause such a change. Her brief

moment of concern soon passed as she saw Taylor talking to a group of six girls and four boys. She thought he

might need some help and decided as such to assist him with his group.

"Do you mind if I double up with you on being a guide?" she asked Taylor tentatively, unsure whether

she had used up all her chances on being a good friend to Taylor because of her fruitless attempts with

Damien.

"Of course not," he beamed. Yes, of course not, she echoed. His sentiment towards her had not

faltered, but in a way it did comfort her. She had been so occupied with the dramas surrounding their new

found world and her constantly wavering emotions towards Damien; she had quite forgotten what it was like to have a mutual interest in someone. Maybe he had noticed the change in the relationship between Damien and her and that had led to a relative boost in his confidence and incensed buoyant attitude.

The girls looked quite disappointed that Brianna had intervened and they remained rather subdued if not sullen as they were led to the stadium. Taylor led them to the seats as Brianna hung back to take in the amazing view of the stadium before he; she felt so at home and in love with this part of the school. At the moment it seemed nothing more than a vast green pitch, but she was not fooled. Truesdale had already informed his club that the stadium transformed when all the riders were in the waiting tent so that there was no unfair advantage on any party.

Taylor returned and bought Brianna back from her reverie with a small tap on the back. He steered her to take the group into the tent before exiting back out of the tent. On their continuous procession back and forth Brianna managed to see most of her friends; Kimberley had paired up with Truesdale and Caleb and Michael were seen joking arm in arm. Even Serena and Alleyen, although not a part of the dragon riding club, gave Brianna a joyful wave as they escorted some more of the students to the waiting tent quickly informed her of their excitement to see her ride and win the competition.

She thanked them, but felt the small feeling of sickness jolt higher up her body. The hope that the students of Merlin had for her had clearly not faltered, but she couldn't see how she was any better than the others; especially as so many had now been trained up.

"Would all the students of Merlin involved in the dragon riding challenge make their way directly to the waiting tent so that we may begin the challenge," rang out the voice of Professor Allard.

Brianna was shocked to hear his voice, until her brain kicked in a gear. Of course the teachers would be watching the event; they would want to show that they cared about their students. This only increased her nervous disposition as she thought that some of the most acclaimed people in the Realm world would be judging her.

Taylor gave her a comforting pat on the back and a slight nudge in the right direction and the pair made their way to what Brianna could only see as her doom. At the entrance Taylor held up the cloth like door and beckoned for Brianna to pass through.

She could barely breathe. The room was packed sure with students from the four schools, she had seen the mortal counterpart in Witchcraft Heights, but the number had multiplied as they had fetched the students that resided in the Realm world. She wasn't entirely sure how anyone had the space to move in this tin of sardines.

"Brianna," called out a voice and Brianna turned to see the waving hand of Kimberley beckoning for Brianna to come over. She dodged her way in and amongst the students, making copious apologies as she made her way through.

"I can't believe how packed it is in here," Kimberley exclaimed when Brianna finally reached her best friend, "there has to be at least thirty people in this tiny little room."

The room continued to hum and buzz until a loud voice finally echoed within the tent.

"Welcome one and all," said the heartening voice of Professor Allard, "it is a pleasure to meet to so many new faces and to know that today we have a wonderful selection of talented students who will be competing for the honorary trophy as champion dragon rider.

"This is a competition set to challenge your physical presence with the mystical and intellectual beings as well as presenting your own mental aptitude. As I call out a competitor's name, they will need to present themselves in the stadium and choose the dragon that they wish to ride. Then it is a simple matter of completing the course in the quickest time possible. Be warned however, there may be a few surprises!"

The voice ceased and all of the hopefuls looked at one another. Brianna noticed as she looked around the tent that Zoe was still holding her contemptuous gaze, but she was not standing with her usual group of cronies who were huddled together over the opposite side of the tent. The ill mannered look and pasty skin that she had noticed from the lunchtime had seemed to worsen, for now her skin looked waxen and stuck to her cheek bones. Brianna couldn't understand how one girl could let herself go like that when her

appearance seemed to be of greatest importance at the start of the year.

"Arbituta Swansdale of Medea," called out Professor Allard and a girl that they had never seen before

made her way to the opposite door of the tent that led out to the stadium. Brianna looked behind and noticed

that the tents entrance had vanished; there was no escape.

The tent was deadly silent but they could not hear so much as a peep from the stadium; Brianna

supposed that the same deafening spell had been put in place so that none of the competitors were given an

unfair advantage. The time seemed to tick by so slowly that Brianna started to wonder how long this course

was actually meant to take. She was sure that Truesdale had said below three minutes equated to a good

score, but she felt as if this Miss Swansdale had been taking hours.

"Astintha Fairwater of Morgana," Professor Allard finally called out and another student who Brianna

had never laid eyes on exited for the stadium. The names continued to be called out and one by one student's

from the four schools went out on to the landing platform to choose their best shot for winning the

competition. Her heart nearly stopped as "Kimberley Aldridge of Merlin" was called out. She gave a tight

squeeze on her best friends arm and noiselessly voiced a good luck. All Kimberley could do in response was to

nod once and turn away to the fateful door.

If the atmosphere has been tense previously, knowing that Kimberley was out there made the tension

almost unbearable. She waited in the silence that seemed to surround her, keeping all her fingers and toes

crossed as her best friend rode for her chance to win the ultimate reward.

"Brianna Eastey of Merlin" the magical voice called out. It took Brianna completely by surprise and it

and only a nudge from Caleb made her realise that it was her name being called out over the tannoy.

She walked slowly under the hanging that lifted without a single touch by an enchantment, to a sight

that she had never seen before. The stadium had been transformed so that it was completely unrecognisable.

The stands circled the cavernous floor that was littered with rocks and cracked jetties of steaming lava. Tall poles of fire wound their way up from the ground and rings of different sizes and colours filled the sky. There were two silver rings placed at either end of the stadium on two tiny stands that were no taller than a basketball hoop.

She turned to see what was on the platform that she stood on and saw four cages, with four entirely different dragons waiting for her. She walked over to the cages and started to think about the best beast pacing slightly impatiently behind the four magic cages. She approached them and knew that the best way to decide was by closing her eyes and sensing which dragon would present the greatest degree of loyalty and commitment during this moment in time. It was a trick that Truesdale had taught them during their training sessions; the only problem was that for it to be effective Brianna needed to be completely calm and switch off any sense of worry that wavered on her mind.

She closed her mind and took in a great breath in. Immediately, a heartbeat seemed to call to her. She followed the sound that was calling and only when her footsteps stopped did she decide to open her eyes. She found herself in front of the cage on the far right and immediately sensed that the most loyal dragon of the group was waiting for her.

"Tresor," she called to out to the Royal Arbonian unlocking the cage and then she waited; it was a far better thing to allow the dragon to make the decision to come out of the cage on its own accord.

Boom... boom... boom. The first footfalls of the dragon rang out and seemed to send out an echoing noise across the stadium. Brianna tried to keep her breathing light and slow as she willed herself to stay in control of whatever came out of the cage.

The audience around her gasped as the beast finally made its debut; a commentator in the stands said something but Brianna had found her sense of hearing muted. All she could concentrate on was the thirty-foot tall Royal Arbonian dragon facing her with its piercing yellow eyes. One wrong move on Brianna's part and the beast, which was well renowned for its doubtful nature, would turn her into ash.

It didn't flinch and after what was only a couple of seconds, but seemed like an eternity in Brianna's mind, she walked up purposefully and climbed onto the great Royal Arbonian. She kicked her heel against the beast's sensitive scales and it responded immediately.

She soared high into the air and the crowd made some unrecognisable call; all that Brianna knew was that atop this beast in mid-air she finally felt a sense of relief. Her mind had miraculously cleared and she was no longer scared; she was back in control.

Spying the first ring to fly through she pushed on the reins and the dragon dived for the ground. She completed a spiralling dart towards the ring, remembering how Truesdale had stated that flashy moves gave points as well as reducing flight time for the dragon.

They skimmed just above the ground and rocketed straight into the air as the next ring lay above their heads. Climbing steeply Brianna heard a noise approaching from behind and tugged for a right hand move in the nick of time. A Jetstream of boiling lava had erupted straight for the tail of the dragon and shot straight past their heads as they continued to climb.

As they burst through the top ring she completed a 270-degree turn and rode along the tops of the stadium, gliding in and out of the poles that stood floating in mid-air. As she darted in and out she could feel a small current of energy and a rise in temperature but fortunately avoided every single one along the way.

Then came the first tricky part of the assault course; she could see one of the tiny gold rings perched on a small platform at the one of the ends of the stadium and knew that she needed to retrieve that ring before the other one would appear. They dived for the ring, but all the while Brianna felt cautious as it hung there twinkling innocently up at her.

A sudden movement up as a water sprite created a sudden barrier between them and their prize. Tresor shrieked and faltered as the fear of water took over its control. Brianna shut her eyes and rubbed the back of the dragon to calm its nerves. Her magic touch seemed to do the trick and she guided the creature over the mounting wall of water. The water sprites was perched on the top of the wall of water and looked up as Brianna sailed over its barrier. She shot a few sparks of clinging fire which caused the sprite to shriek as the flames stuck fast to the translucent face.

The end was in sight and Brianna made the final speedy dash towards the final golden hoop, pulling on the reins to open the dragon's mouth by the slightest touch. Tresor snatched the ring in its mouth and was only then that the roar of crowd was audible. She steered the steed back down to the landing platform and looked up to the erupting stadiums. Students were loudly applauding and stamping their feet; she had never seen such an acknowledgement and couldn't quite understand why she was receiving such a tumultuous applause.

Professor Llewellyn was there to greet Brianna and lead her out of the stadium. Instead of leading her back to the waiting chamber, he took her to another door, which opened onto more rounds of applause and a huge embrace. It was Kimberley; greeting her and congratulating her.

"You were brilliant," Kimberley cried excitedly, taking Brianna's hands and jumping up and down.

"You saw?" Brianna responded, still somewhat confused by the continued overly positive response that she was receiving.

"Yeah, and we were so lucky to see it as well. You flew incredibly," Kimberley answered. As Brianna looked further than Kimberley she noticed the room held panoramic views of the stadium and its audience.

Other people started to come over and congratulate her and Truesdale claimed how rare it was to see someone fly the way she did.

"You are the quickest flier by far," he informed Brianna. "Your time should be announced after the last flier."

"That was Caleb," she said, informing Kimberley more than anyone else that their friend was the final person to fly in the challenge.

294

The time seemed to fly by in comparison to the excruciating wait as she had endured to take on the challenge and all too soon an announcement was made loud and clear within the new chamber where the completed finalists stood looking out onto the stadium and its audience.

"Could all competitors please make their way to the landing platform; all competitors to make their way to the landing platform, Thank you."

Kimberley took Brianna's hand in her own and the two best friends walked out together to the roaring crowd. Professor Allard and Professor Llewellyn were waiting for them by a podium that had been erected since the last dragon rider had taken a stab at the course. He took a small step to shadow above the students and spoke into a circle like contraption that enhanced the volume of his voice.

"Professors," he primarily acknowledged, "riders and students of Medusa, Morgana, Medea and Merlin. We have finally reached the end of the dragon challenge. It has been truly a remarkable event with some spectacular displays of dragon commandeering.

"Many of you have displayed the potential to be talented riders and will do credit to your school. A result in under four minutes is something of a remarkable feat and should be notably recognised; Caleb Williams, Taylor Presley, Jesse Garon, Zoe Harper, Wesley Stanton, Kimberley Aldridge and Kenna Grindel."

A round of applause flowed around the stadium to recognise the achievements of the high achieving students and Brianna gave a warm smile and enthusiastic round of applause in the direction of all her friends. She wasn't too abashed, as she knew how amazing they had been during their practice drills.

"But our attention should be focused on one particular person; a person who managed to completely change the way in which dragon riding is perceived. This rider has not only demonstrated a divine level of excellence in their riding, but also demonstrated a true understanding and unity with the dragon itself; this is a rare gift and a true wonder to witness.

"I therefore wish to congratulate Miss Brianna Eastey, not only on winning the dragon challenge in an outstanding time of 1 minute 53 seconds but on winning the top prize that can be awarded in this challenge; a dragon from the mountains. In the time since the dragon riding challenge commenced between the four

schools only two previous riders have won this prestigious prize."

A great 'oooohh' shivered around the stadium and Brianna could barely register the incredible news.

The highest acclaim known to the magical community was to be awarded to her; she had a gift and for her

talent she was to be presented with one of the greatest prizes.

"Members of the audience, you are about to witness a remarkable display. A display where dragon and

rider meet for the first time," Professor Allard declared, "where two parts become a whole. Brianna, all I need

you to do is step up and take a stand on the podium."

She obliged and went on the podium.

"Close your eyes and let your mind wander. By freeing it of all thoughts and feelings we will be able to

draw the dragon towards you. One will answer your calling, drawn to your aura and talents as a dragon rider.

In a short matter of time we shall see it flying up over the hills and down towards us all."

A hushed silence fell over the stadium as everyone waited with baited breath. Brianna strained her

ears to hear for some sign of an approaching dragon; maybe a beating of the wind as its wings beat closer to

the stadium or a powerful blast of fire coursing over the tops of the stands. People started fidgeting in their

seats as they continued to wait and for a shadow of a moment Brianna worried that her ability as a dragon

rider did not stretch to the gift of receiving a dragon of her own.

Suddenly, Brianna saw a black dot fly over the darkening sky. It sped past the purple and red sky,

getting closer and closer to the stadium. When it was no more than a quarter of a mile away Brianna could

spot two things either side of the dot moving up and down. The air seemed to whistle as it became even closer

until Brianna could most definitely identify the dot to be that of a dragon.

It swooped down towards the stadium ground as the crowd began cheering and clapping in

excitement. It roared out loud as it circled lower and lower before it settled itself on the landing platform. The

only thing that Brianna could think was that this dragon was the most beautiful creature that she had ever laid eyes on. It had a smooth golden head where the scales looked like glistening golden discs. Its wings spread

out two metres each way before they nestled closely in at it sides. The yellow underbelly glistened in a

glittering gold shimmer. Every claw was perfectly shaped and pointed, scratching lightly on the platform. Its

eyes were onyx but sparkled with hints of amber that made it seem a warm creature rather that than the

unpredictable and rather cold quality that the dragon usually possessed.

It looked intently towards Brianna, towards its new master. It stood proudly in the stadium as she took

her first tentative steps to her dragon. She took steps around the dragon and started to look at the dragon

from every single possible angle. Professor Allard stepped down from the podium to join Brianna whilst

Professor Llewellyn went to usher the other dragons away from the landing platform so as not to frighten the

beast.

"What shall you name this fine dragon?" said Professor Allard quietly.

She stood there, feeling suddenly inadequate. She couldn't think of any name that could suit the

dragon; it made her feel unsurpassable to own such a magnificent beast.

"Well, I suppose it could be an idea to give you some time."

"Professor's, witches and wizards, I would like you all to now make your way up to the dining hall

where a feast will now be held," he called out through the sound sonorous, "students of Merlin, could you

kindly escort the students from the other three schools up to the dining hall and make sure that they are well

catered and cared for. Thank you one and all for a truly amazing afternoon."

The crowds started to make their slow procession up to the school. There was a persistent chatter as

the students felt at ease to discuss the on goings of the event. Now that they were far away from any fire-

breathing beasts, the tension of being burnt to a crisp had subsided and they were busily discussing all the

heart stopping moments that occurred that afternoon.

Brianna walked up with Kimberley and Taylor; at the back of the crowd. Although she had been the

main victor she did not want to be the centre of attention and hoped that the students would be more absorbed with their own discussions than able to identify the person that was the centre point of everyone's conversation. She was about to ask Taylor a bit more about his ride before she noticed Damien up ahead. She hadn't considered the possibility that he would have gone to watch the tournament since he stopped turning up to training. As she looked up towards Damien two girls that she didn't recognise and one girl with lank black hair that she most definitely recognised rudely pushed her.

Zoe and two other girls that she supposed attended Medusa from the realm world walked arrogantly in front of Brianna.

"They consider themselves to be so high and mighty," one of the girls said loudly enough so that Brianna, Kimberly and Taylor could hear them.

"Yes," said another, "those cocky members of Merlin. They believe themselves to be talented beyond the likes of any others. Well they shall never understand how very wrong they are. One day it shall be Medusa that produces the most renowned and most accomplished witches. We shall rid of the hideous riff raff that befouls our world."

"Should we not," one of the girls looked round cautiously for the first time, "we shall seek out to awaken the dark power. If the prophecy is true we shall see the times of change, the pieces are in place. It is now a simple matter of turning the cogs of fate. I agree, the riff raff shall be removed from out world."

"It will not be so much of cleansing process, more of a changing of the times and ruling of the Realm World. Long live Medusa; tenenbrarum et erit." The girls placed their hands to their temple at the same point before going to join Zoe who had sauntered up ahead. It seemed, to Brianna, that Zoe was the leader of the group; such as she had been at the start of the year at Witchcraft heights.

Zoe looked around and smirked wickedly in Brianna's direction, but Brianna was not entirely sure if she knew Brianna had heard the conversation or whether it was a simple case of her constant cruelty. The other two girls walked ahead of Zoe, intent on moving to a point and stopping as they reached Damien. For some strange reason they stopped and began talking into his ears. Unlike their proclamations of earlier they

chose to speak quietly to Damien so that all others were deaf to anything that they had to say.

She rather hoped that he would brush them away. However, he seemed interested in what they had to

say and nodded in response as well as making a few quiet comments in return. They carried on up to the

school and Brianna was left with a worrying feeling settling in the pit of her stomach. There were a couple of

questionable matters that Brianna felt needed answering. It was imperative to decode the Medusa witches

conversation and discover the motive behind their interest with Damien.

Chapter 18

Nothing compared to him, she thought to herself. For the next few days Brianna awoke with the same elated feeling as she reminded herself of her triumph. It was almost an unbelievable concept that she had managed to control a dragon around a course in the quickest time, but had also done it so well that she was credited with the highest award.

The fact that she had her own dragon, a dragon that was intrinsically linked to her was a matter that she was still trying to become accustomed to. In a world where dragons ruled the skies and were not fragments of imagination, Brianna felt a true sense of awe at the idea of her owing such a precious jewel. She sat in the school library for days on end, trying to locate the most suitable name to bestow on her most prized treasure.

It had to mean something and reflect how she felt about the new joy in her life. On the fifth evening of her search, after a good hour of strenuous trawling through a mountain of books, she had come across the idea of a name that signified a new era as she started a life with her new pet. To her, the dragon symbolised the dawn of a new life, her life as a witch in the Realm world.

As she searched through the 'Guide to dragons and their beauty' for a word that would suitably represent those feelings she had come across the word aura; the word to symbolise a beautiful glow that surrounds items of beauty and power. As a consequence Brianna decided on the name Aureus. This befitted the golden scales on its back which seemed to reflect golden beams in the bright sunlight.

Since the day of the challenge the dragon had been kept in the school enclosure. Professor Llewellyn informed her that the dragon would return to the caves on the coast from time to time, but for now it would stay in close vicinity to learn more about its master. She visited it every day to become accustomed to the dragon and make a true connection between dragon and master. Now that she had a name for her dragon, she could feel the connection growing stronger between the two of them. She knew that it was another responsibility, but it was worth every ounce of her time and effort. Aureus filled her heart with joy and she knew that no greater prize could be given in the Realm world.

*

She had been escorted by older students to the dragon enclosure every day as first years weren't allowed to visit the enclosure without an older student or Professor present. She could see the logic in this, but she could not help but think that the older students simply wanted to have a look at the dragon for themselves.

Today, when she took her usual route to the dragon enclosure, Ambertia escorted her. Ambertia was a second year student in the dragon-riding club. She was much attuned to the aesthetic elements of dragon riding and once, when Brianna had watched her in action, she had been able to witness the beautiful sky flute turns.

She walked up silently for a long while, passing through the corridors that led to the northern end of the school. She walked by the Viridian Flos expecting to see nothing but the blue heavenly glow that glinted through a crack in the door, but to her surprise she was met by none other than Damien. He sidled past her in an awkward fashion and carried on to the further depths of the school. It jogged in her memory from the previous occasion when she had seen him talking to the students of Medusa and some of the words that Medusa had said resounded in her mind.

She looked at Ambertia and a notion came to mind.

"Ambertia," she said to grab the second year's attention, "I don't suppose you know much about these words: tenenbrarum et erit"

"No, I'm sorry. It sounds like a foreign sort of language, or an unknown spell. Who spoke those words?"

"I don't know who they were exactly, but I believe that they were from the school of Medusa. They were explaining how the times would change and I think they stated something about the rule of Medusa reigning with accomplished and talented witches."

"Well that doesn't surprise me, those cocky students," Ambertia sneered, "it is a well-known fact that the school of Medusa produces some of the most stuck up students of the four schools. They believe that they have been wronged for too long and most of them grow to despise the students from other schools."

"But why exactly? Why are they so different from the students of Medea, Morgana and Merlin?"

"How much do you know of the history of our realm world?"

"A little," she responded a bit sheepishly, wishing she had the deep understanding that the students of the realm world had regarding their history of past witches and wizards.

"Well, throughout the ages, the four schools in the area of Salem have turned out thousands of newly qualified witches and wizards. Some have gone rather unnoticed; some have gone to change the world in which we live in. We cannot link a school to the decisions made by the students after they have left, but through strange coincidence or planned device, Medusa have seemed to turn out more dark witches and wizards than any of the other three schools. In fact, the witches of Medusa have been some of the most notoriously evil witches throughout the course of history.

"They feel, for some strange reason that they have been persecuted and humiliated by others in the witching community. In the realm world many ancestral lines can be traced back and has often been found that the family will attend the same school as those before them. For example, all of my ancestors have attended Merlin.

"For some of the families in Medusa, their families were involved in some of the most awful tales in magical history. I'm sure that you are aware of the massacres of Salem?"

"Yes."

"Well it is rumoured that the descendants of those believe they were wronged, which is of course an absurdity. They believe that Medusa had the correct idea on how the realm world should be ruled and they attempted to replicate the evil fate that once occurred. The idea that those students want to be superior to others, seems to show an echo of the old ideals from the events of 1692 and the first great battle of good

versus evil.

"I'm amazed that those students would say such a thing. I reckon that they were simply bitter at a

member of Merlin receiving the ultimate prize."

Brianna milled the conversation in her mind, drinking in the information that Ambertia had provided.

She didn't want to discuss the interest that the Medusa witches had with Damien, for she had no idea herself.

She did not wish to arouse question or speculation when she couldn't fathom an interest in a student from

another school for herself. She planted a seed of remembrance in her mind as she thought that Zoe had

shown a hungry interest in Madison and now Damien.

Ambertia and Brianna reached the dragon enclosure and could already hear the growling and jets of

fire issuing from the dragons that resided in the school. The heat started to rise as they stepped in and closed

the titanium railing behind them.

"Ambertia," said Brianna "is there such a thing as a dark power?"

She had felt reluctant to discuss this particular matter, but as her book had provided no revelation to

the conversation, she deemed it important to find as much as she could from those that resided in the Realm

World.

"Where did you hear about such thing?" she retorted, whipping Brianna out of sight and out of the

audible range of any other persons. She seemed to have a panic in her face.

"I heard it almost on the wind; I think one of the other students spoke about it when I was walking

back from the dragon challenge. I didn't fully understand what was meant by it."

"It is not a thing that we discuss," she replied almost fearfully, "I am afraid I cannot provide you with

any answers other than to not go asking about it. It fights against the natural course of magic in his world.

There are tales that say if you so much as speak of it could set the wheels in motion that could bring about its return. I will not be one to bring that about and I would suggest that you should not entice matters that you do not fully understand."

Ambertia fell quiet and Brianna thought it best to call out for Aureus. She did not call out for her dragon, she merely focused on her heart and the intuitive link that she knew existed between the two of them. The palpitation sounded louder and louder until she realised that it was not her heartbeat that she could hear, but the huge heartbeat of her dragon. She looked to her right and saw Aureus looking towards her with adoration. She had been informed by Landon the previous day that a dragon would come to its master whenever it called for it, no matter how far away the rider would be from the dragon. The link that the dragon had to its rider was a true treasure, a bond like no other and one that ran deeply.

She didn't spend any faltering time gaining her dragons trust, she had been told and knew that there was an unconditional level of love between her and her beautiful golden trophy. She had spent a couple of days getting a collar onto Aureus and making sure that the claws were well kept. Today she wanted to take Aureus on a small walk around the enclosure; under her control.

She gathered up a rope that hung on one of the poles and looped it through the link on Aureus' chain. Lightly she pulled Aureus around, not wanting to apply too much force, in case she seemed to commandeering or controlling.

She managed to take four laps of the enclosure. Whether out of fear or respect, the other dragons made a wide berth whenever Aureus approached. She stopped on the fifth lap as the dragon swished its mighty tail. It closed in around Brianna, but not forcefully. Instead it drew her in softly and held on to her, almost protecting her master.

"When will you leave me?" she whispered to Aureus.

The dragon looked doe eyed into its master's eyes and Brianna could almost sense the reluctance that was held as it knew it would have to return to the cave at some point. She led her dragon back to its sleeping quarters, gave it a loving stroke against its long neck and removed the chain from the loop in the choker.

Ambertia came and found Brianna soon after and the two of them returned back to the main part of the school. Ambertia headed towards the front entrance of the school and Brianna went to the transporting chamber. Kimberley was waiting for her best friend, much as she had done for the rest of the week. She passed over her bag and Brianna rummaged through its contents to locate her beloved 'Book Estas Orientem Magia Animabus'. She found it and flicked through to see if any further detail had been added since her conversation with Ambertia. On finding no such luck she pushed the door open and headed back into the mortal world and reluctantly away from her new found love.

*

Things had seemed to settle in the Realm World; at last they were keeping up to speed with their workload in both worlds. Her understanding of the spells she had been taught thus far were beginning to make some sense. She was a confident member of the dragon riding club and if truth be told she was something of a celebrity among the other riders. People were in awe that a student from the mortal world had won a dragon and asked for riding tips to better their own performance. Madison, although still a bit baffled after her run in with Professor Allard, was still maintaining a positive manner with Brianna in the mortal world and they were holding a lucid friendship. She had finally come to terms with the negligence of Damien and his cold nature towards her. She had allowed herself to spend more time with Taylor and did so without feeling as much guilt over the whole situation.

Taylor and her would often go to training together and sit with one another in the common room. She had learnt an awful lot about the boy from St. Augustine during their time together. Taylor was born into a family of naval officers. He had lived most of his life by the sea and they had chosen to live in Salem when his dad received a generous donation, which allowed him to lead an early retirement. He greatly enjoyed his time at sea, but the comforts of home and being grounded to one spot was also a great joy.

Taylor had found that the oddities that occurred before he found out his secret emulated from him rather than situations that occurred around him. He seemed to set off sparks whenever he felt a strong emotion and the natural elements would be affected to a greater degree the closer he was to a certain element when he had a strong emotion. One time he recalled how mini whirlpools formed in his bathtub when the water was still. He found his greatest draw of power from the water, which probably explained the link with the naval force.

He had a younger brother called Quentin and Taylor had tried to identify any potential signs that he possessed the magical being inside. As yet, he had not been able to determine anything, but hoped beyond hope that his brother would be able to share this experience with him.

On this particular Friday, one week before the Easter half term, Brianna and Taylor were busily discussing their favourite spell whilst Kimberley and Truesdale walked the grounds at the front of the school. The front of the school led onto a thick block of woodland, which hid the school from the rest of the world. There were some beautiful trail walks that could be taken and on a day like today, when the sun was warming the spring air and the clouds were scarce in the sky, it was rather a romantic affair to be had.

They had finished a discussion over the pros and cons of the disillusionment charm, when Kimberley walked in. Taylor got up and left the two girls to have a little gossip, at which point Brianna noticed Michael and Caleb sitting on the other side of the common room. Caleb was talking to Michael, whilst looking over his shoulder as if checking to not be overheard. Brianna looked couldn't help but notice the uncomfortable body language that Michael exhumed as he sat their fidgeting in his seat. Both Caleb and Michael possessed this same disposition and it was always in the same situation, when they were talking to one another about a matter that was an awkward topic.

"Caleb," Brianna called out loudly across the common room, "do you mind coming over here for a moment?"

Caleb obliged and made his way over swiftly, giving a short nod to Michael as he made his way across.

"Is everything alright? I couldn't help but notice that Michael seems a bit on the edge. I do hope I don't seem intrusive, I am sorry."

"No, no," he brushed away a hand rather dismissively, "everything is fine." She found it rather odd that two people could be so alike in their mannerisms without themselves even realising it. Neither were particularly good at hiding the fact that they knew something and both of them were awful at keeping secrets. His falsetto and attempt to speak lightly did nothing more than spur her first assumption; that he was in fact hiding something.

"Caleb," she called out all the louder, "what is it? Don't start to shut me out, we are friends after all. Maybe it is a matter that I can help you out with."

"Well I don't know if he has definitely gone," Michael said in a faltering voice, as he stood up and went to join the rest of the group.

"Whom are you talking about?"

"Well, it was only something he said in passing," Michael continued almost talking to him and Caleb, "He had that notebook of his and he said that he has finally found out how to get there."

"Michael, tell me what is going on!"

"It's Damien… he's been completing more research in the library and now he wants to find out more information on his own terms."

"He's gone to the village!" she exclaimed, the blood rushing from her face to leave a pallid colour, as she came to the slow realisation, "but what if he gets caught? What if he tells a Professor that we have been there too?

"We have to go and get him and make him see sense."

They sat there mulling over their own thoughts for a couple of minutes. Brianna could see each member of the group trying to come up with some sort of solution. It was Caleb that decided to voice his opinion first.

"But how are we going to get there?" questioned Caleb, "if we all go, it will increase our chances of getting caught. Is it really up to us to interfere with the on goings of someone that couldn't care less about us? I think we should leave him to it."

"I'm going," said Brianna immediately, "it's my fault he's gone on his own, I sparked the interest in going further afield."

"I'll come with you," chipped in Kimberley "you boys should stay her in case he comes back. We can see if Truesdale can drop us into the village, he's still in school at the moment."

Brianna looked surprisingly in Kimberley's direction. As a person that had shown nothing but dislike towards Damien, she was certainly the last in the group that Brianna thought would help out. With a thankful smile, she gave Kimberley a squeeze on the shoulder.

"There is no way that two are going on a wild goose chase after Damien," chirped in Michael, "We will all go together, whether you like it or not, he was our best friend at one point. Plus we can't just leave two girls to fend for themselves; we don't know what Damien is planning on doing."

"Don't be so silly, it's not as if he is dangerous! I'm with Kimberley," Brianna stated, "if too many of us go down there we could draw far too much attention to ourselves. We know the area pretty well now and I'm sure Truesdale will be more than willing to give us some help, he would probably say that you two won't be allowed to come along anyway."

Michael snorted to show he truly doubted this. She turned without another word and Kimberley followed quickly in her wake. She almost believed for a moment that the boys' had succumbed to her reasoning as they made it all the way to the front door of Merlin.

That was when the way was barred as they had run around in a loop and bought in certain reinforcement. Taylor stood there with his arms folded and Brianna braced herself for an even tougher argument.

"Where do you think you're going?" Taylor asked in an interrogative manner. "Taylor...," Brianna began weakly.

"Save it," he cut her short, "are you completely mad?! Caleb and Michael have just told me the whole story and you think that it's wise to go gallivanting around the village in search of someone who has decided that it's okay to wander wherever he wishes?"

"Taylor, it's not like that," she answered back and for some strange reason there seemed to be an almost pleading tone to her voice. "Damien became interested in Salem because of me; he is off by himself because of me. What if he does get caught by the Professors this time?"

"It's not your responsibility Brianna," he responded sharply, "you can't risk your future because of him."

She huffed in frustration; she didn't even understand it herself. She couldn't explain why she was so adamant to look after Damien all the time, but she did. No matter how he treated her and no matter how their friendship currently stood she couldn't leave him alone. Damien had become interested in his ancestry and she had given him more the fuel that led to greater avenues to explore, therefore it was her fault that he wanted to find out more about where he truly came from.

"The graveyard," she said softly.

"What?" Taylor looked confused as Brianna stated the soft three syllables.

"Damien has gone to the graveyard," she expanded her phrase somewhat and as she did it made complete sense. When they had gone to the graveyard before, Damien had shown such a hungry interest in looking for something, one of the tombstones perhaps? To identify which line of witches and wizards he descended from?

Brianna had only one previous conversation regarding Damien's family history, but now she thought about him clearly for what seemed like the first time, Brianna realised that he had never known his home life or where he had come from. Maybe he was looking for answers, but Brianna was unsure as to what purpose that might be.

"We have to go and find him," she said, with a pleading look directly into Taylor's eyes, "when I know where he is I will never think about him again."

She emphasised every part of her sentence, knowing that proclaiming a finality with Damien that would help her push forward in her relationship with Taylor.

"Okay," Taylor responded, just as Brianna knew he would, "but we are still coming with you. I can't let you go without me."

It seemed that they had met a bridge of agreement. The meeting in the middle was the only resolve that Brianna would find and fighting the conversation anymore would just waste more of their time.

"Okay, Kimberley can you see if Truesdale is still around to give us a lift down in his Accipegus carter?"

Kimberley was gone for no longer than five minutes before she returned hand in hand with Truesdale. Kimberley nodded to show that Truesdale agreed to take them down and the five of them headed out towards the front entrance where the Accipegus carter was standing.

After the short trip in the Accipegus carter, passing the beautiful country scenery. Brianna and the rest of the group were dropped off in the village square. Kimberley pecked Truesdale on the cheek and Truesdale, with a slightly questionable look left the group in the middle of the square.

'You didn't tell him?" Brianna said, "How did you persuade him to drop us off?"

"I said we had a little school project and that we had been given permission by Professor Merrydew to visit the Salem records hall," she retorted slyly, "I said that he can pick us up in a couple of hours."

"Kimberley!" exclaimed Brianna in a shocked tone, "what if we are not back in a couple of hours?!"

"Well, we will have to be," she stated simply, "at least it gives you a time limit. If we don't find Damien in that time we shall simply have to leave and get back to Truesdale. It's non-negotiable Brianna"

They went into the Salem records hall, just in case Damien had made the sensible choice to look through records of his ancestral lineage rather than venturing into the eerie graveyard.

They walked through the echoing hall, but after a good ten minutes of searching the empty chambers and corridors it was evident that Damien was not in here. Brianna knew where they would have to look and it was not somewhere that she wanted to walk to.

Brianna rounded up the rest of the group and led the way back out of the Salem records hall. They jogged up the hill that led to the edge of town and closer to the line of trees that bordered the graveyard. They fought their way through the tangled branches and entered the graveyard.

For Brianna, it felt as eerie as ever, even in the warmer spring air. The warmth never entered this place and as Brianna scanned her eyes across the grave stones and larger memorials that littered the area. As she looked to all the corners of the memorial she thought she spied movement; she believed it was of about the same height as Damien but from a distance she could not be indefinitely sure. She most definitely saw movement; of that she was sure. It wasn't rushing so whatever or whoever it was, they had not realised that there were strangers in their midst.

Brianna approached cautiously, deciding which way was best to approach the moving figure. She took a few more steps forward before realising that she was walking towards the memorial of her very own ancestor; the impressive memorial that commemorated the events of 1692. Although she hated the place, she was most grateful that the dim and fading light allowed her to be a pressing shadow towards her target. As she took the next two steps she saw a lighted wand tip and a face became apparent by the light; it was Damien. He looked deep in thought and Brianna thought it wise to walk away from his line of sight.

She took one more step and then Damien's face vanished in a wave of thick sparkling blackness. She panicked, frantically looking around for the face of her lost friend and wondering what this overwhelming and enchanted darkness was. Her eyes continued to focus intently on the same spot until she registered some outlines atop the mass of blackness and as her eyes adjusted she realised that she could see hoods. The

mass had appeared out of nowhere, cloaking Damien from the view of anyone else.

The black was a mass of cloaked figures, their cloaks glittered and as her eyes managed to focus on the

vision before an eerie orange glow emulated from the middle of the huddle. The shuffling of the cloaks against

the grassy floor could be heard and what sounded like an undetectable language was spoken. The voices were

deep and unrecognisable, until one voiced 'ata begulian historia de famiia' and Brianna realised that the voice

was that of Damien's. The orange glow moved and made contact with the memorial and the sound of moving

stone scraped against the stone floor on which the memorial had been erected. At this point the black wall

seemed to engulf Damien and the memorial and she had no opportunity to espy what had just occurred.

She heard fast footsteps behind her and quickly reached out an arm to stop the approaching person.

"What is happening?" whispered Taylor in her ear.

"I don't know, but get the others out of here," she instructed him.

"No, you're coming as well," he said as he grabbed her arm. She shrugged him away and pointed her

wand directly at his chest.

"I will make all our presences known if you do not follow instruction," Brianna stated looking straight

into his eyes, "I will not approach them, but I will not let my friends be seen. Go."

He looked painfully at her, but succumbed by her as he always was, he did as she asked and left her

side. She felt stronger and now that she knew her friends were safe she moved closer to the ominous crowd.

"Accipere eum ad eam," said one of the voices and a murmuring of agreement rang out. It had an

awful sense of clicking approval about it and it sent a shiver of fear running down Brianna's spine. She went to

take another step forward, but at that point a sweeping black, glittering dust seemed to consume all of the

surrounding area.

Brianna could hear the shuffling of cloaks move around in a twister like fashion and she tried to make her way blindly in the darkness. She had to save Damien, but the darkness was like a fog and tar combined, restricting her ability to do anything but struggle in the absolute darkness.

She swiped blindly in the darkness to find out where Damien had gone, clawing and panicking in the deep abyss. She took a sudden sweep to the left which was swiftly followed by fiery orange jets shot out from the middle of the black mass.

"Damien!" she exclaimed, panic struck as she could not work out what was happening before her. In response she heard the shuffling speed up and begin to whirl around and around in a crescendo. She saw the black mist disappear and the cloaked people rounded to face her.

As they dispersed from the memorial their seemed to glow a faintish green light, different to anything she had yet seen thus far. It seemed to emulate from the memorial itself where one solitary person still lingered by its' stonewalls. Brianna could have sworn that it was Damien; the person was of the same height and unlike the others in the memorium, the head was visible. The person brushed against the wall, turned to see who had called out his name and shook his head. She hadn't realised that she had made an instinctive advance in his direction, but at the shake of his head she felt as if she had slammed into a glass wall, stopping her in her tracks. The face of the person glowed ever so faintly as they lined themselves to the green light and purposefully they walked into the memorial, but she had no chance to look at what occurred after the person set foot into the memorial as her brain kicked in and registered the fact that nearly fifteen unknown people were chasing after her, their cloaks whipping loudly behind them.

They rose into the air, like black winged demons rising high above the headstones below and then they started their descent. Brianna turned and sprinted in the direction of the line of thick trees, when suddenly she felt heat brush past her cheek and scorch her face. She chanced a look back and spied the figures shooting spells out from the tip of their wands. She looked forward once more to see the way barred by a couple more cloaked figures, which made her change her course, jumping over the gravestones and scrabbling back up to another higher point.

She used her wand and was instinctively able to send a few blue balls towards the course of her pursuers. All the while she prayed for a way to escape this trap as they managed to speed up, flying in the air by some freak of nature. She knew that people, witch or mortal could not fly, yet here they were defying all sense of reality.

They started encircling Brianna, trapping her on top of the mound where she had positioned herself. She thought despairingly of a way to escape this catastrophic nightmare, thinking whether one of the students in the village would come to the rescue. Maybe Truesdale, Blutain or Landon could help them out. Landon...

A thought sparked in her mind of a conversation that she had with Landon not so long ago; it was a conversation that might just help her out of this awful predicament. How could have taken so long!

Aureus, she thought to herself. Aureus if you can hear me, please come to my rescue.

She opened her eyes but could see only cloaks edging their way forward. They were whispering amongst one another; their faces hidden beneath their black hoods. She continued to scan the skies and then she noticed movement high in the sky. It moved swiftly and started to lower itself, but the cloaks were now towering high above her and blocked any further view of her descending dragon.

"What do we have here?" called out one of them.

"A spy," said another, "one who thinks that they can find out the secrets of the Bituta witches. We do not allow for onlookers to fall through unnoticed."

Brianna thought it would be wise to remain silent; any response could provoke them and she didn't know how truly dangerous they were.

"Who are you?" the cloaked voice said in the middle, something of the voice sounded familiar. It sounded like a girl, but had been altered somehow. Brianna tried to place it while she remained in silence.

"Answer me!" the voice demanded as she bought a hand fast and sweeping, striking Brianna across the face. It stung where a mark had been left but her ears were deafened by another reason altogether.

Aureus had reached the Memorium and was now flying directly towards its master. It held itself in mid-air and flapped its wings in the direction of those trapping Brianna. The current sent from the wings caused all of the cloaked people fall to the ground and Brianna took her chance to jump over the people and climb onto the back of the dragon.

As she jumped over the fallen figures she noticed one of the hoods had fallen away when they had been knocked to the floor. It was a face that she had seen before; it was one of the witches that had attached herself to Zoe that day after the dragon riding challenge. The witch had a shocked look about her as she looked into the eyes of Brianna, but Brianna knew it best not to stop.

She kicked Aureus to go and the dragon took flight. The cloaks rose once more and chased Brianna, but they had no chance against the force of a dragon's wing. Aureus made huge strides away from the group and sailed over the line of trees and finally away from danger.

She directed him into the village square and dropped down in front of the Salem records hall. As she settled him lightly onto the cobbled street, he growled ever so lightly. To Brianna it was a growl to suggest it was pleased to see its master safe of its accord.

"Brianna!" shouted out a voice. Brianna turned to see Kimberley sprinting across the grassed courtyard with relief spread clearly across her face.

She gave Aureus a pat to thank him and told him to return back to the enclosure as the rest of the group run up behind her with Truesdale in their wake.

"We're so relieved that you're safe!" she continued, grabbing a hold of Brianna and pulling her in close. "And… I'm so sorry. Taylor told us that you were just behind us, but when we reached the other side of the trees we looked back to see that you weren't there. I tried to go back in, but their seemed to be some sort of repellent spells that stopped me from getting back in. Caleb and Michael decided that it would be good to go back to the village and find Truesdale to see if he would know what to do.

"We found Truesdale and were walking out of his home when Taylor spotted the dragon in the sky. That's when we thought to follow its direction and ran towards the square."

She looked around to the rest of the group; Caleb and Michael looked warn out but happy to see Brianna safe and sound. Then she saw Taylor and went over to him by some automatic fashion; he looked absolutely distraught.

She cupped his head in her hand, before it may have seemed strange, but for once it seemed natural. "I'm okay," she said soothingly.

"I'm sorry, I'm so sorry," he kept repeating over and over. It took him a good minute before he realised she was holding onto him and looked shocked but it most certainly calmed him. She gave him a satisfying smile and the spark that had been there all along ignited. She had liked Damien, but the attraction had been based on mystery. Here she felt a content sense of attraction and a warm beautiful feeling, bought about by a moment of terror.

"I will never let you go again," Taylor said with sorrow and a deep meaning. "I should never have let you go alone in the first place, but it was awful when we couldn't go back. What happened in there?"

"Yes, please do tell us," Kimberley interjected, bringing Taylor and Brianna out of their little moment, "but maybe we should make our way back up to the school. I think our time is running out before the portal closes."

Truesdale led the way to his Accipegus carter and as he took the students back up to the school Brianna retold the scary tale of the cloaked figures. They were rather tired, so she only told them the basic details, knowing that she would have to go over some of the more imperative questions another time. Her main concern at the moment was the whereabouts of Damien, hoping that he would turn up tomorrow, as she was sure that they would see him tomorrow walking around the school.

Chapter 19

Brianna woke up the next morning after a tormented sleep. She had suffered a night filled with black cloaks, being trapped and the face of the girl that she had seen on the day of the dragon challenge. She went to sit with Gretchen as she made poached eggs for breakfast, smelling in the fumes of the bacon that was to accompany the poached eggs.

"Is everything okay?" her mother asked her with worry. A poor night's sleep was clearly showing on her face so Brianna tried to save a lost cause in as light fashion as possible.

"Yeah of course mom," she said with a false smile.

"Maybe at the weekend you could do with a couple more hours sleep?"

"I will do mom," she said with a smile. Her mom was a person that always tried to make things better, she was very caring and Brianna still after all this time felt guilty that she couldn't confide with her mom about what was truly worrying her.

She made her way to school, hoping that the knot in her stomach would loosen, but as she stepped into her science lesson she found no solace. Brianna had walked into the classroom with the sound belief that Damien would be there, looking sullenly in her direction as she stepped through the door. It would be okay for him not to talk to them, the days of their friendship was clearly not what it once was. All she wanted to know was that the disappearing act was something more innocent than what she first believed. She had abandoned him, believing he would return and now he was gone. She proceeded to look among the rows, doubting her first sighting of the individuals in the room. It seemed almost pointless to look so rigorously around the room when she knew that Damien's presence was something that she was immediately drawn to.

Caleb and Michael entered the classroom and looked over to Brianna, shaking their heads and both brows furrowed with a mild sense of stress. That could only mean one thing; that Damien had not come to school with them.

"We went to his house this morning," Caleb explained as he sat down to join Brianna at their row, "his foster mom opened the door. Apparently she hadn't seen him leave this morning, but she presumed that he had already left for school. We didn't think it wise to extend the conversation and agreed with her story before leaving."

This information did not comfort Brianna in anyway and all that she wanted was for the day to pass and her to do a little bit of searching in Merlin at the end of the day. Throughout the course of the day she looked into every nook and cranny of Witchcraft Heights.

She looked in the library, hoping to see him poring over a book once more. She ventured into the common room, the locker room, out to the sports grounds, into every classroom and even to the crowded canteen. When the time finally reached three o'clock she concluded him to be lost from the mortal world and prayed he had been stuck in the Realm world for the night. The group made a swift dash to pack away all their belongings before made their familiar route to the chamber. She dashed off while the others were still organising themselves. She went to the front entrance, but for the first time since six o'clock this morning it was not Damien that she was thinking about.

Some of the other students from the other neighbouring schools walked into the main entrance hall, but her attention passed every single one of them by. She failed to notice a couple of the girls giving off rather evil looking sneers in her direction, most of it hidden beneath lank tendrils of hair. She waited till she saw the crown of blond hair bobbing up and down as it ascended the stairs, then a pair of hazel brown eyes and finally a dazzling set of pearly whites smiling directly at her.

He didn't seem surprised to see her, which seemed only odd for a fraction of a second as she had never greeted him at the front before, but it seemed as if it was something that she had always done.

He lightly brushed his hand against her back as they turned and headed back towards the chamber while Brianna filled him in with the on goings of today and the fruitless search to locate Damien. They greeted the rest of the group outside Miss Ashdown's history classroom and proceeded down the pitch black corridor

to the transporting chamber.

The overwhelming black abyss sent a flashback of black hooded figures consuming and surrounding her

and Brianna felt her knees buckle and fall swiftly, if not painfully to the floor. Taylor turned sharply and bent

down to pick her back up.

"Are you alright?" he questioned her, with worry ringing clear in his voice even if she could not see the

worry on his face.

"I'm fine, it's just…," her voice tailored away as she heard the sound of footfalls in front of her and a sure

sound of murmuring. Normally they rarely saw or heard the other students making their way into the realm

world. She didn't want anyone to overhear their conversation in case they guessed that they had been out of

school grounds. Today they were surprised with the presence of someone that they, especially Brianna, were

not particularly fond of.

Zoe was standing with a couple of girls at the gateway that linked the mortal world to the school of

Medusa. The sound of the approaching footsteps must have been heard by Zoe because she stopped from

walking through the portal and turned around to see who was approaching. Her translucent skin seemed even

more hollowed out as it received the flickering light from the flaming brackets. It was pulled so tightly across

her face that parts of her skull jutted out and the pits of her eyes held a depthless and dead look, that was

filled with a mixture of pleasure and something else far more disturbing. It seemed as if a great darkness was

taking over her. For all her changes since the start of the year, one element of Zoe remained the same. She

gave her usual contemptuous glare that grotesquely and somewhat shockingly transformed into a triumphant

looking grin. She beckoned the other Medusa witches and without so much as one syllable they turned away

and walked through the chamber door. The grin unnerved Brianna and she felt an instinctive feeling that Zoe

had some knowledge about Damien; he had been on her mind all day after all.

They all continued their usual journey and stepped through the portal. She knew that they would be rushed for time, but she begged for a quick trip to the Merlin common room before they made their way to their lesson. She pressed on the face of merlin as the door opened and she scouted around the room; he was not near the fireplace or the small collection of books that the room had to offer. She ran back out to the lockers, but there was only a tall lanky boy with jet-black hair accompanied by a girl with tight red curls. Addressing his absence once more, the five of them proceeded to their remedies lesson with Professor Vita.

They were fortunate that this was their first lesson, for among all the loud noises and commotion that filled the room, it allowed them the opportunity to talk to one another without a fear of being seen.

"Did you manage to see him at Witchcraft heights today," Taylor started off the conversation.

"No and we looked everywhere. Caleb and Michael went to his foster home in the morning, but she stated that he had already left."

"Maybe he was really ill and tucked up in bed. Maybe the foster carer was telling fibs so that you two didn't go to disturb him," reasoned Taylor.

"I don't think so," retorted Brianna, "why would she do that?"

"Maybe he has told her that you lot are no longer friends with him; she wanted to protect him and considered exposing him to you lot might make his illness worse."

"No, I don't think it was that," more to herself than anyone else. In her mind she was trying to piece together everything that had happened the past night, things that she had told the others and things that she needed to piece together before she jumped to any conclusion.

"I think…. I think he has been taken."

The group looked at her with intense gazes, each one of them gasping or putting their hands to their mouth to stifle their surprise.

"Abduction?" Kimberley said incredulously, "impossible. There is nowhere to go in the memorium; it's surrounded by a thickset of trees. When they were chasing you he must have attempted his own escape. He could well have past us without our knowing; we were so focused on finding you after all. Maybe he didn't

get back to the transporting chamber in time because he was still intent on searching around for whatever is

so important to him."

"No, there are a couple of things that I have missed out; things that I don't fully understand."

"Well tell us!" Kimberley exclaimed, "Maybe we can help you."

So Brianna stood there among the fumes, explaining what she sworn had been the disappearance of

Damien. How she had noticed a change in him in recent times and then it came to her like a bolt of lightning.

He was changing, changing like someone else that she had seen alter throughout the past year.

"Zoe."

"I'm sorry, what did you say?" questioned Kimberley.

"Its Zoe," she repeated, slapping a hand against her forehead, "of course. When I last looked upon him his

complexion was growing steadily paler, like the waxy and translucent colour of Zoe."

"Zoe hasn't changed," Michael joined into the conversation, "she's the same awful looking person that

she has always been."

"You're looking at it from an attraction point of view," she said dismissively, "if a girl is unattractive to

you, you will barely notice of the changes that could have happened to her. She has become more of a

skeleton nowadays ever since she joined …. Medusa! You see it all makes sense!

"The girl's hood that had fallen off, she was one of the girls that was with Zoe on the day of the dragon

riding challenge. I hadn't seen her before because she belongs in the Realm World, it must be Zoe's new

friends."

"New friends?" asked Caleb, "what about her cronies in Witchcraft heights? She could barely function

without one of them nearby. She was with two of them just now."

"She has been sitting by herself in the canteen every day, just watching people." Watching Madison she

thought to herself. "She doesn't talk to the girls from Witchcraft heights anymore; she must have been taken under the wing of students from the Realm World, like we have been with Serena and Alleyen. The two

girls we saw in the transporting chamber aren't from Witchcraft Heights; I don't know where they are from…"

She wondered if they were even from the mortal world, but even that notion seemed too farfetched for

the likes of Zoe. That would run the risk of losing the chance to ever become a witch and Brianna didn't think

that Zoe would take that sort of risk.

"Then that means that Zoe was one of the cloaked figures. They must have taken Damien away."

"Brianna this is all sounding a bit ridiculous," Kimberley said, interrupting Brianna's train of thought. "You

have had a vendetta against Zoe for the way she had treated you from day one; there is no link to a reason

why she would abduct Damien. Why would she need to take Damien?

"It seems to me like you are jumping to conclusions without any real proof."

"Well where is he?" Brianna couldn't help but snap back. She couldn't understand why Kimberley couldn't

see how obvious it was that Damien had been taken away. One of the questions that did spark from

Kimberley's interruption was the purpose behind it all. Why would Zoe and a bunch of cloaked figures be

interested in one person?

They finished creating a deferio potion, which kept a fire going for the light but took away the heat so

that the witch or wizard would not burn. Brianna took up a cauldron spot near Taylor as Kimberley had

annoyed her. They didn't talk much while creating the potion, adding a branch of fillywig to the potion and the

seeds from a poprey corn. These ingredients were in the classroom cupboard, dried and hung for the students

to take of their own accord. She looked up at Taylor, but even he seemed a bit uncomfortable in her company.

She supposed this was more due to her obsession with finding Damien rather than her crazy conclusion.

By the end of the lesson Brianna knew that there was only one way that she was going to get piece of

mind on the mysterious case of Damien. She was going to have to return to the graveyard and work out where

the cloaked figures had taken him.

Before she would have asked her friends to come with her, but as she had a received a less than warming response to her idea behind Damien's whereabouts she didn't think they would want to come along for another trip. All day she considered how she was going to elude her friends and sneak off to the village, she wouldn't be able to do it today because the conversation was fresh in everyone's minds. As well as their obvious dismissal, she had been in a terrifying ordeal in the memorium and it was something that she didn't want to drag the others into, they had already done so much to help her out with the predicaments of Damien. They had just seemed angered by his attitude towards them and if she was honest with herself, she didn't blame them.

*

The school year was whirling past in such a flash. Brianna had had so much to deal with over the course of the year that she had forgotten about one of the key parts of the school year; the end of year exams. She had spent much of her time preparing for the dragon riding challenge, looking after Aureus and then keeping a watch on Damien. Well, she thought to herself, she supposed she had managed to take care of two of those things.

Sitting in the common room with the other first year students, she could not help but feel quite unprepared. She could see Caleb and Michael busily rifling through a couple of the books and there were Serena and Alleyen practicing the Illicio charms. She saw this as an opportunity to distract her friends, even if it meant forfeiting her own learning in the process.

They made their way to the first lesson, wand lore with Professor Eldridge where they knew they were to revise all of the wand trees that they had learnt thus far. He spoke over the main properties of the oak, cedar, linden, willow, pine and walnut tree. She tried to take in as much information as was possible, but it was hard to do so with Professor Eldridge's difficult to understand vocabulary and she was attempting to plot her escape for later on.

After their lesson had finished the five of them went to sit in the common room for Professor

Llewellyn had announced that his lessons were no longer necessary in the run up to the exams. They used this

time to continue revise and waited for the time when they could return to the mortal world. Brianna took a

seat next to Taylor; the tension between Kimberley remained rather high so she decided that it would be

better to stay away from her. She looked down and twiddled her thumbs before she considered a good way

to shake off her friends.

"I just need to pop down to the library," she said as she quickly rose from her seat.

"That's perfect; I need to look for a couple of books myself. I was hoping to find one on perfecting

transporting spells," responded Taylor.

"Oh, I shan't be long in the library, but I do need to go to the ladies room afterwards," she thought up

quickly, "there wouldn't be much point in you coming along."

"Okay, well if you're sure," he replied as Brianna quickly made her escape. She had had the most

fortunate luck and didn't want to extend the potential of it not lasting incredibly long. She had expected a

bombardment of questions, but then she thought to herself that her excuse was rather mandatory. They

couldn't read into her mind after all and what a fortunate piece of luck that was as well.

She couldn't rely on the help of Truesdale so she would have to walk into the village by foot. Thinking it

through, she knew she would have to break one of the rules that the first year mortals had to abide to; she

would not be returning to the mortal world tonight. Even if she managed to get down and find Damien fairly

quickly the journey up would place her in the situation where the portal connection would most certainly be

shut.

She quickly thought of one object that might help her in her escapade; her beloved book. She swiftly

retrieved her bag from her locker before making her next move. Meandering through the corridors to the

front entrance she attempted to keep as inconspicuous as possible. Fortunately, the inside of the main building always seemed to remain rather dark and full of hidden spaces, so she flitted from one dark spot

to the next.

Feeling like a brilliant spy, she ventured all the way to the front doors without being noticed.

"And just where do you think you are off to?"

The voice sounded so suddenly that it made Brianna jump at least four foot into the air. Her heart

pounding in her throat she turned to see Taylor, Caleb, Michael, Kimberley and Truesdale standing behind her.

"Ermmm," she faltered, knowing this would only injure her case, "I was… was just, erm, looking to see if

there was another ladies facility. The… er… one near the library was packed and I desperately needed to go."

"And your journey just happened to lead you to the front entrance? What were you hoping to find on the

other side of the door? A toilet with a scenic view?" Kimberley said in an accusing manner.

"Well, I… er…"

"Brianna, do you honestly think that we wouldn't have figured out what you were going to do?" she said

shaking her head.

"Well, yes," she retorted in a rather sulky voice, "or rather I hoped that you wouldn't figure it out."

"And do you suppose we would have just let you go and think only of ourselves? When we have to go

back to the mortal world, do you think we would just leave you behind? You are such a fool sometimes

Brianna, one day you will understand that there are people that deeply care about you… I care about you,"

Kimberley finished off somewhat lamely, but Brianna knew that it was her way of apologizing for being

annoyed at her.

"I don't want to bring you into further danger. The last time I took you lot down to find Damien we were

chased out by those awful people. I can't bear to think about how I would feel if one of you went missing as

well. I can't risk losing you too, but I can't leave Damien when I know what I saw. He has been taken, I'm sure

of it. Whether it has something to do with Zoe or not I have to go back to the graveyard and find a way to get

him back from wherever he has been taken."

"Well, I suppose...," Truesdale nudged Kimberley to continue, which she did with a little bit of effort. "Regardless of what you saw, we should go back and have another look. After all, there was a time in the year when we were all good friends with him. I'm sure that the good in him can come back just like it has with Madison."

"Well that's settled," Truesdale intercepted, "I suppose I should grab the Accipegus Carter and drop you off in the village square. I would take you closer to the memorium, but my pets get spooked out by that place even more so than us."

She gave a grateful nod and smile towards Truesdale as he darted off and she turned to face her dear friends.

"I don't need...," she began.

"Now don't start that again," said Taylor, taking her hand in his. "We are all coming with you, we are a team and that will never change. We are not just doing this for Damien; we are doing it for you as well."

"Thank you for understanding how important this is to me," she said softly, looking directly into his eyes and feeling a sudden jolt of the heart as their eyes connected. As they held their gaze Brianna was bought back out of her reverie as she heard the stomping of hooves outside the front entrance and knew that Truesdale had pulled up.

They parted hands and assembly rushed down to hop onto the vehicle. As soon as Michael had seated himself inside the carriage Truesdale whipped the creatures so that they soared quickly down to the village. They had travelled quickly before, but that was like a snail pace compared to the blurred fashion in which they were now being driven. They reached the village square in less than five minutes and hopped down from the seats at the front or out from the carriage. Caleb looked a little queasy, but that was not a surprise. Brianna, although grateful for the ride, did not feel too peachy herself.

"I'll wait for yours at mine, in case I hear anything from this end," Truesdale informed the others, "Kimberley, you know how to reach me should you need to."

Kimberley nodded and started to run off in the direction of the memorium. Brianna and the others followed suit and Brianna sprinted to run alongside Kimberley.

"How can you contact him?" she panted, knowing that a phone would suffice, as technology would not work in the realm world.

"He taught me a spell," she said through deep breaths, "the 'ventum' spell... allows me to... send messages... on the wind. I call the name... and the message will travel."

The ingenuity of it pleased Brianna and now that she felt safer at having some contact in the village, she increased the speed to reach the brow of the hill. She had to wait a little while on the top of the hill, looking down at the line of trees, as some of the less athletic members of her company followed behind her.

They walked through the same thickset trees as they ran down the other side of the hill as one and came face to face with their least favourite place in the realm world.

The memorium looked as ominous as ever and the fog, that never seemed to disperse, lingered around every headstone and memorial in the site. She led the group directly over to the 1692 memorial and tried to recollect what side she had seen Damien looking intently at, if it was Damien that she had seen. No, she thought to herself, it was definitely him. He went through here somehow and now it is my job to rescue him.

Every side that she stood facing, she looked over to see if it was from here she had approached him. On her third turn she stopped and knew that this was the one. She lit the side up with the Illicio spell and looked intently at the inscriptions on the stone.

She noticed, once again, that some of the letters were inscribed in a different way to the rest of the letters. She looked around the other three sides, but they all had the same font. This puzzled her and she beckoned Caleb over, asking to get a second opinion.

"Caleb, can you see that some of the letters are different to the majority of the letters?"

He drew out his own wand and traced the stone side. "Yes," he responded finally, "The calligraphy is different on a few of the letters, I wonder...

"Why don't you try and read the letters from the top left down to the bottom right."

She squinted as she used the glow from her wand to light the letters, "M... E... D... U... S... A. Medusa!" she cried out, "the letters spell Medusa! This must lead to the school of Medusa; it is too much of a mere coincidence for different letters to just randomly spell the name of a school."

The others ran up to see what she had read and they all nodded in agreement.

"Why would the school of Medusa be carved on a memorial stone?" questioned Kimberley.

"It must lead to the school," Brianna responded. She called out Medusa again, but nothing happened. She stood their pondering what else had to be done.

As she stood their looking for something she might have missed an odd pale glow shone, much like it had done on her first visit to the memorium. It made a letter Z against the stone and circled on a word in the bottom right corner. The pale blue light zoomed away from the stone and dispersed into nothingness.

"Bituta...," Brianna muttered as she read the encircled word. "That word rings a bell... where have I heard it before?"

The thought lingered for a moment, when Taylor interrupted her. "Whatever that was, I think it was telling us how to open up this stone gateway. Brianna could you stand aside please, I don't know which way this will move."

Brianna obliged as Taylor began to repeat what he had just witnessed.

He cast the 'lurida' spell to send out a blue beam from the end of his wand to help identify any key cryptic messages before her and called out "Medusa," loud and clear. As he called out the name of the evil witch he sent the blue beam in the shape of a Z before encircling the name and calling 'Bituta' out loud.

He withdrew the blue light and as he did so the sound of stone against stone resounded as the stone side moved to reveal a green light.

"You did it!" Brianna exclaimed, embracing Taylor while the others came up to pat him on the back on account of his brilliance.

"Well let's not dawdle and gape at the opening of a door. Let's see where this gateway sends us."

Chapter 20

As soon as all of the company were inside the stone memorial, the door closed itself on them and the green light, which had blinded them from seeing any further on, went out as if it had been snuffed out. They all recited the Illicio spell to light up the black abyss and registered that they were at the end of a very long tunnel. Its rough stone walls resembled those that lined the way down to the transporting chamber in Witchcraft Heights.

"What do we do now?" asked Michael, unable to hide the fear in his voice.

"We go through the tunnel and find out what's on the other side," Brianna replied assertively. "I shall lead at the front of the pack, everyone else fall in behind. Keep your wits about you and stay quiet, we do not know what is waiting for us on the other side."

They travelled in silence along the stone corridor. The uneven floor made it difficult to keep a good pace as many of the group kept tripping over a sudden pile of rocks or lost their footing in a small puddle of water. Their feet echoed along the floor and as they continued down the way they started to hear the faint sound of water droplets splashing against the rocky floor. Brianna felt the wall and noticed its damp surface as water trickled down the side. Placing her wand light up to the side she saw little trickling streams of water running down the side of the wall.

"We must be under a lake or a river," she announced to the others and they continued further along. As they descended further and further into the corridor the temperature significantly dropped and Brianna could feel her teeth chattering and the involuntary action of all her muscle contracting in an attempt to keep her warm.

Time seemed to carry on and on, she thought it must be the dawn of a new day and she worried whether they would ever find out where this tunnel led to.

Unexpectedly, she felt the path rising up and she noticed a faint yellow outline up ahead. She picked up the pace a little and realised that the outline was shaped against a door and that the light was from a torch bracket on the other side of the door. She pushed lightly on the door and was shocked to find it was open.

She beckoned the group to close in tightly behind her and they simultaneously blew out their wands so that the only light came from the other side of the door.

They found themselves in what they supposed was a building. The darkened walls were only visible due to the flickering glow cast from the brackets on the wall. The shadows that were cast on the walls were eerie and as Brianna put together the pieces that surrounded her she came to the conclusion that they had made their way to the school of Medusa. It was a stark contrast to Merlin, where everything in this school made the atmosphere have a far colder quality to it rather than warmer as the likes of her beloved school.

"We should leave behind a trace," Brianna informed the others, "the concealment of the door against the wall will make it extremely difficult for us to find it again."

She thought back to rhythmic charms and remembered how they had personalised a block of wood that was exactly the same size, weight and colour as everyone else's. The Subscripus spell created a personal signature on the object; the witch or wizard merely directed the course of the spell to leave their mark.

"Subscripio," she whispered and focused on the power travelling down her arm to the tip of her wand. She began to trace something that was personal to her; a dragons wing. She didn't do a particularly good drawing, which was probably a blessing in disguise as it would be far more difficult to link the mark to its originator if it looked like a misshapen blob.

She nodded to the rest of the company when she was done and decided it best to search around the school. She hoped to find Damien in one of the parts, hidden or ambling about with a great relief at being rescued. Brianna and the rest of the group tiptoed around the school, hiding behind the divides that sectioned off the corridors. As they ventured around a corner of one of the strictly angled corridors they noticed an unknown silver glow moving ahead of them. Brianna edged her head around one pillar and watched as the

silver glow floated through a wall. They were ghosts. She continued to hide behind her post and saw a

procession of more and more ghosts burst through one wall and exit through another. All of the ghosts that

resided here looked miserable; some they saw were chained, whilst others were covered in silver droplets.

Brianna had never seen a ghost before, but rather than feeling scared of the ethereal beings she found

herself being oddly entranced by the way they moved around. It was as if they were trying to imitate the

humanly movements that they had once done in their living times; they did not float as Brianna had originally

believed. She wondered why they existed in this particular place, as far as she was aware there were no ghosts

residing in the walls of Merlin. Three ghosts that walked together seemed to be muttering amongst one

another, but either they were speaking too quietly to understand or in a language that was not entirely

recognisable than for a few select words.

"Witches fuzzedly wigging atem again. Saw shurip indiny boy, truol taken fors adlib hidden," she heard

one say as they went past them.

"Did you hear that," Caleb whispered into Brianna's ear. "I think Damien is here, some of the words

they said connected to saying a boy that has been taken is here."

She quickly hugged Caleb, appreciative of how quickly his clever mind worked and spurred on this

notion they sought to carry on and locate the stolen Merlin student.

It was nothing like the layout of Merlin, but as she thought more and more about it she noticed that

some of the features and corridors resembled those of the Merlin building back in Witchcraft Heights.

They started to notice some doors on either side of the corridor walls and snuck a peek into each one,

hoping to find Damien confided in one of them. Time continued to pass and luck seemed to be wearing thin

for the troupe. They were lucky not to bump into anyone else as they slipped silently around the school, which

supposed that they were most definitely held in the Realm world for a whole night.

It didn't seem as large a school as Merlin, for within an hour of searching Brianna noticed that some of the places they were walking in appeared to be awfully similar.

"I think that we have been here before," she whispered to Kimberley, "I think that we are starting to go around in circles."

They had searched through the school and her head dropped at the realisation that Damien was not in fact here, he had eluded her somehow and now she felt angered that she had led the other four on a pointless quest.

"Let's have another look."

They darted around the very strict corridors, straight with sharp turns. There were only a few paintings along the way, which helped the troupe to remember the spots that they had ventured into. They pressed on every door this time, sure not to miss one. They all creaked open a little bit and the panic rose every time a noise echoed reverberated off of the walls. The floors muffled the sound a little with the shabby and worn out carpet that covered the floor. They looked into the very small dining area, its barren outlook easy to identify that no one was in the vicinity. The boys checked the boy's lavatories and the girls checked the girls counterpart. Throughout their whole journey only one door remained steadfast, only one door refused to move. The second trip gave no relief and then everyone turned to face Brianna.

"He has got to be here," she said, getting more and more frustrated with the situation and touching every part of the wall, searching for something they may yet have missed. "I saw him come through this way. He is here somewhere!"

She continued moving frantically around until she felt a force pushing against her. She finally saw clearly and knew that she was overreacting as Taylor looked at her with a concerned disposition.

"I know you did Brianna," he said soothingly, "but we have looked through this school twice and have found nothing. Maybe, just maybe, Damien doesn't want to be found."

"Why would he go here, of his own free will when he knew he would break one of the rules and not return before the portal closed? How could he do this to us? How could he lead us to look for him?"

There it was, the real reason why she had gone searching for him. She believed it was his cry for help, his way of reaching out and demonstrating the fact that their loss of friendship had deeply affected him. She still believed there was some good in him, but she could now see that there was none. A true friend would not lead another blindly to a place that reeked of danger and the unexpected. True friends would not have left another to fend for themself when chased by others. A true friend would never have abandoned their friend in the first place and that was when the light bulb glowed brightly and painfully in her mind.

He had been a friend with her, with every single one of them, whilst he wanted to gain information.

Or, rather information from them; courtesy of her beloved book she thought to herself.

She recalled his keen and somewhat overwhelming attraction towards the book and his constant thirst for answers. She didn't know what he wanted to find out exactly, but whatever it was he was now gaining the information from another source.

"Let's just head back to the village," she said in a resigned voice. She felt annoyed that she had led the group on yet another fruitless journey to recuse Damien and vowed to herself that she would never go looking again. They started making their way back to the hidden door, skirting the corridors as silently as was possible.

"Going somewhere are we?" a voice hissed in the shadows. "I don't think so!"

The group looked left and right, but no one could be seen. She looked up high and as she did so she saw five or six of the cloaked figures she had seen in the graveyard descend on the group.

"Laquem!" they shouted out in unison and a rope protruded from each wand, tightening the group together in one big circle. The ropes then proceeded to bind their hands behind their backs so that they were completely defenceless.

"So what do we have here," one of the voices jeered, the face completely hidden beneath the overhanging black hood. "Trespassers, thieves, or a silly bunch of first years thinking they can do what they wish."

"They aren't from Medusa," called out another, "there are boys with them."

"And… look," another said pointing Brianna with a finger hidden underneath a long black sleeve, "this can't be the winner of that ugly dragon? I think it is!"

They all tittered in unison, pleased by their catch of the night.

"The boss will be impressed, we have an Eastey," the first voice exclaimed. She moved around the group and for stopped in her tracks as she came face to face with Kimberley.

"No… it can't be."

The others rushed to face Kimberley and they all looked delighted as if they had found the prize jewel.

"This one is coming with us," said the first voice, "she could do with a little reunion. As for the rest… lock them in the dungeons."

Brianna tried to move to Kimberley, but fell immediately to the floor as she hadn't realised her feet had also been bound in the meantime. The group whipped Kimberley away from the rest and two of the group stole her away.

"Well, the boss wouldn't want us to leave them in a state such as this," one said tauntingly and the others agreed with shrill laughs. "We need to make sure that they won't be able to find their … old … friend."

With the end of 'friend' a blinding combination of spells were sent in the direction of the defenceless company. Painful fiery shots seared past the faces of the group and they yelled in pain as it caused the skin to boil and burn. Then Brianna head the sound like gun shots protruding from the wand and making connection with the group. Shattering pain split through her as she realised they were breaking their bones. They fell into crumpled heaps on the floor before the cloaked figures resorted to mortal fighting, just for good measure. She tried to stay awake but a swell blow to the head made her see bright shining starts before all the world

was consumed into a great black abyss.

Chapter 21

Brianna fluttered her eyelids open and it took her a good while to understand where she was. She tried to roll out of her bed, but she didn't remember her bed feeling so uncomfortable and hard on her spine. As she tried to push herself up with her hands she found that her hands seemed unable to move. One appeared to be strapped down and the other one was in excruciating pain. Pain... it was as she thought of pain that her brain started to piece together where she was and why she was strapped to a hard cold table.

The reason she was trapped was because she had been captured. She had been captured by a group of masked individuals who had ambushed herself and her friends and put them in here; in this dark and cold room. She wanted to call out and find out if any of her friends had been placed in the same room as her, but what if her captors were stationed in the darkness, waiting for their next attack.

She shifted her head left to right, but there was not even the slightest change in the colour surrounding her. It was probably the first time in her life where Brianna understood what it was to be blind and with the sense of blindness came the horrible sense of vulnerability and danger.

The only thing she felt was safe to do was make a 'psst' noise and hope that one of her friends would recognise her tone of voice.

"Psst," she called again into the darkness, where her voice echoed against the walls.

"Hello," croaked a small voice, "who's there?"

"Caleb, is that you?" Even with the croaking struggle, Brianna was still able to identify the voice of her good friend Caleb. She didn't want to cause any sense of distress as he didn't sound in a good stead at all.

"Yes," he whispered in response, "is that you Brianna? Are you alright?"

He sounded distressed and Brianna could hear the agitation in the small amount of shuffling that he seemed capable of doing. She didn't know what was nearby her or who may be listening in on them.

"Yes, how long have you been awake?"

"I'm not too sure," he responded. She could hear the strain in his voice and knew that he was in far worse shape than she was. "Where are the others?"

"I don't know…" she responded hesitantly, it was a growing concern that she couldn't find her way in the complete abyss and in the looming blackness no other human, friend or foe, could be heard. She tried with all the effort she could muster to move herself on the stone table. As she tried to move one arm she registered that the other arm was strapped to the table, but the other seemed to have a bit of freedom. As she shifted it across her body to free her other hand the excruciating pain returned and she realised that the unstrapped arm was probably broken. It was useless, which suggested as to why her captors didn't strap the other limb down. The next step was to wriggle her feet; they moved.

The relief of this lifted her hopes by the slightest degree, but they were no way in fighting order. She could feel a stinging sensation from the hips down and wasn't completely sure what state her legs were in. In her mind, her main concern was that she needed to find the way out of wherever they were and find the others.

"Can you move?" Brianna asked Caleb. She heard some struggling and cries of pain as he failed in his attempt to move.

"My arms are strapped down," he responded, "I'm not too sure that I can move my legs either."

She began to realise that what they had woken up to; torture. The point at which she had blacked out she could not recall, but she had not blacked out in such a dishevelled state. This had been done to her whilst they had been unconscious and the mere thought of it disgusted her.

"It will be okay, we are getting out of here," she said in attempt of comforting her wounded friend. The next thing she needed to find was her wand; it would be the only thing of real use at the moment as her body was in such a sorry state. Feeling around blindly and biting against the excruciating amount of pain that was protruding through her arm, she failed to locate her wand.

If it wasn't too far away she may have a small chance at locating her wand. The connection would still be there if it was close by, so she called out quietly into the dark "locant virgula".

A small red light flickered in the corner of her eye; some luck at last! They had left a wand clumsily in the corner of the room, which seemed almost too good to be true. Then again, the sorry state that she was in, they probably hadn't counted on them being mobile enough to escape and retrieve the wand.

"Pertraho virgula," she commanded, instructing her wand to come towards her. The power that emanated from her command and the effort that coursed through her veins to draw the wand to her. It rolled over slowly and climbed up to her free hand. She shot a burning flare across her body to free her clasped wrist. The burning sensation reduced the ache in her wrist and she found that she could support her body with the freed hand.

As she got up to a standing position the pain ran through her leg, but she persisted nonetheless and lit the room with a low glow from the tip of her wand.

She took a great gasp as the wand light fell on Michael, who had been silent up until this point. The light cast over the body of her friend and she saw that one of his arms was sticking out in a completely obscure angle; it was completely unnatural and sickened her to the core.

"Caleb, I've found Michael," she called out, trying to disguise the sadness that was welling up and she sent the light around the room to locate Caleb. It stopped on him and she could see that his legs were badly broken, hanging limply from his sides.

"Brianna, is that you?" a new voice questioned into the darkness.

"Taylor?" she called out and her heart pained as she looked desperately for Taylor. It was a desperation that she had never known before, a new sort of feeling for someone; someone that was important for her very being.

"Where are we," he said with a panicked voice that suggested he had only just awoken to this horror.

"We don't know exactly," she started, "but I promise I will get us out of here."

"I'm meant to be the one to save you," he replied with an attempt at a chuckle.

"Well you have saved me plenty of times. You just haven't known it," she answered, "I'm returning the favour. Do you think you can walk at all?"

She heard another attempt at someone struggling, "well, I'm strapped down, but my body doesn't feel in too much pain."

That bought a warm sense of relief to her and she decisively went over to him and freed him from his shackles.

"So that's me, you, Caleb and Michael," she counted off the people that she had discovered in the darkened chamber.

"Where's Kimberley?!"

Frantically she swept the light around the room, but in neither nook nor cranny could her best friend be found. She forced the power of her waning light in the far corners of the room, but her wand was flickering and dying through her exhaustion. It was then that Brianna heard a most frightful sound.

A high pitched scream, a torturous sort of scream, echoed in some place from above. What was worse, was the fact that Brianna immediately what was the source of that pained voice. Kimberley.

She no longer felt the pain. She no longer felt the exhaustion. She no longer felt the cold. Her mind was driven on anger and the desperation to find her best friend. The wand glow flared back with a fiery intensity and standing in front of her was Taylor.

"Let's go and get her," was all that Taylor said before he turned and cut the bonds that tied Caleb. He then broke away the table from its locked down hinges. Michael limped to grab one end and Taylor held the other.

"Brianna we have to send him back," Taylor explained, "we cannot go on a rescue mission with Caleb in this condition."

"But how do we send him back?" Brianna questioned Taylor, focused completely on finding Kimberley and desperate for them to hurry up in their escapade. In a strange sort of response something seemed to rustle in the chamber. Brianna sent the light searching for the source of the noise and it fell on her forgotten bag propped against a pillar.

With a sense of puzzlement, Brianna approached the bag, and opened its contents to discover what was causing it to rattle. Her hand pulled out The Book Estas Orientem Magia Animabus. As she did, it fell out onto her hand and turned the pages swiftly as if caught up in a wind.

Words formed at the top of the page, 'Journey to the Mage' where the book then jumped out of her hand and fell flat on the floor. Something started to grow from the pages, higher and wider, with a swirling mass gathering at its centre; just like the mass Brianna looked upon as she moved from the mortal world to the realm world. It was a transporting doorway.

"Quick," Brianna called out, "we can send Caleb through there."

"And where does that lead to?" Michael asked, "We can't send him to somewhere that we don't know."

"We have to trust the book," Brianna responded and somehow, she didn't know how or why, but she knew that she was right. It was all a matter of trust; this book would not lead her astray. "It has only done good deeds for us before, it will protect Caleb."

Her firm belief and resolution meant that Taylor immediately succumbed to Brianna's argument. She knew that he would do as she wished anyway, but this was definitely a good time for him to be so responsive. With a simple nod in her direction, he started to lead the way with Caleb. Michael had no time to respond and found himself pushed by the large wooden plank.

As they reached the swirling mist the plank seemed to rise off of the boy's shoulders and began carrying itself to the mist. It picked up speed and as it touched the mysterious substance, the mist changed to an electric blue and looked more like a series of fast track lines, pointing to its destination. A sound like a whip cracked in the chamber and a current carried Caleb through. Caleb vanished and with it the portal. Brianna picked up the book and placed it safely back in her bag, before running to the door and pulling on it. Oddly enough it opened; Brianna cared not for what reason and sprinted towards the source of the screams.

The dimly lit walls seemed to carry on for an eternity as she rushed to find the location of her best friend and the screaming continued to echo horribly off of the wall, reverberating into her ears and locking into her brain. As they climbed another flight of stairs she saw a flickering light of a strange purple; that was no ordinary light.

She held out an arm to slow down the other two as she thought of the necessity to remain inconspicuous to their captors. As they crept towards the door that presented the slither of purple light they heard an awful sound of what was laughter, but it did not fill the heart of Brianna with comfort. Instead the level of fear mounted within her.

"Listen to the traitor," one of the captors said. Brianna per chanced a glance through the crack in the door and saw a wall of black cloaks looking down on something before them. Her eyes quickly took in the room and she saw a couple of pillars that had a good view onto the wall of cloaks.

She beckoned the boys in close to her and spoke in a voice that was barely more than a whisper, "We need to hide behind those two pillars. Well two of us, one will need to stay outside and when it looks like we are on the way back they must open the portal in the book. It's the only way that I can see us getting out of here."

"You get the book open for us then Brianna," Taylor suggested.

"No I think Michael should do that," she stated firmly, "I have to go in, I don't think I could bear to wait for the outcome. Taylor you go to the left hand side and I'll go to the right."

This was not the time for debates and Taylor could see the resolute decision within her eyes so he once again succumbed to her wishes. As he nodded in agreement Brianna made her dash, fortunately being unseen by any of the cloaks. She looked right around the pillar and saw that the cloaks were not encircling their prey they were looking down a slight pit into the poor dishevelled form of her best friend.

She looked completely broken; her clothes were peeling away from her skin with some parts almost looking burnt. Her face had a series of burn marks mingled among deep cuts and around her eyes were deep purple and blue bruises. She could see the tears that had been running down her face, but were dried onto her skin that she was unable to wipe away as her hands were bound to the floor by shackles.

"So traitor, what are we going to do with you?" the voice from earlier on announced. Brianna gathered that it was a female voice, but it sounded almost non-human, as if the voice was consumed by something else.

Kimberley made a feeble sounding cry and the group sent their chilling round of laughter to link in one terrifying jeer.

"The traitor doesn't agree with our hospitality," the voice declared mockingly to the rest of the group, "she doesn't realise that because of people like her we have endured pain and suffering unlike she has ever witnessed. You must see that this is fair payment for all of those that have been unrightfully imprisoned, punished and killed for what should be the right way to rule."

"Please," Kimberley tried to plead with the relentless group, "I don't know what I have done, I come from the other world."

"Bingo," the voice said, "there begins my reasoning. How can we have those of you from the other world learning our ways when your ancestors wanted to be rid of the magical world? Also, you must know of the family from which you descend from."

An evil hissing went around the room at this _.

"The Aldridge's….the Aldridge's," the voice repeated with venom in her tone, "Now where do I begin with that traitorous family. You dearie, need to read up on your family history to understand the destruction that your family caused to our magical world. Then you will see that what you are receiving is nothing short of apt compensation for the likes of us."

Brianna felt panicked at the thought of what they were going to do to Kimberley. They had already caused so much damage, she needed to get her friend out and she needed to think fast.

The shackles could easily be broken, but getting past a wall of people would not be such an simple task. She needed the captors to be distracted and she thought frantically of a way to do so. They wouldn't budge for a small amount of noise; they needed to see and hear something that would make them want to move.

It hit her; she could send a hologram version of herself to send off to another part of the room. She had been practicing the spell in case she wanted to venture in the village and needed to have a pretend image of her up the school. The only problem was that the image was not very powerful and would not hold for a very long time. She would have to cast quickly and react even faster than the spell that she could cast.

She pointed the wand at herself and created a pointed figure of eight sort of motion before drawing away from the middle point.

"Effingo, Effingo, Effingo," she said in a whisper before turning to point the created image in a direction away to the far corner of the room. She made a quick sound of moving footsteps as if the image had moved swiftly to the other side of the room.

"What was that?" one of the other people in the group called out.

"Look, over there, one of them has escaped!" another proclaimed in a shocked voice. Unfortunately for Brianna they did not all go to investigate the source of the noise; two of them stood guard over Kimberley. Quickly Brianna looked over to Taylor and all he did was nod once more at Brianna before charging out and sending to sparks of spells at the guards, it was a simple soap spell but it hit them squarely in the eyes and caused them to cry out in pain.

As they stood their rubbing their eyes in pain, Brianna quickly ran to Kimberley and broke her friend free from the fetters. She draped her fragile friend's arms around her shoulders and lifted her up. A piece of torn paper stuck to her shoe but she didn't have the time to remove it.

"GET THEM!" shouted one of the other _.

"Run Taylor!" Brianna exclaimed, "CALEB… NOW!"

She ran in the direction of the door and saw Caleb opening the book. A door grew bigger and opened for them. She passed Kimberley to Taylor and made the others go through first. She saw the others sending spells her way and wondered how she would shut the portal. As if in response to her worries a voice said "hold onto the book and jump through."

She did as commanded and with one swift leap and an angry outcry she felt the sucking sensation as she was transported through the door and landed with a thump in a room that she had never seen the likes of before.

Chapter 22

Brianna found herself in what could only be described as a dumping ground. She was swamped in stacks of papers, objects that teetered precariously on one another and bits and bobs the likes of which she had never come across before. The light quality was very poor, hidden behind dusty rusting lamps. She couldn't see the depth of the room, where the walls were, where the door was or for that matter, where any of her friends had landed.

She hoped that, although not the ideal location, the book would have at least led them all out to the same place.

"Hello," she called out tentatively, the words muffled and absorbed by the unsurpassable mounds. "Taylor, Caleb, Michael?"

"Do not worry dearie," a voice suddenly answered, "they are all being taken good care of."

"Who said that?" Brianna replied cautiously. She squinted in the dim lit room, "where am I?"

"You are in the house of Eastey," the voice answered, "well my house I should say. I am the Mage that owns this house; or rather I have been given living rights to guard the secrets of the house. Tressle is my name, if you want to know that as well."

"Show yourself!" Brianna remained guarded after everything that had happened so far this evening and did not warm to the stranger's voice, "Why do you lurk in the shadows?"

"Completely unintentional I assure you," the voice chuckled a little, "if I could just move… ah there we are! Hold out your hand child and let me pull you somewhere a little more spacious."

She held out a hand and quickly she found it grasped by another hand. It was warmer, but somehow felt more fragile than her own hand.

"There we are," and as Brianna felt herself being pulled through she looked into the eyes of the owner of the house of Eastey. She was a very old woman, hunched over a little where time had taken its gravity on her fragile bones. Her grey hair was pulled into a bun that rested on the nape of her neck. She was draped in a comfortable red woollen robe that trailed across the floor behind her. She held a wand aloft in the other

hand and lit the tip of it without so much as the tiniest mutter.

"You have got yourselves into a bit of bother this evening haven't you?" Tressle said, shaking her head

with concern. "What have you been up to on this little adventure?"

"I was... now wait a minute," Brianna suddenly stopped in her tracks, "How do you know of my

adventures?"

"The book dearie, the book! Please keep up!" she said rather sharply, tapping her wand on Brianna's

out held arm. "The book that you cling so dearly to; I thought you would have learnt a thing or two about it by

now! How do you think all that information magically appears in the book? Books can't think for themselves

you know!"

Brianna looked incredulously at Tressle; considering everything that had gone on tonight Tressle had

made no attempt in lightening the load. Thinking that that particular conversation could be saved for another

day, Brianna looked back to the old woman and reiterated one of the first questions she had asked.

"Where are the others?"

"I told you they are safe. They are currently in my healing quarters; unlike you, some of them haven't

had such a fortunate escape. One of them, the girl... well I'm afraid that she will have to stay with me for a

couple of days."

"Can I see them please?" she asked Tressle, feeling a lump rising in her throat as the tears threatened

to take over from sorrow and guilt.

Tressle nodded and with a wave of her arm she beckoned her to follow. They tiptoed past a careworn

sofa with what looked like a stuffed vulture perched on top of it. They meandered through stacks and stacks of

old parchment, before pushing aside some hanging willow branches.

"Why do you have all this stuff?" she couldn't help but ask.

"You can't think that this stuff is all mine?! Surely not! No, I do not own this house, but I do belong to it and so do the things that reside within it. Everything that you see here has been collected from the Mages of the past; when I first came to inhabit this place, oh some forty years ago I tried to do a bit of spring cleaning. Needless to say, the house did not agree with my plans and I have had to deal with the mess ever since."

"Why don't you just move away?"

"Move, ha! Now that's one that I haven't heard. One can't simply move away, once you have been assigned to a house that is where you shall stay until your last day."

"And what happens after that?"

"Oh, I become a part of the house you might say. I become the whispers, the information; the aide to the next Mage that enters into the house. It is part of our duty; to be ever filled with the knowledge of what has been and to be the gift of enlightenment to the someone anew."

They left the main clutter in the living room and proceeded down a corridor. It reminded Brianna of a tree, where they were walking down the trunk of the tree and all the branches were protruding from its core to other parts of the house. There were no stairs however, so it seemed that the house was built on one level, and as she passed a few glass portholes and saw the stars burning brightly overhead, she knew her assumption to be correct. For a one floored home, it was much larger than Brianna had first anticipated and she wondered just how much space was inside this rather magnificent house.

"If you live in the house of Eastey, then you must be an Eastey!" she said, almost forgetting her recent turmoil at the jubilation of finding one of her family members.

"Oh no, a Mage of a house does not need to be an ancestor nor a descendent from a family line. It is a gift you see, not a lifestyle choice. I didn't choose to be a Mage, but the Mage in me led me to look after the house of Eastey and all of the Eastey's that live in this current lifetime. Which is why dearie, I set the path for you to find the book. For a chance to discover what you truly are primarily, to be a wealth of information secondly, but thirdly to be a source of guidance and assistance ever should you need it."

"Thank you," was all the reply that she could give for they had both left the main corridor of the houses and proceeded down a corridor to their right. The Mage pressed on ahead and placed a palm on the door as they reached the end. It glowed a faint golden yellow around the spot where she had touched the door, similar to the way that Professor Merrydew pressed his palm to open the door in Merlin. Maybe, there's some fairy blood in a Mage, Brianna thought to herself.

As she stepped into the room she saw a small circular window in front of her, with the moonlight and starlight streaming in. In the middle of the room was a circular bed, almost for visiting and viewing purposes, as everyone who entered would be able to grab a spot in which to watch the person that was laid there. In this case it was Kimberley.

"Kimberley!" she exclaimed as she rushed over to her. She could see Kimberley squinting from the glow that was outside and she went to pull the curtains across to rest her friend's eyes.

"Leave the curtains dearie. The moonlight and starlight hold magical healing properties. It's best to let Kimberley drink up what light she can."

Brianna looked at her friend lying in the bed and had to hold a hand to her mouth. Her face was bloodied, puffed and heavily bruised. A liquid seemed to be seeping from her hairline and dribbling into her mouth. Brianna wiped it away with one hand and placed another near her friends shoulder. She heard a slight crunch and lifted her hands up high into the air, realising that she had just moved a broken collarbone from its fragile position. There was no sheet covering her body as there was too much blood covering her and too many open cuts that would stick to the first thing that it touched.

"This was the worst casualty to pass through my chamber," Tressle said shaking her head and looking sadly onto the body of Kimberley.

"Will she make it through?"

"Of course dearie, it will just take a little while longer for her to return to her full health. Fortunately they resorted to mortal violence with only a couple of slicing hexes. If they had only used magic to injure this poor soul it would have been a great deal harder to reset the damage that has been caused. This makes me question the magical prowess of the culprits. Most individuals in the Realm world would rather use magic than resorting to cold mortal violence."

That thought did not stir in Brianna's mind as she stood hovering above her friend, simply horrified by what lay before her.

"Would you like to see the others perhaps? She won't wake for quite some time and I believe the others may be stirring."

Giving one short nod, Tressle led the way back to the main corridor and off to another of the rooms. As they stepped through this room there were three beds lined up in a row against the back wall; once again the light was streaming through the window to allow the starlight and moonlight to work its magic.

"Brianna!" called out the voice of a person that she most certainly knew.

"Taylor," she said with utter relief, expelling a little bit of her worry as she saw the smiling face of Taylor. The injuries to his face weren't as extensive as the ones on Kimberley's, but there was enough for his to resemble a person who had been stung by thousands of bees.

"Thank you," he said as she took a seat next to him, noticing the leg that was stuck out rigidly and tied to a splint.

"Why would you say thank you?" she replied placing her head in her hands, "it's my fault that you are all in this state."

"Brianna, look at me. If I was lost and I knew that this is what you would put yourself through to know that I was safe, that would make me the most grateful and honoured person across both worlds. Simply because we did not find him does not mean we did the right thing; those that choose to live their life for themselves and not others people have not the life that they truly want or necessarily deserve."

"Who told you that?"

"I made it up, but I think it sounds rather impressive and it is fairly accurate if you don't mind me saying so." He lifted up his arm, wincing as he did so, before placing it around Brianna. As his hand lightly touched her she broke down and sobbed away. He pulled her in tighter and they held there embrace for what seemed an eternity.

As she pulled away to wipe away the tears Taylor placed his other hand up to her face and wiped away the tears for her. She smiled weakly at him and at that point she knew, regardless of all that was going on around her, her feelings for Taylor certainly were far more than friendly fancy. Her affections for him were incontrovertible, a deep and meaningful relationship that had bloomed from the turbulent life that they had dealt with over the course of the past few months.

Lost in the moment, she almost failed to register Caleb and Michael both stirring in the beds next to Taylor on either side. "Oh!" she exclaimed as she saw four eyes gazing in her direction.

"Oh," she said even louder as she realised for certain that they had come to, "Caleb, Michael your awake!"

"Yes," said Caleb, "I have been for a good couple of minutes, but I didn't wish to burst the bubble that was blossoming between the two of you." He couldn't help the smile from spreading across his face as Brianna felt a crimson blush flush profusely across her face.

"Well," she composed herself after being embarrassed by her friend, "how are you both? I'm..."

"Don't even think about apologizing Brianna," Michael interjected.

"It would seem that there is a bit of a link running through with this matter," Taylor added into the conversation, "as you can clearly see no one seems to believe that you are to blame for the incidents that have occurred from this evening. So, the sooner you stop apologizing, the quicker we can get on with the more important matters."

"Like what?" Brianna stated feeling completely bemused.

"Well to start off we need to question why there are a group of psychopathic witches torturing witches with particular ancestors of interest. Why were they so hell bent on attacking Kimberley? Why have they taken Damien or what could they have possibly said to entice them into their quarters?

"Then there is the matter regarding a group of witches, part of a cult I would hazard a guess, running amok in one of the local schools. Maybe you could look in your book. Now that we have been in close vicinity your book may reveal greater details regarding the matter."

"I wouldn't bet on that Taylor, it turns out that I haven't been getting information from an unknown power. In fact, it has been from something most definitely living and breathing and right from within this room."

"Who?" the three boys called out in unison.

"Tressle, the Mage that lives within this house, or rather the House of Eastey. She has been feeding information and keeping a close watch over me throughout the course of the year. She is something of my guardian, or least a guardian of the Eastey's in this world," Brianna explained. She wanted to carry on explaining what she had learnt from Tressle, but the boys had both all rested their head on their pillows and were on their way for a good night's sleep.

"Let them rest," Tressle called out unexpectedly, having managed to creep up on Brianna without her knowledge. "They will be free to go in the morning, but for now you should take a nap and allow yourself to wash your mind away from all that has happened tonight. Please place this offluant plant next to your bed; it will help you to sleep."

After being directed to her bed from another side corridor Brianna laid her head against the pillow; positive that after all that happened she would not be able to free her mind and fall asleep. She felt for something that was crumpled in her pocket and found the piece of paper that had been taken before she

had been transported. She didn't bother to reads it, but folded it carefully back into her pocket and rested her

head once more on the pillow. As she turned to look to the plant on her bedside table next to her she felt

overwhelmingly exhausted and with one long blink she fell into a dreamless sleep.

Chapter 23

When the sun shone down on Brianna and woke her it took her a good couple of minutes to realise where she was. She rolled over and saw the bedside cabinet with a potion fuming on the side. It had a little note underneath which she grabbed a hold of and read.

'Drink me as you rise and mix with a morning drink. I am afraid I cannot tend to you this morning as I have several things to be getting on with myself. Please take the potion and make your way back to the school.'

She followed the instructions on the note and tried to work out when she could head back up to the school; she didn't want to return too soon in case any of the teachers noticed a mortal based student in the realm world.

She roamed the corridors in the morning, her mind a little groggy from the night before, as she tried to recall the route that would lead her to her friends. On her fourth attempt she pushed on one of the doors and found the three beds lined up in a row. Of the three beds, one was unoccupied, and Brianna turned around to see Taylor throwing a coat over his back. He winced a little as the pain had not completely left even though it seemed he looked completely back to normal.

"I'm ready to go," Taylor decided to start the conversation; "the Mage left a note for me. Michael and Caleb should be alright to leave tomorrow; it says that she wants to keep an eye on them as they came into a full fire of a couple of the particularly nasty curses."

Images, bought up by the word curses, flashed through Brianna's mind. Sharp bursts of light, searing pain, the braking of bones like gunshots. She shivered ever so slightly before readjusting her attention back on Taylor.

"I think it's safe for us to return to the school," was all she could manage to say, the incidents of last night flashing and haunting her mind.

"Yes, I should think so. We will have to walk as Truesdale will still be up at the school and I'm sure he will want to stay at the Kimberley's side once he has made his way down here. We could make our way up the main valley and then enter the woods; approach the school from the side so that we don't make so much of an entrance."

The two of them left the others in the care of Tressle and made their way out of the House of Eastey. It took them a good ten minutes to find their bearings once they had left the front gates of the house. They were on the far western side of the village, the opposite side of the Memorium and a place that Brianna never wished to go near again. As they walked a short way along a cracked path their view opened out to a downhill slope that led to the centre of the village. They made their way to the centre, as they needed to find their bearings before they went back up the valley to the direction of Merlin.

They walked from the centre of the village, up the path that they usually sailed down in the Accipegus carter, but now were faced to trek up on foot. They had always travelled at the speed of light, so in a way it was a gratifying experience to look on the different buildings that made up the village. She found that the buildings had more uniformity to them as they walked away from the unique qualities of the village square. A lot of the homes had signs at the front of their lawn and the gardens seemed to have a beautiful country garden feel to them. The long grass played host to a number of wild flowers and in the warm spring air the creatures milled about their daily business, including a couple bread and butterflies that Brianna happened to notice.

They wended their way to the top of the village where the houses started to disperse as the landscape gave way to the open country. She knew that the space between the village and the school was an open expanse, green as far as the eye could see, until the floor touched the mountains that encompassed the area of Salem. She and Taylor walked silently in this space, still keeping to the road, but wishing to venture off to the unknown that the Realm world had to offer.

After a good hour since they left the house of Eastey they finally found themselves up against the woodland that sheltered the school of Merlin from the rest of the world. Brianna felt apprehensive as she made an advance towards the woods, haunted by the woods that lined the Memorium. Taylor noticed the shudder that had taken a hold of Brianna and he consoled her by placing a hand on her shoulder and guiding her back to school. They walked cautiously through the woodland and although it held no ominous quality, every time a leaf rustled or a twig snapped under foot she could not help her heartbeat from fastening ever so slightly.

The light eventually became clearer as they waded through the trees and soon enough the front of Merlin stood facing Brianna and Taylor. They felt afraid of being caught by a Professor and decided to skirt the side of the building, hoping for some small entrance that they had not yet discovered from their many adventures. As luck would have it, not twenty foot from where they stood, a door hid itself precociously behind some dangling ivy.

"Let's try our luck through here," Taylor said to Brianna.

They pushed on the door, but were put out to find that the way was shut. She wondered if it worked the same way that the transporting chamber door worked and recited the enchantment that unlocked the door. She had no such luck.

"Let me try," Taylor suggested, sensing Brianna's irritation rising. "Recludo clavis," he said brandishing his wand at the point of the keyhole. She heard a clicking sound and the door swung open to admit them.

"Where did you learn that?" she asked with rapt at Taylor's knowledge.

"Well... I don't like to bring it up," he came over rather red and shied away from Briana for maybe the first time ever.

"Come on, you can tell me."

"Well, when you were spending all your time with Damien I decided to learn as much about magic as possible... as a sort of distraction. Looking back it was silly, but in a way it did help me to learn an awful lot of spells that I would never have considered before."

She looked away equally as embarrassed and the two of them found themselves walking in silence through the corridors of Merlin; heading in the direction of their history lesson with Professor Benethon.

They rounded the corner, still looking away from one another, but what they saw when they faced the new corridor made them look at each other in utter shock.

Damien.

Damien was walking down the corridor, without a care in the world and acting as if he had not seen them approaching him.

"Damien!" Brianna could not help but shout out.

He pretended to show surprise at being addressed and with some obvious reluctance sauntered over to the two of them. As he advanced Brianna couldn't help but notice how different he looked; his eyes no longer shone, his hair wasn't as well kempt and his stance was more gloating than it had ever been before.

"Where have you been?" she demanded, feeling no need to act on accord or hide away from the obvious.

"What do you mean?" he hissed rather menacingly.

"You weren't at school yesterday."

"I'm here now," he snapped back, "besides I was stuck at home yesterday, ill, not that it's any of your concern."

"Caleb and Michael went to your house," Brianna stated, glad of this information, "they were told by your foster mom that you had already left for school."

"What are those nosey twits doing checking in on me," he spat back, "never bothered to knock for me when I was their friend. Why the sudden interest? Why do they feel the need to spy on me? Some ridiculous idea that has been put into they're mind by you no doubt."

She felt as if she had been slapped around the face, but for once she was not going to let Damien have the upper hand.

"Well are you going to tell us where you have been? I saw you down in the Memorium, I saw you pass through a memorial, where did you go?"

"Ha… what on earth are you on about?" his laugh was bitter and shrew, "Like I have said, I was ill. You are talking utter nonsense and quite frankly, you're wasting my time. I have a lesson to get to."

"You're not going anywhere until you give Brianna some answers," Taylor stepped in, placing his arm across to stop Damien from carrying on.

"Ooh, look. It's Brianna's knight in shining armour, come to save the day," he made a mock curtsey in Taylors direction and Brianna could see Taylor clenching his fists as Damien angered him.

"We saw you," she said quietly, lowering the volume to break the tension, "We saw you walk through the memorial and I saw you surrounded by those cloaked witches. One of their hoods fell down and I recognised she was from Medusa. What do they want from you?"

"Nothing," he shouted suddenly, his attempt at cool mockery no longer kept, "just leave it, I've told you why I've been off. Stop trying to act like my girlfriend because you're not. You don't need to look out for me because I don't want you to."

He swung his arm to knock Taylors out of the way and stormed past the both of them. She didn't like him in that way anymore, but his words stung her like a blade cutting across her cheek nonetheless. She found Taylor pulling her in for a hug and she found herself unable to stop sobbing into his shirt. All that effort, time and suffering, had been wasted on a complete monster.

*

It took Kimberley five to recover in the House of Eastey. Tressle would not let her leave until she had completely returned to normal, but Tressle did allow her visitation rights for her best friend. Every day Briana would go down with Truesdale and update Kimberley on the on goings at the school. Taylor would often come down, but give Brianna and Kimberley the space that best friends so often craved. She explained her run in with Damien and all Kimberley could do was respond with many things to say on the subject, but not things that she wished to repeat to anyone.

Other than the confronting episode, Brianna kept Kimberley well informed on the exams that were soon to take place. The timetable had been handed out, giving a list of all the times for the practical and theoretical examinations. Too her slight dismay, the exams were to begin the following week, so most of the time Brianna found her friend buried in a book or two.

When Kimberley was finally given the all clear to return back to Merlin, Tressle bid them a fond farewell before sending them on their way.

"Remember, I shall keep an eye on you and should you ever require my guidance or aid you need only use the book. It's the fastest way to contact me."

As they journeyed back in Truesdale's Accipegus carter they busily discussed what was to happen with the last days of their year at Merlin. They had tried hard to remember all that they had learnt over the past year, but they panicked that they may not pass the exams. They wondered what would happen if they didn't pass the tests, they wondered whether they would be allowed to return and try to learn for another year. Brianna secretly worried that they would no longer be able to learn magic and would be cast out of the Realm world forever.

As Truesdale dropped them off at the front gates, he gave Kimberley a kiss on the cheek and tight hug. He had most definitely perked up since Kimberley had made a full recovery, and if it were at all possible, he had become more openly affectionate than he had ever been before. Kimberley blushed, but held Truesdale's face and gave him a kiss on the lips in return.

"Kimberley!" came the voice of Serena as soon as they stepped through the main entrance of Merlin, "it's so good to see you! Alleyen and I have been so terribly worried about you. Where have you been for the past five days?"

"Ermm...," Kimberley faltered.

"She came down with a horrible flu," Brianna quickly interjected, "she finally managed to get out of bed yesterday and is fighting fit once more."

"Oh... well we are so happy to see that you are a lot better now," Serena responded, "I'm not too sure what a flu is, but five days of being ill most definitely sounds like no fun at all."

Brianna felt almost fortunate that Serena and Alleyen didn't know what the flu was. If they did they would have probably expected a pale complexion and a Kimberley that looked far more tired out than Kimberley's current state.

As it was the last day before the examinations, all lessons had been cancelled to allow them further opportunity to revise. The five of them made their way to the library and found a corner to sit in, drinking in as much information from the books as they possibly could. They finished their two hours in complete silence before Kimberley, Brianna and Taylor made their way back to the mortal world, to continue their studies in the comfort of their own homes.

She looked up as she got out of the door that transported them to Merlin and back and was met by a most undesirable site. Zoe stood by the door of Medusa, her darkened stare bored into Brianna's eyes and she seemed almost triumphant in a way.

"Haven't seen you around lately," she changed her stare and made a direct comment to Kimberley, "where is it that you have been hiding these days."

"Like you wouldn't know!" Brianna exclaimed as the anger rose from the pit of her stomach and exploded like a dragon breathing fire. She blamed Zoe and although she couldn't prove it yet, she was sure

Zoe had some part to play in that terrible evening. "How dare you speak to us! How dare you address

Kimberley!"

"What on earth are you shouting about," she sneered in return, "you ought to be careful, someone

might hear us."

"As if you care, you concerned that your new best friend Damien might see you for what you truly

are!"

"Damien… why on earth would you bring up that waste of space? He has done nothing but humiliate

himself and annoy me from day one. I have no concern over someone from *Merlin*."

"Come on Brianna," Taylor said consolingly, "she's not worth it."

She turned and walked with Taylor, fighting the fumes that were threatening to engulf her as her

anger for her enemy reached boiling point.

"Of course Brianna, run away. I can wait; I'm not going anywhere soon, just watch who you go

shouting at in the future. Not everyone in the world is as tolerable as me."

Brianna turned to look back and maybe even say something, but Zoe had vanished. All that remained

was a cold space and chill that passed right through her.

*

The week passed in a long string of painfully difficult exams. They were tested in their knowledge of

wand lore and were asked to create the potion to form mini rainclouds. Professor Benethon tested them on

the five fundamental laws of the Realm world and Professor Llewellyn had them complete a test on the

different sports that entertained the magical beings of the Realm world. Further to this, their ability to

perform elemental and rhythmic charms was tested in an hour long session of wit and cunning. They were

placed in the middle of an enchanted woodland and only through the power of magic could they escape the

trap. Of all the challenges they had been set thus far, the charms test was by far the most difficult and trying

of all the tests that they completed. For flora studies they had to show the way to care for five different magical plants and Professor Merrydew made them identify the best way to care for a unicorn and what foods were necessary for feeding a griffin.

By Friday, when all of the exams had been taken, Brianna felt that she had truly given it her best. She hoped from the true depths of her heart that she had done enough to pass her exams, for after all that had gone on throughout the course of the year, her feelings and wishes for becoming a true witch had not faltered.

She went with Caleb, Michael and Kimberley to the locker room before they retreated back to the common room, to rest their minds for a little while before they had to venture back to their mortal world. They stepped through the carved door, but were stopped by a crowd that were congregating around the notice board. After siting a couple of the first years standing by it, Brianna decided to make a move to the board and read it for herself.

'Dear first years,

On Monday I would very much appreciate your company in the main hall. It contains some vital information regarding your progression as students within this school and the future for you as a training witch or wizard.

Professor Allard'

Brianna finished reading he note and immediately made an advance for her friends that had managed to find seating in the rather crowded common room.

"What was all the commotion about?" Kimberley enquired as soon as Brianna had taken a seat next to her.

"We have been given an invitation to see Professor Allard on Monday. I believe he is going to explain what is going to happen to us at the end of the year."

For perhaps the first time, no one in the group managed to come up with anything more to say and the group sat in complete silence as they pondered over their potential future. All the fears and worries that had clouded her mind at the start of the year began to flood through her mind once more. She fretted over the possibility of her magical career coming to an end and where that would leave her if she were to never pass through to the school of Merlin.

*

"Thank you all for coming here today," Professor Allard announced to the group of students when they had finally all sat down in the main hall. "For those that did not manage to see the notice on Friday, there are a couple of items that I need to discuss with you.

Professor Merrydew, the very first Professor that Brianna laid eyes on floated at the front of the hall next to Professor Allard. He smiled the same warm hearted and kind smile that she had been welcomed with on her first day. It bought back so many memories and she could not believe that she had now been here for eight months. June has dawned so fast and quickly on her and she had learnt so much in such a short period of time.

"As students of Merlin and members of the Realm world you understand that magical education is vitally important. The tests that you have taken in the last week demonstrate your competency as members of the magical community and identify if you are well suited to this world."

Brianna looked around the crowd and noticed Damien looking at Professor Allard without a care to a word that he was saying. He soon trunked his attention away from Professor Allard; where his attention flittered aimlessly around the room. Fortunately it avoided her direction.

"Those who live in the realm world, the future is more straightforward. If you are to fail this year, you must spend another year at school. You have been bought up in the Realm world and therefore your identity and competency is clearer than that of the students from the mortal world. Your results shall come

through in the summer via troll mail. That is all the information I have to give for Realm based students. You

are free to leave.

"Mortal based students, I request for you to stay a little longer."

Serena and Alleyen rose from their seats and gave Brianna and Kimberley encouraging pars on the

shoulder.

"It will be fine," Serena stated encouragingly, "we believe in you. We have seen what you can do; you

shall not be leaving us so soon."

They left the hall along with the other Realm based students so that only a small handful remained,

including Brianna, Kimberley, Caleb, Michael, Taylor and Damien.

"Thank you, my dear Mortal based students. You have bought us such light and joy since your arrival

all those many months ago. From the wand _ ceremony you have evolved and grown. Some of you have

demonstrated exquisite skill in your lessons, of which the Professors have reported and fed back to me. Others

of you have settled in well with the extracurricular activities we have on offer here at Merlin.

"But now I have some further information for every one that' sits here in his room. As you know, the

Realm world is sworn to secrecy, where the mortal world cannot know of our existence. You have carefully

and cautiously visited this world for a year but it is not something that will go unnoticed. We cannot risk that

and as such a decision must be made by each and every one of you."

It was only at this last sentence that Damien bothered to look up in Professor Allard's direction.

"Every student that belongs in the mortal world must decide whether they wish to continue their

education in the Realm world. If you choose to do so there is one heavy price that you must pay; you will no

longer be able to visit the mortal world on a daily basis. Since the events that surrounded the dark power, in

times of our history, we have felt the need to protect both worlds. This is the only way to do this.

"You will no longer be able to visit family and friends back in the mortal world, save but once a year. Your parents will be placed under a spell, fed a story that explains your absence; your family will become those in the Realm world.

"If you decide that this sacrifice is too great you shall return to the Mortal world, but there is also one consequence to this decision. You will never remember anything regarding the Realm world; your time spent in the Realm world will be magically drained from your memories.

"You must make a preliminary decision today a decision that will be sealed in magic and unchangeable once you have passed through the door. Your results from the test will affirm whether you can return should you choose to. Even if you wish to continue studying, but do not pass, you cannot return. It is an unfortunate affair, but it demonstrates that tour magical desire is not as great as originally thought and will better you and your future."

Professor Allard stopped his speech and Brianna looked at the rest of the group. She had always believed that magic was the only way forward, but she had never expected that magic would come at a price. How could she abandon the two people who she loved more than anyone else in the whole wide world? But how could she refuse her true calling?

She would see her parents, but only once a year, which seemed cruel in one way. On the other hand, would she wish to have her memories wiped; all knowledge of her magical existence taken away from her? Then there was the matter of the prophecy that Tressle had made small hints about; could her decisions, like the decisions of Madison and Damien truly affect the future of the Realm world. She knew that there was only one choice that could be made from all of this.

She rose and stepped over to Professor Allard and Professor Merrydew who were standing by the door.

"You have made a decision Miss Eastey?" Professor Merrydew asked.

"I believe so Professor," Brianna replied, "I wish, if my fortune allows it, to become a witch in the Realm world like so many before me."

"Very well. Proceed through the door, once through you cannot change your decision. It is, as one might say, a decision set in stone."

She passed through and felt a layering, like a cloak, surrounding her as she passed through the door. She didn't wait for the others; it was a time that she wished to spend alone. Instead she decided to pass through the transporting chamber to the mortal world, for maybe the last time, alone.

It was with a heavy heart that she turned away from the world that she had grown accustomed to, unsure whether she would step through to it once more. Brianna knew it; that in her heart of hearts her life had changed forever. She was no longer Brianna of Salem, Massachusetts. She had come so far, found out so much, but only felt as if she had scratched the surface on something that was unfolding before her. She was Brianna, witch of Merlin in another world awaiting her fate and what the future could possibly hold for her.

8586254R00217

Printed in Germany
by Amazon Distribution
GmbH, Leipzig